LITTLE GHOSTS

GREGG DUNNETT

Storm
PUBLISHING

To request permissions, contact the publisher at rights@stormpublishing.co

Ebook ISBN: 978-1-80508-066-4
Paperback ISBN: 978-1-80508-068-8

Cover design: Henry Steadman
Cover images: Henry Steadman

Published by Storm Publishing.
For further information, visit:
www.stormpublishing.co

ALSO BY GREGG DUNNETT

The Rockpools Series

1. *The Things You Find in Rockpools*
2. *The Lornea Island Detective Agency*
3. *The Appearance of Mystery*
4. *The Island of Dragons*

Standalone thrillers

The Wave at Hanging Rock

The Glass Tower

The Girl on the Burning Boat

The Desert Run

To my daughter Alba, who came up with the idea of this book over her morning Weetabix, and her little brother Rafa, who just had to be part of it too.

PART ONE

ONE

"Gale, we're going to be late." Rachel heard the way her voice rose in pitch and tried to calm herself, the way her therapist had shown her. But she gave up on the very first breath. She turned away from her son, to where her husband loitered in the doorway.

"It's 9:30 that we're seeing Miss Townsend, you know that don't you?"

Her husband froze, triangle of toast hanging from his mouth. He always took the time to cut his toast into triangles; it was one of the things that had endeared him to her, back when life was a happy thing. Not like now.

"I told you about my meeting." He wouldn't meet her eyes.

"Yes, and I told *you* we were seeing Miss Townsend today." Her voice was stuck now, its higher pitched note of incredulity. "It's Layla's anniversary day tomorrow." Her hands found her hips, but as she spoke she had a vague memory of him saying there was some event he hadn't been able to move, and asking if she could speak with the headteacher alone on this occasion.

"Rachel, I'm the chief *financial* officer. I can't *not* be there for a finance meeting. And we're seeing DI Clarke later this week..." He put the toast down now, so he could rub a heavy hand over his face. All the while, poor Gale sat on the hallway bench still trying to get his shoes on. Rachel dropped her head into her hands. Ten years old and the kid still struggled with tying his shoelaces. Where had they gone wrong? Where had they gone *so* wrong?

She grabbed at Gale's shoe, too quickly. He glanced up at her as it slipped from his hands. His face was a picture of pure misery, and yet so reminiscent of Layla. For a second Rachel had to stop and stare at the ceiling – a neutral place. A space without emotion. She let a few moments pass in the fantasy that this was two years earlier. Back in the full-colour version of her life, when there had been *two* children rushing to get ready for school. Bickering and squabbling but everything fundamentally right with the world.

Rachel got Gale's shoes on and bundled him into the car. She had told him he could sit in the front seat now, if he wanted to, but he preferred the back, taking the same side he'd sat in when Layla was still alive. As if she might still climb in beside him.

Neither Rachel nor Gale spoke during the mile and a half drive to school. The parking was limited, but since Layla's death, Rachel had been given access to the teacher's car park. A sympathy perk, exclusively reserved for the horribly bereaved.

"I'll drop you off and then go in to see Miss Townsend, OK?"

Gale nodded and pushed open the door. He was small for his age. So small it still took him both hands to get the heavy door to move.

As they walked to the classroom door, Gale seemed to be in a different place to the other children, who yelled and chattered with their parents. He felt limp as he accepted her hug, and then disappeared inside. His class teacher, a young woman named Miss Evans, offered Rachel her characteristic awkward smile.

Rachel had learned that the world, post Layla, could be divided into those able to express real compassion for the family's situation – the minority – and those who felt so uncomfortable that they reduced their interactions to a series of supposedly sympathetic expressions. Miss Evans was of the latter group. It wasn't all bad, though: Gale had been assigned an SST – or *Specialist Support Teacher*. Mrs Gibbons was older and more experienced, and she was able to look Rachel in the eye and understand that there was more to her life than a dead daughter, but that it still touched *everything*.

Rachel peered past Miss Evans into the now busy classroom, looking for her son's helper, needing to see a friendly face. But she couldn't see her.

"I'm sorry that Mrs Gibbons isn't here today..."

Suddenly Rachel registered that Miss Evans was speaking to her. "I'm sorry?"

"Mrs Gibbons – she's poorly." Miss Evan's pretty mouth crumpled into a faux look of sadness, as if this was a shame, something that *couldn't be helped*. "Didn't the office tell you?"

"No." Somewhere inside Rachel a familiar cocktail of panic and rage began to mix itself together. "No, they didn't."

For a few seconds, Rachel saw a possible future. She could demand to know who would take Mrs Gibbons' place, who would support Gale until she returned. But she knew the answer would be nobody. The school didn't have a limitless supply of staff – they'd told her that many times in the meetings and support sessions since Layla had died. So, instead of complaining, Rachel simply let her soul shrivel a little more, then turned away.

.   .   .

She waited in the reception for the headteacher, trying not to think of the first time she had been in this space. The three of them – Rachel, her husband Jon, and the precocious, bright, *wonderful* four-year-old Layla – had sat on the very same chairs, waiting for the same Miss Townsend to take them on a tour of the school.

It was crazy, she'd been there dozens of times since, before Layla died too, but it was always this image that came to her. It was something to do with the hope she had felt then, the sense that *this* school was the one. The place where Layla would grow and meet her friends, build the foundation of her education, act in Nativity plays. *These* were the spaces that would mould Layla into the teenager she would become, the beautiful young adult after that – and beyond, who knew?

They'd felt – Rachel and Jon – that their daughter was somehow selected for a very special future, though they knew not what it would be. There had been something unique about her from the very beginning, and it didn't feel irrational to think that perhaps she had something approaching a destiny.

And now, this morning, Rachel found her mind filling up with memories of how her daughter had gripped her hand that day.

Before she knew it, Rachel was weeping; not the full-blown crying that sometimes still happened – even in public – but the quiet tears that were just enough to ruin her make-up. She swore under her breath as she regained control and dabbed her eyes with a tissue. And then the school's automatic front doors swished open, and her husband walked in.

"Jon? You said you had a meeting."

"I did. I asked Charlie to stand in for me. If they have any questions they're going to phone, but I told them it was important I was here."

She smiled and felt a now familiar, but still confusing, swirl of emotions. A wave of love for this man, who stood so handsomely before her, in his dark blue suit, but also a peculiar emptiness, as if that wasn't enough, not anymore, and perhaps never could be again. The thought stayed, unresolved, until Miss Townsend walked through the other doors a moment later, and invited them through to her office.

"Rachel, Jon," Miss Townsend paused to send them what was presumably meant as a comforting look, but then it was down to business. "You asked to see me?"

Rachel couldn't remember the point that Miss Townsend had started using their first names. She'd offered her own in return – Emma – but they hadn't taken to it. Maybe that was for Gale's sake – he had to keep to her official school name.

Rachel took a breath to gather her thoughts. "Yes."

There was a combative edge to Miss Townsend's body language which caused Rachel to frown as she went on. She sensed the argument to come.

"As you doubtless know, tomorrow is a very important day for Gale, it's the day he becomes the same age as Layla, and we wanted to ask whether you would mark it by saying something to the children." She paused. "As you know he's still... struggling a little. And it might help him to know how much his sister is still thought of as a part of the school community."

Miss Townsend had begun by giving the appearance of listening carefully, but now she actually seemed confused.

"I'm sorry, are you saying it's Gale's birthday tomorrow?" Her forehead crumpled.

"*No.*" Now Rachel felt confused. She'd been quite clear, hadn't she?

"Because I thought Gale's birthday was in August," the

headteacher went on. "And it's not Layla's, because we marked her birthday in March?"

"*No.*" Rachel glanced at her husband in frustration. *Help me.* "Yes. Yes, I know we marked Layla's birthday. I don't mean..." She stopped. *Breathe.* "No. Tomorrow is the day that Gale becomes the same age as Layla was... on the day... you know."

Still the headteacher frowned, not getting it.

"Layla went missing when she was ten years and three months exactly. Tomorrow Gale will be that same age."

The frown lifted from the teacher's face. "I see. Yes, now I understand."

There was another pause, while Miss Townsend flashed a range of expressions, as if considering which to go with. In the end she opted for a quick smile.

"Of course. Well, I can say something in assembly." Then, as if remembering similar conversations, she went on. "Was there anything in particular you'd like me to say?"

Rachel fumbled in her bag, pulling out a folded sheet of paper.

"Yes, I wrote down some thoughts, and I found a prayer..." The Martin family were not, and never had been religious, but the school was.

"I thought it would be nice for Layla's friends to hear it while they're thinking about her." She held out the paper for Miss Townsend to take, covered in her neat, small print.

Miss Townsend hesitated. Her mouth fell open as she appeared to check her reply. When it came, her wording was careful, measured.

"Of course." Her eyes scanned the paper, and it was obvious she was taking in just how much was written there. She turned it over, to find more text. She raised a finger to her lips and tapped them a few times.

"Of course, it is important to remember that most of Layla's closest friends are no longer here on the lower school site..." A pause, in which Rachel felt herself tensing. "I could perhaps ask the headteacher of the upper school if he would be able to read this?" Miss Townsend paused, then must have registered Rachel's face, because she added quickly: "As well as here?" She smiled as if reassuring that the suggestion was in no way an attempt to evade the request in her own school. But then she seemed to gain courage.

"I should also say that..." She slowed, picking words as if treading through a minefield. "There does come a point when it's important to let the children... not move on exactly, but not dwell too closely on such a terrible tragedy."

In Rachel's brain the shutters began clattering down.

"We do have the Layla Garden, the two rainbow benches, and we did dedicate the whole assembly to her memory in March, on what would have been her birthday." Miss Townsend opened her hands. "As I say, most of the children here now won't have known her that well."

"But they know *Gale*." Rachel countered, the tears springing back. "He's her *brother*. And they know what happened. *Everyone* knows what happened."

At this point Jon stepped in. He had a knack for knowing how far to let Rachel push things, and when to intervene. He held out a tissue to her and turned to the headteacher.

"How is Gale getting on?" he asked. "You said there were still some concerns."

Miss Townsend looked like she might reach out and touch Rachel for a moment, but settled for letting her face crumple again, this time into a look that was clearly supposed to indicate compassion. Then she turned to Jon.

"He's still a little way behind the other children, of course, but academically he's beginning to catch up." Miss Townsend replied, and Rachel dragged herself back to the conversation with a flash of anger. Gale had been 'beginning to catch up' for months now.

"We are still a little concerned about the social side," Miss Townsend continued. "Obviously he's been through a terrible experience, and it will take a while. But he's still very isolated, very quiet. Unwilling to join in. He seems to want to spend as much time as possible on his own."

"Is there..." Jon rubbed a hand across his chin. He hadn't shaved that morning and even though you couldn't see the stubble – his hair was even fairer than Layla's had been – it made a rasping sound in the small office.

"Is there anyone else you can try sitting him next to?" The question smacked of desperation to Rachel. The same tactic the school had suggested back in the early days, when Gale had gone back a few weeks after Layla's murder.

The school, the police, the grief counsellor they had first worked with, had all reassured Rachel that the other children would be able to compartmentalise. To understand that, even though Gale's elder sister had been abducted by a stranger, and then her naked, battered body discovered three weeks later, Gale himself could still play 'tag', could still take part in lessons.

Yet it was Gale himself who wanted nothing to do with the other children. He went into school obediently enough, but when he was there he would stay the whole day almost completely silent. At break and lunchtimes he would wander to the far edge of the school field. Moving away if anyone else came too close.

The conversation moved onto familiar ground. The measures the school were taking to support him, the things they could yet try. How Gale's own sessions with the grief counsellor were going. But there was nothing new to say, and eventually a short silence settled in the office. And then the headteacher asked what was on her mind.

"Is there any news from the police? Any progress?"

Jon bit his lip. He glanced at Rachel, who gave the slightest shake of her head, small enough that Miss Townsend missed it.

"They're still looking into it?" the headteacher said, sensing something, but misunderstanding. "I mean, they're doing something?"

"Of course." Jon nodded, and Rachel knew he was going to launch into his standard explanation. His easy-to-understand guide to life as a parent of a murdered child. He was so good at it, she'd thought he should write a book on it. *The Dummies' Guide to a Dead Kid.*

But then, with the letter that had come last week, it seemed he might have to add a whole new chapter.

"It's not quite like you see on the TV," he began. "There's no team of detectives in a big room with lots of white boards... I mean there literally is – but they're not only working on Layla's case." He sighed, shook his head, and in a flash she saw how tired he was, how much this was taking out of him, too.

"What they don't show you is just how overworked the police are... They have budgets, just like any organisation." He shrugged, defeated.

"But there is still someone working on it?" Miss Townsend persisted. As if she were more outraged than they were. Layla's actual *parents.*

"Yeah..." Jon nodded. It seemed to take a big effort. "There's a DI – Detective Inspector Kieran Clarke. He's responsible for the case, and he's doing a lot. He's really trying to keep the focus on the case, but..." Rachel shot him a glance, warning him not to tell the headteacher the latest chapter of their horrors. He backed off.

"Kieran's doing a really fantastic job. All the police are," Rachel cut in, the lie feeling better than the truth. "Actually, we have a meeting with him later, to discuss it."

She shared a look with Jon, but it was interrupted by his mobile phone sounding. The ring tone was the chorus of a song by Ed Sheeran – Layla had selected it, and he hadn't yet changed it back to something more suitable. Rachel knew why not. He quickly apologised, indicating both to Rachel and the headteacher that it was something from work, that he had to take it. Then he answered as he backed out of the room, already explaining where a file could be found.

When Rachel was left alone with the headteacher, the atmosphere suddenly changed. There was a silence, until Miss Townsend spoke again.

"Well, again Rachel," she gave a large sigh, "I am so, so sorry this has all happened to you." She glanced down at the paper on the desk. "And I will be sure to mention this in the assembly. Thank you so much for bringing it in."

But as Rachel looked at the headteacher, firmly nodding her head, she realised she no longer cared.

TWO

At the end of the school day Gale Martin waited for his name to be called out by his teacher. When she did, he stood and went to collect his bag, and then made his way outside to where his mother was waiting for him, a little way apart from the other parents. He avoided her gaze as she squeezed him to her.

"How was your day?"

"Fine." Gale gave the same answer that most of his classmates gave to their parents, but with notably less expression. It never occurred to him to say how it had *really* been, without even Mrs Gibbons to offer a few moments of warmth.

And then his mother had put her hand behind his back and propelled him out of the school gates towards the car, the two a little bubble of unhappiness amid the end-of-day release and excitement of his classmates and their parents.

"We've got pizza for dinner," his mother told him as they came in the front door. He'd been silent in the car.

"OK."

"Do you have any homework?"

"No."

"OK, well would you like to watch some TV? Or play some Minecraft?"

"No. I just want to go to my room."

It was the longest sentence Gale had said for hours – possibly the whole day – and the words felt strange in his mouth. He swallowed, while his mother nodded sadly. And then he went upstairs. He closed the door to his bedroom behind him and sat down on his bed. He took a deep breath. Then another.

"Hello," he said.

The room fell silent, but Gale looked around, first to the left where his wardrobe stood next to the door, then the right, towards the window.

"Hello?" he said again. This time there was an answer, of sorts. In the air by the wardrobe there was a kind of disturbance. Had Gale been observing closely, he might have described it as a silvery shimmer, that deepened and darkened, and then slowly resolved itself into a near-human shape. But he wasn't watching closely, he was just waiting, until the disturbance-in-the-air became something recognisable, a semi-transparent, floating image of his sister Layla. She hovered a while in front of him, then she sat down next to him.

They stayed like that for a long while, perhaps half an hour, neither moving, nor speaking. And then Gale, feeling a little better now, lay down on his tummy on the carpet and began playing with his Lego bricks. Layla moved with him, laying facing him. The room wasn't large enough to give room for her legs, but it wasn't a problem – they just disappeared where they met the wall.

Gale focussed a while, constructing and de-constructing a crane that he'd got for his last birthday, and then robbing the wheels to make a car. Every now and then he glanced up to check that Layla was still there. And she was. Silent. Watching him. Exactly as he knew her in life, except that her eyes were now filled with sadness.

It had been like that for months now, and had come to seem quite normal. Gale first became aware of Layla's – he didn't know what word to use, but perhaps 'presence' covered it best – just a few weeks after her body had been found. In the beginning, it had been barely noticeable amid the pain and sheer bewilderment of everything that was happening. He had caught her reflection in the bathroom mirror, but when he looked again to check, there was nothing. He'd seen her from the corner of his eye when he moved through the house, but when he turned, she wasn't there. But there *was* something that only he could see. A flash of colour that brought to mind one of her dresses, or the things she used to wear in her hair. And a wobbly patch in the air that somehow seemed to blur whatever was behind it.

It happened infrequently at first, and was easy enough to ignore, or put down to him being tired, and sad. But gradually the glimpses became more common, more vivid. Longer lasting. He would turn to see whatever caught his attention, and there she would be, her outline in the air, hanging for a moment, before dissolving away. Each time the vision would last longer, grow stronger, and settle into what was unmistakably her shape.

Eventually he had found himself able to stare right at her. Through her. Look into her face and feel her looking back. For months now she had been stable, a near-lifelike apparition he could conjure almost at will, when he was in the house. And he did so; whenever he could be alone he would look for her, and more often than not she would come. Yet no matter how realistic this see-through version of his dead sister appeared, there was one thing she had never done. She had never spoken a single word.

She had simply watched him. Been with him. Waited.

Early on, he had told his mother, though he'd been scared she might be angry, such was the unpredictability of her grief. But she had been understanding, and encouraged him to also tell his counsellor, Karen, whom he saw every Saturday. Karen had explained that it was quite natural and quite normal and nothing at all to worry about. He wasn't really *seeing* Layla, she explained, but a part of his brain called the *subconscious* was *creating* her. She gave an example. Imagine sitting in a cinema and watching Evil Knievel jumping his motorcycle over the Grand Canyon. It would be very dramatic and exciting, but he wouldn't really be doing it *in* the cinema – it would simply be an image created by a projector, hidden in the darkness.

The analogy had almost fallen flat, since she'd had to explain who Evil Knievel was, and for a while they'd sat watching YouTube videos of this crazy American jumping over all sorts of things on his motorbike. But Gale got the idea.

The way Karen explained it, seeing Layla was something that would happen for a little while, and would gradually stop happening as he began to feel less sad and less lonely – and that this would be a good thing. As he healed from the trauma of his sister's death, she would cease to appear. But that part never made much sense to Gale, because he actually felt *less sad* and *less lonely* when Layla was there with him.

And so, despite the visitations continuing to grow in strength and frequency, he stopped reporting them to Karen or to his mother. When they asked if they still occurred, he lied, and told them they didn't happen anymore. And then a year passed, without him even mentioning her, and it felt as if both Karen and his mother had forgotten he had ever seen anything at all. But secretly, the silent vision of Layla he saw, nearly every time he went to his bedroom, looked almost as clear as a real person.

And no one but Gale knew she was there.

· · ·

From downstairs Gale heard the sound of his mother's voice calling out that dinner was ready. Carefully, and a little reluctantly, he set down the Lego he had been working on.

"I have to go for dinner now," he told her automatically and he pushed himself to his feet. But then something quite new happened.

"OK," Layla said.

THREE

Detective Inspector Kieran Clarke checked his watch, then raised his arms into a deep stretch. He rolled his head around his neck a few times, wincing as it cracked alarmingly, then cast an eye around the mess of his small office off the investigation suite. There was a pile of files and paperwork on one of the chairs he kept for visitors, so he got up and hefted them onto a battered grey filing cabinet. He brushed crumbs off the seat of the second chair, then gathered the half-dozen empty cardboard coffee cups and dumped them into the waste bin. He glanced around at the rest of the room. It would have to do.

He arrived downstairs in the reception area of the police station just as his visitors were coming in from outside. Rachel and Jon Martin were pushing their way through the glass double doors, their faces set with thin lips and downcast eyes. He approached, laying his hand on Rachel's arm in greeting. She nodded, and he did the same with Jon.

"It's good to see you." There was compassion in his eyes, a moment when the three of them seemed to connect. He let it last.

"Let's go through." He said finally.

He indicated to the desk sergeant to buzz open the door, then allowed them to lead the way back upstairs. It wasn't like they didn't know the way.

"How's Gale?" he asked as they walked, directing the question to Jon. He sensed Rachel was in the more fragile mood.

"He's..." Jon Martin seemed to consider glossing over it, but chose honesty. "He's not great. Not really any change."

"He'll get there." Clarke said, meaning it, and wanting them to believe it. "I've seen it. He won't get over what happened exactly, but he'll learn to live with her loss. I promise you." They came to his office, at the far end of the investigative suite, and he called out to one of his detectives to fetch coffee. She already knew how the couple took it.

Back inside the room Clarke closed the door.

"Sorry for the mess, I did do a basic tidy." He offered a rueful smile, then gestured at the chairs. "Please."

"So what's this about?" Clarke asked when they had sat down and been handed their drinks. But he already knew the answer.

"We've received a letter," Jon Martin began, "from Detective Superintendent Starling."

Clarke kept his face without expression, but he nodded. "A letter."

"Yes." Rachel Martin pulled it from her bag, and passed it over the desk to him. It had the crest of the police force at the top, and DS Starling's flamboyant signature taking up most of the bottom. Clarke recognised the pen, could almost see his boss signing it, filled with his own sense of self-importance. Clarke read it slowly. Even so, it didn't take long.

"He wants to close the investigation?" This was Rachel.

Clarke read the lines a second time, but said nothing.

"He wants to shut it down?"

"No —"

"Well, that's what it sounds like." Rachel Martin leaned forward and stabbed a finger on the letter, right at the point where it said pretty much exactly that.

"We're not stopping the investigation," Clarke replied, glancing at the letter again, and wincing at the words his boss had used. "It is being reclassified – but..." Clarke paused. "But *I'm* not stopping."

There was a knock at the door; it opened at once and a man's head appeared. Clarke flashed a look of apology and glanced up. The man asked a question, clearly about another case. Clarke answered it quickly, and the man retreated. There was a short silence.

"With respect, Kieran," Rachel went on. "It doesn't sound like it's your decision to make."

The couple hadn't touched their drinks, and it had seemed disrespectful to Clarke that he be the first to do so, but now he gave up. He needed the caffeine. He took a deep gulp of the bitter black liquid, then set the cup down.

"Look, I'm really sorry you got the news this way. I wanted to tell you, but Starling thought it should come from him. I don't know... I understood that he would talk to you in person but..." His eyes dropped to the letter again. "But regardless, you should see this as more of a formality than anything else. It's just how these things have to be run within the structure of the police force."

"You sound just like him." Rachel spoke into the silence. She said it like an insult.

Clarke took off his glasses – black rimmed spectacles with lenses thick enough that they slightly magnified his brown eyes – and cleaned them on his shirt. He put them back on.

"He's not a bad guy, Starling, you know?" He looked appealingly at Rachel, and stopped himself from turning to her husband for support. He was the more level-headed of the couple. "He has to take a budgetary approach – that's his job.

Just like mine is to catch the man who did this. *I'm* the one who's failed, so far..."

"I don't blame *you,*" Rachel interrupted him. "You've been tirelessly helping us. You've pushed for more resources the entire time."

Clarke was silent, but Rachel didn't go on. Eventually he felt he had to reply.

"It's been two years since Layla's death, and the investigation has been one of the largest this force has ever carried out. At some point it has to be scaled back. At some point, the case has to be reclassified to a... a less active status." Clarke paused, then found he almost couldn't bear the look in her eyes. Both of their gazes went back to the letter on the desk.

"It seems that DS Starling has decided that's the point we're at."

There was a silence.

"But I don't really care what it says." Clarke went on again now. "You should believe that. You really must. *I'm* going to keep searching, and my core team will as well, both during work hours and outside. We're not giving up. Nor should you."

Rachel closed her eyes and looked sharply away. Her husband watched her, then turned back to Clarke.

"What exactly is the significance of this in terms of the number of detectives you'll have working the case?" he asked.

Clarke considered bullshitting him, but he knew Jon better than that. He deserved better than that. "Officially it means I'll have fewer resources to draw upon. But that will change, as and when we get new information to follow." He wanted to go on. To tell them his idea. But he couldn't yet.

"How many?"

Clarke drummed his fingers on the desk. "If I could give you a number I would, but it doesn't work like that. The reality is this has been such a large case, we've already followed up every lead we've had. But I promise you, Jon, should we find new information, we'll have detectives looking into it. As many as we need." He wanted to say it now. But he had to be sure that it wouldn't do more harm than good.

"But that's what I don't understand." Rachel cut in again. "You haven't found a suspect, you haven't made any arrests – surely that means you ought to be looking *harder*, with *more* officers? Not waiting for something to land in your laps?"

Clarke was silent. He considered the meeting he'd had with Starling. In it, he'd made pretty much the same argument that the couple were making now. Now, he was careful with his reply.

"It's just a name: 'inactive' refers to how the case is classified on DS Starling's spreadsheet. It's not going to change anything about how I work. I promise you that, I give you my word."

"But you *report* to Starling. He's going to want you working on other cases? He'll have expectations?" Jon pressed.

Eventually Clarke had to concede. He nodded.

"And you have other crimes? There have been other murders since Layla was killed?"

Again, he had no choice. "Yes."

"So *how* can you promise us you'll keep looking into Layla's case? Why would you prioritise this case?"

Clarke didn't answer out loud, but as he took another gulp of coffee he considered the question. Why was this case special to him? There were many answers. Almost every murder was brutal and sad. But there were things about this case he hadn't been able to get out of his head.

Even though the girl's body had been found a few weeks after her abduction, the post mortem had failed to identify her actual cause of death. There had been strangulation marks around her neck, but they were light. She'd had part of her ear removed, and another part of her skin around her waist removed, apparently by a blade of some sort, but again, neither of these wounds were enough to kill her. Yet her heart had stopped. In the end, the best guess from the pathologist was that the girl had actually died from fright. She'd been terrified to death.

Clarke felt the knot of too-much-caffeine in his stomach grow tighter.

"Because I gave you my word."

The couple seemed broken, defeated, and Clarke watched them sadly for a few moments. He considered his next words very carefully. The last thing he wanted to do was give them false hope. And yet, in his mind this wasn't over.

"Look... there is one thing."

"What?" Rachel's eyes had flicked back to his face, shiny with a thin film of tears coating them.

Clarke shifted a little uncomfortably in his chair. "It's... look I don't want to sell this as a done deal, but it's a possibility."

"What is?" Rachel frowned through her tears.

Clarke considered Starling's less-than-enthusiastic reaction to the idea. He pressed on regardless.

"OK. Last week, DS Starling called me in to tell me about the change of status, and I wasn't... I wasn't best pleased. We clashed a little, but basically he told me this was happening, until and unless I came up with some more leads to follow. So, I had an idea. But it's a long shot – a real long shot."

"What is it?"

"I'm sure you've seen the television programme, *Crimebusters*?"

There was a silence. Clarke wasn't sure what it meant.

"I know we've done some TV before. We've put out several appeals for information, but I think there's room for more. I think there's a real chance that someone out there is sitting on information that could help us. And if we could encourage them to come forward..." Without thinking his hand went to the letter again. "If that happens, then the case becomes active again." Clarke waited. "Whatever Starling says."

He saw the range of emotions flow across Rachel Martin's face and knew exactly what he was asking. TV appeals were hard on everyone, but particularly the parents. In reliving the horror of the crime in such detail, it blew away any healing they had managed to achieve. They had to start again.

"What does DI Starling say?" Rachel answered, carefully. "Will he even let you do that?"

Clarke hesitated. "I have to admit he didn't love the idea, at first. The department would need to cover half the cost, which isn't great for his budgets. But on the other hand," Clarke allowed himself a half-smile, "I reminded him how *Crimebusters* likes to feature a senior officer from the case on the show, which in this case would be him." He shrugged. "And that's a pretty good way to raise your profile, just ahead of when the Chief Super is casting around for promotion prospects. Long story short, he told me he'd consider it. *If* you agree to put in an application, and it gets accepted."

There was a silence, and he leaned forward.

"The way it works is, *Crimebusters* will feature a reconstruction of the crime, and put it out on primetime TV. Perhaps twelve, fifteen minutes long. In real detail. With the work we've already done – what we already know about what happened that day – we'll be able to put together something really accurate. I think it could jog someone's memory. I believe there's someone out there with the information who can help us catch this guy."

Rachel shook her head. "It shouldn't be DS Starling they feature; it should be you. You're the one who's kept this alive."

Clarke waved this away.

"That's not important. What does matter is what you think. I can put forward an excellent argument to feature Layla's case, which is why I'm bringing it up. I think it's worth a shot.

Clarke hesitated. There it was. The ball in their court. Squarely and unfairly.

Clarke glanced at them over the rims of his glasses. He saw the dark look that had come over Jon's face. It was hard to read, but looked somewhere between anger and a form of dread. Clarke turned to him, trying to keep in mind how this would feel from their perspective.

"Look, it'll be hard, I know it will," he said. "On some level it will be like reliving that day, and that will be painful." For a second he couldn't meet Rachel's eyes, but he made himself do so. Then he shook his head. "But *someone* must have seen something. Layla was taken from a busy beach in broad daylight, and she was a bright girl – very bright. No question she knew not to just climb into someone's car that day. So there must have been *something* out of the ordinary that happened. And somebody must have seen it. Getting a feature on *Crimebusters* would give us a real chance to find them."

Clarke realised he'd been imploring them, exactly what he'd told himself not to do. He quietened his voice, lowered his eyes. He raised a hand in part-apology.

"I really think it might help. I really do."

"And you can get us on it?" Jon asked, ever the pragmatist. "You said you had to get it accepted? How hard is that?"

Clarke hesitated.

"I can't guarantee it. We'd have to make an application. And there are certain criteria that we'd have to meet in terms of how the reconstruction would look, how likely it would be to bring in new and useful information. But I know we meet the requirements. Easily. I think we'd have a very strong chance." He was probably overstating things a little, but they certainly had a *good* chance. Clarke fell silent. Giving them the opportunity to respond.

Jon looked to his wife. She was staring straight ahead. He turned back.

"But there's every chance it *wouldn't* get on? That this would just be raising our hopes for nothing. Dragging out the agony. And even if we did, it's going to bring it all back. We'd be right back at the start. Reliving that day."

Clarke was quiet a moment. "There's no guarantee, you're right. But if we get accepted, we'll make it as easy as we can on you both."

Jon Martin turned to face the wall. He sighed loudly. "And what for? What would this be for? Everyone already knows about Layla's case. Anyone with information would have come forward by now."

Clarke's voice was quiet. "Maybe," he conceded. "But maybe not." He went on after a few moments. "We would make it about what happened on the beach that day – we have so much more information now on what happened than when the case was first in the news. I think it might help."

"No." Jon shook his head. "The answer is no."

Clarke bit down on the disappointment that rose instantly in his mind. But he hid it. He didn't want to show the couple how much he'd been hoping they'd like the idea.

"Okay. Well, we'll find another way," he began. "There'll be other opportunities."

"We'll do it," Rachel Martin suddenly spoke.

The little office fell silent.

Clarke's eyes flicked up off the table, where he'd been looking. He looked into hers.

"Are you sure?"

She nodded. "Of course I'm sure. We have to find who took Layla. *We have to.* We can't ever move on with our lives until we do, so what choice do I have?" She began to cry now, fat tears that she didn't bother to wipe away until they reached her chin.

Clarke nodded slowly. But he knew he couldn't accept what she said. Not after Jon's reaction.

"Thank you, Rachel. I really mean that. And I think it might help. But..." He glanced at Jon, and sighed. "Clearly, I agree with you, but this isn't a case of two against one. I'm going to have to ask that you talk it through, and come back to me when you're in agreement." He winced, as if anticipating how difficult this might be. "I'm sorry."

He paused as the couple glanced at each other. Then he went on.

"You need to give it proper thought. It's a big decision, and it will be difficult for you both. But I do think it will help. So if you decide to say yes, then I'll put in the application. And I'll make it the best damn application they've ever had."

He almost broke at the look that crossed Rachel's face, but he held himself together. He let his gaze move to Jon, and he held the husband's eyes for a few moments, then finally nodded. Throwing it back to them was the last thing he wanted to do when he had no idea which way it would resolve. But it was the right thing to do. It was Rachel and Jon Martin who had lost their daughter. It had to be them that made this decision.

"How about I give you a ring over the weekend? Once you've had a chance to talk it over?"

For the third time Clarke's eyes fell to the letter on his desk. Somehow, he knew that Rachel was looking at it, too. And this time he picked it up and handed it back to her.

FOUR

Gale froze, not sure if he'd heard properly. Or *what* he'd heard, because it kind of sounded as though his dead sister had just spoken to him.

"Did you say something?" he asked.

It felt silly to ask the question. Because he knew she didn't speak. In fact, he knew she wasn't even there, it was just his imagination, a projection – like Evil Knievel. And when she didn't reply he felt reassured, as if things were better when they were simple.

But then she spoke again. "*Yes.*" She looked nervous, too.

Gale stared at her. Today she was wearing a long baggy hoodie and blue-and-red patterned leggings that he remembered from when she was alive, and might even still be in her chest of drawers in the room next door.

"Yes," Layla said again. "I've been waiting."

Gale considered what to do. Even though he had long since stopped admitting to anyone that he still saw Layla, the situation concerned him. He knew that his seeing her was a sign that he wasn't getting better, and therefore – logically – him seeing her more meant he was getting worse. What did her speaking to him mean? It probably wasn't anything good.

"What were you waiting for?" he asked.

She gave a small, sad smile. "For you to be as old as I was, I suppose."

"What?" Gale didn't understand. But then the significance of tomorrow's anniversary – the day when he would be the same age as Layla when she died – was heavy in the family. So, he kind of did. And then again, she only existed in his subconscious, so of course he understood. She *was* him, on that level. So he went on. "Why?"

She shrugged. "I don't know. It just seems a big thing, to actually talk to you. I thought you might be scared or something. But then I thought, I could probably have coped with it, at my age. When I was taken, I mean. So I figured I should wait until you're the same age as I was. And then you'd be OK with it."

Gale considered this explanation. He was slightly pleased at the logic he had hidden inside him.

"It *is* quite a big thing," he told himself; or her – he wasn't quite sure. "And I'm not the same age as you, not until tomorrow."

Layla sort-of-smiled. "I know, but you're nearly there. And it's been quite hard waiting. Just sitting here in silence, watching you."

There was an interruption from below, and then Gale heard the sound of his mother's footprints on the stairs. His door opened without a knock.

"Gale, love? Dinner's ready."

At once Gale twisted to see his sister, noticing how she had suddenly become less solid. Now he could see the wall and the edge of his curtain quite clearly through her. He turned back to his mother. As usual, she seemed completely oblivious to Layla's presence. Or semi-presence. But then of course she would be. Because Layla wasn't really there, she was just in his own head. *A projection.*

All the same, he wanted to ask her if she would still be there when he got back, and more importantly if she would still be able to speak. Only he couldn't ask that in front of his mother. He realised he didn't need to: Layla seemed to know exactly what he was thinking.

"Don't worry," Layla said. "You go. I'll still be here."

"Really?" Gale said out loud.

"Yes *really*." His mother looked at him funny. "Didn't you hear me shouting up the stairs?" Gale looked from the image of his dead sister who wasn't really there, to his living mother, who was. He had no choice but to get up and go downstairs.

FIVE

As soon as Gale had eaten enough pizza that his mother wouldn't complain, he'd said he was full, and hurried back to his room. He called Layla's name softly, not wanting his mother to hear, and quite aware that what he was doing was sort of mad.

"It's a mess in there. Why don't you fold your socks together when you put them away?" she asked as she floated out of his wardrobe.

He stared at her. "You can talk?"

"Well, I always used to be able to... Don't see why I can't now."

"But you haven't – not since you came back."

"No... You've got more odd socks than even socks. And some of *my* socks." Perhaps it was a subject she didn't want to talk about.

They both looked down at Gale's feet. He was still wearing his school uniform, and he had on a pair of grey socks. He bent down and peeled them down to look at the name tag. *Layla Martin*. They both laughed out loud.

"So why are you wearing my socks?" she teased.

"I... I didn't mean to. They were just the first ones I pulled out of the drawer." He looked up and saw she didn't believe his little lie. "They're comfortable..." He felt himself blushing. "I just like wearing them."

She smiled. "It's OK. I like that."

"So do I."

They were both quiet for a little while, before Layla spoke again.

"I'm glad I can talk to you now."

"Me too." Gale replied.

From downstairs came the noise of the front door closing, and then the sound of their father greeting Barney, the dog the family had bought almost a year previously. Their mother had hoped it would become Gale's dog, and obviously not *replace* Layla, but go some way to filling the enormous hole her murder had left in the family. But even though Gale liked the puppy, it had taken most obviously to Jon, who took it out sometimes on his mountain bike rides. Now a young dog, it seemed to spend its days watching the front door, never happy until Jon returned home. When he did, it would bounce around the hallway, its thin tail whipping backwards and forwards. The two children listened from Gale's bedroom.

"Dad's home," Layla said. Her voice was sadder again.

Soon afterwards there was a soft knock on the door, and then Gale heard his father's voice.

"Hey there, mind if I come in?"

Gale looked at Layla, but before she could answer, the door swung inwards.

"Hey kiddo, how's it going?" His father's eyes glanced around the room, taking in the pile of Lego spread out on the carpet. But as they swung over where Layla stood – she had turned to face him now – they passed across her without any hesitation. Gale looked from his sister to his father.

"Hi Dad," he said, his voice quiet and kind of sad.

Absently his father reached down and scratched at Barney's ear, who had followed him upstairs and now gazed up at him adoringly.

"How was school?"

"School?" Gale frowned. He'd forgotten about it.

"OK?"

"Yeah. It was OK."

"Wotcha doing? Lego?"

For a second Gale wasn't sure about this either. But the Lego model he'd been building before dinner, before his dead sister began speaking to him, was still there, at his feet.

"Yeah. I guess."

"So what're you making?" Jon Martin squinted at it, then said something unusual. "You wanna hand with that?"

"Erm..." The offer threw Gale. There were times he would have jumped at the chance. Too often he'd been left alone, to fend off his grief in his own lonely bubble. But this time he wanted nothing except the space to continue his conversation with Layla.

"Alright," his father held up a hand. "No bother. I better go see Mum anyway. There's something we need to talk about." He made a face now, but stayed a moment, his hand still scratching the dog's ears. Finally, looking somewhat unsatisfied, he retreated from the doorway.

"Dad still can't see you," Gale began, but his sister shushed him with a hissing noise and a finger at her lips.

He waited, to see if their father had heard, but he didn't come back. Instead, there was the sound of his footsteps on the stairs, and then his voice downstairs, too low to make out the words.

"Dad still can't see you." Gale said again, softer this time.

"No."

"I thought that now you could talk it might have changed things."

"It hasn't. And I could talk before. I just didn't want to. I guess it's quite a big thing, being murdered."

Gale stared at her. He'd never heard her use that word before – he couldn't even remember her ever saying it when she was alive. It frightened him.

"What was it like?" he asked, cautiously.

She shivered and shook her head. "It was horrible. I don't want to talk about it."

Gale was silent, but his eyes grew wide and round.

"What?" Layla challenged. "What did you expect? That it wasn't so bad?"

"No." Gale heard how defensive he sounded, and he was confused. "I don't know. I guess I didn't expect you to know, since you're just me."

Layla shook her head and gave him a stern look he remembered well.

Gale turned away; studied his hands a moment. Chewed fingernails. Bitten down so much they sometimes bled.

"I'll tell you about the bit before. But not the bit at the end. Not that..." Layla said to him.

This didn't make sense. All his life he'd been told how Layla was the one with the big imagination, so how was he doing this?

She gave a small laugh. Almost an embarrassed laugh. And then she began, "Well, after I was taken, I cried a lot. In the beginning at least. But I didn't know then he was going to kill me, so after a while I calmed down."

Gale thought about this, and it seemed to make sense. "What was he like?" he asked, a moment later.

"I don't want to talk about it."

"Course..."

This time it was Layla who didn't seem satisfied with the

response. "What? You wouldn't either. Not if it had happened to you."

"I know. I get it." But then he couldn't leave it. "Except that's not the real reason, is it? It's just that you don't *know* what he was like, because you're me, and I wasn't there. If you tell me, then you'll just tell me the picture I have in my head."

"Gale..." Layla was calm now. She'd turned to face him. "I'm not you."

He waited some more, but she didn't go on. "OK..."

"No, I mean it. I'm *not* you. I'm not part of your subconscious."

"You are part of my subconscious. Like Evil Knievel jumping over a double decker bus... Like Karen said."

"Who's Karen?"

"My grief counsellor – surely you know that?"

"Oh yeah. I heard Mum talking about her."

"But..." Gale was confused. "You're me, so you must know about Karen. We see her every Saturday."

"*I* don't see her. Because I'm not you and I can't leave the house. Not... not easily."

Gale stared at her. "You *can't* be real."

The conversation was interrupted from downstairs by an all-too familiar sound – his parents' voices, raised in anger. It wasn't something he could remember from before Layla's death, but now it happened quite often. Hushed accusations fired backwards and forwards, sometimes even the sound of something being smashed. It wasn't that bad now, but the noise still silenced both children.

They listened for a few minutes, picking out the odd word. Their mother insisting the school wasn't doing enough for Gale. Some decision the police told them they had to make.

"I can prove it," Layla said after a while, after their father's calmer voice seemed to have settled things down.

"How?" He brightened. "Can you move things? Like a poltergeist?"

She shook her head, and he looked around quickly, then thought of a better argument.

"Dogs can see ghosts. Barney would be able to see you."

"I don't think Barney is the brightest dog in the world. And anyway, they can't."

"How do you know?"

"Same reason, dumbo. I *am* one. He can't."

Gale wouldn't let it go. "But *you* can see *him*?"

"Dur!" She said, then went to land a whack on the side of his head. It was something she used to do when she was alive, never hitting him hard. But when she did it now, he felt nothing. He stopped though, taken aback. It was the first time the ghostly apparition of his sister had tried to touch him – and they both realised it.

"Ow," Layla said.

"Did that hurt?"

"No. Not hurt exactly..." She looked pained.

"What then?"

"I don't... I don't know the right word. There *isn't* a right word."

Gale thought about this, but then shook his head. "What you mean is, *I* don't know what it's like, so my subconscious doesn't want to explain it. Because it doesn't know."

"Will you stop going on about your subconscious? This isn't all about you."

"Except it is, isn't it?"

"No. It's not."

"Yes it is."

Gale sighed, it seemed silly to get into an argument about it. With himself. Almost like old times, when they could get into arguments about pretty much anything. Though they'd soon make up again.

Layla stared at him, her cheeks colouring in the same way they used to do when she was alive.

"I'll prove it to you," she said again, after a while. "I can tell you the last thing you said to me – when I was waiting in the queue at the ice-cream stand. You said you were going to go back to Mum and build the 'S' base."

Gale stayed very quiet. He stared suspiciously at his sister, and searched his memory. Not for the words – she was right there, word for word – but for whether he'd told them to anyone else.

He had been interviewed for a long time about what happened when Layla went missing. The detective, a woman whose name was Jennifer, asked him over and over for every detail he could remember, and told him how important it could be. But somehow Gale had felt that the exact details of the game they'd been playing were not relevant to her, and were something that should remain *private*.

Suddenly he got up and walked to the window. In the street below, their neighbour's red car was pulling onto his driveway.

"You know about the 'S' game?"

"Of course I do." Layla had joined him at the window. "The 'S' stands for 'secret'."

Gale felt the blood pumping through his body. He stared out the window, forcing himself to focus attention on his neighbour climbing out of his car and shutting the door, then shuffling over to his front door. He glanced up at the window just before he opened it, eventually raising a half-wave to Gale. But Gale simply turned away.

"That doesn't prove anything. It just hurts." He was angry now. Close to tears.

"Why? Why does it hurt?" Layla asked.

"Because I know I'll never play the 'S' game again. That's why." He wouldn't look at her, but she replied anyway, her voice soft as loose sand.

"No. I mean why doesn't it prove anything?"

A tear leaked from Gale's eye, and he angrily wiped it away. "Because I know about the 'S' game, so of course you know about it. I'm the only one left who knows. Because you're not here."

Layla didn't answer for a while. She just watched as a few more tears leaked from Gale's eyes. He wiped them quickly away.

Then suddenly her own eyes widened. "If I could think of something that you *don't* know, but I did know. Then you'd have to believe me, wouldn't you?"

She glanced at his Lego and a slightly guilty look came over her face. She bit her lip, hesitated. But finally she went on. "Do you remember you used to have a Lego submarine that you really, really liked?"

Gale was frowning again. But at least he'd stopped crying. "Yeah."

The guilty look on Layla's face deepened.

"And do you remember how it got lost, about... about six months before I died?"

Gale looked perplexed. "Yeah."

"You cried about it and everything."

"Alright, you don't have to—"

"What if I knew where it was?" She cut him off. Her eyes were glinting now, excited. Her lips pulled back, revealing a smile he remembered. Remembered loving. A smile reserved for when she had a really good idea. "I mean, *you* don't know where it is, do you?"

Gale thought about it. He'd searched over and over for his submarine. But it was lost.

"But you do?" he asked quietly.

The guilty look reappeared on her face. She nodded. "I might have... Well I only meant to borrow it. But then you made such a fuss, that I thought I'd get into trouble. Mum always sided with you over things like that."

Gale said nothing out loud, but his face was screwed up in confusion.

"I kind of hid it." Layla said, quietly. There was a silence.

"You *hid* it?"

"Yeah."

"*Where?*"

She was silenced by this. Just for a second.

"In my room. Under the floorboards in my room."

They were both quiet now. Both children knew exactly what Gale would say next, whether they were really the same person or not.

"*I can't go into your room.*"

SIX

Police Constable Ellen Cross opened her eyes and noticed the damp patch on the wall opposite her bed had grown. Joe – her ten-year-old son – had been the first to notice it. He'd thought it looked like a map of Italy. But now it better resembled the whole of Europe, with the beginnings of Africa underneath. She stared at it a while, wondering whether she had the energy to report it yet again to the letting agency.

When they'd first moved in, she'd known the old man who owned the flat. He was a bit of an odd bird, but nice enough. But then he'd died, and ownership had passed to his son who lived abroad. He had brought in the letting agency – a smarmy outfit, as Cross had discovered. The sort of place that promised everything would get sorted out until you'd signed the contract, and then never returned your calls.

Her bedroom door creaked open now and Joe mooched in, still wearing his Spiderman onesie. He was small for his age, and could still fit into size eight to nine years clothes. At least that helped with costs – she was able to get hand-me-downs from some of the other mums at school. And Joe, bless his heart, never complained. He climbed onto the bed now and sat there, without saying anything.

"Sleep well?" Cross got out of bed, tucking her feet straight into slippers. The flat was cold too, the insulation too inefficient to keep the heat overnight, and the bills too high to leave it on.

Her son shrugged and yawned.

"Good. Go and have some toast. You've got breakfast club today."

Joe's face was blank. "Is Dad picking me up after school?" he asked.

"Not today. He's got a gig."

Joe seemed to think about this and come up with a fair objection. "It's Friday," he said. This time Cross shrugged her shoulders.

"Well, that's what happens when you have a famous musician for a father. He has gigs on a Friday."

Joe's expression didn't change. "I don't have a famous musician for a father."

"No. You don't. But he's still got a gig. My shift finishes at five, so Grandma J will pick you up. I'll be there as soon as I can."

The boy nodded again, accepting but showing no emotion to the familiar solution. Then he sat staring at the patch on the wall until she ushered him off the bed.

"It's getting bigger."

"I know it is. I'll call in at the agency on my way to work. Now go and have some toast."

Joe shuffled out of the room, and through the thin walls she heard the sounds from the kitchen, the cupboard opening, the cutlery drawer. She dressed quickly – jeans. She would change into her uniform at work, and shower there too, which helped with keeping the water bills down.

"Mum!" Joe called from the kitchen, his voice different now. A bit more engaged.

"What is it?"

"There's no water in the tap."

Cross stopped what she was doing and sighed. Then she went to investigate. She found her son standing by the sink with a confused look on his face, turning the tap on and off to no avail.

"What do you mean there's no water?" She brushed his hand off the tap, only to repeat what he'd been doing, with the same result. She frowned, and for a few seconds another image filled her mind. Their previous flat – Joe's first home, when he was a baby – that she and Geoff had actually *owned*. Not outright, of course, there'd been the mortgage to pay, but she'd been able to cover it on her wages, and whatever Geoff had brought in helped with the other bills. It wasn't exactly luxurious, but the plumbing worked.

From somewhere in the walls there was a gurgling sound.

"I'm thirsty," Joe said, helpfully.

Cross considered, not for the first time, that maybe she should have done what Grandma J wanted, when she and Geoff split up. He was the one who said their relationship wasn't working. That he didn't have enough 'bandwidth' in his life: not for her, baby Joe *and* his music. And since Cross had more or less agreed with this analysis – at least if that was the way *he* felt – she'd agreed that the fairest thing to do was sell the flat and go their separate ways with whatever cash was left over. Grandma J had fiercely disagreed. In her view, Ellen and Joe should keep the flat, and Geoff could go and sleep under a blooming bridge until he grew up and learned how to be a responsible father.

Perhaps that might have been the way things would have gone, had Cross not been so familiar with the people who actually were living under bridges – her patrol took in the underpass where a number of the town's homeless kept their cardboard boxes, sleeping bags and few other possessions. She would check on them most mornings, just to make sure they were OK, and on a few occasions had been the one to discover that they weren't – either succumbing to an overdose, or the cold during the winter months. But it wasn't just that. Cross also suspected there was something in Grandma J's tough attitude to her own son that had made Geoff turn out the way he had in the first place.

And then there was Grandma J's latest idea, presented the other weekend when they went round for Sunday lunch, with almost as big a flourish as the roast beef: *Why didn't Cross try for a promotion?* She had been a Police Constable, the lowest ranking officer, getting on for ten years. If she got a promotion, she would also get a pay rise, and then maybe she and Joe could buy their own place again. And wouldn't it be fun to be a detective? Investigating real crimes, rather than what she did, moving on the drunks and checking up on the homeless?

Cross crouched down now and opened the cupboard under the sink. She stared at the pipes, wondering if they might offer a clue as to the problem. But if there was a clue there, it completely escaped her. She reached in a hand and waggled the pipes. They wobbled a bit, but nothing else happened. So much for her detective skills. She stood up again.

"I'm thirsty," Joe said again.

"I know. Go and see if the tap in the bathroom works," she told him, and watched him pad away out of the kitchen. Again, from somewhere in the walls, came a gurgling sound.

"I've got a card for the letting agency somewhere," she called out, more to herself than to her son, as she pulled open the drawer filled with old clothes pegs, rubber bands and Post-it notes – but despite a good rummage, there was no business card. She stopped and remembered it was probably in the other drawer in the bedroom, where she tended to dump all her important papers. She went there now, pulled the drawer open and sighed at the disorganised mess of old mortgage documents, gas bills and signed divorce papers.

"It doesn't work," Joe said, from beside her.

"What doesn't work?" Cross asked, until she saw the empty glass in his hands. "Oh."

The wall gurgled again, and Joe stared at it.

"It's getting bigger."

Cross drew in a calming breath, turning to her son again.

"I know it's getting bigger, Joe. I'm trying to find the number of the agency, and I'll ring them, and they can send a plumber."

"No I mean, it's getting bigger *now*." Joe held the glass up, using it to point at the damp patch on the wall, which was now significantly larger than it had been when Cross got up. And which was now getting dramatically darker with every passing second. The two of them stared at it for a few seconds. And then the surface of the plaster began to change, to almost dissolve in front of them, as the liquid trapped behind it found its way out.

Cross had time to open her mouth, but not say anything as the wall suddenly gave way. A cold spurt of water fired out, hitting her square in the face and soaking her top. She stood there a moment, stunned, before stepping back, so that the stream from the broken pipe missed her, but landed on the bed. Joe gave a small scream, then looked to his mother, as if he had no idea how to react. And for a second, Cross didn't know either.

SEVEN

"I can't. I can't go in there."

The argument downstairs had burst back into life. Loud enough now that had Gale cared, he could have picked up every word, but he was entirely focussed on Layla.

She looked at him, her eyes wide. "You could sneak in now, while they're busy shouting?"

Neither child needed to explain the problem. After Layla had gone missing, the police had asked the family not to go into her room, in case there was evidence there. And afterwards, when they were allowed back in, and Layla's body had been found, dumped in some woodland, their mother had kept the rule in place. She went into the room, to lay flowers on the bed, and sometimes light a candle. It had become a ritual, that she didn't like disturbed.

Then, about a year ago, there had been a *massive* row when Dad had suggested they clear the room of Layla's things and move Gale in there. It made sense, he'd said, since it was nearly twice the size of Gale's little bedroom. But their mum had gone absolutely mental. Even worse when Dad admitted that part of the reason for the idea was because he wanted to put his Peloton bike in Gale's room.

The argument had scared Gale so much that he'd cried out how he didn't want Layla's room, that it seemed disrespectful. So even though it had never been spelled out exactly, a firm rule had slowly emerged. No one was allowed into Layla's room except Mum, to light a candle every night, and keep the flowers fresh.

"Where is it?" Gale asked.

"What?"

"*My submarine.*"

Layla's eyes grew wide now. Slightly translucent, yet in an expression that he recognised oh so well.

"Do you remember I used to have the bed on the other wall? When I first had Fudge?"

Gale nodded. Fudge was Layla's hamster and had died a few months before she did.

"Well I told Mum and Dad I wanted to change things because of how my old room layout reminded me of Fudgie. But that wasn't true." She shook her head. "The real reason was that Fudgie ate the carpet by the wall, and I knew how angry Dad would get if he found out. So I moved the bed to hide it."

Gale stayed quiet, waiting for her to go on.

"But he ate enough carpet that you could see the floor-boards underneath, and there's a bit that was loose. And when I pulled it out, there was a hole there. So I used it to hide stuff there.

"What kind of stuff?"

"Stuff like your submarine."

Gale tried to think it through. He wanted to check, but the last thing he wanted to do – the absolute last thing, on a night when Mum and Dad were arguing – was to get caught in Layla's bedroom. But on the other hand, they could be at it for hours yet. And if there really *was* a loose floorboard under her bed... if he really *could* find his grey Lego submarine there... Well wouldn't that prove what she was saying? Wouldn't that prove everything?

So even though he was scared, it wasn't like he had a choice.

"Can't you go and get it?" he asked. But she shook her head.

"I can't."

As if to demonstrate, she reached out and touched the wall. Her whole hand simply disappeared through it. Gale nodded.

"All right. I'll do it."

He opened his own bedroom door and stepped out into the hallway. Here, he felt exposed. His parent's voices were louder.

He put his hand out to grip Layla's bedroom door handle. He hadn't even touched it for over a year. Before he did so now, he turned to check she was there. She was, but there was something about her posture that didn't seem right.

"Aren't you coming with me?"

"If you like." Still, she was reluctant.

He thought about this. "*Can* you go in there?"

"Yeah. Sort of."

Gale paused, whispering now. "What do you mean, *sort of?* I keep trying to see you at school, but you're never there. Are there some places you can appear, and others you can't?"

"Sort of."

"So can you go in there? Into your room?"

Layla looked frustrated. Embarrassed. "I *can*. But Mum doesn't really want anyone in there, so I feel like I shouldn't."

"But that's crazy! It's *your* room."

"I know." She half-smiled and waggled her head from one side to another, something she used to do often, but which he hadn't seen for two years.

The sight of it comforted him. The fear and anxiety he'd

felt at the idea of entering her bedroom himself seemed to drain away. A little.

"OK."

"Maybe I should stand watch," Layla offered now. "I'll tell you if anyone's coming."

Secretly Gale thought this was a pretty stupid idea, given that she was really just his subconscious, and therefore couldn't see anything he couldn't see. But he didn't want to offend her by telling her – and he'd only be calling himself stupid if he did. This was a tricky concept, but he was getting the hang of it.

"Alright. But come in a little way so I can see you."

Layla nodded.

Gale took a deep breath, pushed open Layla's door, and stepped inside. As usual the lights were off, but there was a yellow, flickering glow from the candle that burned in there. It smelled of perfume. From downstairs came the sound of raised voices.

"Shall I turn on the light?"

"Yeah, if you like."

Gale did so, then looked around.

Immediately it felt weird, actually being in there. It used to be such a familiar place – albeit one that Layla would regularly kick him out of. Now it was like he'd forgotten the contours of the space. He'd grown too, since he'd last come here, so that it felt noticeably smaller. Or perhaps it was just that the room *was* different now. Layla had been quite tidy, but it had still been rare not to see toys and discarded pairs of tights on the floor, or piles of school uniform to put away on the dresser. Now everything was in its place, the bed perfectly made, except that Mum had positioned a large tray on the top of the duvet, where she placed the candles, alongside a large framed photograph of Layla. Gale glanced around, taking it in.

"Urgh," Layla said, looking at the tray of candles. Gale didn't ask why.

"Where's the submarine?"

Layla took a second to respond, but she jerked her chin at the bed.

"Over there. You need to pull the bed out from the wall." Layla pointed. "Move the... I don't know what you call it, the shrine thing."

Gale looked at her.

"Can't you help me?"

"No. I told you."

A memory passed through Gale of years before, when they'd been told to lay the table – or clear it – and Layla hadn't helped because she was talking to Dad, or had some other reasonable excuse, but he had complained and argued bitterly that it wasn't fair. He felt a hot shaft of regret at the arguments now. What a waste of time. How easy it was to waste, when it seemed to stretch on forever.

He nodded carefully, trying to focus now. He moved closer to the bed and inspected his mother's tray. He tried to lift it. It wasn't heavy, but he was worried the candle would fall.

"Careful."

"I *am* being careful."

"Well be more careful." She followed him. "That's it. Put it on the desk."

He did what she said.

"Good." They both stood back, pleased with Gale's work, but Layla turned around again. "Now move the bed out."

Gale went to the headboard and tugged it. He was small, but he'd got stronger recently – and the bed rested on carpet. It moved a little.

"*Quietly!*" Layla warned. "They'll hear."

"I could do it quieter if you helped," Gale said quickly. Then he saw her face, and wished he hadn't. "Sorry..." He tried again, more gently this time, but still managed to drag and slide it away from the wall. Finally the bed was moved enough that he could get in behind it and access the wall.

"It's there in the corner," Layla told him. "I cut off the worst bits of the carpet where Fudge ate it, but you can peel the whole thing back."

Gale saw she was right. The carpet edges were frayed and chewed. The sight of it made him remember Fudgie for a while. It made him sort of sad, but sort of happy. He and Layla had spent hours in her room with the little creature running around freely, and him begging to be allowed to handle it. And eventually, only when Layla was satisfied the animal was properly tamed, and Gale wouldn't squeeze him, or scare him, she'd allowed him to do so. Then he would make an endless staircase by letting Fudgie climb from one hand to the other, over and over again, feeling the cold feet, and the warm, fluffy tummy.

"What are you doing? Come on!"

"Oh. Sorry. I was just thinking."

"Well don't! They've gone quiet downstairs. You know what that means."

Her words, or his words – he didn't know – were enough to prompt him back into action. He knelt down and began tugging at the carpet edge. It came up easily, and soon he had the whole corner lifted up. He looked over at Layla in amazement.

"I didn't know about this. I really didn't." As he spoke, a question began to form in his mind, asking if this were really true. But in the excitement of the moment it was easily brushed aside.

"I know," Layla replied. "Be careful of those edge bits." She came close to him now, and pointed at the red-painted strips of wood fixed by the edge of the floor. "They're called carpet-grippers. They've got—"

"Ow!"

"I was going to say they've got nails in them." Layla looked apologetic as Gale stuck his finger in his mouth to suck on it.

After a while he took it out and inspected it. A bead of shiny red blood formed on a scratch.

"Are you alright?" Layla asked. He ignored her. For a second it seemed he might start to cry.

"Are you OK?"

A deep, determined yes formed on Gale's face. "Yeah. I'm fine." He licked the blood off his finger again, then went back to work.

"You need to be quick. I can't hear them downstairs anymore."

"Yeah, I know."

"I used to do the same sometimes," Layla said now. "With the nails."

Gale ignored this. It was all too weird – the whole thing was weird. It almost felt like this was a dream he was going through, or at least *had* been going through, right up until he'd cut his finger. But now he knew for sure he was actually in here, where he wasn't allowed to be, and now he also just wanted to get it finished. To get back to the safety of his own bedroom.

So, being more careful this time, he lifted the carpet as far out of the way as he could, until he could see the floorboards underneath. He had no idea if there was a loose one or not.

"There. That's the one that comes up."

It was a bit tricky to get his fingers underneath, especially with one now injured. But Layla told him how to move it, and soon Gale had the board worked loose, and then prised up completely. Then he put his hand in to the small space below. He felt around, and his hand touched something, its shape and touch instantly and weirdly familiar. He stopped at once, then let his fingers envelop it. He pulled it out, and as he did so, he wasn't sure if he could trust what he was looking at. In his hand there was a small grey plastic Lego submarine. *His* plastic Lego submarine. He stared at it, utterly and completely bewildered. He actually considered pinching himself. Instead, he turned to his sister. His actual sister, except that she was now a ghost.

"I don't understand."

"What don't you understand?"

"What is— how did—? " He tried to bring ten years' experience of existence to bear on a situation that made literally no sense. No sense at all. But then, a fair amount of those years had been spent in front of Netflix shows that featured ghosts, dragons and monsters of all types. "You're real? You're actually real?"

"*Yes, I'm real.* Like I said. But more important than that right now, you've got to hurry up."

Gale paused a little longer, looking from the toy in his hand to his sister – both things which had seemed eternally lost to him, yet which now seemed inexplicably returned.

"Come on!" Layla urged, and he heard the fear in her voice. It snapped him back to reality. Or some form of it.

He got up, then pushed the floorboard back down, and then the carpet after it, all the while with Layla in his ear telling him to *come on, come on.* And then he heard the unmistakable sound of footsteps on the stairs – the fifth from the bottom had a squeak that you could only avoid by walking right on the edge. He still hadn't even moved the bed back.

"Oh right – just walk away, like always." His mother's voice sounded clear and angry. The footsteps on the stairs stopped.

"I'm not walking away, Rachel. I'm just exhausted. OK?" Their dad's voice. Another footstep up the stairs.

"Do the bed. You've got to do the bed!" Layla hissed.

Gale didn't need telling twice this time. He grabbed at the leg of the bed, and shoved it back into place. All the while expecting one of his parents to put their heads around the door and ask what on earth he was doing in there.

"The shrine! Don't forget the shrine thing," Layla said, her voice sounded so panicked it made Gale even more anxious, but she seemed to try and help him, shadowing his movements as he picked it up, and much less carefully, dumped it back on the bed. It was as if she had become his shadow.

"Come on. *Get out! Hurry up!*"

Gale grabbed the Lego submarine, and rushed for the hallway. But he only made it to the doorway as his father appeared at the top of the stairs.

"Gale? What are you doing?"

EIGHT

"I keep telling you, there's no need to apologise, I would just like it fixed as soon as possible." Cross took another biscuit from the plate in front of her, and dunked it as far as it would go into the tea.

"Of course. Absolutely." The young man from the letting agency nodded, his mobile phone stuck to his ear, and a nervous look on his face. His name was Paul. The same Paul who had got her to sign the tenancy agreement years before, and who had been avoiding her calls about the niggling issues ever since. What a strange coincidence that he was being so much more accommodating this morning, Cross thought, as she dusted biscuit crumbs from her police uniform.

With Joe's help she'd found a valve that cut off the water, and then – still laughing – had got him changed and then herself. Then she'd left him in the capable hands of Jane, who ran the Tiny Pickle Café, just down the road from the flat. And while Joe was tucking into a cooked breakfast, she'd been to the station, explained the problem to her sergeant and begged for the morning off to get it sorted. Then she'd changed into her uniform, gone back to the café (thanking Jane for looking after

Joe and promising to meet her for a drink later, since she was suddenly off work), walked Joe to school (where she'd had a quick coffee with Mrs Rogers, the receptionist, because she always liked a chat), and then called in at the rental agency in person. She'd already phoned about the problem, but had a suspicion that turning up in person might speed things up. It had taken Paul quite a while to understand that she was there only as one of their renters – with a flooded bedroom – and not on official police business.

"OK," Paul got off the phone. "So, the plumber's there now, and we're going to put in a new boiler, too. And if there's anything of yours that's damaged, just let me know. It's all covered by insurance."

"Thank you, Paul." She smiled at the man, contemplating taking another biscuit, but it was the only one left and she'd had several. Instead, she got to her feet.

"Well, it's really nice to meet you *properly* at last. But I'd best be on my way." She put the mug down on the desk. "After all, I've got criminals to catch!"

She smiled as he gave an anxious laugh. And then she helped herself to the last biscuit after all.

NINE

"Were you in Layla's room?" Jon Martin asked.

Gale froze. He couldn't deny it; he was still in the doorway. His father's eyes went from his face to the inside of Layla's room, the light still on.

"What were you doing in there?"

Gale considered lying, then telling the truth, but in the end silence seemed the only option. He dropped his head and stared at the floor, the metal bar that marked where Layla's green- and blue-flecked carpet met the beige wool of the hallway flooring.

"You know your mum doesn't like—" his father stopped mid-sentence. Then he squeezed his eyes shut for a moment. "I guess you heard us downstairs, huh?" He switched off the light, and moved so that Gale could step into the hallway. "Come on. Get out of there."

Gale moved, his eyes flicking up now to see where Layla was, but he couldn't see her.

"Gale, it's nothing to worry about. It's just a grown-up thing. There's a... difficult decision we have to make, about your sister's case. And we're not quite agreeing over it. At least, not yet. But it's nothing you need worry about."

Still Layla was nowhere to be seen. Gale's father put a hand on Gale's head and ruffled his hair.

"Come on. It's late. You should be asleep. You've got school tomorrow." His father's fingers laced their way through his hair, but putting pressure, guiding him.

Gale let himself be moved, still trying to see where Layla had got to. But she seemed to have melted away, disappeared. For a few seconds it made him think that everything that had just happened had been in his imagination, that he had invented her, but then he could also feel the familiar shape of the submarine clenched in his fist. He dared to take a peek at it now, keeping it hidden from his dad. It was there. It was real. Layla was real.

"Come on. Back to bed."

His father followed him into his room, and Gale had no choice but to climb into bed, and let his father tuck the duvet around him. But he wasn't tired. Sleep was the last thing on his mind. For a minute he feared his father might decide to sit with him until he fell asleep – they'd done that in the weeks and months after Layla's death, but not so much recently. But then his father's phone had beeped in his pocket, the sound it made when a WhatsApp message came in, and he pulled it out and read what it said.

"OK Gale, you get some sleep now, huh?" His dad leaned down and kissed his forehead, then turned out the light and softly shut the door.

Gale waited a few moments, then turned on his side light. Layla was right there, waiting for him. He pulled out his hand, opened his fist to show her the submarine.

"You're real!" He spoke in his normal voice, and Layla hissed at him.

"Keep your voice down. Dad'll hear you."

"Sorry." Gale replied, his voice only a little lower. "But you're really real."

She half-smiled, then shrugged her shoulders. "Told you so."

For a long time he kept his eyes on her, as if seeing her like this for the first time. He noticed how the light from his lamp passed through her, as it had since she'd come back, but now there was a kind of beauty to it. He was reminded suddenly of an ornament his grandmother had in her house, a blown-glass bird he loved to pick up and stare into. He could almost feel the weight of it in his hands.

"Is it nice, being a ghost?" he asked, after a while.

She took a long time to respond, and several expressions passed over her white face. In the end she simply shrugged.

"It's nice to see *you*."

As she spoke Gale had been examining her feet, which were about ten centimetres up from his carpet, but he suddenly flicked his eyes to her face. They gazed at each other for a long while. Layla looked like every photograph they had of her, every memory he liked to run in his mind.

"It's nice to see you too. Really nice."

She reached out a hand towards him, and without thinking he did the same so that their fingers nearly touched, or at least came together. But then they both paused.

"Doesn't it hurt?" Gale asked.

"It's not... not hurt exactly. It's something else." They both kept their hands up, their fingers almost coming together, and then Layla moved her hand closer towards his. But at the point where the tip of her finger should have come up against his, her hand simply kept going, so that Gale found his fingertips somewhere inside Layla's hand. She winced as she did it, but she kept her hand there.

In the end it was Gale who pulled his hand away. When he spoke, his voice had a new edge. Almost reverent.

"You're really here."

"Yep."

"Or really *not here*."

She shrugged, tipping her head from one side to another. Her hair shimmered as she did so, as if merging with the waves of light that flowed from the lamp.

"You're really, *actually* a ghost, standing in my bedroom."

"Uh-huh. Not really standing, if you've noticed. I can float."

"I *know*. Is that what you call it? Floating?"

"I guess so."

"Can you go up and down, like flying?"

"A bit." She did so.

"Can't you go higher? Like right up to the ceiling?"

"I'm a ghost, Gale. Not a bird."

He looked disappointed for a moment, but it quickly passed.

"It's so cool that you can float." His eyes lit up. "Is that what you ghosts call it? Do you say you're going out for a float?" Gale giggled at his own joke, but she didn't join in.

"I don't know."

He frowned at the response. "Do you mean—" He didn't like the thought that had come to his mind. "Do you mean you haven't met any others?"

She shook her head again. "No. I haven't."

"But why not? There must be lots of you. Everyone dies – it's a normal part of life – and we're just not very good at dealing with it. Or that's what Karen says."

"The grief counsellor?"

"Yeah. She says we should all talk about death a lot more."

"She sounds fun." There was sarcasm in Layla's voice, but Gale missed it.

"Not really, but what I mean is, if everyone dies there must be other ghosts, so why can't you see them?" Suddenly Gale looked around the room, as if he might suddenly notice they were surrounded by an audience of ghostly figures watching their conversation.

"I don't know."

For a moment Gale felt frustrated. "I don't understand."

"Nor do I." His sister's voice was serious.

Gale stared at his sister. He was tired now.

"I don't understand it either. I only know there's no one else *here*. Except sort of you."

He caught the emphasis she'd placed on the word and thought about it.

"When you say 'here', what exactly do you mean?"

"I don't know. I know this is your room, only for me it isn't really. It's not where you are." She stopped, but Gale gave her space to continue.

"It's like..." she swept an arm around suddenly. "It's like... all this is my house, but it's not a real house anymore. It's not made of bricks and stuff, it's just made of... energy. And you are too. That's why I can go through things. Because it's all just energy."

"And you're energy?"

Layla shook her head firmly. "No. I'm something else. I'm the opposite. I'm like... a space where there isn't any energy. Where energy can't *be*. And that's why... that's why it kind of hurts."

They were both quiet for a moment. "I wish I could hug you." Layla's face crumpled, like she used to do when she was about to cry. But she didn't.

"Me too."

"We could try." She looked coy, as if a thought had chased away the threat of tears.

"What?" Gale was lost again.

"I kinda..." She stopped, noticing his frowning face. "I kind of already tried."

"When?"

"When you were asleep, before. When I first got here. I tried it with Mum as well, and it just doesn't... well it doesn't really work. It's like hugging air."

Gale looked thoughtful. He opened his mouth to reply, then stopped, then said it anyway. "Well maybe it's better when the other person isn't asleep?"

She thought about this too, and finally nodded. "We could try I suppose?"

Gale pulled back his duvet and sat up in his bed, he was dressed now in pyjamas so didn't feel cold.

"Shall I stand up, or will you?"

"I can come down to you." Layla floated closer until she was on the bed next to him. Nervously Gale held out his arms, and when Layla did the same he carefully laced his through where hers would be, if they were physically there. Then he leaned in. At first, he almost tipped over, expecting there to be something to lean against. Layla did the same, and it took them some moments to each find a position that worked. But then they did. Sort of.

And for the first time in nearly two years, since she was abducted, raped, and brutally murdered, Gale gave his big sister a hug. Then after a while he spoke again.

"I need to go to sleep now."

TEN

"This is pretty nuts," Gale said, the next morning, when he'd woken to find Layla still in the room with him. She'd reminded him of what had happened. But hadn't needed to. He'd remembered.

"Spectacularly nuts."

"It is pretty crazy," Layla agreed.

"What are we going to do? I mean, we don't have to do anything but, think of all the things we *could* do! We could have loads of fun."

Gale had just finished dressing, telling Layla she had to turn away. He'd never bothered when he'd thought she was just a part of his subconscious, and that thought did mildly concern him now, but there were bigger things to worry about.

"Yeah," she said. "Yeah, there is that."

She sounded far from convinced. Finally, Gale picked up on it.

"What's wrong?"

Layla stopped now, her chest rose and fell in a sigh, and Gale wondered how that was possible; if she was a ghost, why was she breathing. But as he noticed, it seemed to make her breathe less, then not at all – as if he were the one making her breathe in the first place. It was a scary thought, that he might control her, and maybe even kill her just with his thoughts. He didn't like it and pushed it from his mind.

"How much do you know about ghosts, Gale?"

The question confused him, and he didn't answer for a while. When he did, it was with a shrug. "I don't know. They're dead people. Dead people who..." he tailed off. Another thought was appearing in his mind. He didn't like this one either.

"Go on."

"Well, I was going to say they're dead people who haven't... I dunno, *gone through* properly. But I don't really know what that means."

"Gone through what?"

"You know, to the other side."

"OK. And why not?"

"I don't know. They *need* something. I suppose."

Layla nodded now; she seemed satisfied. "That's what I remember, too."

Gale waited for her go on, but she didn't.

"So, is it true? You need something?"

She watched him carefully as she answered. "All I know is I've had a long time to think about it. And I think I might."

"OK. So, what do you need?" Now the thought had fully arrived, Gale decided that maybe it wasn't such a bad one after all. If there was something his sister needed, he could help her. It might even be fun.

But Layla took a long time before she replied. And when she did speak her voice was grave.

"A horrible thing happened to me Gale, a really horrible, disgusting, despicable thing."

She paused.

"And I think that's why I'm... here. Here and not there."

Gale's smile slowly dissolved away. "I know."

"No." Layla shook her head. "No you don't know. No one knows, not really," she paused.

"So tell me."

Layla looked away. After a few moments she turned back to him, shaking her head a second time.

"I can't... I can't tell you."

"OK." Gale thought. "So where is *there*? The place you ought to be?"

"I don't know. I just know I'm supposed to be there."

They were both quiet.

"So what do you need?" Gale asked after a while. "To get there?" This morning was quickly getting back into the too-weird-to-cope-with territory of the night before, but he was doing his best to keep up.

"Well, isn't it kind of obvious?" Layla replied. "The police haven't caught him. The man who..."

"...killed you?"

"Yeah."

They looked at each other for a long while.

"I didn't know it was a man. I mean, everyone kind of thinks it must be, but they keep saying the person, like it could have been a woman that—"

Layla interrupted him. "I thought they would. Catch him, I mean." Her words stopped Gale speaking. "When I was first here. When I was weak, I thought they'd catch him, and that would help me, you know. Pass through. But the police *haven't* caught him, and now they're not really... they're not even looking properly, or that's what Mum says. So..." She looked at him again. Her expression was different now. Determined. "So, I think I have to help them."

Gale stared at her, feeling how the remnants of his earlier emotions had withered, and were now being swept away. Near-happy thoughts – so unfamiliar these days – breaking up and being flushed away, like they were vanishing down the plughole of the bath. And in their place, new thoughts, scary thoughts. One in particular, that came out of nowhere but pushed everything else out of the way and seemed to fill his mind, until it was too big not to say it.

Gale dropped his head for a minute, his face screwed up as he considered the thought, tried to see a way around but there wasn't one.

"What is it?" Layla asked. Clearly she recognised the look on his face.

"It's not *just* you," he replied in the end. Then he lifted his head and stared at her. "There's no one else who can see you, right? Only me?"

Layla nodded. "I think so."

"So it's not just *you* who has to help them. It's both of us. *We* have to find him."

ELEVEN

There was a scratching noise from the metal cleats moulded into Jon Martin's cycling shoes as he entered the kitchen. Rachel turned from the sink to look at him. In one hand she held a half-peeled potato. It was the weekend now, and they'd mostly avoided each other since their argument, including by Jon tactically leaving the house for a cycle.

"I'm sorry," he began. "About last night."

Rachel nodded, turning away. Almost, but not quite ready to do this.

"I didn't mean to... look we both said some things, some stupid things. I didn't mean to shout." He looked pleadingly at her, the pain deep in his eyes. "I just sometimes wonder what we're gonna be like in years to come. You know? Are we gonna be one of those couples whose child died and they just *never* let it go?"

"I can't let it go. Not until we've done everything we can. *Everything*."

Jon was silent. Then he gave a deep sigh.

"I just don't know if it's worth it, that's all. I don't know if that's the *wise* choice. I don't know if it's best for us. Or best for

Gale." He stopped, but into the silence he added. "I don't know what Layla would have wanted."

Rachel put down the potato. She recognised the mood her husband was in. *Conciliatory*. She knew she was going to get what she wanted.

"What Layla would have wanted is justice."

"Sure." Jon nodded after a few moments. He watched her get a tissue from the drawer and dab at her eyes. "I know that," Jon went on. "She had a really strong sense of what was fair and what wasn't. But she wouldn't have wanted..." He swept a hand around the kitchen, as if it symbolised their latest row. "This."

Rachel felt herself drawing up her energy again. For a moment she felt ambushed, like he was playing a trick on her.

"So you don't think we should do the *Crimebusters* show? That's what you're saying? I thought..."

"No, that's not what I'm saying." He answered, then fell silent, inspecting the floor. Rachel waited. Unsure now.

"I caught him, in her room," Jon went on. The change of subject surprised Rachel.

"What? Who?"

"Gale. When I came upstairs, after we were... rowing. He was in her room."

Rachel felt her forehead crease. She'd been in there herself to check the candles. She'd thought there was something was out of place.

"What was he doing?"

"Nothing... I don't think he was doing anything."

Both of them were silent a while.

"Look, I'm going to agree with you. That we should do the show. But I think we should also agree it has to be the last thing. We can't go on like this forever. *I* can't. We need to learn how to be a family again. The three of us. Or accept that we're not."

His last words were spoken quietly and Rachel never heard

them. All she heard was that he was agreeing to the reconstruction.

"Really? You think we should do it?"

Jon looked troubled, but the expression drifted off his face.
He nodded.

"I don't believe it's going to help much, not after all this
time. Not after all the publicity we've already had. But maybe
there was someone on the beach that day from across the
country – and maybe they saw something?" He shrugged his
shoulders.

Rachel surprised herself by what happened next. Without
thinking she crossed over to where he was standing and
wrapped her hands around his shoulders, burying her face in
the folds of his cycling top. She stayed there a while. Then
pulled away.

"And you'll appear on camera, if they ask?"

Jon nodded. "They won't, though. They'll want you.
Emotions laid bare."

Rachel burst into tears at the suggestion – but managed a
laugh at the same time. "That's not exactly an issue for me,
is it?"

TWELVE

"Do you eat?" Gale asked Layla. They were in their kitchen as he made his breakfast. Their mother had gone upstairs, and Dad wasn't there – he'd left earlier for a bike ride with some of his riding friends. At least they seemed to have made up from their row.

Gale and Layla had continued to talk in every moment when they weren't observed, but it was difficult with the comings and goings of the morning. Now things had calmed a little.

"No," she said.

"Why not?"

"I don't get hungry." She shrugged her shoulders, watching as he spooned Weetabix into his mouth.

"Have you tried? Does it just fall straight through you?"

"I can't put a spoon in my mouth. I can't pick it up."

"Oh yeah." Gale ate more Weetabix while he considered this.

"How about sleeping? Do you do that?"

"No."

"So what do you do all night, do you get bored?" Gale felt

like he had a limitless number of questions, and for the time being Layla seemed happy to try and answer them.

"Not *bored* exactly. Time is sort of different now. It's like you can just sort of... retreat from it. Just step back, to where time isn't really a thing. And then step forward again when you've stopped laying there snoring."

"I don't snore!"

"You do. Not as much as Dad does. But you do."

"Really? Do I really?"

"Do you really what, honey?" Their mother came back into the room carrying the laundry basket, almost overflowing with dirty clothes.

"Nothing," Gale said quickly, and she glanced around, as if there might be someone else in the kitchen, but of course it was empty.

"Well, hurry up. It's nearly ten, and you have Karen at eleven o'clock."

"Yeah." He nodded. "I know."

She walked through the kitchen to the utility room, and they could hear her puffing slightly as she bent down to load the machine.

"So how are we going to do this? How are we going to help the police catch him?" Gale asked the question in a low whisper. Layla lowered her voice too, though there was no actual need.

"We could try telling Mum?" suggested Gale.

They both looked to the utility room, where their mother's back was visible through the open door.

Layla shook her head. "She's never going to believe us."

"We could try? I mean, I don't see what else we can do."

"Well, how about telling your grief counsellor woman? She must know loads about death."

"I already tried that. She said you were my subconscious. And worse, that I'll only start getting better when I can't see you anymore. So if we tell her, or Mum, it'll just make her even more worried and stressed than she already is."

"What was that?" Their mother's voice came from the utility room. "Who are you talking to?"

"Nothing," Gale replied. "No one." And then he added, as his sister suddenly started miming dancing around the kitchen. "I was just humming to myself."

"OK..." Rachel looked through the open door, studying Gale with a confused expression on her face. "Well, it's nice to hear you're in a better mood. Perhaps the sessions are beginning to work?

Gale didn't reply, but shrugged his shoulders, until she turned back to the washing machine, which at that moment began to make a convenient noise.

"Are you *sure* she can't see you? Have you really tried?" Gale hissed the question to his sister. But Layla didn't have time to answer before their mother emerged again, this time carrying a basket of clean washing.

"Watch," Layla said. And while before, when their mother had passed through the room, Layla had backed herself towards the wall, and faded in intensity a little, this time she did the opposite, glowing stronger, and standing directly in the centre of the room, blocking their mother's path.

"MUM!" she cried out loudly, as Rachel Martin crossed the kitchen, passing directly through her daughter. There was no hint on Rachel's face that anything untoward had happened.

"Make sure you put your bowl in the dishwasher when you're done. And don't forget to clean your teeth." She left the room to go upstairs.

"Ouch." Layla said, when she was gone.

"She really can't see you. Or hear you." Gale said.

"No, but I can feel her, and it kind of hurts.

Gale contemplated this a while. Then he had an idea. "Is there anything like my submarine? Something you know about, that she doesn't. But she *would* know you were real, if you told her about it?"

It took Layla a while to untangle this. But in the end she shook her head.

"No."

"Are you sure?" Gale looked disappointed, but Layla just shrugged.

"Well, are you sure about your grief counsellor lady? She must know about this stuff? What does she make you do?"

"She talks to me a lot, and wants me to talk. But I don't say much, so she makes me draw pictures."

"Pictures of what?"

"Pictures of... how I feel. It's called art therapy." Layla didn't look impressed, and Gale felt a moment of disappointment. "I can show you if you like?"

Layla still looked dubious, but she shrugged her shoulders in an accepting kind of way. So Gale went to the hallway to get his bag. He pulled his drawing pad out and put it on the table. For a second he waited for her to open it, but then realised, and began turning the pages. A little too quickly for Layla's liking.

"Whoa, slow down." He did so, turning the pages carefully to show her the pictures he had drawn of the family, sometimes with her in them, more often without. He was quite proud of how good some of them were.

"What's that black blob there?" She pointed at something nearer the ground.

"That's Barney."

"That's a *dog*? Why's it got six legs?"

"It hasn't. That's his tail."

"That's still only five, and you've drawn six."

"That's his lead. He's on a lead."

Layla made a face, then sighed. Then she turned away from the book. "So what are we going to do? How are we going to catch the man who killed me?"

"Come on, Gale." Their mother was suddenly back in the kitchen, tutting at the Weetabix bowl still on the countertop.

"Have you cleaned your teeth?"

Gale didn't reply, but then Rachel saw the art pad.

"Oh. I'm sorry, honey, I didn't know you were looking at your grief diary." Her voice was suddenly much softer. "But we've still got to go, or we'll be late." Gently she closed the book and put it back in his backpack, but was then back in mum-mode, hurrying him up the stairs.

Layla followed, then stood behind him in the bathroom while he brushed his teeth, so he could see her in the mirror. When he finally finished, spitting the used toothpaste into the sink she asked: "Maybe you could try asking the counsellor lady?"

"Come on, honey," their mother stood in the doorway. "I don't want to be late."

He managed to give her a look.

"I'll try," he mouthed, as they left the room.

THIRTEEN

Ellen Cross didn't have her own desk, but there was a row of computers for the Constables to use when typing up reports. She felt a little guilty, using work time to be reading what she was, but in a way, it was work related.

Awkwardly she typed the words *Detective Promotion Exam* into the police intranet, which held all the forms and documents. And, just like on Google, when she hit return, a long list of results came up. The third said:

Information and sample questions for officers considering taking the DPE or Detective Promotion Examination.

She looked around. There were a few people in the office, but the other computers were empty, and no one was paying her any attention. She clicked the link. The screen changed and filled with text.

The Detective Promotion Examination (DPE) is designed to assess the candidate's knowledge and skills in the areas of crime investigation, problem solving, decision making, and leadership. The examination will consist of multiple choice and essay-based questions to evaluate the candidate's ability to analyse and inter-

pret evidence, conduct thorough and efficient investigations, and make sound decisions under pressure.

Cross felt her heart rate climb as she read. *Could* she do this? Should she? Suddenly a noise behind made her jump, and she turned to see two plain-clothed officers speaking loudly as they crossed the room. They were both actual detectives, the first a man in his late forties who Cross knew, but had never spoken to. The other was a woman, younger than Cross was and a fast-track graduate. Cross had chatted to her in the canteen and she'd seemed nice enough. Neither of them noticed her now, or if they did, they ignored her, and soon disappeared out the door. Cross checked again that she wasn't being watched, then turned back to the screen.

To prepare for the DPE, candidates are strongly encouraged to review the latest investigative techniques, including forensic science, crime scene management, interview and interrogation methods, as well as being familiar with all relevant laws and regulations.

The DPE is a rigorous examination, and only those candidates who demonstrate the highest level of knowledge and competency will be considered for promotion to the rank of Detective.

She wavered. The *highest* level of knowledge and competency? There was a link to *Sample Questions*, which she clicked next.

Question: How do you ensure that all aspects of an investigation, including interviews, interrogations, and surveillance, are conducted within legal and ethical guidelines, while also ensuring that the investigation is conducted in a timely and efficient manner?

Beneath this was a large blank space, as if whoever wanted to answer it would have a lot to say in response. Cross swallowed. Exams hadn't been her thing at school – one reason she'd decided against going to university. She scrolled down the screen with the mouse, feeling grateful when she saw another button, marked *Next*. She clicked it, and a new question appeared.

Question: How do you handle a complex case involving multiple suspects and a large volume of evidence, while ensuring that the integrity of the evidence is maintained and admissible in court?

Again, there was a large space for the respondent to answer. And again, she quickly clicked *Next* to move on. This time she was presented with a sample multiple choice question:

Question: In a complex and high-profile criminal case, what is the most effective approach to managing and organising large volumes of evidence and information?

A) Using a simple spreadsheet or document to keep track of the evidence and information.

B) Creating a detailed flowchart to visually organise the evidence and information.

C) Implementing a specialised case management software program with advanced search capabilities.

D) All of the above.

This was better. She read the options carefully, thought a moment, then selected the answer D. Right away the page came back.

Incorrect. The correct answer is C. Specialised case management software programs are able to handle large amounts of data, with advanced search capabilities and organisation tools that make it the most effective approach to manage and organise large volumes of evidence and information in a complex and high-profile criminal case.

"But that's... My answer *included* C, so how can it be wrong...?" She only noticed that she was speaking out loud when she heard a chuckle from behind her. She turned to see Paddy O'Brian, a career Constable, looking over her shoulder with a large mug of tea in hand.

"First sign of madness, Ellen. Talking to yourself." He chortled again and leaned closer to see the screen better. Even though it was too late, she closed the window, so the computer now showed the report she was supposed to be filing about a bicycle stolen from outside the Tesco Express by the station.

"You looking at the DPE exam?" He sucked air in through his teeth. "Nasty."

Cross felt her face flush red.

"No, just filing in an LP3 on a stolen pushbike." She indicated the screen now. "Whatever that was, it was just open when I sat down." She stopped herself talking, but Paddy wasn't listening anyway.

"I tried it a couple of times. Failed, obviously." He lowered his heavy frame into the chair next to hers and blew the steam off his tea. "Sorry, did you want a cup?" He settled himself more comfortably on the chair, as if not expecting her to take up the offer.

"No, I'm just off out." Cross turned back to the screen.

"You can learn to do it. Pass, I mean. How else do you think them upstairs get through? It's certainly not cos they're super cops. Just know the tricks, what *they* want you to say."

Cross didn't stop to wonder who they were in this context.

"I suppose."

From somewhere Paddy produced a packet of sandwiches, white bread, wrapped in clingfilm. He carefully unwrapped it and lifted the top of one sandwich to check the fillings. Cross was unable to avoid glancing down at the exact same moment, and the sight confirmed what her nose was already telling her. Sardines in tomato sauce, with rings of red onion. It smelled like he'd made them a week ago.

"You just have to put the work in," Paddy continued, replacing the top of the sandwich with deliberate care. "You know, in the evenings and that. Before your shift in the mornings. I could teach you if you like, I've still got the books somewhere."

Suddenly Cross laughed. Not at Paddy, but herself. Who was she kidding?

"Thanks, Pad." It wasn't a come-on, he just had a generous heart. "But I don't think it's really me, do you?"

She smiled now, feeling a sense of relief flow through her, and he shrugged as he took a bite and chewed noisily. And then she turned to finish the form on the bike, while he got on with own work, pecking at the keys like a large bird. But just as she got up to leave he spoke again.

"I think you'd make a damn good detective, personally." He spoke quietly, making Cross freeze as she stood. "Course, no one listens to me." He gave a rueful smile, then turned back to his screen.

FOURTEEN

"Well, did you ask her?" Layla asked. It was late afternoon, the next time they were able to speak freely.

"She didn't know anything."

"Did you *ask* her?"

"I asked her if ghosts were real, and if it was possible that you might be one."

"And what did she say?"

"She gave me a hug, then said I should draw a picture."

Layla stared at him. "How does that help?"

"I did warn you."

Gale opened his backpack and pulled out his pad. He'd drawn a family scene again. He peered at Layla thoughtfully. There was a question he'd pondered over lunch.

"Are you quite sure you're not at all poltergeisty? Have you tried?"

"Of course I've tried," Layla snapped. Then she softened. "Look." She glanced around the room, and settled on a Lego brick that was sitting on the edge of his bookshelf. She put her finger near it, and then screwed up her face in a scowl of concentration. Slowly she pushed her finger forward, and right into the block.

"There. See?"

Gale moved closer to see more clearly. "Well. That's pretty cool anyway." He bit his lip. "What does it feel like to be *inside* Lego?"

"I don't know... It just doesn't *feel* like anything. Nothing does."

Gale looked disappointed, but only for a moment. "But it doesn't matter. We can still do it. We can still catch the man – we just have to work together. You can tell me what you know, and I can tell the police."

"Yeah. Only they won't believe it. They won't believe it's me saying it, because they don't believe in me. So there's no way they're going to believe you."

Gale picked up the Lego block himself now. First, he examined it to see if Layla's attempt had changed it in any way, and then he tried to repeat her trick, unsuccessfully.

"Well, we'll just have to prove it. We'll have to get evidence."

She stared at him a long while.

"How?"

Gale shrugged. "I don't know yet. Tell me what you remember about the man who took you."

Layla kept watching him for a while, and then floated down to hover in a sitting position on the only chair in the room. They had time now – it was ages before dinner – and their mother had the radio playing downstairs.

She nodded. "OK. I'll tell you."

She got up again and stood – floated – by the window, looking out at the street below.

"We were on the beach, you and Mum and me. Dad was off on his bike somewhere. He was supposed to meet us down there later."

"Yeah, I know the bits with me in."

"I know you do." She glanced around. "I'm just... setting the scene." She scowled slightly, then carried on.

"We'd been there a while and it was hot, so Mum said we could get ice creams. She didn't come with us, because she could see the kiosk from where she was sitting. So, she stayed there, reading her book."

Gale nodded. "I remember." He didn't admit he'd relived that day hundreds of times since her disappearance.

"And we were playing that game, the 'S' game, and we kept playing it in the queue, but it was busy and we had to wait a long time. So you said you were going to go back to Mum and wait for me there," Layla said. "It was almost an argument, but not really. Not a proper one."

Gale bit his lip, her words were taking him back there. The last few moments of seeing his sister alive.

"So after you'd gone back to Mum, I waited there a while – a long while. It must have been ten minutes nearly. And that's when the ambulance turned up. It was driving along the promenade, and then it stopped. And that made lots of people move, to see what had happened. But not me, I didn't want to lose my place in the queue. Then, because of all the people looking at the ambulance, suddenly I couldn't see Mum anymore. But I wasn't worried. It didn't occur to me that it might be *you* that was injured."

"Huh?" Gale interrupted, "I wasn't..." The story had unexpectedly diverged from what he knew, or thought he knew.

"I know. I know that *now*. But that's when he came along. The man." Layla stopped.

Gale felt a chill in his stomach. It was strange how this – whatever it was that was happening with his sister – could swing from fun to deadly serious so quickly.

"What happened then?" He'd wondered about the moment Layla was taken so many times. Everybody had, because she was a sensible girl, and she knew not to go off with strangers. But if that was the case, then how did whoever it was get her off a busy beach without anyone seeing?

Layla didn't answer.

"What was he like?" Gale tried again. "The man?" In his mind he couldn't help but picture an *actual* monster. A kind of hairy giant with green skin and evil red eyes, who physically lifted Layla off her feet and carried her away, tucked under his arm, as she fought and screamed. But Layla seemed to sense this and shook her head.

"He was quite normal looking. It's hard to describe."

"Did he grab you?" Gale asked.

"No." Layla looked frustrated for a second. Or maybe embarrassed. "No, he... he tricked me. I was stupid. He didn't have to grab me."

That made Gale swallow. His sister had always been the smart one. The idea that she could be tricked scared him.

"How?"

As Layla went on she kept her eyes locked onto her brother. "I wouldn't have listened to him at all, but he knew my name. He asked if I was called Layla, and then he said that Mum had sent him..."

"How did he know your name?"

"I've thought about that a lot. I think he must have heard it when we were arguing. I think we were shouting it at each other..."

Gale's eyes went wide, and Layla saw it at once.

"It's not your fault. I don't blame you." She stopped. "He knew your name, too."

"My name?" As cold as he already felt, Gale's body turned to ice.

"Yeah. But he said you'd been hurt. That's what the ambulance was for."

"No it wasn't." Again the confusion hit Gale, where her

story differed from the one he'd gone over so many times with the police lady, and with Karen, and with his parents. "It was because someone had fallen down the cliff. The police said so."

"I know. I know that *now*, because I've heard Mum and Dad talking about it. But that's not what *he* said. He said you'd been hurt – not badly, just enough that you had to go in the ambulance, and Mum had to go with you. And that was why I had to go with *him*. He told me that Mum had asked him to find me and take me to the hospital. She was going to meet us there."

Gale was silent a while, thinking about this. He tried to imagine himself back on the beach, with their situations swapped around. Would he have fallen for it? Would he have been even easier to fool? He didn't like the answer that appeared in his mind.

"Why *him*?" Gale suddenly asked. "Why would Mum have picked a random stranger?" But Layla shook her head.

"He *wasn't* a stranger. That was the point. Or at least he said he wasn't. He told me that Mum happened to notice him on the beach, just after the accident, and she was really relieved, because they knew each other from work. That's why she'd trusted him to take me along to the hospital.

"So he knows Mum?" Gale felt a mix of hope – this would make it easier to catch the man, but the idea that it was someone their mother knew was unsettling too.

But Layla shook her head again. "No. He doesn't. At least, I'm pretty sure he doesn't. He didn't look like a solicitor. Plus, when we were in the car, driving to the hospital, he changed his story.

"What did he say then?"

"He asked if I wanted to see his snakes."

Gale's eyes widened in sudden surprise.

"*His snakes?*"

Layla swallowed, but nodded her head.

FIFTEEN

"Snakes?" Gale asked again. "He asked if you wanted to see his *snakes*?"

"Yeah. I know. That's when I first thought there was something weird about him. Before then he was talking about the hospital and telling me you'd be alright, and I was kind of scared for you, but not really thinking about me, but then suddenly he turned to look at me and said it."

"What exactly did he say?"

"Something like: '*Hey, I just thought, my house is just around the corner, would you like to stop by? I can show you my snakes?*'"

Gale was quiet, trying to imagine the moment.

"And what did you say?"

"I said no, of course. I said I wanted to go straight to the hospital, to see you and Mum. But I thought it was weird and I guess he realised that, because that's when he changed."

"Changed how?"

"He wasn't friendly after that. We were on a quiet road – we weren't going the quick way to the hospital – and he stopped the car and then he suddenly lunged over to me and put something over my mouth and nose."

Gale was silent for a few moments, except for the sound of his breathing.

"What was it?"

"I don't know. It was some sort of cloth, but with something in it, something chemical."

"Like how we saw in that show? The one Mum stopped us from watching?"

"I guess so. Not exactly like that. But sort of."

"That was scary. That show, I mean."

"It's even more scary in real life."

Gale was silent again, thinking about this.

"What did it taste like?" He asked in the end.

"I don't know. It wasn't nice."

Gale thought a moment, then nodded in agreement.

"Then what happened?"

"Well, that was the thing. For a long time we were like that. Him leaning over me, with the cloth on my face. Me not really able to breath. It was horrible."

"Did you fight?"

"I tried to. But he was heavy. And then eventually I got dizzy – you know when you see stars, and it all goes black around the edges?"

Gale stared at his sister, horrified. He managed to nod.

"Well, that happened, and what I could see just got smaller and smaller, and I really panicked. I was terrified, but there wasn't anything I could do, and then I just sort of gave up and let it all go black. I didn't mean to, I really didn't. Then the next thing I knew, I wasn't in the car anymore. I was in this... this big room. This underground room. Without any windows."

Gale tried to make himself think, to be helpful. "The police say they think you were kept somewhere, for around two weeks before you died."

"Yeah, I know."

"And that you were sort of looked after. You were fed and things."

"Sort of."

"So did you see him again?"

Layla turned to face him again. She was still, but after a moment she nodded.

"Yeah. I saw him lots."

Gale just stared at her and waited until she finally went on.

"At first, I was just confused. I didn't know where I was, or how I got there, and I felt sick, really sick."

"Were you scared?"

"Yeah. I was but... well I wasn't *that* scared. I mean—"

"I'd have been terrified," Gale said, meaning it. "I kind of am now, just hearing it."

"No, I *was* scared. But I didn't really believe anyone could do what he was doing. Not for real. And he kept telling me he was going to let me go. I never believed he was going to kill me. Not until..."

They were both quiet for a few seconds. Layla didn't finish the sentence.

"What then?" Gale asked. "What was it like? The room?"

Layla glanced around Gale's bedroom, as if comparing the two spaces in her mind. "It was really bare; the floor was just concrete. But it had a bed in it. When I woke up, I was in it. He must have put me to bed, and taken most of my clothes off when he did it." She turned away, as if not wanting to meet his eyes.

"I don't know if he'd done anything to me by then... I don't think so."

Gale half-recognised what she was referring to, but it wasn't a subject he understood well.

"Were you...?"

"No." Layla replied firmly. "But the door was locked, and there weren't any windows. The door was at the top of a set of stairs, so I think it must have been a basement, or something like that. I didn't have any shoes on, and the floor was cold."

"So what did you do?"

"At first? I cried a lot. And I tried shouting, but he didn't come. I don't think he was even there, at first. So mostly I just kind of waited, in the bed."

Gale suddenly cocked his head onto one side, then got up and went to his shelves.

"What are you doing?" Layla asked.

"We're doing it wrong."

"What?"

"I've been interviewed by the police lots. They always record it, and then they write it all down afterwards. So the next time, when they ask the same questions, they have it all as notes. We need to take notes too. And then we can work out which bits are the most important."

Layla looked dubious, but Gale ignored her and pulled a notebook out, then rummaged around his untidy desk until he found a pen that worked.

"We need to go back. What did he look like? Tell me again."

Layla paused. She seemed both irritated yet relieved to have had her story interrupted. Then she seemed to choose the latter, and nodded.

"OK. He had black hair, and a little beard."

Gale wrote it down. "And you said he was normal looking? What does that mean?"

"I mean he was... like a normal man. Quite strong, but he didn't *look* particularly strong."

"OK. Was he tall? Or short?"

"I don't know. He wasn't a midget." There was a poster on Gale's wall, sent to him from their American cousins, whom they had seen only the once. It showed LeBron James, the basketball player from the LA Lakers. Layla looked at it now. "He wasn't a basketball player either."

Gale looked at it now, too. "Was he black?" But Layla screwed up her nose. "*No*. He had really white skin actually. Like he didn't go outside much." She breathed heavily, while Gale wrote this down.

"Anything else?"

She was quiet.

"What was he wearing?"

"Jeans. Black jeans. And kind of... I don't know what you call them... like, cowboy boots?"

"With the things at the back, the silver bits?"

She shook her head. "No. They just looked like them otherwise."

Gale thought for a moment. "Did he tell you his name?" She stopped still, then stared at him.

"He told me to call him Kenny, but he said that wasn't his real name."

Gale thought for a while, then looked up to see Layla had moved closer and was twisted around trying to see what he had written.

"What about the car?" Gale suddenly asked. "Do you remember that?"

She moved away, shrugging her shoulders. "Some. I don't know the type exactly, but it was quite big. And it was green." Gale wrote this down.

"New? Old?" He asked hopefully.

She twisted her mouth sideways. "It was dirty inside. There were crisp packets on the floor."

"What type?"

"Normal crisps. Ready salted."

Gale took another note.

"Did you get the number plate?" Gale asked afterwards. He didn't expect her to say yes. "I'm only asking because the police have talked about them a lot. They say they can find who owns the car from the number.

"Not all of it. I tried. Just before I got into the car I looked at it, because I thought I ought to remember it just in case. But then I didn't remember the whole thing."

Gale was suddenly animated. "Well how much did you remember?"

"The first bit. BN12."

Gale blinked.

"Is that a lot? Is that enough?"

"I don't know, but it might be." He wrote it down, feeling a shaft of excitement that this might be their first real clue. "Are you sure about it? Are you sure you can't remember any more?"

"I think so..." Layla squeezed her eyes shut in concentration, then opened them again. She held out her hands. "It's what I remember."

Gale looked over what he'd written, then looked up again.

"When you were in the basement place, did you see him again? Did you talk to him?"

Layla nodded. "Yeah. He came in. After a couple of days, he was there a lot."

"What did he do?"

"Not that much mostly. He brought me food. Like, microwave food, in plastic tubs. They were really hot and I burned my tongue the first time he brought one, because I was really hungry by then. Then he kept saying how I didn't need to worry, and that I would be able to go home soon, I just had to be good and wait. I sort of believed him, because he didn't seem particularly nasty then. There was like..." her voiced tailed off.

"Like what?"

"It was like, there was a good side to him, and a bad side. And I never knew which it was going to be."

Something about this stopped Gale from asking her to explain in more detail.

"What did you do? When you were in there."

"Nothing much. I kind of daydreamed really. There was

nothing to do. Except that... At one point he brought me some magazines."

Gale gave this some thought.

"Oh, and he did show me his snake too."

"*Really?*"

"Yeah. One time when he brought me food, he just sat and watched me eat it, not saying anything. And then when I finished he said the snake was upstairs, and I could see it if I wanted."

"And did you want to?"

"No, not really. But he went and got it anyway. And then he came back in, and there was this snake wrapped around his arms."

"What did you think?"

"I didn't know what to think. I was kind of used to being there by then, but I didn't know when he was telling the truth and when he was lying. Because I kept asking if I could go home, and he said I could, but not yet. So, I suppose when I saw he really did have a snake, I thought it was good news, because maybe he was telling the truth about me going home too."

Gale considered this; the logic seemed to make sense.

"He said I could touch her."

"*Her?*"

"Yeah. That's what he called it."

Gale screwed up his face. "Yuck. And did you? Touch it?"

"I didn't want to. But I thought if I did what he wanted then he might let me go. So I did."

"What was it like?" Gale had touched a snake before, on a trip to a wildlife park with his parents, back when Layla was alive. At the time it had been a kind of victory for him, since Layla had refused to do the same, and for a short while it had sparked an interest in snakes for him. He wondered if she remembered, but said nothing. In a strange way it almost felt disloyal now.

"It was drier than it looked. But it kept sticking its tongue out."

"It was smelling you. That's how they do it."

She pulled a face.

"What else happened?"

"Nothing much. He asked if I wanted to hold her, and I said not really, and I told him I was hungry. He only brought me food once a day, so I was always hungry."

"Was there a toilet down there?" Gale changed the subject suddenly.

Layla nodded again.

"Yeah. In a little room off the main room. And a sink. That's where I drank from." She waited. She seemed to sense that, now Gale had the notepad, he was the one in charge of what they were doing.

"Did it have a name?" Gale asked. He noticed the power shift between them too, different to when she'd been alive. But he wasn't able to think about it now. He was too busy. "The snake, I mean."

Layla's eyes rose as she thought about it. "No, he just called it 'his girl'."

"No, not that type of name," Gale persisted. "Did he say what type of snake it was?"

"Oh. Yeah." Layla nodded. "He said it was a Mexican kingsnake. He told me it wasn't poisonous. But – like I said, he said he had more. He told me he had a poisonous one upstairs that he couldn't show me because it was too danger-ous." Layla grew quiet as she said this, but Gale didn't notice. Instead, he wrote *Mexican kingsnake* on the pad, then looked up.

"Did he say what the other one was called?"

"Erm... Oh yeah, I think he called it a pit viper." She stared at him, then swallowed.

Gale wrote this down as well, then sat back and thought.

"Is there anything else you can remember? Anything else that might help us to know who he is?"

Layla spent a moment thinking too, but then shook her head. "There's... there's what happened at the end. But I don't really want to talk about that, if it's OK."

"Why not? What happened at the end?"

She sort of smiled, then looked uncomfortable. "It's not easy. Like I said, it wasn't a nice thing that happened. I don't want to... to re-live it."

Gale stared at her for a while, then he nodded, and put down the pen.

SIXTEEN

They broke for Gale to eat dinner. Layla followed him down the stairs and hovered by the window for a while as they ate. But after a while she drifted off. Gale used the time to think, only giving the briefest of answers to his mother as she tried to make conversation. As soon as he could, he slipped upstairs again, this time to go to sleep, so he had to go through the usual routine of cleaning his teeth and putting on his pyjamas.

"What we need to do –" he began, once he was finished, and he saw that Layla was back, "is try to work out what information we can use to find him."

Layla nodded in agreement. "How?"

Gale answered by opening the notebook. Layla moved to look at it – she'd been wanting to do so for a while – but was unable to turn the pages herself. Gale leafed through until he found the part about the number plate.

"Do you remember what I said about the number plates?" he asked.

"If we have the whole number the police can tell us who owns the car?"

"Or *we* can. On the internet."

"But we only have a part of the number plate."

"I know. We can still try."

Layla looked dubious, but she shrugged her shoulders. "We'll have to look tomorrow. Mum doesn't let us take the computer upstairs at night-time."

For a second Gale looked triumphant. "She isn't as mad about that now." He crossed to his desk, and lifted a copy of *The Adventures of Tintin: The Black Island*, a large book that he'd placed over their mother's old laptop before she'd put him to bed. "Plus, she didn't see me take it." Gale smiled.

For a second it looked as though Layla might object. The no-devices-upstairs rule had always been pretty strictly enforced when she was alive. But even if she was going to object, her curiosity got the better of her.

"Go on then, type it in."

They tried putting the letters directly in Google, but it didn't seem to work. They discovered there was a BN 12-inch naval artillery gun, that it was a name for an acupuncture point, whatever that was, and a postcode in West Sussex. But when Layla suggested adding the words 'number plate' after the letters, they got somewhere.

"Birmingham," Layla read off the screen. Despite being dead for two years, she was still a faster reader than he was.

"Where's it say that?" Gale asked.

"Here, look. Number plates beginning BN are registered to Birmingham. It's just a link, though. Click it and see where it goes."

Gale did so, and they were taken to a website called CarScan. At the top was a box inviting them to type in a number plate for a "vehicle search". Gale typed the letters again and clicked the button.

Sorry, we couldn't find a vehicle with that registration plate.

They went back and tried several other pages, until they got a little closer, clarifying that the BN part was a code that referred to where the plate was issued – where the car was first sold to someone, Layla explained – and the '12' part referred to *when* it was sold. It took a while to figure it out, not least because Layla herself was unable to control the computer to show the right bit she needed to read.

"He bought the car in Birmingham, in 2012, and in the first half of the year?" Gale clarified, when he'd finally understood. "Between March and August 2012?"

"Yeah. I think so."

Gale wrote it down.

"But it doesn't necessarily mean *he* bought it in Birmingham?" he said, sucking on the end of the pen. "Someone else could have bought it, and then sold it to him?"

"I guess so. Like when Mum bought her new car? It wasn't new at all."

"Yeah..." Gale looked disappointed. "So what you're saying is, he could have bought the car any time, and pretty much anywhere, and we don't know where or when it happened?"

Layla looked thoughtful, then seemed to agree. "So we don't know anything at all." She suddenly looked incredibly sad. And Gale saw how this mattered to her – really mattered.

"Yes, we do," he stood up forcefully, sending the notepad sliding onto the floor. He began pacing up and down his bedroom. "We know lots of things. We know that he lives quite close."

"How?" Layla asked. "He could have driven for hours after he used that stuff that made me go to sleep. I could have been in Scotland!"

"No," Gale shook his head. "He said he lived just around the corner, remember? When he suggested showing you his snake. He really did have a snake, so he probably wasn't lying about where he lived either."

Layla stayed quiet, considering this.

"Plus, we know he probably lives alone."

"How do we know that?" She screwed up her face.

"Because everyone who keeps snakes as pets live alone. And you said you were screaming quite a lot."

"I did, but—"

"So, if he had a family, or children, wouldn't they have wondered what all the noise was? Wouldn't they have wanted to play in the basement?"

"They wouldn't," Layla said at once. "It was horrible down there."

"Well it was for *you*, but that's because he was a sicko who lives alone. If he had kids it would have been a cool den, or maybe like a home cinema. Or something like that. Think about it. *We'd* have played in the basement, if we had one."

Layla contemplated again, and finally accepted the logic. She looked impressed with her brother. "What else?"

"Well..." Gale paused now, thinking hard, and not wanting to disappoint her. "We know he's *not* called Kenny, because he told you so."

"So he could be called any other name except that. I'm not sure that's a big help."

"Unless he was lying? It could have been a double bluff."

Suddenly Gale returned to the computer, pulled up a new internet search page, and typed in *'men with beards'* and *'Kenny'*. When the results came up he clicked on the images, so that dozens of pictures of men with beards came up.

"There. Any of them look familiar?"

She leaned in to take a good look, but shook her head.

"Scroll down."

Gale did so, and they spent some time looking through the pictures that came up.

"These ones?" Gale asked hopefully, as each new batch of faces came up. But Layla just shook her head again.

"He was much younger than that one," she said in the end,

pointing to a photograph of Kenny Rogers, a musician who had died in 2020. "More like that one, but the beard was smaller."

Gale thought. "Maybe we can work out how old he is, more or less, from the pictures. Was he as old as Dad?"

At once Layla shook her head. "Definitely not."

"OK, how about Uncle Jim?" This was their mother's younger brother, the one who lived in the US.

"I don't know, I haven't seen him for ages."

"Well how about Mr Jones from school?"

It took a while, but eventually they decided upon an estimate of Layla's killer's age: that he was somewhere between twenty – he wasn't a teenager – and forty – the age that grown-ups tended to be parents and either lose all their hair, or have it turn grey like really old people. But within that range they weren't able to narrow it down.

"So we know the man who killed you is between twenty and forty years old. He keeps snakes. He drives an eleven-year-old car that's quite big and dark green. He probably isn't called Kenny and he lives nearby in his own house," Gale concluded. He was pleased with how it had gone. "If we know all that, he can't be that hard to find."

"Yeah, but how?" Layla asked.

SEVENTEEN

"It's good news." Detective Inspector Kieran Clarke began, as soon as the call from his office phone connected. "I wanted to tell you right away."

"OK." On the other end Rachel Martin's voice sounded disorientated for a moment, in the background there was the sound of a dog barking. "What is it?"

"The application for the *Crimebusters* program. I asked the producer to let me know as soon as they made the decision, so that I could let you know. She's just phoned to tell me – they've agreed to feature Layla's case." He paused, wondering if good news was quite the correct term, in the circumstances. "I'm sorry, that was insensitive, I know this is going to be difficult."

"No, it's fine. I'm just out walking the dog." There was a silence.

"That's not all."

"What?"

Clarke wished for a moment that he had made another appointment to meet with them. It might have been a better way to break the news. But then he'd wanted them to know right away, so they wouldn't be left wondering. He took a deeper breath.

"They've agreed to make it the lead item. They always have one case that makes up the bulk of the programme, then a couple of smaller ones as well. They've made Layla the lead."

"That's... that's great." Rachel managed.

In his office, Clarke got to his feet and moved towards the door. The cable on the desk phone stretched out as he opened it and looked out over the investigation suite. He carried on talking, knowing the half dozen detectives working there could hear his words.

"Which also means Starling's had to reclassify Layla's case again, so it's no longer technically inactive. And that means we've the whole team back working on it." A couple of the detectives looked up from their work, and Clarke smiled at them. He pulled the door to, and sat back down behind his desk.

"Were there any questions you had? Or would you like some time to think it over? We can meet up next week if it helps?"

"No that's... That is good news. When will it all happen?"

Clarke nodded, as if this were an excellent question. "Well, there's a fair bit of work to do now, our end. We have a very accurate idea of what took place on the beach that day, but we have to help the production company to translate that into a twelve-minute reconstruction. That'll take a while, and then there's filming. All told, they're looking at a date about five weeks from now."

"That's great." Rachel said again, and Clarke sighed.

"I'm sorry, Rachel. This is going to be a very difficult time for you, and I understand that. But I promise you, I'll do everything I can to make it easy for you. If you want to be involved, you can; if you want to stay out of things, that's fine too."

"Thank you, Kieran. That's..." Her voice changed,

becoming more positive. "Actually, it's really great. And thank you for letting me know."

"No problem," Clarke replied. "Enjoy the rest of your walk. And give my regards to Jon."

"Thank you, Kieran. For everything you're doing."

Clarke smiled. "You're welcome."

He hung up the phone, placing the receiver back carefully in its cradle. And then he drew in a deep breath, held it a moment with his eyes closed, then breathed out again.

After that he got back to work.

EIGHTEEN

"Snakes!" Gale said, the next night, as he burst into his room. There had been no time to talk over breakfast, and then he'd had his swimming lesson, and after that a family walk with the dog. After that their mother had insisted upon the family eating around the table, which was as painful as ever.

"Snakes?" Layla looked uncomfortable, but she still grew brighter and vibrant as she came more fully into Gale's bedroom. Gale paused pulling on his pyjama top to watch.

"What about them?" She asked.

"That's how we can find out who he is."

"How?"

Gale grinned. He'd had the idea at school. "Lots of people have dogs, right? And cats? But hardly anyone keeps snakes as a pet."

"So?"

"So, he must have bought them from somewhere – from a pet shop – and he must feed them something. Like dog food, but snake food."

Layla looked slightly ill still, as if the whole topic was difficult for her. But Gale was enthusiastic.

"Do you remember the way Dad used to take us to school, through the short cut?"

"Hmm. Yeah, sort of."

"Mum does a different route, because it was hard to turn onto the main road with all the traffic, but Dad still goes that way sometimes. And do you remember that weird pet shop there?"

Layla didn't seem to want to answer, but it was clear she remembered it. "Yeah. I remember. It was called The Reptile Room."

"*Exactly.*"

She watched him for a while, and finally seemed to engage with the idea.

"And you think he might have bought his snakes there? Or his snake food?"

Gale's eyes were bright. He nodded. "It's worth a try, don't you think?"

Layla frowned, but in the end she nodded too, with a shrug.

"But how does that help? We can't exactly go there."

For a second Gale looked at his sister, aware of how their roles had almost reversed. It used to be her who had the ideas, and he who followed on behind, waiting to see what she'd come up with. He took a deep breath, embracing the change, as strange as it was.

"OK. Do you remember when I was younger, I told Mum and Dad I wanted a snake as a pet? It was after we went to that zoo place, and I held one and you wouldn't?"

"Yeah. Sort of."

"And I did that project on snakes, for school? And Dad helped me, he took me to the shop. I even got to interview some of the reptile owners about how to care for them."

"Did you?"

"Yeah, you didn't want to come."

"OK, though I still don't get how it helps?" Layla continued to look doubtful, but Gale pressed on.

"Well, back then Dad said I couldn't actually have one, but it's all different now. They're really worried about me, so maybe this time they will let me!"

Layla stared, clearly confused, or at least expecting more. "You want a snake? Don't you get it, the man who *killed me* kept snakes. They're disgusting—"

"I don't *want* a snake. I just want to go to that snake shop. So we can ask them if there's anyone local who has snakes."

"Ohhh. OK." Her head fell on one side, thinking. "But Mum's still not going to let you keep a snake."

"She bought me a puppy."

"Gale, there's a bit of a difference." She shook her head. "No. We need another plan."

Gale felt disappointed. Maybe their roles hadn't reversed as much as he'd thought they had.

"Maybe there's another pet I could ask for? That the pet shop has too."

"Like what?" Layla turned back to him, as if she thought this idea was more promising.

"I don't know."

"Does it have a website?" Layla asked. And since Gale still had the laptop in his room, they were able to look straight away. He picked it up and typed the search.

"Yeah," he said, when The Reptile Room's website came up.

Welcome to The Reptile Room. We sell a range of exotic pets and essential supplies including live and dead prey.

There were lots of pictures of different animals along the bottom of the screen.

"Look." Gale turned the laptop to show her.

Layla shrank away a little at the snake pictures, then said, "OK." She sounded more hopeful. "Why don't you go downstairs and ask Mum. But use the school project idea again, she's never going to let you have a lizard or anything disgusting. Just tell her you've got to do research on exotic pets and you want to have a look."

Gale felt good, but then something changed. It was one thing to think about it in his own head, or talk about it with Layla, but then actually going to do it, speaking with Mum... that was different. But on the other hand, if he really was going to help his sister, and not just talk about it, that meant actually doing things. Maybe things he didn't really want to do. He understood that now.

"Mum?" Gale paused as his mother, who was watching TV, her legs up on the sofa, twisted her head around to see him.

Layla had followed him downstairs, and now stood behind him, nodding encouragingly.

His mother smiled, but it looked forced, like she'd been mulling things over.

"Yes?"

Gale took a deep breath.

"I've got to do this school project, and I need to go to the pet shop – you know the one on the way to school? It's called The Reptile Room?"

"Really?" Her forehead crumpled into a light frown of confusion. "I didn't see anything about that on Facebook."

Gale felt a moment's concern. Neither he nor Layla had thought of Facebook. The way his mum seemed to get her information there was a mystery to him. He went on anyway.

"I don't suppose it will be on there yet," he guessed. "Because it's the next project coming up. I just find it interesting, so I wanted to get ahead." Gale tried to ignore his sister as she nodded encouragingly.

"Oh." Still their mother didn't look particularly convinced, but she didn't seem against the idea either. "Well, OK. If you like." She thought a moment. "We don't have anything on after school tomorrow. We can go then?"

"Yeah, that's great. Thanks, Mum."

NINETEEN

The Reptile Room was a tatty looking place, with a grid of bars over windows which had been painted to not let any light in. It was in one of the dodgy parts of the town – as Mum liked to call that end of the high street.

"Are you sure about this?" she asked, as they paused just outside the door. "It looks a bit..." She pulled a face to indicate 'yuck'. But Gale's reason for hesitating was that he was looking around for Layla. She hadn't been there at school, and though he'd spend the whole lunchtime walking the grounds trying to sense her, she was nowhere to be found. And now he was here, he didn't quite know what he supposed to do.

"You could always just look on the internet," she suggested. But Gale shook his head.

"I just need to have a look. For school."

"OK." His mother nodded.

There was an electric buzzer attached to the door that sounded when it opened, presumably alerting whoever worked there that customers had arrived. No one came at first, leaving Gale and his mother standing in the small, dimly lit shop front, surrounded by walls of metal shelving, filled with glass tanks and pumps and small electric heaters. A second room led off from the one they stood in, where pale-blue lighting cut through the darkness. There was a strong smell to the place. Hay, and something else. Not pleasant. Eventually a man came from another room, behind the counter. He was large, his gut forming a bulge in the front of a well-worn Metallica T-shirt.

"Hi."

"Oh hi," Gale's mother sounded embarrassed, answering before Gale got a chance. "We're just looking around, thank you."

The man sniffed, as if this wasn't a surprise, nor particularly welcome. He kept his eyes on them, as if suspecting they might be the types to grab something and run out, but managed to look bored at the same time.

Gale moved a little closer, bracing himself to speak, but his mother was standing protectively close, which put him off from saying anything. Plus, he still didn't know what he wanted to ask. He began to feel deflated. All day at school he'd thought about this; now, it wasn't going to work. He looked around for help. For Layla. Where was she?

It was so dark in the shop he wondered if she were there, but he just couldn't see her, so he took a risk, speaking quietly, but loud enough that she would hear him.

"I can't see you," he muttered, hoping to hear her reply.

"What?" his mother replied, irritated.

"We use UV lights," the shopkeeper answered, as if Gale's comment had been a question to him. "A lot of animals are nocturnal."

Then, somewhere in his mind, Gale heard Layla. But not like she was there – more a memory of what she would say, or had said before.

I'm here. Just not in the same way. Remember what I said

about being outside the house? It's not as easy. But I'm still with you.

Gale looked around again, as if confirming, but he still felt better.

"OK, I get it."

"You get what?" Rachel asked.

"Nothing."

She gave him a look.

Gale waited for his sister to tell him what to do, but nothing else came. Even so, he had the beginnings of an idea now. He thought a moment, then turned to the shopkeeper.

"Um, I sort of need to know what animals you have." As he spoke, he sensed his mother's disapproval, but at the same time, his sister willing him on.

The shopkeeper answered. "Sure. Most of the stock is in here." He pointed to the second room, with the blue light. "We've got dragons, stick insects, praying mantis. You have any idea what you're after exactly?" The question was part aimed at Gale, part aimed at Rachel, even though she'd been clear they weren't buying. He said it almost as a challenge. Gale glanced at his mum. He took a deep breath.

"Erm. Do you have any... snakes?"

"Gale! We're not—"

"We've got a few in." The man turned his attention fully to Gale. He seemed to enjoy cutting Rachel off. He nodded again to the second room. "We had some corn snakes come in last week. They're good for beginners." He seemed to appraise Gale for a moment, but apparently was satisfied with what he saw. "You wanna see one?"

"Yes, please."

The man lumbered out from behind the counter, and Gale followed him deeper into the shop. They stopped in front of some more tanks, larger than the ones in the front, and lit by fluorescent lamps. Up close they hummed quietly. Inside one, several yellow-and-orange snakes were curled up and sleeping under fluorescent tubes. Each one was about the size and thickness of a finger.

From behind him, Gale heard his mother make a disgusted sound. She tapped him on the shoulder. "I think I'll just wait in the front." She backed away.

The shopkeeper watched her go. "You like snakes?" he asked Gale.

"Um, yeah, sort of," Gale lied.

"Some people don't." He indicated with his head towards Rachel's receding back. "But if it helps you work on your parents, you can explain how they're really misunderstood. You can handle these little guys. They're super friendly."

"Do you—? Erm." Gale stopped. He tried to remember everything that Layla had said, and focus on why they were there. "Do you have any Mexican kingsnakes?" Gale thought quickly. "Or pit vipers?"

The change in the conversation clearly surprised the man.

"Woah. OK. Yeah, we *can* get Kingsnakes in. A couple of times we've had Mexicans too but..." He peered at Gale in the semi-darkness. "Pit vipers are a bit of a different animal." He chuckled at his own joke. "They're not quite so friendly, if you get my gist. Why the interest?"

"A friend of mine has one. Or wants one. So, I just wondered."

The shop assistant watched for a moment. If he didn't believe Gale, he seemed willing to go along with it. "Okay... if your *friend* wants a pit viper, he'll need to wait a few years. Until he's eighteen, at least. And then he'll need a licence."

"A licence?"

"Totally. Pit vipers are covered by the Dangerous Wild Animals Act. They have to be registered."

"Have you ever sold any?"

"What? Animals covered by the Act? Course we have. We have a Gila monster over here, if you want to see—"

"No, I'm just interested in pit vipers. Have you ever sold any of those?"

The man turned back from the tank, which Gale guessed housed the Gila monster – whatever that was. He was looking intrigued now, peering through the darkness at Gale, who wished Layla was there to help him.

"What's the fascination with pit vipers?"

"Erm," Gale had no idea what to say to this, but it turned out that saying nothing did the trick.

The shopkeeper smiled, his teeth glowing a blue-white colour from the lights. "You know your snakes, huh? That's cool." He nodded enthusiastically. "Super cool. I was like you when I was your age."

Suddenly Gale had an idea of what he was going to say next, that if he played his cards right, he might end up like him, actually able to work in a shop like The Reptile Room, but he didn't. Instead the shopkeeper grinned deeper.

"Actually we do have a couple of local guys into their vipers."

Gale drew in his breath. "Really? Do you know who they are?" He was unable to keep the excitement from his voice, which seemed to confuse the man again. It was like the conversation wasn't following a track that felt natural.

He scratched at his face. "Yeah. I know who they are." But then he seemed to anticipate Gale's next question. "And I can't be telling you."

Gale searched his mind for what to say next, but he had no idea. He turned to his mother, but she was in the other part of the shop, out of sight. He turned back to the shopkeeper, and yet his mind was empty. A sense of panic began to rise up inside him. Then, he heard his sister's voice, weakly in his head.

Ask him if they have to keep a record? Tell him it's for the school project. Like we said.

Gale nodded in the darkness. He felt the panic recede. His voice sounded natural again, when he spoke.

"Can you tell me more about the records of who buys the pets, like the pit vipers? I need to know for this school project I'm doing."

"School project?" The shopkeeper sounded unimpressed now, like he'd misjudged this kid, and now he was worried he might get thirty visits just like this one, wasting his time. He turned and led the way back towards the counter. "Yeah, sure. We got a register right here. You wanna see it?" There was a clear note of sarcasm to the question, as if it was wasn't a serious offer, but Gale answered at once.

"Yes please."

The man stopped at that, then burst out laughing. He turned to look at Gale, like he couldn't figure out what was going on. But perhaps The Reptile Room didn't get too many customers – or visitors, since Gale wasn't a customer exactly – and he was happy to be indulge him.

"Well, OK then," he said, with mock enthusiasm. "Let's take a look!" He bent down behind the till to pull out a black notebook, then placed it on the counter between them.

"There you go. The register. Happy now?"

Check it for Mexican kingsnakes, Layla said at once. *And pit vipers.*

I know, Gale said, inside his head, and he went to open the book, but the man immediately snatched it back.

"Uh huh." He shook his head again. "It's got customer information in it. I can't let you see it."

"Of course not," Gale heard his mother's voice from behind him. He'd almost forgotten she was there, but she was, and she was clearly getting angry judging by her tone.

"I think we should be going Gale, don't you?"

We need to see inside that book, Layla's voice sounded in his head. Gale tried to focus, to ignore them all.

"So if someone buys a Mexican kingsnake," he said as confidently as he could, "or a pit viper, it would be in there?"

The question silenced all of them, except the shopkeeper, who paused, and then answered.

"No. Not the kingsnake. We don't have any requirement to record that. But a pit viper, yes. All vipers are covered by the Act. We put it in the book here, then I have to upload the information to a website. Seriously, kid – you happy now?"

Gale wasn't, but he had no idea what to say to get into the book. But again, it turned out he didn't need to. The man suddenly seemed to think of something, and opened it himself. Absently, he leafed back a few pages. Then, with his face crunched up in concentration, a few more.

"You know, now that you mention it, I remember..." He went back several more pages. When he spoke again, he sounded satisfied. "Here you go. I thought as much. We did sell a pit viper on..." He checked the date, having to lean down close to see the entry in the poor lighting. "January fourteenth. Three years ago."

He looked up. "Beautiful animal. I remember it."

Gale felt his eyes widen. He was nearly there! He swallowed carefully.

"Can you tell me who bought it?"

"Nope." The man shook his head again. "Data protection and all that." He tapped the book, his fat finger obscuring the name that had been written there.

"*Gale.*" His mother called from behind him again. She sounded actually angry now, like she'd had enough of whatever was going on now.

Gale felt frustrated. He was so close, he just needed that name. But then he felt his mother's hand gripping his shoulder, and begin to pull him away from the counter. Yet as she did so, Gale saw something else.

In the semi-darkness a shape flowed through the air, and his sister began to materialise next to the shop assistant. She bent down as he did, and studied the still open book. "I can't see the name, his finger's on it!" she called out, as Gale's mother's hand tightened on his back. He resisted, which just made her grip firmer.

"Come on," his mum said. "We're going."

"Make him move his hand!" Layla shouted, frantic.

"How?" Gale replied out loud, too desperate to care that his mother and the shop assistant would hear. Both paused in surprise, but neither answered him.

Instead Rachel turned to the assistant. "Thank you for your time."

It gave Gale an idea. "Time! What's the time?" He blurted out, spinning out of his mother's grip. He looked at the fat man's wrist, hoping it might bear a watch, and to his relief, saw he was wearing a large digital watch, which even incorporated a minia-ture keyboard. For a second he saw the man's own eyes fall on the device, as if he were about to read out what it said. But then he didn't, he just left his hand there.

"Please, the time. I really need to know the time!"

"Gale! What are you doing?" Rachel asked.

The man's eyes rose to a clock on the wall. "Quarter past five," he said.

"Gale, will you come with me right now?"

She had a firm grip now, and pulled him away from the desk.

"We're very sorry to have bothered you," she said to the man, who didn't move, still didn't pull his finger away. Instead with his other hand, he slowly closed the book and watched them leave. Gale kept his head turned, to watch the book as long as he could, but it was no good. He was propelled firmly towards the door. And then Layla was there too, coming out of the shop with them.

"I didn't get it!" Layla wailed. She was crying now. Desperate tears.

For a second he didn't care that his mother would hear. "I know."

"You know what?" their mother replied, but Gale ignored her and listened instead to his sister, who was still sobbing and shaking her head.

"I didn't see his name! He didn't move his finger." Tears dripped down her pale face.

Gale's mother got into the car, but he hesitated before opening the passenger door.

"I didn't get his name either," he said. "But there was an address underneath it. I got that."

TWENTY

"You got the address?" Layla was still breathless, when they finally regrouped back in Gale's bedroom. "I didn't see anything; the man wouldn't move his finger."

"You were looking in the wrong place. The next column had the address. 42 Kingsley Avenue."

"That's it?"

"That's all I saw."

Gale pulled out a notepad where he'd written it down when he got home. He looked at the note now, as if unsure what to do next.

"How come you were there?" he asked suddenly. "I thought you couldn't go anywhere outside the house?"

"I can't. Not easily anyway." Layla replied. She looked as if she didn't want to discuss it, but then relented.

"I *can* be in places where you are. But..."

"It hurts?"

"It's not..." She stopped. After a while she nodded. "Yeah."

Gale bit his lip, and went back to the notepad. "Well, what do we do with this? We don't know where it is."

"Just look on the computer!" Layla said. "On Google Maps."

The computer had been discovered in Gale's room and put back in the living room, but their mother was making dinner now, so Gale was able to retrieve it again fairly easily.

"Go on, type it in," Layla prompted. Gale did so, and the map zoomed in to a street. He didn't recognise it.

"I know where that is!" Layla called out, her head close to the screen. "It's near where I used to play netball." She turned to him, excitement on her face. "Remember?"

Gale thought about it and decided he probably did. He'd only gone a few times, though, when Dad had been cycling and not able to look after him, so he'd had to go and watch. It was funny, though; he'd moaned like crazy at the time, but now he'd love to spend his Saturday mornings watching her play netball.

"Come on, put the little man there," Layla instructed, apparently unaware of his thoughts. She pointed impatiently at the icon of the person that Google used to indicate its Street View service, and the screen changed, morphing from a computerised image of the street to actual photographs taken from the road. For a second they were disorientated.

"Spin around," Layla went on. "There." She pointed at the screen, where the front gate of a house had a number written next to it.

44

"It must be next door."

It took Gale a few seconds to manipulate the computer to show them, and then it was difficult to see the house next door, since it was set further back from the road than the other houses on the street.

"Well?" Gale murmured. He still felt the confusion from

his earlier thought: wanting to be with her, when he was with her.

Layla leaned in again and stared at it, but when she pulled back from the screen she shook her head.

"I don't know."

"What do you mean, you don't know? Don't you recognise it? Is it the right place?"

"I don't know. I didn't see the outside, remember? I was drugged or something, when he took me inside."

Finally, Gale focussed properly.

"And dead when he took you out." He finished the thought, then he realised what he'd said and glanced at his sister. "Sorry."

Layla looked crestfallen.

"It's OK. It's true," she said finally. "Can you..." She put her hand onto the trackpad of the computer, but of course it went straight through. Frustration filled her features.

"Can you move it around a bit? Get a better look?"

Together, they spent a long time trying to see the house and managed to agree on several factors. It was a big house. It was quite well hidden from the road by large trees and bushes in the front garden. It also had a garage – which Gale reasoned could have been how the killer got Layla into and out of the house, so that the neighbours wouldn't have been able to see anything. But it was impossible to tell if it had an underground basement or anything similar, and Layla was certain that the room where she was kept had no windows.

"So now what?" Gale looked at his big sister. He was happy now to let her be in charge – they'd fallen comfortably back into the pattern in which both of them had grown up. Her leading, and him following faithfully behind.

Layla looked thoughtful.

"We have to go there," she concluded. "We need to get a better look and see if there are any clues."

It was the answer that Gale had expected, but that didn't mean he was happy to hear it.

"How exactly? I can't really have another school project."

"No..."

"And there's no way that Mum's going to let me go there on my own." Some of the other children in his class were now allowed to walk to school on their own. But not Gale. He understood, though it frustrated him. "She won't let me go anywhere on my own."

Still Layla looked lost in thought. She stood up from the computer and drifted over to the window, looking out on their quiet cul-de-sac street below. Gale watched her, remembering how the two of them had been allowed to play out there on their bikes in the summers before she died.

"I'm not even allowed to do *that* anymore," he said, assuming she'd understand him, and she did.

"I know. I'm sorry."

"My bike's too small for me now anyway, I grew too much," Gale went on, but Layla wasn't listening now.

"How about Becky?" Her face lit up at the idea. "I bet she'll let you go with her!"

Becky was their older cousin, eight years older than Gale. She was the daughter of Auntie Erica, their mother's sister, whose family lived close enough that they tended to visit once or twice a month, and had done so throughout Gale and Layla's childhood. Despite the age difference between the children, Becky and Layla had been close. The family had continued to visit regularly since Layla's murder, but Becky didn't always come any more. Now she was eighteen, had passed her driving test, and was preparing to go to university.

"I dunno..." Gale began.

"You could tell her about me!" Layla's eyes lit up at the

thought. "She might actually believe you. She's the only one who might."

Gale looked dubious.

"Oh, come on. Aren't they coming this weekend anyway? Didn't Mum say?"

Gale had to concede this was the case.

"Well then. Tell Becky about me, and she'll help. She'll take us to see the house. I'm sure she will."

Layla looked firm. The idea was settled.

TWENTY-ONE

The week ground by, and on Saturday morning Gale found himself in the living room ostensibly watching TV, but actually keeping more of an eye on the street outside for the arrival of his auntie's car. When it finally arrived, and Erica and Becky came in, they were arguing about whether Becky had been paying proper attention as she drove.

His aunt Erica kissed him on both cheeks, as she always did, but Becky only gave him a brief smile before ending the discussion and seamlessly started to tell Gale's mother about her latest plans for university. At the same time, she unloaded a plastic shopping bag filled with food they'd brought along.

"You need to get her alone," Layla suggested to Gale, who was watching uncertainly. He puffed out his cheeks.

Aunt Erica set herself up in the kitchen, roping Gale into peeling potatoes. He did so quietly, listening as his cousin talked non-stop about her friends and all the night clubs they'd been too. Layla listened too, a serious look on her face. When he was finally done, and Becky paused for breath, he steeled himself, and took his chance.

"Becky," he began. "Can I show you something? Something important."

Becky glanced around at the kitchen and the table which still had to be laid. Then she turned happily to her younger cousin.

"Sure." She beamed.

Gale led her upstairs to his room, then closed his bedroom door. She lifted her eyebrows, then asked.

"So what's this about?"

Gale looked at Layla, who was standing beside the window, rubbing her hands expectantly. He shifted his weight from one foot to the other.

"I kind of need you to help me with something."

Becky waited, then glanced around the room. "Sure. What?"

"It's... it's a bit odd." He was worried. He was actually fairly sure that Becky already thought he was a bit strange. When Layla was alive, she'd been much closer with her.

"Okay..." She held out her hands. "Go on? You're freaking me out now."

Gale didn't go on, and Becky frowned suddenly. "Is this about girls or something? Is that why you wanted privacy?"

"No." Gale glanced at Layla again. "Well not exactly. Not in that way." He paused.

"Just tell her," Layla said, unhelpfully. "I think she might believe you."

Gale shook his head, then unfolded the picture of the house they'd printed out from Google Street View.

"I need you to go with me to look at this house." He held out the paper.

Becky took it and studied the photograph.

"OK... Why?"

"Just tell her!" Layla urged.

"*OK, OK!*" Gale tried to ignore the look that had appeared

on his cousin's face at this outburst. Then he took a deep breath and told her. "It's about Layla."

At once the smile fell off Becky's face. "Oh." But she kept her eyes on her cousin and her impatient look transformed into one of compassion. "Oh. Babe. Oh, I'm so sorry. Are you still feeling sad? Is that it?"

Gale hesitated again, and Becky took that as a yes. "It's totally normal, you don't have to hide it, or feel embarrassed. I'm still really sad about it."

"No, it's not that—"

"*Just tell her!*"

"It's... it's that she's actually come back. Sort of."

There was a silence. Becky even looked around the room again.

"Come back?"

Although Gale had told both his grief therapist and his mother, much earlier, about his visions of Layla, and Rachel had talked about them with her sister, she'd asked Erica to keep it to herself. It had never got back to Becky.

"Come back how?"

"I mean, I can see her," he said. He swallowed.

"Oh." Becky seemed to have no idea how to react. For a few moments she didn't even try to hide the look on her face. Clearly she feared her cousin might be crazy. But then she offered him a smile.

"Well, maybe that's normal too. Or at least *sort of* normal." She wrinkled her nose, and then seemed to warm to the idea. "I mean, sometimes I think *I* see people too. Actually, I was in this club the other night, and I thought I saw my friend Jessica, from school, even though she left in like year nine or something. They went to Germany because her dad's from—"

"No, I mean I can see her *right now*," Gale cut in. "She's right here. In the room."

Layla waved her hand at Becky, a goofy grin on her face.

"She's waving at you."

Becky was silent.

"*Hellooo!*" Layla said.

"She says hello."

Still Becky was silent.

"I can hear her, too," Gale explained. "I should have said."

There seemed no way that Becky could seek refuge any further in the idea that Gale meant he *thought* he could see his sister. Gale waited as she worked this out, and was then surprised that her solution was to open her arms and engulf him in a hug.

"It's alright Gale, it's alright babe!" She clasped him tight and stroked his hair. He waited, a bit uncomfortable, until she let him go.

"Tell her I'll prove it," Layla said, when she did.

Gale nodded almost imperceptibly. "She says she'll prove it," he repeated, and Becky smiled a little. She seemed to have realised now that whatever this was, Gale wasn't sad in the way she had first thought.

"OK... how?"

"Give her your pad and pen," Layla went on. Gale did what she said, not knowing where this was going.

"She said I have to give you this." He held out the notebook.

"And then tell her to go to the other side of the room and write a number. But don't let you see what it is."

"Go over there and write a number. Don't let me see."

"Any number?"

"Yeah."

"Is this like a magic trick?" Becky asked. "I like magic tricks." She grinned again, as she did what he said. The room wasn't big though, and they couldn't go very far apart.

"This is no good. You can see what I'm writing from how the pen moves," Becky complained, so she turned to the wall to finish what she was writing.

"I can't see it, I promise," Gale said to his cousin's back.

A moment later she turned around.

"Done." She had her hand over the number.

Gale looked expectantly at Layla, but she seemed a little confused.

"She can't see it with your hand over it." Gale interpreted.

Becky gave him a goofy look, but when she moved her hand she made sure the pad was kept at an angle so that Gale couldn't see, and that there were no reflections in the window that might help him.

Gale looked again at Layla, as she leaned in close to see what was written. But still, from her frown it was clear something was wrong.

"Well? What is it?" Gale asked.

"I'm not going to tell you!" Becky replied incredulously.

Gale ignored her. "What's wrong," he asked his sister instead.

"Nothing's wrong," Becky said, in the background, but it was only Layla he had ears for.

"I don't know."

"What do you mean you don't know?"

"It's like, I can see she's written something... but I can't..."

Gale waited.

"I don't know," Layla said. "I can't see what it says."

"You can't read her writing?"

"No. It's not that. I can't... it's like... I'm not *meant* to see it. I'm not meant to *prove* it. Not to anyone else." Layla wore a questioning look. "Not to anyone but you."

"Shall I show you?" Becky asked, a second later. It seemed she was tired of waiting. And before Gale could reply she had turned the pad around. On it she had written the number eight hundred and eighty-eight, in large, clear letters. Becky shrugged. "I think you need to work on your magic, babe."

"Eight hundred and eighty-eight," Layla repeated quietly. "I can see that now." She turned to her brother. She looked scared. Scared and saddened. "Why couldn't I see it before?"

There was a silence, interrupted by Becky's mobile. It was remarkable they'd managed to talk for so long without it announcing a message, or new TikTok notification. She pulled it out, and her thumbs flashed as she replied, then slipped it back into her jeans pocket. Her attention returned to Gale.

"I really do miss her too, you know," she said. Gale just stared at her. "Like, she was really important to me." She said something else, but Gale didn't hear. His eyes had slid across to his sister, who was standing invisibly next to Becky, as the older girl continued to say how much she missed her.

"Yeah," he murmured in the end.

"So why do you have a picture of this house?" From the bed Becky grabbed the paper that Gale had showed her earlier, but Layla interrupted her. Or tried to.

"I've got another way," she called out, and again Gale looked from one to the other, choosing which to listen to. For a few seconds he didn't know what to say.

"She wants to try another way," he said in the end. "To prove she's real."

Becky, hesitated, drawing in a deep breath. "OK." She shrugged, then waited.

Layla was silent though.

"Do I need the pad?" Becky prompted, but Gale just waited, sensing this was hard for his sister.

"When I was alive, and Becky came to visit, sometimes we would go up to my room, and not let you in," she began.

Gale repeated it, not sure where this was going.

"Yeah..." Becky was uncertain too.

"And the last time, or around the last time, we came up with a new name for you," Layla hesitated. "A secret middle name. It was really mean."

"You came up with a middle name for me," Gale repeated. "A mean one."

"Oh." Becky's face was folded into a deep frown now.

Gale listened as Layla told him what it was. Then he nodded.

"You called me 'adopted'. Gale Adopted Martin." He sniffed, and his sister mouthed *I'm sorry*.

"Oh hun, you knew about that? I'm so sorry," Becky began to gush. "We didn't mean it. Layla was just... she was in this bad mood, and that got it off her chest. But she totally loved you, you must believe that. She never thought that about you. Not really."

"I'm really sorry," Layla said again, louder this time. "It was just a stupid thing..."

"It's alright," Gale told her – or both of them, it didn't seem to matter. "I know I'm not adopted. And even if I was, it's way better to be adopted than dead."

Layla smiled at him and Becky came and wrapped him in another hug, this time not letting go for a long time.

"Oh, hun. I'm so sorry, I really am. I can't believe you've been holding that in for like, two whole years."

"I haven't." Gale gently pushed himself away. "Layla just told me. Just this moment."

Becky stopped speaking and looked properly now at the space where Gale was looking. But clearly she saw nothing there but empty air, and then the bedroom wall. She drew in another deep breath.

"Have you told your mum about this?" she asked slowly. "About seeing Layla?"

Gale shook his head.

"Or the grief counsellor? You're still seeing her right?"

"They won't believe me. We thought you might, well... Layla thought you might believe me, because you and she were really close."

Beside Becky, Layla was nodding her head hopefully. "Ask her."

"Do you believe me?" Gale asked.

Becky's phone beeped again, and she went to grab it, but stopped herself.

"Not... not exactly. But I believe it's important to you."

Gale sat down on the bed, feeling defeated, while Becky checked her phone. When she was finished, she returned her attention to Gale.

"I mean, would you believe *me*? If it was the other way around?"

He thought about this, then shook his head.

"You'd think I was going crazy! I mean, think about it, Gale."

He did, for a moment. "So you think I'm going crazy?"

"Not *going* crazy." She suddenly flashed a smile. "You've always been crazy. My crazy little cousin." It was what she'd called him sometimes, in the life they'd shared before Layla's death.

The smile faded, and her eyes went to the paper on the bed again. "But I don't get where this house fits in? What's the deal with that? You want me to take you there? What for?"

"I just..." Gale replied as if it didn't matter anymore, because it wasn't going to work. "Layla thinks this is where she was taken. We want to check it out to see if there's any clues."

Becky's eye's widened as her face turned white. "Whoa! *Okay*..." She looked at the paper for a long while. "Well, is it far?" Now she turned the paper over, where Gale had written the address after they'd printed it out. And before Gale could reply she was typing the postcode into Google Maps on her phone. Seconds later she had the route on the screen.

"Oh. It's just five minutes' walk. Let's tell your mum we'll take Barney out. We've got time before lunch..."

Gale and Layla were both silent.

"OK? Well come on? Let's go look." Becky stared at Gale, and then laughed as his expression changed. Suddenly he nodded gratefully. He tried to speak, to thank her, but she stopped him.

"Aww, come here, babe. It's alright." She wrapped Gale up in another hug.

"Come on. Your mum will let you go with me. I'll keep you safe."

TWENTY-TWO

Barney wasn't used to walking on the lead. Perhaps it had something to do with his puppyhood being spent in a house where his owners were drowning in an ocean of grief, or perhaps they just hadn't trained him properly. Either way, his normal walk was just a couple of streets away to a park where he could run free and chase his ball. But the route to the killer's house was in the opposite direction, which meant Barney spent the whole way pulling and tugging, and nearly slipping his collar.

He was too strong for Gale, so Becky took him, spending most of the time shouting "heel" at him and yanking at his neck. She had to give Gale her phone and told him to lead the way it showed. It was unnerving to Gale just how close the murderer's house was to where he lived.

"It's this street," Gale said. "Number 42."

"OK," Becky said. "Well, that's number 122, so it's a little way down – Barney will you *please* stop pulling my arm off?"

They walked on.

"How exactly did you find this house?" Becky asked, as they continued down the road. "Or... how did you and Layla find it?"

Gale explained what Layla had told him, about how her killer had promised to show her his snakes, when he took her in his car, and then actually shown her them in the basement. And then how they'd got his address from the pet shop.

"Woah." Becky replied. "That's like, totally insane Gale. You know that, right?" She seemed to think for a moment. And then like she wanted to ask something, but maybe shouldn't. In the end she gave in. "So, um, is... is Layla here with us right now? Can you see her?"

The question surprised Gale – he'd been concentrating so hard on the phone with its map, and on not tripping over Barney, that he hadn't noticed. He looked around now, then shook his head.

"Not right now. She finds it hard to be in places outside the house." The realisation that she wasn't here left him with a sudden lonely feeling, even though his bubbly cousin should have been company enough.

Becky looked almost disappointed. But she let it go.

"48, 46..." She read off the house numbers they were passing, and then stopped. "Well, you've managed to pick the nicest looking house on the street!" She grinned.

She probably meant it sarcastically. Or maybe she didn't – Gale wasn't sure. It was a nice big house, just a bit run-down looking. It was a bit different to most of the other houses on the street, which were quite close to the road, with tiny front gardens.

Number 42 was set back, with a driveway on one side, and a large oak tree that hid the upper part of the house. It looked older than the other homes too, as if it were one of the few original houses from when the street was laid out, with the others having been knocked down or extended and turned into flats. But it didn't look creepy or anything like that. Still, Gale shivered just from being there.

"What now?" Becky asked.

"Erm..." Gale didn't know what to say. He looked around, but still there was no Layla.

"There's no car on the drive," Becky went on, after a while. "I suppose it could be in the garage, but hardly anyone actually puts their car in a garage, so it probably means he's out. If he's got a car."

"He does have a car. A green one," Gale replied, but then he thought. "Or he did have. He might have sold it by now."

"Well, there's no green car here now," Becky replied. "Shall we go and knock on the door?

Gale was horrified. "*No way.* There's a murderer who lives there. It's dangerous."

Becky looked up and down the street, as if it didn't look particularly dangerous to her. "We could try the neighbours? Ask if they know him. If he's dodgy and that?"

"But what if they like him? What if they don't tell us anything, but then go and tell him we asked? Then he'll know we were onto him."

"OK." Becky looked mildly frustrated, and she swapped her phone for the dog's lead. Then she snapped several photos of the house, from different angles.

"Evidence." She smiled.

When she was finished, she spoke again. "It's quite a cloudy day, and the other houses have got their lights on. But there's no lights on here. So I reckon he's almost certainly not in."

She seemed to be justifying something, but Gale wasn't sure what. Not least because he sensed now that Layla *was* there after all, or at least that she was *trying* to appear with them. Like in the pet shop.

"So..." Becky reached down and unclipped Barney from his lead.

"What are you doing?" Gale asked.

Becky didn't reply. Instead, she pretended to take the ball, which she'd been carrying in her coat pocket, and pretended to throw it into the garden of the house. Barney knew the movement on an almost instinctive level, and immediately followed where he thought the ball had gone, despite the fact it had never actually left her pocket. He bolted in through the open gates of number 42's driveway.

"Oops. I appear to have accidentally made the dog think I threw his ball into this garden." Becky said now, a triumphant note to her voice. "I'm going to have to go in there and get him back."

"Why?" Gale asked this time.

Becky lowered her voice. "I'm going to go and look in the windows. See if there's anything I can see. Are you coming?"

Gale didn't at first. Instead, he watched as the dog sprinted from bush to bush in the large front garden, hunting for the ball that wasn't there. His tail swished back and forth, loving the task. Meanwhile Becky was completely ignoring him and was walking calmly towards the largest window in the front of the house.

From where he stood, on the pavement outside the property, Gale couldn't see much. He watched for a second, then turned to Layla's outline.

"Is this it? Is this the place?"

She didn't answer, and it took him a moment to work out she wasn't able to. She was only there as a disturbance in the air. Without knowing how he knew, he was aware this was the most she could do.

He hesitated further. Now Becky was at the window, leaning in and using her hands to shade the outside light. Gale looked up and down the street, but it was deserted. In some ways it was more scary waiting there, and he sensed his sister building up to something. Finally, Layla released whatever it was, a single word, hissed directly into his mind.

Go...

He put his head down and went through the gate, moving towards the house where his sister might, or might not, have been killed.

TWENTY-THREE

"Can you see anything?" He was breathless as he joined Becky at the window. She didn't reply, but kept looking, and he adopted the same position as her, their faces pressed against the glass.

Inside there was a living room. A leather sofa and matching armchair faced a large TV. A large-leaved plant of some type took up much of one corner. A bookshelf occupied another. It was neat and tidy, the floor the only thing that really caught Gale's eye. Instead of the carpet that covered his house, this one had bare wooden floors, but polished so that they shone.

"Looks pretty normal to me," Becky said beside him. She held up her phone and began to snap more pictures. Gale went back to studying the room, desperate to spot something that might be important.

There was a coffee table in front of the sofa. On it were a couple of magazines, and some papers that looked like the sorts of things that Mum and Dad got sent – bills or letters from the school. Did that mean he did have children after all? *No*, Gale corrected himself. Mum and Dad got letters that looked the same, from the council and lots of other places, not just school.

And the room didn't look like the sort of place where there were children. There were no toys, games. No photographs of kids on the walls.

In fact, now he looked, the pictures that were on the walls – paintings, not photographs – were weird, almost creepy. They looked like – he thought about it – they looked like they were meant to be naked people, naked women, but they weren't quite; they were just brush-stroke outlines.

"Stop staring Gale," Becky joked, noticing where he was looking, but she was interrupted by a sharp noise from behind them. Gale jumped, before he realised it was just Barney. The dog had tired of his fruitless search and given one loud bark. Gale turned now, to see him wagging his tail.

"Barney," Becky admonished him. "You nearly gave me a heart attack." She pretended to throw the ball again, and the dog hared off a second time, easily daft enough to fall for the same trick twice. But then Becky seemed bored of looking through the window. Instead, she went to the front door. She lifted the letterbox and looked through.

"What can you see?" Gale joined her, anxious.

"A hallway." Becky replied, sardonically. She held up the flap with one hand and snapped another photo. She showed him the picture that appeared on the screen. It was wonky, and dark, since the flash hadn't fired, but there was a coat rack, and several open doors leading off the space. But from one of them there came a strange blue light that seemed suddenly familiar to Gale.

"What's that?" He asked, pointing at it. She zoomed it in, but shrugged.

"I dunno." Becky stepped back, inspecting the house. There were more windows upstairs, out of reach, darkened by the cover of the oak tree's leaves. To the right, a garage was attached to the house, and beyond that, a side gate stood ajar.

"Maybe that goes round the back? We could look in the

back windows?" She didn't seem very confident about the idea. Gale felt even less so, but he thought again of why they were here.

"OK..."

If Becky regretted suggesting it, she didn't say so. But this time she wasn't willing to go alone. "Right. Stay with me," she said.

They walked in front of the garage, both of them glancing back at the street, fearing the house's possibly murderous owner would appear at any moment. But he didn't. Becky pushed open the gate and led the way down the side of the property, beside a tall wooden fence.

Soon they came to the back of the house. The back garden was large and also filled with large bushes and trees that gave the house a lot of privacy from its neighbours. A bonfire was ready to be lit, in the middle of what should have been a lawn, but was really just bare earth. Closer to the house there was a stone patio, half-buried under moss. Becky led the way.

"He's not a gardener, is he?" she said, but then added. "Hurry up. We really shouldn't be here."

The first window they looked in was obviously the kitchen. It just looked like any other kitchen, though Gale still tried to make himself remember details. The cupboard doors were a kind of white wood. There was a laptop computer on the work surface, its lid closed. Next to it stood an empty coffee cup.

"Looks pretty normal," Becky said, from beside him. "Come on."

They went to the next window, and there Becky stopped. The room was presumably supposed to be a dining room, but lining the far wall, and giving off the same strange blue glow as Gale had seen from the hallway, there were two enormous glass tanks. Gale felt himself go cold as he saw them, and he knew at once what was in them.

"The snakes."

"What the hell?" Becky said. "Oh shit."

They looked more closely at the rest of the room, and now they noticed a third tank. Inside this one was a bed of sawdust, and a tangle of white fur. On closer inspection they saw it was filled with white mice.

"Ewwww. That's so gross." Becky said.

Between the two windows there was a door. Now, Becky moved towards it.

"We should get that computer," she said. And before Gale could stop her, she tried the handle, but it was locked. She briefly appeared frustrated, but then her courage seemed to quickly desert her.

"Actually, maybe we should just get out of here. Like, right now."

Gale didn't answer, but he liked that plan better. He felt sick. Cold. Suddenly very scared.

But then his cousin swore again.

"Gale! Where's your stupid dog?"

The answer was, he was now searching the back garden for the lost ball. Even though Becky had pretended to throw it in the front, the animal had followed them around the side, and simply recommenced his search, as if the ball might have magically made its own way there. Now, he was running between the bushes, and suddenly he stopped by the unlit bonfire, and buried his head in it. As it happened that turned out to be lucky, since Becky was able to run over to him, and clip the lead before he could run away again. She pulled him back, so hard he let out a small yelp.

"Come on." She was breathless as she led Gale back beside the garage. But halfway down she stopped.

"*Shit.*"

"What is it?"

"There's a car coming. Into the drive." She turned and pushed Gale back, towards the rear garden. It scared him – the thought of going back towards those snakes.

"Where are we going?" he asked. He could hear the car, but not see it.

"He's just pulled into the driveway. He might see us."

"What car? What colour?"

"Blue. But I don't think that really matters right now."

"What are we going to do?"

Becky was silent for a second, thinking. "OK. We'll wait in the back garden until he comes in the house. Then we go out round the side. That way he won't see us then." Her lips were thin. She didn't seem to like the idea any more than he did, but Gale didn't have a better one. So, they stood there, flat against the back wall, by the kitchen window.

The street was quiet again now, the car's engine silent.

"What if he comes in through the back door?" The thought suddenly occurred to Gale. "Some people do. They use their back door like their front door."

"I don't know," she replied, her voice miserable.

They waited, breathless moments, expecting to be caught at any second. But instead, suddenly, the kitchen light flicked on.

"*Now.* Let's go." Becky grabbed Gale's hand and pulled him and the dog back to the passageway, this time not hesitating as they broke from the cover that the garage itself gave them from anybody watching from the house. They passed the car quickly. A blue Audi. Gale noted it, thinking he should get the number plate, once they were safely back on the road. But then a voice stopped them dead.

"*Hey!* What are you doing?"

They both stopped, wheeled around. From the open front door of the house, a man was staring at them. He had dark hair. A beard. In his hand he held the key fob for the car. Now he pressed it, and it bleeped at them, the indicator lights flashing.

"What are you doing in here?" the man asked again. "This is private property."

He wasn't friendly. He wore jeans and a tight, dark blue top. Maybe in his thirties – Gale wasn't sure – but older than a teenager, and younger than his dad. He seemed stronger, too. Tougher.

He looked angry and started walking towards them.

"Sorry," Becky said to him. Gale was too scared to say a word. "My dog escaped into your garden. We were just getting him."

It seemed the man hadn't noticed the dog – from where he was standing the car was in the way – and Becky tried to pull up on the lead to show him. She only succeeded in tightening his lead and making him yelp again. This clearly wasn't the walk Barney had imagined he would be getting.

The man stopped moving now and looked from Becky to the dog, as if assessing whether to believe the excuse. Then, as the eyes began to turn towards him, Gale heard a sound in his head.

Look away!

It was Layla again, and Gale did what she said, partly to see where she was. Then, when he failed to see her, he looked down, as if he were embarrassed, or just unable to meet the man's eyes. Gale heard what the man said next, but didn't see him say it.

"He better not have crapped in my garden. I'm warning you—"

"He hasn't," Becky said. Her voice had shrunk, so that she sounded like a little girl. As scared as he felt. "I promise."

Gale looked up now, to see the man was walking towards

them, fast, taking large strides on his long legs. But as he did so, his cousin pulled him again, and they broke into a run together.

After a few moments, when they were a few houses back down the road, Gale stopped and turned, to see the man just standing there, watching them leave.

And Gale couldn't see Layla, but he could feel her within him, shivering with fear.

TWENTY-FOUR

They couldn't go straight home. Not least because they still had the dog to walk, but also because Becky declared that she needed space to chill out. So instead they took Barney on his normal walk and strolled along the far edge of the park, far from where anybody could hear them.

"Did you *see* the way he was looking at us?" Becky asked. It was the third or fourth time she'd asked it – Gale had lost count.

"It was like he wanted to grab us, like he wanted to *murder us*, right there and then."

Gale wished she would stop talking like this, but he couldn't disagree. *On the other hand* – a portion of his mind kept arguing – they *were* in his garden, so maybe it was normal he was angry?

"Do you know him? Do you recognise him?" Becky said suddenly. "Like, have you seen him around anywhere? Hanging about by your school?"

Gale forced himself to listen to her. He didn't think so. But then, how could you actually know these things? The man might have been outside his school every day, and he just hadn't seen him because he hadn't known to look. And now that Gale tried to think about how the man looked, he found it was impossible to bring a picture of him into his mind. It wasn't like a computer, where you could just see a photograph.

Gale's memory of the man wasn't really anything other than selected details. His anger. The evil, piercing eyes. The strange contrast between the neat front garden, and the decay and mess around the back. The room with the snakes.

"That just wasn't a normal reaction," Becky went on. "You should tell someone, you really ought to." She was shaking her head. "I'm serious." She stopped suddenly, forcing Gale to do the same.

"Look Gale, I don't exactly know what's going on here, but you know the police haven't caught whoever took Layla? Which means *he's still out there*." She spoke as though Gale might not know this.

"I mean it's probably not this guy," Becky went on. "But it *actually might be*. I don't know where you got the idea that whoever killed her keeps snakes, maybe it's like – just some creepy idea that got into your head – and maybe that guy is just the local weirdo, and you've just seen him hanging around. But even so, the police need to check him out. You know what I mean?"

She paused, thinking over what she'd said.

"You said that Layla told you she was in a basement, yeah? Well, if it is possible that she's somehow communicating with you, from the dead – which is totally mental by the way – then it'd be way easy for the police to check it out. If that house has a basement, then they'll be able to find out if Layla was ever there." She was breathing loudly from talking so fast.

As Gale listened, her speed-talking was doing nothing to slow his still-racing heart. And even less to ground his response in common sense.

"How?"

"You probably don't know about this stuff, because you're really young, and your mum wants to protect you. But the police have these forensic people, and they can like, find hairs, and tiny little bits of skin, and fingerprints, and it doesn't matter how hard criminals try to clean up, they can never get it all. So, if they were to search that guy's basement, then they'd find evidence if Layla was there."

Gale nodded. He did know about that stuff. Grown-ups always thought kids didn't know stuff, but there were loads of science shows on TV and YouTube that explained all that kind of thing. And before Layla died, they'd often watched things on Netflix that they weren't supposed to.

"Seriously. You have to go to the police." Becky's nostrils were flared and she looked excited. Scared.

"How?" Gale replied. It took a while to realise his cousin didn't understand the obvious problem. "They won't believe me."

Becky was silent for a long time, and in the end she started walking again, absently kicking the ball for Barney. Finally, Gale couldn't take any more, and broke the silence.

"I could tell them about Layla. About what she told me?"

Becky stopped again and shook her head. "No way. You can't do that."

"Why not?"

"Because they'll think you're mental, and then they won't do anything. Except maybe lock you up. No. We need another way." She reached down and picked up the ball. Normally she didn't want anything to do with it once it got slobbery, but this time she threw it and then wiped her fingers on her jeans. Her phone chirped. She pulled it out.

She read the message, her face unchanging. But then her eyes widened. She started a reply at once, but turned to Gale as well, explained as her thumbs flashed on the screen.

"It's my friend, Sara. Her boyfriend's parents are going away and she wants to stay over with him. She's like, the only one of my friends who's still a virgin. And she wants to tell her mum she's staying with me, so that she can..." Becky stopped, as if suddenly realising this was something she'd never normally discuss with Gale. The thought seemed to disturb her more.

She finished her reply and hit send. And then looked up at Gale, suddenly sure.

"You have to lie. You have to make something up about how you've seen this guy, hanging out, looking dodgy. No— " She pointed at Gale. "You have to say you *saw* him, hanging around Layla. Say you were with her somewhere, and he came up to you and started asking funny questions. Say he asked if you wanted to come see his snakes, that's *super* creepy."

"That *is* what he said to Layla."

"I know. I mean, I know that's what *you* said she said. But if you tell the police that you see Layla, they'll just stick you in the loony bin. But if you tell them this guy was hanging around, looking dodgy, when she was still alive. *Then* they'll definitely look into him."

Becky put her hand on Gale's arm. "Tell them he told you to come and see his snakes *in his basement.* Then they'll have to check if he's got one. If that's where he held her, then they'll find evidence." She stared at him, as if willing him to agree.

Gale tried to make sense of it. "When would I have seen him? Won't they ask *where* it happened?"

"Yeah." For a moment Becky looked defeated. As if this would scupper the idea, but then she brightened. "You need to think of a time when you and she were alone somewhere. Somewhere public. Just before she died."

Gale thought hard, and almost at once an idea came to him. At first, he tried to dismiss it, because it seemed silly, or at least not real. But it wouldn't go away.

"There was one time, when we were at swimming lessons, and Mum was late picking us up. We had to wait outside the pool."

"That's *perfect.* We can say he came up to you then. He was probably looking through the window, at all the kids in their swimming gear." Becky looked genuinely disgusted at this, as if it had actually happened. "And you'll need to say you saw him again today. And that's why we followed him to find this house."

"*We?* I can say you were here as well?"

Becky was silent for a second, but when she answered her voice was very serious. "Yeah."

They walked home, further talking through their plans.

"There's something else," Becky said.

"What?"

"We need to do this right away." She hesitated as Gale looked at her anxiously.

"Why?"

Becky was solemn. "It's the way he looked at us. If he did take Layla, then those sort of people don't just do that once. He lives so close to you it's dangerous having him there. Or he could escape." She took a deep breath, thinking.

"Look, I don't know how much you know about this," Becky went on. "But Mum – my mum I mean, she talks to your mum. And sometimes I'm there, and sometimes I overhear what they're saying. Or sometimes mum just tells me. But anyway. There's this detective who's leading the investigation. I can't remember his name, but your mum really likes him – he helps her. So if we both speak to your mum now, when we get back, then she can phone this detective and she can tell him. And then he'll get it all sorted. He'll look into this creepy guy."

Gale nodded. He didn't know what else to say. Without thinking he bent down to run his fingers through the dog's fur.

TWENTY-FIVE

"Mum, there's something I need to speak to you about."

Rachel had sensed there was something up with Gale. He'd been out with Becky, walking Barney, for longer than expected, meaning the roast was probably overdone, and after they returned they'd gone straight up to his room, whispering about something. And now he'd come practically tiptoeing into the kitchen, with Becky stood in the doorway, her eyes wide.

"What is it?"

Gale bit his lip, then glanced around at the table; a bowl of greens stood there, steam rising off it. Becky waved her hand, as if egging him on.

"Gale, can this please wait until after lunch?"

"It's something really important. It's about Layla."

At the mention of her name, Rachel felt a shift of emotion, not just in herself but for Gale, too. Suddenly she had time for him.

"What is it," her voice was softer, and she crouched a little to get closer to his height. "What is it, honey?"

Gale swallowed, his eyes flicked left and right, not able to keep them fixed on his mother. He took a deep breath.

"Erm. You're probably not going to believe this, but I think I might have found who killed her."

Rachel Martin froze. Only the expression on her face moved as it morphed through shock to disbelief. For a few seconds she was literally speechless.

"What do you mean?" She was hollow now, all emotion drained away.

"I just saw him. Just now. Out with Barney."

Rachel felt her mouth drop open. She looked up to see that her sister Erica had also heard, and also had her mouth open. Becky stood up and moved closer to Gale, as if backing him up.

Rachel took them all in, as new emotions filled up her insides. She knew she had to form words, but which ones? She didn't know.

"Well how... why would... *What do you mean Gale?*"

And she watched her son take another deep breath and tell his lie.

"I never told anyone this before, but before Layla was taken we saw this weird guy. He was weird because he had this beard, and we were at the swimming pool – you remember that time when you were late, and me and Layla had to wait outside? He wanted to take us to see his snakes. He said he had them in his basement."

There was a pause, as Rachel took this in. The first emotion was guilt, at the time she'd been late. But then she exploded.

"What...? He said— Why *on earth* wouldn't you—"

"I didn't think... I was scared."

Gale *was* scared, she could see that, and on some level, below the tsunami of anger she felt, she knew she had to calm down, had to think through how to handle this.

"I didn't know it was important."

"You didn't know it was—" The rage peaked, and then suddenly vanished, as quickly as it had arrived. It was like some kind of magic trick. For a second it was all she could do to contemplate it. But then she saw her son again, standing miserably in the kitchen, beginning to cry.

Telling her he had the answer.

"Oh, honey." Rachel dropped lower. "I'm sorry. I'm so sorry. It's not your fault. *It's not your fault.*" Breathlessly she swept her son into her arms and pulled him close, inhaling the smell of him. After a moment she pushed him away to see him better.

"And this was in the swimming pool? Did you tell one of the lifeguards? Did they see him?"

"No. It was outside." He'd stopped crying out, was struggling to be clear. "Outside the pool, that time you were late."

"Oh." Rachel's emotions began to bubble up again. In her darker hours she still thought of that time, perhaps even feeling some guilty sense of relief, that *that* wasn't the time when Layla had been taken, because on that occasion she *had* been at fault. She breathed hard. Trying to think.

"Oh my gosh." She hugged Gale again, almost as if to buy herself time. "I'm so sorry. I'm so, so sorry."

Her sister had taken Rachel's arm now, in a generic act of support. Automatically Rachel smiled her thanks, then pulled away, indicating she was OK. In control. She crouched again at Gale's level.

"You said you saw him again, this man? Today?"

"Yeah. We went to his house."

"You WHAT?"

She couldn't help exploding again, but this time it was easier to roll back. She glanced up at the ceiling to take a second, then turned back to Gale, who kept talking.

"We... we followed him."

"Who's we? *Becky?*"

Rachel stood again, swinging around to confront her niece, who apparently decided this was the moment to defend her role.

"We... I didn't know whether to believe him at first, so we

watched him go to his house, just so we knew where he lived. He didn't suspect anything."

Rachel blinked. "So you have his *address*?"

"Yeah." Becky nodded. "Yeah. And I *saw* him too, and he definitely does look creepy as hell." She nodded encouragingly, as if willing the adults to believe her. There was a moment when no one spoke, and Becky decided to go on.

"I kind of... I kind of sneaked up to have a look at his house, and he really does have snakes. It's the same guy from the pool."

Gale pulled out the sheet of A4 paper from his pocket. He handed it to her.

"We found it on Google Maps."

Rachel took the paper and unfolded it. It showed a photograph in black and white of a street, above it was a map, and then some text from a webpage. She looked at the house. It was just a house, an ordinary house, not so different from theirs. And from the map, it was only a few streets away. And the man who lived there had approached Layla.

This really could be it.

"OK, OK." She stared at the paper, playing for time again. Then she turned to look at Gale, at Becky. They were watching her, waiting to see what happened next, and Rachel knew she needed a plan.

"OK, OK..." She knew she was saying the same thing over and over again. But in her mind only one other word kept forming. *Kieran.* She needed Kieran.

"Erica, are you able to look after Gale while I speak to the police?"

Her sister looked relieved, as if she was fearing that something more might be asked of her.

"Of course. Absolutely. We'll eat, and I'll save some for you. I can be here as long as you need." She gave a reassuring smile, then seemed to think of something else. "Or just until Jon gets home."

"Jon will come with me," Rachel replied, then she remembered he was off on one of his cycling trips, and a burst of anger flared within her. There was no way she was going to wait for him. "This is…" She stopped, looked at Gale again, the fear turning to hope.

"This could be the moment we've been waiting for. The thing they need to catch this—" She didn't finish the sentence, but laid a hand on Gale's slender shoulder, before crouching again at his level.

"Gale are you *sure*? Are you sure it was the same man?"

He nodded, his face still frightened and miserable. And perhaps it was that which broke Rachel. She felt the tears before they arrived, like the roar of a dam breaking, before the floods arrive. But when the tears came they were less a flood, and more an almost sweet release. The end of two years of praying for this monster to be caught. Two years of fighting against the bitter injustice of what was taken, from her, from her beautiful daughter. She felt Erica rushing forward again, to catch her, and this time she let her sister hold her up, and then guide her to a chair.

And from there she saw Gale, standing quietly, as if just watching what he had unleashed.

TWENTY-SIX

"Hi, Kieran, is that you?"

DI Clarke knew it was Rachel Martin from the ID on his mobile phone. "Rachel. What's up?" He hadn't been expecting a call.

"Something's happened, something important."

Clarke eyes went to the sandwich he'd just made for himself, but hadn't had a chance to bite into. "Go on."

"It's Gale. He's just told me something. I think he might know who took Layla."

The sandwich was instantly forgotten, as Clarke slowly got to his feet.

"Excuse me? What did you say?"

"I think Gale might know who took Layla."

He'd heard right, but still it made no sense. None at all.

"What do you mean? What's happened?"

Rachel Martin was breathless, and Clarke was nearly too impatient to give her space to talk. There was no doubt from her voice that this was serious. But it was hard to get the details.

"He says he and Layla were approached by a man, a few weeks before she was taken. At the swimming pool. He tried to get them to follow him... and Gale says he saw the same man on the beach *that day*. And then today, he saw him again, out walking, and he followed him home. *He knows where he lives.*"

To Clarke it felt as though the blood in his veins was fizzing, but he forced himself to stay calm. To stay logical. In his mind he began running over the testimony that had been taken from the boy. He'd read it so often it was virtually stored in his mind, word-for-word. And he trusted the female detective who had taken the testimony. She was specially trained to work with children and one of his best officers. In fact, his faith in his colleague made him cautious.

"Gale was asked about this several times," he replied, slowly. "He was very explicit that he didn't see—" Clarke didn't get any further before her voice cut him off.

"He was scared. He thought he'd done something wrong!"

"OK," Clarke thought again. "I'm sorry, I didn't mean that as a criticism. You've caught me by surprise, but clearly this could be extremely important." He paused, taking deep breaths and trying to let the situation crystallise in his mind. "Let me get to the station. Maybe we can meet there and talk this through properly?"

Rachel was crying again. "You're not at work?"

"No. I'm not on this weekend, but that's OK. That's not a problem."

"I'm sorry to disturb you—"

"Don't be silly. Don't be sorry." Clarke stopped her at once. "I told you to call me any time." For a moment he allowed himself to believe this might be real, that they might be on the verge of a genuine breakthrough. "Believe me, Rachel, I've been as anxious as you are for a development in this case."

"Yes, I know you have." Rachel half sobbed down the phone; Clarke hardly even registered it.

"But let's be cautious," he went on. "Take things one step at a time. Are you and Jon able to meet me there in an hour?"

"Yes – no. Jon's away on his bike. He's in Wales. But I'll come in." There was a pause. "Shall I bring Gale as well?"

Clarke thought about this. "How much has he told you? Do you have enough to give me the details?"

"I think so. I'm not sure. I have the man's address." Again, Rachel wasn't able to prevent a sob from catching in her throat, and Clarke felt his eyes widening. *They had an address.*

And DI Clarke made a decision. "OK. My DC who interviewed him before – Jennifer Robbins – she's away this weekend and I can't get her back in at short notice. But it would be better for Gale to speak with her again. Easier for Gale, too. So, let's begin with you telling me what you know now, and Gale can speak with Jen on Monday? How does that sound?"

On the other end of the line Rachel Martin sobbed a little more, then agreed.

"OK. I'll see you there shortly." Clarke hung up the phone and stared around him. The room he was in suddenly seemed different. He saw his sandwich, but now he had no hunger at all.

They had an address!

TWENTY-SEVEN

The call with Jon had annoyed her. Rachel understood that she'd phoned him when he was on his bike, presumably many muddy miles into his ride, but he was slower than he should have been to register what she was saying, and at first he appeared to suggest that he shouldn't cut short his day out, but finish the ride and then come back. He'd quickly backtracked, but still insisted there was no other way back to his car than by riding the bike, and it would take him an hour at least – perhaps more – and then he had a three-hour drive to get back. There was no way she was going to wait for that. Not when she had the *actual address* of the man who could very well be their daughter's killer. No way on earth.

Rachel met DI Clarke in the reception area of the station. There was no mistaking that *he* understood the significance of the moment – he was pacing up and down, and his eyes were wide as he signed her in and led her in silence along the corridor to the interview rooms. If it hadn't been for small details, the chill in the air – perhaps they turned down the heating on weekends – the squeak of her shoes on the hard, lino floor, then she might have mistaken it for a dream.

She had spent time in several of the interview rooms, and knew that some were very bare and spartan, while others were arranged more comfortably. Presumably the former were designed for suspects, supposed to intimidate them, perhaps hint at the prison to come. And the latter were for witnesses, to coax clues out of them. Clarke had booked one of the comfortable ones, but today Rachel barely noticed. She sat at the table, her eyes on the clunky, tape-driven audio recorder, the only thing on the surface.

"I've asked for a female police Constable to sit in with us," Clarke held the door open as a woman in her thirties entered the room. "This is PC Ellen Cross."

She had short, spiky hair, and was dressed in uniform. She nodded kindly as she saw Rachel, but again Rachel barely registered it.

"Hello."

"Ordinarily I'd have asked one of the detective team, but we're a little short this weekend, and PC Cross was... available." There was the slightest hesitation in Clarke's voice, as if he'd been about to use a more complimentary term, then changed his mind.

"From what you said on the phone, I think we need to have a third party sit in with us."

Rachel nodded. She clutched her bag in her lap. Glanced at the PC, then shifted her eyes back to Clarke. He sat down opposite, his face lined with concern.

"It's also important that this conversation is recorded. Are you OK with that?"

Rachel glanced at the machine again, then nodded. Clarke watched her, then nodded back. He pressed the two buttons that made the tape start recording. Rachel listened as he gave his name and hers, then waited while the Constable spoke as well. Then he nodded to Rachel again. They were ready.

"Ms Martin – Rachel – you told me on the telephone that

your son, Gale Martin, remembers himself and his sister Layla being approached by a man some time prior to her abduction. Is that correct?"

A pause, then Rachel nodded. "Yes."

"Can you tell me what he said?"

Rachel steeled herself, leaning forward. She still had both hands holding onto her bag, clutching it like a shield.

"It was outside the swimming pool. They were there waiting for me to pick them up after their lesson. Gale said a man came up to them and tried to get them to go with him. And then he says he saw the same man today..." Her words were accelerating and rising dangerously in pitch.

"OK." Clarke held up a hand. "Let's slow things down. Take a deep breath. There's plenty of time."

Rachel did so.

"OK," Clarke's voice was calming. "Which swimming pool are we talking about?"

"The one down by the station. It's..." Rachel felt baffled, suddenly flustered. "I've forgotten the name? The big one, does it really matter—"

"Waterdown swimming pool?" the PC interrupted.

Rachel turned to look at her. She gave an anxious sigh. Then a fast nod.

"For the tape please, Rachel," Clarke reminded her.

She looked up suddenly. "Yes, Waterdown swimming pool."

Clarke paused. He seemed lost in thought for a moment.

"Are you able to say what day that was? Do you know the time?"

"No, but I know where he *lives*," Rachel replied. She began fumbling with the clasp of her bag, meaning to get the paper that Gale had given her, but Clarke interrupted her.

"Rachel, we'll come to that, I promise. First, I want to get every detail I can. A lot of time has passed since Layla's death, which means there may not be much evidence left to find. If this man *approached her* before, and we can find a witness to that..." He had to pause, the significance seemingly too much for him for a few moments. "It could be extremely important in convincing a jury."

Rachel understood. But she kept working on the clasp, and when the bag opened she pulled out her mobile.

"I can give you the date. It's on my calendar. I had an appointment with the— it doesn't matter who, just it overran horribly, and then the traffic was awful, and I was late to pick the children up. That's the only reason they were there. Oh God..." She fell into her own silent misery as she accessed her phone, then scrolled rapidly backwards in time through the appointments app. Then she looked up.

"June 4th. My meeting was at two thirty, but I didn't get out until nearly four. A friend of mine, Sue, she takes them to the swimming pool, but she had to go off somewhere. I asked if she could take the kids too, but she couldn't. So, I had no choice. I asked if she could tell them to wait outside. I thought I'd only be a few minutes, but you know what the traffic is like around there." Rachel took another breath, composed herself. "But I spoke to Layla. I told her to wait by the entrance, where the receptionist could see her."

"And what time was that? What time did you get there?"

The information wasn't on the mobile and Rachel held up her hands helplessly. Then she reminded herself just how important this was. She had to concentrate.

"It was about five. The news had just come on the radio."

"OK. OK, that's good, Rachel. That's really good." Clarke stopped to think. "And do you know where they were waiting? The exact spot?"

"Just by the entrance. I told Layla not to go anywhere else."

Clarke's eyes flicked across to the Constable. Something seemed to pass between them. Rachel didn't know what, until the woman spoke.

"They've definitely got CCTV there," PC Cross said. "Joe does lessons there." Then the woman aimed a slightly sad smile at Rachel. "Joe's my son."

Clarke meanwhile was shaking his head thoughtfully. "It might have it, but it's been more than two years. Almost no chance they'll have kept it that long."

"I can check if you like?" the PC offered. "You never know."

Clarke shook his head. "No. I'll get one of my team down there. I don't want any mistakes." He turned back to Rachel.

"Go on. What else did Gale tell you?"

Rachel was finding it difficult to keep her concentration, but she was doing her best, and the calm of the room was helping her. She thought for a long while. Then she spoke.

"He told them he had snakes."

There was a silence. A look of confusion mixed with distaste passed over the face of the Constable, but it was Clarke's face that took Rachel's attention. Suddenly he wore an expression she had never seen on him before.

"*Snakes?*" His voice had changed too. The pitch wavered. Everything about his calm and reassurance had vanished. It was like something had knocked the air out of him.

"Yes." Rachel remembered what Gale had told her. "He offered to show them to Layla. That's what he said to them. He said he had *snakes in his basement*. That was how he tried to get them to go with him." Rachel could almost see the scene in her mind as she spoke, and suddenly she was horrified that her daughter had had to go through it.

There was a long silence, until Clarke broke it, his voice still filled with something – incredulity, disbelief?

"You're sure he said *snakes?*"

"Yes. Snakes. But they didn't go. They both knew about not getting into a stranger's car."

A few seconds after she said it, Rachel saw the implication of what she'd said – that this was probably exactly what poor Layla had done, when she was taken, those few weeks later. She couldn't stop herself whimpering out loud, as she thought it. But Clarke himself seemed to entirely miss the moment. It was left to the PC to offer her a compassionate look.

"OK, Rachel – Mrs Martin..." Clarke held a hand out in front of his chest, hanging in the air. He screwed his face into a frown. "You've told me that Gale says he saw this *same man* today? That he followed him home? Gale thinks he knows where he *lives*?"

"Yes."

There was another pause. Clarke didn't look happy about this.

"He has an actual *address*? *You* have an actual address?"

"Yes." Once again Rachel reached into her bag, and this time she pulled out the piece of paper that Gale had given her, the printout from Google's Street View.

"This is a picture of the house, he took it from the computer." She handed the paper across the table to DI Clarke, then waited.

Kieran Clarke took the paper, unfolded it, and looked at it. He held the paper for a while, just staring, and saying nothing. Then he looked over at Rachel again. She looked back at him, as if expecting him to leap into action. His eyes went back to the paper in his hands.

It took a long time, but finally he turned back to Rachel Martin.

"Is this some sort of joke?" he said in the end.

The question stunned Rachel into silence for a few bewildering seconds.

"A joke?" Rachel stared at him. From the corner of her eye, she registered the confusion on the PC Cross's face too.

Clarke seemed to register how inappropriate the question was, and he half-held up a hand, as if to apologise. But still he seemed baffled. Eventually he regained the power of speech.

"Mrs Martin, the picture you've just handed me... it's *mine*. This is a photograph of *my* house."

PART TWO

TWENTY-EIGHT

"Seriously, is this some kind of joke?" It made it worse to say it again, but Clarke simply didn't know what else to say. Rachel Martin had just handed him a Google Maps printout of his house, telling her she thought Layla's killer lived there. It was absolutely insane.

"*A joke?*" Rachel Martin stared at him, bewildered pain etched deep into her face. "Why would it..." She glanced at the Constable for help, but she too seemed stunned, unable to make sense of the turn the interview had suddenly taken.

"That's *your* house? But it can't be..."

Clarke shrugged helplessly. He felt like he was a child again, being admonished for something by his parents. "It's my house," he said. Then he studied the paper again, as if he might have made an error, but there was no mistake. The address matched, the little section of the Google Map was centred on his house.

"That's my address, too." Clarke heard himself speaking, and a part of his brain screamed that this must be some kind of crazy dream. He'd been working hard on this case now for over two years, maybe too hard. Most of his colleagues considered him somewhat obsessed. Had he simply cracked?

"But this man has *snakes*." Rachel's voice interrupted his thoughts, bringing him right back into the room. And what she'd said was worse. Everything was getting worse.

"*I* have snakes." Clarke could sense the expression on his colleague's face changing. He'd had to grab PC Cross for the interview because none of his detectives were available that weekend. He turned to her defensively, unable to consider what he said before the words tumbled out of him.

"What? I can't exactly have a dog, not with the hours we have to keep." He felt his face heat up, as the blood rushed to it, and knew he would be turning red, too. He fought against the moment, remembering now that the tape was still running. Everything here was being recorded.

"Mrs Martin..." He paused, playing for time, for the room to stop *spinning* so wildly. "Look, Rachel. I really don't know what is happening here, but yes, you've just handed me a photograph of *my* house." He stopped for a second, but not long. "Yet I can assure you – absolutely categorically – I have nothing to do with the disappearance of your daughter. *Nothing*. Except for the fact that I've dedicated the last two years of my life trying to find out what happened to her."

There was a silence, in which each person in the room tried to make sense of the moment. In the end, Rachel was the one to break it.

"You have snakes?" she asked again.

Clarke forced himself to breathe before answering. He was calming now, enough to talk at least.

"I do. It's a... it's just a hobby. I know some people don't like them, but they're actually very friendly. They make good pets, and they cope well with the hours I put in here—"

"I didn't know that," Cross interrupted, from his left, and

Clarke turned away from Rachel to look at her. The look on her face alarmed him. There was clear accusation in her voice when she went on. "You never mentioned you kept them."

"Well, no." He stared at her, chest tight. "It's not a *crime*. And you know what the rumour mill in here is like." He felt sick. The beginnings of anger, too. "For what it's worth, PC Cross, I have to say I'm unaware what pets you have as well."

"I rent my flat. We're not allowed pets." This time there was an unmistakable edge to her voice. Unmissable. But this was *ridiculous*. This whole thing was *insane*.

Clarke scrambled to keep thinking, as another silence descended. He still had no idea what was going on, and clearly the mother felt the same. Then, suddenly, his mind locked onto a thought. It was like a lifebelt being thrown to him in a raging sea.

Maybe there was a simple explanation.

"Mrs Clarke," he leaned forward, still breathing hard. "Rachel. I can promise you I have absolutely nothing to do with what happened to Layla. Surely you know me well enough to believe that?" He held her gaze as a range of emotions registered on her face. Finally, she swallowed and gave a nod, but she looked far from convinced. He pressed his fingers against his forehead, and tried to keep hold of the thought that might explain this.

"OK, let's try and work out what's happening here. You said Gale told you he *saw* this man. Today? That he followed him to this address? To *my* address?" He stopped, still thinking. He was thinking now of the incident that had happened in his garden. The girl with the dog. She was with another kid – he never saw him clearly, but *could* that have been Gale?

He'd never actually met the boy. He only vaguely knew what he looked like – when Gale had been interviewed, Clarke had asked Jennifer Robbins to conduct the interview. Since then, the parents had been adamant they wanted to protect their son as much as possible. And he'd done everything he could to facilitate that.

"What if Gale saw *me?*" He went on. "Gale doesn't know me, but my face has been clearly associated with the case. The TV appeals on the news – I gave many of them. And my photograph has been in the newspapers several times..." He opened his hands. "Could Gale have simply got confused?"

Rachel opened and closed her mouth several times, before finally speaking. She still sounded utterly baffled.

"I don't see how that could have happened. We haven't let Gale watch anything about the case on TV. And we don't read newspapers. We didn't want him to see." She was slowly shaking her head.

There was a silence.

"But it must be," Clarke heard himself protesting. *It had to be the explanation. What else was there?*

"Does he have access to any devices, Mrs Martin?" It was Cross who asked the question. Clarke glanced at her. She wasn't supposed to speak. Just come in and fill the damn seat so there was a second officer present. How hard was that? But he watched now as Rachel turned to look at her, her face blank.

"Why?" There was a hard edge to Rachel's voice, a hint of accusation.

"Well, it's possible that Gale's been searching for details of the case online. He might have seen photographs of DI Clarke that way."

Her logic filtered through to Clarke, accompanied by a rush of gratitude. "Yes. *Of course.* It's possible." He turned to Rachel. "Does Gale have access to the internet? If so, he must have looked up details of the case. Anyone would."

"I... Yes, we do let him go online sometimes..."

With the two police officers looking straight at her, Rachel Martin looked crushed.

"So this isn't... This isn't going to help catch him?"

Clarke felt his breathing coming back to normal. It was the first realisation he had that he'd been out of breath in the first place. The first moment too when he realised what this meant for *her*.

"Look Rachel, I'm so sorry. This is a blow. A real blow. When you called, I really thought this could be a breakthrough. What we've been looking for." He shook his head, dropping it down towards the desk, still trying to think.

"What about the man at the swimming pool?" Rachel replied, and Clarke's head snapped back up. He'd forgotten.

"Gale told me a man approached them at the swimming pool? He said the man tried to get them to go with him. He said he had snakes in his basement." She held out her hands in a shrug. She looked at him with fear in her eyes.

The atmosphere in the room seemed to change. The mystery solved, yet now suddenly back. Clarke felt it on his skin, a pressure change, and his brain clamoured for an answer. But it was like wading through syrup. There was no answer, at least nothing he could come up with.

"This was... We have the date for that?" he glanced again at PC Cross, who had been taking notes. She nodded at once.

"June 4th, sixteen hundred hours to seventeen hundred."

Clarke turned back to Rachel. "I... I don't know. I can absolutely assure you that it wasn't me, but I have no explanation for why Gale thought it was... Perhaps it's a case of mistaken identity? Perhaps the killer in some way resembles me?" He shrugged too.

He simply didn't know what else to say.

"Ms Martin," Constable Cross seemed to have sensed that some responsibility had landed on her following Rachel's revelation, but her voice was stiff, awkward. She cleared her throat.

"Rachel." she smiled. "Can you tell me how old Gale is?"

It took Rachel a while to answer. First, she had to tear her eyes away from Clarke's face. When she did so, she was blinking, as if suddenly facing a bright light.

"He's ten."

"OK." Cross nodded. "And how's he been coping? With everything that's happened?"

"What's that got to—" Rachel began, but she seemed to stop herself. She sat up straighter, as if literally pulling herself together. "He's coping fine. *Really well* – with everything considered." Suddenly she burst out into laughter, a wild sound, almost hysterical. "Considering that his sister was abducted and murdered."

There was a silence. Then Cross went on. "Rachel, is he seeing anyone? Is he getting any kind of counselling?"

Rachel didn't answer at once. But then she nodded. "Yes. He sees a grief counsellor once a week."

"And how's that going?"

Rachel rubbed at her eye. She changed her answer. "Not so well," she admitted. "She says he's still bottling a lot of things up inside."

Cross turned to Clarke, and she met his eyes. Then she turned back to Rachel. "I've got a boy, Joe. He's only a little bit older than yours. And he's a good boy, but he's not always honest, and sometimes I think he's lying to himself just as much as he's lying to me. Do you know what I mean?"

Rachel stared at her, and Clarke stared at Rachel. For a moment he thought she was going to start shouting, or laughing again. But instead, she nodded.

"So maybe it's possible he got confused and mixed up DI Clarke because he's seen a photo of him online. And maybe he saw something about the snakes online too?" She turned to Clarke. "Are you on any forums? Facebook groups about snakes, things like that?"

Her calmness surprised him. Cross didn't exactly have the

best reputation in the station – she was the woman you sent out
when a cat got stuck up a tree. But she was helping him now,
and he was grateful for that.

"Might that explain it?" Cross went on. "He saw DI Clarke
online, associated with the case, and then discovered he kept
snakes, and that's what made him put two and two together, and
come up with five?"

But this time Rachel dropped her head and covered her
eyes. She snuffled a while, then blew her nose into a handker-
chief. When she looked up, Cross was still watching her.

"Um... I don't... I suppose it's possible."

Clarke retreated into his head for a few moments. He
needed space to think, and he didn't even know if he'd missed
any of what was said next, or if so how much. Then he jumped
back in. He was starting to see light where there had been only
black.

"Rachel, I'm so sorry for this," he said. "When you called
me I really thought this could be the moment we've been
waiting for, working towards. But it still might be. I want to get
Gale in as soon as possible. I'm going to call DC Jennifer
Robbins right away, see if she can find out some more details of
the time this man approached them. Maybe there is still something we can get from this. Maybe there's something there,
underneath all this... confusion."

Without thinking he reached out his hand to Rachel. It was
a subconscious movement, but Rachel's response was considered. She looked at it, almost with fear written on her face. But
after a few moments she reached out her own hand too, and let
his squeeze hers.

The touch fired through Clarke's body, hope and relief. A
thought occurred to him.

"You said something about a basement, didn't you?" he
asked.

Rachel Martin nodded, and Clarke's tight hold on his body relaxed a notch. He shook his head and allowed the briefest flash of a smile.

"Rachel, I don't even have a basement."

TWENTY-NINE

"Well, this is an odd one." Detective Superintendent Starling wore a bemused look, his greying hair in need of a trim. "I'm fairly used to hearing accusations against my officers, but they normally come from known scumbags, not ten-year-old children."

"Yes, sir," Ellen Cross replied.

Minutes earlier Clarke had suspended the interview and removed the tape from the recorder. She'd noticed how much his hands were shaking. Then he'd asked Rachel Martin to wait in the room, while he led Cross up to see the Superintendent in his office. She'd thought it was good luck that he was there – normally on a Saturday he'd be on the golf course. After that, Cross had sat waiting outside the Super's office for nearly ten minutes, with Clarke inside, before she was called to join them. Then Starling had asked her what she'd witnessed in the interview. All the while DI Clarke was sitting beside her, watching what she said.

Now the super had told DI Clarke to wait outside, and it was just her and Starling, alone in his office.

"A very, very odd one." The super seemed lost in thought

for a long while, and Cross wondered what he was going to do. How on earth did you handle a situation like this?

Finally, he spoke. "Well. As unlikely as it seems that there could be any truth in this, it's going to need to be looked at." All the while he kept his eyes on the surface of his desk, where everything was neat. He had his laptop computer open – one of those fancy ones, super thin, with carbon fibre effect. It looked a bit ridiculous next to his large hands.

"But we need to do it very, very carefully." He looked up at her. "Mud has a tendency to stick, and this is a seriously impressive load of mud." He stopped again, apparently lost in thought.

"For the time being, I'd like to keep this as confined as possible, do you understand?"

Cross nodded. "I think so, sir."

"To be specific, you're not to speak with anyone about this development... which presents me with a problem." He looked doubtful for a moment, but then seemed to come to a decision.

"Normally I wouldn't be asking this of a Constable, but this has rather fallen into your lap, so I'd like you to stay on it. I want you to get down to the swimming pool and check out whether there is any CCTV of the incident the boy talked about." He paused. "You applied to take your detective exams, didn't you?"

"No sir. I didn't."

"Oh. You've been a PC how long? Six years?"

"Eight years."

"Hmmm. OK, well I don't suppose it matters. It's highly doubtful they'll have anything after this long. But if they do have anything about this approach, then I want you to get it, and bring it back, reporting only to me. Do you understand?"

"Yes, sir."

"Do you actually understand what I'm saying here? It's almost certain this accusation is false, but if it gets out it will destroy DI Clarke's career. At this point the only people who know about it are Clarke, me and you. I hope I don't need to explain the implications, if word does leak."

"No, sir, I don't think you do."

Still blinking in amazement at how her shift was going, Cross left the Super's office.

She began by calling the Waterdown swimming pool on the phone. She might not have been a detective, but it wasn't such a tall ask to go and pick up CCTV – that was something she was very familiar with. And she'd done it enough times that she knew the law, too.

There were no statutes that covered how long footage had to be kept – at least for a sports centre – but most systems automatically recorded back over the footage after anything from two to twenty-eight days. A system covering public areas, such as the cameras that overlooked the entrance to the pool, would usually be at the upper end – but two *years* on? In most cases it would only be the proper tinfoil hat brigade that kept footage that long. The only hope Cross had was that, in her years as a police officer, she'd come across a fair number of those.

After explaining what she wanted several times, she finally managed to get her call routed through to a man named Gary, who was apparently in charge of security at the centre.

"No chance," he told her, when she told him what she wanted.

She pushed down the sense of disappointment that appeared inside.

"Can I get you double-check, it's June 4th. Two years ago. Just to be sure?"

"No need," Gary replied. "I already know. What did you say it was for again?"

"I didn't say," she thought a moment, remembering the super's slightly chilling warning. "But it's for a serious, ongoing investigation." A silence followed her words, and Cross wondered for a moment where they had come from. She'd sounded just like one of the detectives.

"Well, I'm sorry I can't be more help—" the man began, but Cross cut in.

"Gary, can I just ask you to *triple* check it, just as a favour to me?" Automatically she fixed a smile on her face, hoping it would translate to her voice. Someone had told her once that she was good with people – actually, lots of people had told her that – but that time, they'd said the reason was because she naturally smiled when she spoke. And because she always seemed to remember people's names. The comment had confused her slightly – how could people *not* remember other people's names? Surely it was only common decency?

"Sorry, love, but there's no chance. You see, we have a fully automatic digital system these days. It keeps the date for a month, and then simply overwrites on the same disks."

Cross sighed, but it was what she'd expected. CCTV was what they called a 'golden hour' enquiry. You had to grab it before it was gone forever, hence why she was frequently sent out to claim tapes and disks and bring them back to the actual investigators working the cases.

She vaguely wondered whether she should get herself down there and check if anyone remembered seeing the incident. Sterling hadn't mentioned that, but surely it was the natural next step? If she had been a detective, then surely that was what she would have done. But then she wasn't a detective, and she wasn't even going to try to become one – she was only doing this because DI Clarke had grabbed her to sit in on his interview, because no one else was around and then... the confusion of what was happening overtook her for a moment, until she realised that Gary was speaking again.

"What date did you say exactly?"

"Mmmm..." Cross checked the note she'd scribbled down.

"June 4th. We need the footage for the afternoon, say between three and six."

"Hang on."

The line went quiet. While she waited, Cross's mind returned to the drama that had taken place in the interview room. It was a standard enough request to be asked to sit in on an interview, but even so, she'd been pleased. For one thing, she wasn't often asked, and for another, a lot of the girls in the station had a bit of a thing for DI Clarke. He was good looking, and a fine copper too. But then the meeting had unravelled, and descended into – what? Confusion? Farce? She wasn't quite sure she even knew.

And *snakes*? She'd had no idea that DI Clarke was into weird pets, let alone snakes. The thought put her off him a bit. She searched her mind for anyone she knew who also kept snakes, as if that might make it more normal. She remembered there was an old school friend who'd dated a guy who kept them. But then he was a bit of a creep.

Then again – she was still hanging on the phone – perhaps that actually explained it? Why Clarke had kept it quiet? Perhaps everyone who had snakes kept it a bit of a secret, just because of the way people instantly formed an opinion on it. As Clarke himself had said, it wasn't a crime – at least, as far as she *knew* it wasn't a crime. She was aware that some snakes would presumably be covered by the Dangerous Animals Act. But presumably, even if Clark's snakes *were* covered, then he would have the required permits, because in every other respect he was a completely normal guy – a well-respected detective. *Wasn't he?*

She shook her head, trying to stop the thoughts chasing their own tails. This was all just a moment of weirdness. She wasn't familiar with the Layla Martin case, but it had been long-running enough, and high-profile enough. too, that everyone who worked from the station knew the basics. And there was nothing to suggest snakes had *anything* to do with it. She marvelled at her ability to lose sight of that. Perhaps another reason why she wasn't an actual detective, or cut out to be one...

"You still there, love?" The man's voice sounded on the phone again. She'd almost forgotten she was waiting for him.

"Still here."

"Well. I've got some good news."

"What?" She'd had so little hope for success, she'd almost forgotten what she was waiting for.

"I *might* have. I can't say for sure."

"What?" Cross didn't get it. "What are you saying?"

"Well, I told you we had a modern system, didn't I? What I didn't say is we still have the old tape-based system we ran before. It's in the storage room – you can't sell it, see. No one wants the old tech anymore. It still works just fine, but you can't get rid of it..."

"I'm sorry, but what exactly are you saying?"

"Oh. Sure. Sorry. Well the *old* tape system. We kept it. Well, *I* kept it actually. Just in case the new system wasn't reliable, because you never know—"

"*Gary!*"

"Yeah?"

"Can you please just explain what you're talking about?"

"Sure. Right. Well, for a while, actually for the *exact week* you're looking for, I happened to run the two systems side-by-side. But once I saw that the new system worked as it should, I stopped using the old system and put it in storage. And like I said, you can't sell it." He paused. "So it's still there."

Cross held her breath.

"And it still has the old tapes in? With that week recorded?"

"Well there's no reason it *shouldn't* have. I'd have to get it set up to know for sure."

"Can you do so? Right now?"

"Well..." He sounded doubtful now, but she cut back in.

"Gary, it's really important that you set those tapes up. And that you don't show them to anyone. In fact, don't even tell anyone what you're doing. And I'm coming to see you right away." When Cross hung up, her eyes were as wide as they went. She was going to be a detective after all.

Cross didn't have a car of her own, and she wasn't able to access the pool of unmarked vehicles assigned to more senior officers. Or at least, she wasn't without consulting Starling first, and she didn't want to do that. More importantly, there was no need. She knew pretty much everyone in the building, and certainly everyone who worked patrol. So she got on the radio and begged a lift, and minutes later was dropped off outside the swimming pool entrance, with a promise to be picked up whenever she needed.

When her lift had driven away, she looked up and saw the cameras. Beside them was a second set of rusted mounts, which the old units must have been secured to.

Could they possibly have recorded something? Was it even possible that they'd recorded DI Clarke?

The thought sent a shiver down her body.

THIRTY

"Hello there, I'm here to see Gary. In charge of the security. He'll be expecting me." She smiled at the receptionist, who looked at her uniform with a mix of alarm and suspicion.

"Who?"

"Gary. He looks after your CCTV here." Helpfully Cross indicated the bank of three screens behind the woman's desk.

"Oh, Gary." The woman looked as if she wasn't used to hearing his name, but she pressed the button on the centre's radio system.

"I'll put in a call for him."

It took two calls, but eventually Gary answered, giving her directions to where he'd set things up. Then, after hiking up and down several wrong corridors, Cross finally arrived at the tiny storeroom where a man in his sixties was waiting for her. He was clearly excited, hopping from one foot to the other.

"That date you wanted, I've only got the *whole day*," he greeted her. "I've watched it through from 3 p.m., but I wasn't sure what we're looking for."

Cross felt an urge to tell him, but reigned it in. "I'm afraid *we're* not looking for anything Gary, I'm sorry." She gave him a conciliatory smile. "As I said, this is a very serious case, which means I'll have to review the tapes on my own. But you've been incredibly helpful."

"Oh." The man was visibly deflated. "But how are you going to operate the system?" Cross glanced down at what he'd set up. She'd seen dozens like it. But instead of saying this, she held up the radio she'd borrowed from the lady on reception, in case she got lost somewhere.

"How about I call you on this if I get stuck?"

She watched as he departed, then looked around for somewhere to sit. The storeroom was filled with old gym equipment: narrow wooden benches, which looked too low and uncomfortable, and a vaulting horse which was too big. The smell of it brought back her own school days, a distant memory of kissing a boy in the school gym. *Darren something...*

She found a chair and brushed the dust off, then sat on it and inspected the system Gary had set up. He'd had to unpack the device from a stack of boxes, and he'd pulled out one of the original screens – they'd obviously replaced both the front and back ends of the system. This set up looked a little like an old-style VCR machine, with heavy, clunky magnetic tapes. It was already on and had been paused on a still image of the footage of the entranceway she'd just passed through. It was empty, but her hopes were raised when she saw the camera was fairly wide angle and covered most of the space. The quality wasn't too bad either. Black and white, but clear enough.

She pressed play, feeling how her heart was beating fast, fluttering almost. Was she about to witness the moment that DI Clarke was revealed to be a child-killer? It seemed impossible. And yet she was here.

She watched for ten minutes before she saw the children. Unmistakably Layla – she'd seen the poor girl's image hundreds of times. She didn't know what Gale looked like, but it was obvious who he was, too: a smaller figure, figuratively and literally in her shadow. She led the way, and seemed to be in charge of him. They came out of the building through the door she'd just gone though, then sat on the wall together, kicking their legs, and presumably talking.

Cross couldn't hear what they said, but the quality was good enough to see their mouths moving. A few times, Layla pulled out and checked a mobile phone; once she took a short call (incoming, the girl didn't appear to have dialled a number).

As she watched, Cross found herself holding her breath, waiting for the moment that the man approached, and praying that when he did so, he would be facing the camera, at least for long enough that she could freeze the frame and get a decent look at his face. But minute after minute passed and no man appeared. She kept half an eye on the time stamp in the top corner of the screen, feeling her anxiety increase as it crept closer to five o'clock, the time the mother had said she'd finally appeared. And then finally Gale jumped off the wall, in a way he hadn't moved before, and a figure *did* approach.

Cross leaned in closer, readying her finger to hit the pause button. But the figure wasn't a man. Even from behind, which was all Cross could see at this point, it was clear that the adult who had approached was female, and from the children's reaction, that they knew her. And then, when she turned around, Cross was able to recognise her – the same woman she had sat opposite in the interview room earlier that day. The children's mother.

Cross slowly sat back in the chair – she hadn't even realised she'd leaned closer to the screen. She exhaled slowly, trying to push back her disappointment. And then acknowledging it *was* disappointment that she felt. But why?

Had she wanted to see DI Clarke approaching the children? *No.* But she *had* wanted to find a breakthrough in the case. She bit her lip. Why? Had she wanted to be the hero, breaking the case wide open? She knew that wasn't it. She'd just wanted the poor girl to get some justice.

She rewound the tape and watched it a second time, this time noting down the key moments like she should have done the first time. There were the children leaving through the exit door of the pool and going to wait by the wall. There was the phone call. And nothing else happened. They never left the screen, and nobody approached them or even came near, until half an hour later, the mother appeared, and the three left together.

Which meant... Cross engaged the analytical part of her brain. There *was* no man with snakes in the basement. And then the motherly part.

Gale Martin was telling fibs.

THIRTY-ONE

One hour later, DI Kieran Clarke was back outside Superintendent Starling's office, waiting to be called in and find out what the hell was going to happen next. As he sat there his mind played and replayed the bizarre series of events that had marked the day.

First the call from Rachel Martin – completely unexpected, but clearly exciting and hopeful. He hadn't known what it meant when she'd told him, but if the girl's brother had been approached by a man prior to Layla's death – and if he *had* seen the same man on the beach – well that was enough dynamite to blow the case wide open.

But then the whole thing had exploded in *his* face. He shuddered as he recalled the total sense of shock he'd felt when Rachel Martin handed him a Google Street View picture of *his* house. His childhood home, the only house he'd ever owned, right back from when his parents died, all those years ago. His mind went back to that time now.

He was living then at his university halls, getting ready for an evening out, when there was a knock at the door. Two policemen stood there. He remembered the panic in his friends, because they had cannabis in the house, but that wasn't why they were there. They'd asked to speak with him, in private. And then in his college bedroom, they'd stood and explained how his parents had been passengers on a jet that had crashed somewhere on the Baja peninsula. A crash with no chance of survivors.

He hadn't even known they were on holiday. Sure, they'd talked about travelling more, now that he was at uni, but they hadn't mentioned that specific trip. Or if they had, his mind had been on other things.

There was a particular sense he'd had then, that was similar now. A sideways wrenching from one reality to another. One moment his parents were this fixture in his life – perhaps a little dull and unexciting by that age, yet ever-present, and young enough that the idea of them *dying* was something he wouldn't have to face until long in the future. And then suddenly, instantaneously, gone. All in the few words of a police officer, who didn't even take the time to sit down. And as his world shifted, it was like a glimpse that reality itself was just a stage set, a mask covering the roaring void of chaos behind. That's how it had felt when Rachel handed him the photograph of his house. For a second the void of chaos was uncovered again. He shuddered at the memory.

What happened after Rachel gave him the photograph? He struggled to remember, but knew it was important. He'd asked PC Cross to accompany him to see Superintendent Starling, floating up the stairs like he was in a dream. That was the right thing to do – a good call. He didn't want to hide anything, or make it look like he was trying to. Before that he'd asked Rachel Martin to wait in the interview room. *Oh shit* – he didn't even know what had happened to her after that. He hoped she wasn't still there, waiting.

But no, Starling would have handled her. He'd said as much.

Kieran had explained what happened, first to Starling, with Cross out of the room, and then he'd sat there, while Starling asked Cross to come in and go through it again. He'd watched them as she spoke, praying that they would believe him. It was totally unbelievable, and yet, the way it had happened, he knew that if the positions were reversed, he'd be wondering.

To his credit though, the super had realised the gravity of the situation right away. It wasn't often a serving police officer was accused of a crime, much less a serious one, but it did happen. Clarke remembered a time when he was in uniform, and an older officer was arrested for the murder of his wife. Clarke had been a junior member of the arrest team, asked to secure the scene. But he remembered the sense of shock in his colleagues, the sense of betrayal, that had spread through the force.

Superintendent Starling had got Cross to check out the CCTV at the pool. There was little hope it would yield anything, but it had to be followed up. At the same time, Starling himself had taken his own house keys – Clarke's keys – to literally check on Clarke's claim he didn't have a basement.

Clarke shook his head again. The whole thing was just *nuts*.

Suddenly the door opened.

"DI Clarke, would you follow me?" Superintendent Starling left his office and walked towards the lifts. He didn't make eye contact, nor speak as they walked, a little faster than was comfortable.

Eventually they reached one of the interview rooms on the ground floor. When Clarke got in, he saw PC Cross was already sitting behind the desk. He nodded a hello to her while Starling sat down.

"DI Clarke, I've decided to tape this meeting in case it becomes necessary to have a record. Do you have any objection to that?"

"No." Clarke shook his head, his own voice sounding

strange. Then he watched while the equipment was started. Starling gave his name and rank, then waited as Cross and then Clarke did the same.

As he listened, he wondered what this was about. Had they found something they thought was incriminating? But how could they have done?

"Let's start with your house." Starling began. "I've just been to the address given by Rachel Martin as the location where her son believes Layla Martin's killer lives or lived. That's your address, correct?"

"It's my address but—"

Starling held up a hand to silence him.

"Just answer the question please." Starling fixed him with a stern gaze.

"Yes."

"The information from Mrs Martin was regarding the possibility of Layla having been held in some sort of cellar or basement at that address. I can confirm I have inspected the house carefully and found no evidence of any such room."

"Well of course, I don't have—"

Starling cut in. "Furthermore, PC Cross here caught a break with the CCTV at the pool. It seems they do still have the footage from June 4th two years ago."

Clarke felt his eyes widen.

"And?"

"And it shows nothing." Starling shook his head. "PC Cross has watched it through twice. I've watched it once. The children are in full view for the entire time, and at no point are either of the children approached by anyone." He paused. "We still have Mrs Martin waiting down the hall, is that correct?"

"Yes sir," Cross answered. "I checked in on her when I got back. Brought her a sandwich since she missed out on lunch."

"Thank you, Constable. I'll speak with her in a moment." Starling paused as he considered what to say next. "It appears quite evident that there's nothing, at all, to substantiate the accusation she's made against DI Clarke. Therefore, I don't see any value in putting this matter forward to internal enquiries, nor to place any kind of sanctions upon DI Clarke. It's not clear what has happened, but it could be a case of mistaken identity, some kind of misguided prank or simply a mistake by the boy." He paused again, giving his officer time to take this in. And the bad news that was still to come.

"Nevertheless, depending upon Mrs Martin's wishes, it may be necessary to move you off this case, purely as a result of what's happened, but with no fault attached to you."

Clarke felt a hollow opening up in front of him, a glimpse of the void, and how he was about to pitch forward into it.

"Sir – no. I've worked this case for *two years*, I know it better than anyone—"

The detective superintendent held up his hand again. "I don't doubt that, Kieran. I don't think anyone doubts that. Your commitment to this case has been noted many times. But I have to consider this from the Martins' point of view. Their son has made an accusation, albeit indirectly, against you. It seems very unlikely to me that this won't change things."

Clarke hesitated, then nodded. "I understand, sir." He tried not to close his eyes.

"That said, I want to understand something myself. In the event that the Martins do not have an objection to your continuing to lead the case, are you willing to carry on?"

"Yes." Clarke gaped at the question. "Of course I am."

"I can give you some time to consider that answer if you need it."

"I don't need time."

Starling gave him a moment anyway, but then nodded. "Good." Then he suspended the interview. When the tape was stopped, he glanced over at Cross, who was still setting up the swimming pool's video equipment. She caught the look and nodded back, indicating it was ready.

"Thank you, Kieran. That's the answer I was hoping you'd give. But for now, if you can make yourself scarce, we'll get Rachel Martin in here and show that her boy's been making up stories. It might still be she wants you off the case, but let's put that choice in her hands."

Clarke nodded dumbly, and stood up. He went to the door, but Starling stopped him.

"Clarke."

"Sir?"

"Look, this is an odd one, but I've worked a few cases with kids, and they can throw up the strangest things sometimes. Go home, and don't dwell on this too much. I'll let you know what she says as soon as I know."

Clarke nodded again. He thanked the Super and left the room.

THIRTY-TWO

Rachel Martin ignored the cup of tea that had been placed in front of her. She used to drink tea, but since Layla's murder had switched to only coffee – at least three cups a day. Now her focus was entirely on the small, black-and-white video screen that had been set up in the interview room. The same woman who had sat in on the interview earlier was operating it. She'd told Rachel her name was Ellen, and she seemed nice, though Rachel hadn't been in any state to reciprocate.

The other officer, Detective Superintendent Starling, whom she knew reasonably well, had already told her the tape didn't show anything. He'd also said he'd personally been to DI Clarke's house that afternoon and confirmed there was no basement, nor any sort of room that met the description Gale had given them. He'd stopped short of saying that Gale was lying – but the clear implication was that her son had at least made a terrible mistake.

But it wasn't Gale's honesty, or otherwise, that was consuming Rachel Martin's thoughts. Instead, she was simply staring at the image of her daughter on the screen. *New* footage. After Layla's death, she had gathered and filed every video on her and Jon's phones, and asked friends to email or WhatsApp her with any footage they had. But here was something new, an image of Layla alive and well, just a few weeks before her death. It was, in a way, as if she had come a little bit back from the dead.

Rachel sat in silence and watched the entire thirty minutes of footage that began with Layla and Gale coming out from the doors of the swimming pool, and ended with her coming to pick them up. She remembered the guilt she'd felt as she fought through the traffic to reach them. The call she'd made to Layla as she drove – even though she wasn't supposed to – and the irritation that all three of them had shown when she'd finally got there. At the time it had seemed like being late for the swimming pool pick-up was a big deal. How wrong that was. How little they all knew, at that point, about the horrible realities of the cruel, cruel world. She mourned her own innocence.

"We're very fortunate the pool kept the footage," Starling's voice cut softly into her thoughts. "They happened to be changing over to a new CCTV system. Had you given us any other week, we wouldn't have this." He paused long enough that she had time to follow the unspoken logic – that in such a scenario there would have been nothing to show that Gale was mistaken. Or lying. Her face reddened.

But he didn't quite say that. Instead, he spoke gently, watching her carefully.

"As you can see, there's no sign of anyone approaching the children, and they're in the frame the entire time." He stopped, until she acknowledged him, and nodded.

"It means that, unfortunately, there's nothing to corroborate what Gale has told you. It's not something that's going to be any help in catching Layla's killer. I'm very sorry."

He paused, but no one else spoke, so he continued. "I don't think there's any reason to be angry with Gale. Strange things like this do happen from time to time. Layla's death will have put a huge stress on all of you, perhaps especially onto Gale, and he will be as desperate as you are to find out what happened."

Rachel Martin nodded again.

"It's quite possible that he completely believes what he's told you. That he hasn't meant to mislead us." He paused. "It's likely he's not even aware he's misled us." This time he shook his head. "But he *is* wrong."

"I can see that." Rachel suddenly found her voice. "I don't know what's got into him. He's just a boy." She held a hand over her eyes and closed them too, as if trying to black out the room. Then she slid her hand down. "Will you still need to speak to him?"

Starling glanced at the other officer, and a look passed between them. "I don't think there's any need to take this any further, no." He paused again. "But there is one more question we need to address."

Rachel held her breath until he went on.

"We need to ask whether you're prepared for DI Clarke to continue leading the case. He's indicated to me that this doesn't change anything from his point of view, but I've explained to him – and he's accepted – that this will be entirely your decision. And you don't have to answer that right away. It's something you should discuss with your husband."

Rachel nodded, her eyes downcast.

After a short while, Starling made his excuses and exited the room. It was left to Ellen Cross to show Rachel out of the station.

THIRTY-THREE

As Rachel pulled into the drive, she saw Jon was back, his mountain bike strapped to the back of his car, and both splattered with mud. She pulled up close, too close, almost touching it with her bumper, then cut the engine. For a moment she listened to the silence. But not for long. She left the car and opened the front door of the house. At once Jon came out of the kitchen to meet her.

"Well?"

Her sister Erica was still there too, her hands wrapped anxiously around another cup of tea.

"What did they say?

Rachel managed to shake her head just enough to communicate that all wasn't well, and then went into the kitchen, fixing Jon a look that he should follow. Gale was already in there, sat at the table, as if he'd been undergoing his own interrogation. Rachel didn't ask him to leave.

"What happened?" Jon asked, but she ignored him.

"Gale." Rachel's mouth was dry; she felt the anger fizzing off her like electricity. Way too much for her to think clearly, to consider how to handle this. For now, she was a storm.

"I don't know..." she began, but was too angry even to speak. She had to calm herself a little. "I don't know what you thought you were doing this morning, but it didn't help. It really didn't help. You've wasted a lot of people's time."

"Rachel—" Jon started to speak but she cut him off at once. Holding up her hand to his face. Fingers trembling.

"*No.*"

She didn't even glance at her husband. In the silence that followed, her eyes never left her son.

"The man you followed, the man whose *house* you went to; he's not the man who took Layla. He's the man who's trying to catch him."

Gale looked confused. Not shocked, not yet. He simply didn't get it.

"What do you mean?" Gale's voice was quiet against the hard rage of Rachel's.

"The photograph you showed me. That was Detective Inspector Clarke's house. The man who's leading the investigation."

Jon was frowning now, understanding, but not understanding. He tried to speak again, but this time she simply ignored him. Her attention was wholly on Gale. Yet he was – somehow – not quite giving *her* his full attention. Instead, he was looking at the window, no – the wall by the window. Then suddenly he turned to face her.

"But... *that* is the man."

"No. No it's not."

"It is, Mum. I promise—"

"*Gale!*"

She screamed his name. Almost out of control. He became quiet.

But then he wasn't.

"Mum, I promise you. I really do," Gale continued, his voice weirdly in control, given the situation. "That's the man who took Layla. He kept her in his basement. He's the one who talked to us at the swimming pool."

As Gale kept talking Jon started speaking too, louder this time, as if refusing to be ignored any longer. But Rachel's anger silenced both of them.

"*No!* No. *I will not take this anymore.* And please Jon, don't go trying to insert yourself in this – the voice of *reason* – because you weren't there. You were... cycling up a stupid hill, while I was in the police station, accusing the very man who's doing his best to help us, who's done everything for us, of being a freakin' murderer!"

She breathed heavily. Automatically. As if her body sensed her anger was too much, and was working on its own to calm her down. She glanced at Gale, but he still wasn't looking at her. Still staring at the infernal *wall*.

"No," she said again. Calmer now. She took several more deep breaths, drinking in air to blunt the worst of the rage.

"I don't know what you're doing Gale, I don't know if you *think* you believe this, or if you're just mistaken. But it's *not true*. You need to know that, and you need to accept it."

"Rach—" Jon began softly, and though she ignored him again, she did at least glance at him this time, before turning back to their son.

"*Is it?* Gale? You told me this man approached you, at the swimming pool. With some story about coming to see his snakes. Is that the truth?"

Now he was looking at her.

"*Is it true?*"

Gale opened his mouth to speak, but she cut him off again, as if she couldn't bear to hear him lie any more.

"And bear in mind, Gale, I've watched the whole thing on CCTV, and there's *no one* that comes to speak to you. Not Kieran, not *anybody*. So, you may as well admit it, because I know the truth."

She watched him staring back at her for a few moments, and then glancing again at the wall. What was so fascinating about that wall all of a sudden? And then he turned to look at Becky, who was now standing in the doorway, as if seeking her help.

Finally, he spoke.

"That bit wasn't exactly true..." he began, then carried on quickly – as if this was just a tiny detail. "But the rest was. The bit about the snakes, and the basement..."

"Kieran keeps snakes as pets," Rachel burst out. "I admit it, it's a bit weird," she went on, since the room had fallen suddenly silent. "And I don't have the first idea how you found that out, but I assume it has something to do with that weird trip you made us take to the pet store? Am I right?" She didn't wait for a response. "But it really doesn't matter. Yes, you saw snakes in his house because he keeps them as pets. For God's sake, it doesn't make him a *murderer*."

Gale's head dropped now. For a while it seemed he might be crying, but when he lifted his head, his eyes were clear, though his voice was so quiet she almost didn't hear him.

"But what if it does? What if he is?"

And the innocence in his round, brown eyes. The fear that penetrated so deep into his expression, right back into his soul: it burst her anger like a balloon. From that moment on, it was only compassion she felt.

"He doesn't even have a basement, Gale. The police sent someone to his house today, while I was there, to search it. They checked his house because of what you said. And there is no basement." She took a deep breath, and touched the top of his head. It was damp.

"So please, promise me you'll stop making up stories?"

THIRTY-FOUR

DI Kieran Clarke pulled open the door of his dark blue Škoda Octavia and climbed inside, finally shutting out the rest of the world. A world that had, out of nowhere, threatened to explode out of control. He sat for a moment, looking out into the police station car park. A squad car came in, and two officers pulled out a young man – clearly drunk – and steered him with some difficulty into the rear entrance of the building.

Clarke stared at the scene, unseeing, while moments from the day bubbled up in his mind. They were disconnected, isolated, like puzzle pieces that didn't fit together. Eventually, he reached across his shoulder for the seatbelt, and pushed the engine's start button. It growled into life, a comforting noise to draw a line under a wild day. He drove home more carefully than he typically would.

When DI Clarke arrived home, and shut the front door behind him, he put the chain on the door. His eyes darted about his hallway. He remembered how Starling had been here. It sent a prickling feeling across his skin. Like his home had been violated. Without him even being able to clear up first.

He dropped the keys on the hallway table and walked through to the kitchen. He ran his eyes around the room. He didn't know what he was looking for exactly, but already there was some relief that he'd left the place orderly and clean. The same for the living room, the leather armchair arranged in front of the TV was a sign that he lived alone, that he didn't expect visitors. *Well, so what?*

He went to his bedroom – there was no reason for Starling to have looked in here, but then again, had the situation been reversed, he would have done so. Clarke had made the bed that morning, leaving a triangle of duvet folded back revealing sheets that he'd changed that week. Nothing of concern. But why would there be? He'd done nothing wrong.

Then he went to the room that *did* concern him. He kept the snakes in what had been the dining room when he was younger, when his parents were still alive. But Clarke never entertained, and certainly didn't have dinner parties, so the room now housed the two large, temperature-controlled glass tanks, as well as the various other containers and paraphernalia that went with them.

He wasn't ashamed of his snakes – in fact, quite the contrary, he took pride in their welfare and in particular how skilfully he was able to handle what could be, in the wrong hands, dangerous animals. But it was *private*. They were private. A hobby – he hated that word – that he hadn't looked, nor expected, to share with the world.

Yet somehow – and in a way he simply couldn't get his head around – that expectation and intention had been utterly shattered. Out of nowhere. By a kid.

He went into the room now, his nostrils twitching at a smell that was unfamiliar. It took a moment to place it, a musky odour that the animals didn't usually give off, but which happened when they were stressed. The last time he smelt it was when there was a problem with the vivarium and the heater failed to maintain the temperature. This time it would have been Starling, Clarke knew. He imagined his boss entering the room, crouching down to inspect the animals. Judging them, *judging him*. Clarke's skin crawled at the thought.

Working automatically and expertly, he began his usual routine of checking that the vivarium's conditions were as they should be. The kingsnake – the larger of the snakes – was due its feed, and he made a quick count of the mice that were visible in their own tank. He bred his own mice – it was easy to do, and required fewer visits to the store.

He reached in now and caught a young white mouse by its tail. It wriggled and writhed as he gently pulled it from the nest in which it had been sleeping. Then he used a second hand to cradle the creature. That stilled it, and he took the moment to inspect it, staring closely into its pink eyes. It was useful to check each mouse for obvious signs of disease, but more than that, he liked to look for signs of the terror that the animals felt. He deliberately kept their tank in a position where they could see the predators that they so feared. He enjoyed that they always nested as far away as possible. But today there was no pleasure. Today he was too distracted.

He opened the lid of the vivarium, and casually dropped the mouse inside. It twisted in the air, landed on its feet, and quickly looked around. It spotted the large, coiled snake at once, but there was nowhere to go. Nowhere to hide in the domain of the reptile. Clarke closed and secured the lid, then pulled up his chair to watch. The snake was already uncurling herself, tongue flicking in and out in excitement at the scent of the mouse, the sour note of its fear. Clarke felt at least some of the tension of the day slip away, as it slid slowly forward.

But then the mouse backed itself into a corner behind a rock, and Clarke knew the snake wouldn't exert any effort to drag it out. She'd be happy to wait, knowing the outcome was not in doubt.

As such, Clarke's distraction didn't last long. Within minutes he was back, replaying the key moments from the day, and assessing how he had handled them.

How the hell had the kid got his address?

Could it be a case of mistaken identity? There were some facts he knew: it certainly wasn't him who had approached the two children at the swimming pool. But then, there hadn't been anyone. Cross had discovered that from the CCTV. What were the chances of that? Low, but it was a stroke of luck, nonetheless.

But then what did that *show*? Well, it showed the kid was lying. But if he was lying, then how in the hell had he identified Clarke's house?

And where did he get the idea that the killer kept snakes?

None of it made any sense. And while he'd fought the fire as well as could be expected – and he thought he'd left the station with things more or less under control – the whole thing was unsettling. Damned unsettling.

He realised suddenly that the drama taking place in front of him had finished, and he hadn't even noticed. The mouse was no more, the only thing to show it was ever there was a smear of blood on the glass wall, and a large bulge in the girth of the snake. He felt a stab of irritation, but pushed himself up to his feet. Then he left the animals to it, and went back into the hallway.

He almost started up the stairs – he knew he should sleep – but at the same time, he doubted it would come. Not until he felt more secure. So instead he picked up his car keys again, fought his way into his coat. Then made his way back to the Škoda.

. . .

Clarke drove out of the town – not on the main road, but a minor route, that wound its way eventually to a town to the north. Once he left the streetlights behind the road was dark, and the road was empty enough that he could relax with the lights on full beam, until he picked out the wood. He slowed to find the entrance, and then took the car down a small farm track.

Here, he dipped the lights, though there was no one for miles to see him. A few minutes later he pulled up in a small empty courtyard between two dark rows of industrial units. Their exact history was a mystery, which he'd never taken the time to investigate in any great detail. The farmer who rented them had told him they were built as bomb shelters in the 1970s, and then been adapted for storage. All Clarke cared about was that they were perfect for his needs.

He'd told the farmer it was storage he was looking for, and was pleased that the old man hadn't been the least bit inter-ested. He only wanted the rent, six months in advance, and ideally in cash, presumably so he wouldn't have to pay any tax. It was an arrangement that Clarke was more than happy with.

There was no one about that night, neither in the rental units themselves, nor in the two buildings that could be seen from the units, both over a mile away across empty farmland. This late, there was no reason why there would be anyone, and Clarke felt secure enough to leave the Škoda's headlights on until he'd unlocked the twin padlocks that secured the door. Once inside, he flicked on the ceiling light, then went back outside to turn off the car's lights and lock it. He locked the door of the unit, too, this time with him inside. Then he set to work.

He'd cleaned the place before. And done a good job. After he'd dumped Layla Martin's body he'd disinfected the entire unit, jet-washed the floor and walls, and left heaters on for a week until it was dry. Then he'd vacuumed. And then he'd repeated the whole process. He must have done it half a dozen times, until he was as sure as he could possibly be that no traces of her remained. He'd gone over every inch of the space with an ultraviolet light, looking for traces of blood, and when he found anything, he zeroed in on that point and scrubbed it all over again.

He looked around now, as if there might have been something that he had missed. Something that, somehow, the boy had discovered. But if there was, he didn't know what it was. He looked around again, trying to solve the puzzle.

Suddenly Clarke was angry. None of this made sense.

How had the damn kid known it was him?

There was no need to clean again, but doing so made him feel better anyway. He grabbed a spray bottle of bleach, and then went downstairs into the underground room below his unit. This part was the bomb shelter, constructed from half-metre-thick slabs of concrete, and buried in the earth. It was apparently strong enough that it could withstand the kind of nuclear strike that people were scared about at that time, but Clarke knew nothing about who had built it, nor how they planned to live when the world above was a radioactive wasteland. He didn't care. All he thought about was how perfect it was. What a lucky find it was for a man like him. For what he dreamed to do.

It looked different now to when Layla had come, of course. She'd been his first, back when he hadn't really known if he would go through with it, or if the whole idea was simply a fantasy he was indulging in. Back when he hadn't known, until the very last moment, if he would actually cross the line.

But he had. Sort of. He sat back suddenly, rocking onto his heels, and trying to bring to mind the two weeks he'd had her there, the feeling it had given him. *Such* a feeling. The power of it was deeply intoxicating. Simply glorious *power*. Impossible to sample that once, and then not want to taste it again. Even so, he had tried to find other ways to recreate the feeling.

That was why he had worked so hard to manoeuvre himself into the position of investigating the case – it was his way of reliving the feeling it had given him. And it worked. Up to a point. Every day that he worked on the case he got to experience again the sensations that holding her here had given him. The thrill. And it helped him too, in forgetting the slight sense of shame that lingered over what had happened during the girl's actual death.

But something else had happened, too. As those wonderful weeks slipped further and further into the past, his ability to bring them to mind faded. It was like a film that could only be watched so many times. He could still remember every detail of Layla's time with him, but the colour of it had gone, the vitality of the feeling had slipped away. The power was gone. There was no question now that he had to experience those feelings again, no doubt that he would kill again. And he was sure, in his own mind, that the mistakes he made the first time would not be repeated.

That was why the room was different now. Since Layla had graced this place he'd cemented iron manacles into the floor. He'd lined the walls with sound-insulated tiles, and he'd greatly improved the technology. For Layla he'd only had a basic camera covering the door, so he could check she was nowhere near when he came to open it. Now he had a state-of-the-art system that would record everything, for his future pleasure.

He stopped thinking and let the tiredness wash over him. He allowed a moment of delicious anticipation, free from the discipline of planning, or contemplating what had happened. He focussed only on what he would *do*. He would take another. He would overwhelm her with his power. He would bask in her terror and pain. And then he closed his eyes, anticipating the final part, the most glorious part. He would witness the struggle. The fruitless and delicious struggle. As her life slipped away under his iron fingers.

And whatever the *fuck* had happened today – however that kid had gotten his address – perhaps because of a mistake he'd made when taking Layla... whatever had happened, *it didn't matter*. Because he was still in control. *He was still in control.* There was no suspicion on him, and he would keep it that way by making damn sure the bitch mother let him continue to lead the investigation.

And his plans to take the next girl? Well, they were on track.

Better than that, he was nearly ready.

THIRTY-FIVE

Clarke woke in his dungeon feeling refreshed. After Layla's murder he'd got into the habit of sleeping there. Not often – because he didn't want to run the risk of someone spotting the car there overnight – but as a kind of special treat. It was as though spending time there, where she had died – where others would die – somehow managed to reach that part of him that caused him such agony. That roaring void which had first opened up when he learned of his parents' death. Just being there soothed him.

He got up and climbed the steps to the ground level of the unit, where there was a small kitchenette. He made coffee and found a bag of only slightly stale bagels. He ran one under the tap now, then microwaved it for a few seconds. It didn't improve it much, but he took a bite anyway, and chewed it contemplatively. He was still, he knew, suffering from shock. He had been hit with a massive wave of fear, thinking that everything was about to unravel. That he'd made a mistake from which he couldn't recover. But then, when that hadn't happened, and he had slowly worked to regain control of the situation, there had been moments when he'd actually enjoyed himself. Perhaps even more than he had for a very long time, since he'd actually had Layla.

It was only natural, after he had killed Layla, that he be assigned to work her case. The murder was in his patch, and it was such a prominent investigation that all available officers had been drafted in. But it had been a stroke of real good fortune to find himself promoted as deputy lead of the investigation, and from there to the lead.

Initially it was only a temporary role, covering another detective's maternity leave. But he had thrown himself into it with a sense of enthusiasm born of relief. His leadership gave him the opportunity to tidy up the few little slips – the cut-off ear for example – and disguise them beneath a veneer of professionalism. It made an impression on the parents – particularly the mother, who genuinely seemed to like him – and helped convince the oh-so-stupid DS Starling that the role should be made permanent. A promotion *and* a pay rise. Not that he needed the money. With no brothers or sisters, he'd inherited everything from his parents, and received a significant sum from the airline, too.

At first he had worried what would happen when his team of detectives couldn't – for obvious reasons – catch the culprit. Yet he soon realised something rather wonderful. Their very failure convinced the top brass of his own brilliance. The lack of progress was seen as proof of what a complex investigation he was running. And his constant clamouring for more resources, more detectives to send out on pointless errands, more space in the building to construct his oh-so elaborate investigation suite – well that only served to further ingratiate him with the dead child's parents, which in turn kept Starling on side. Or, mostly on side.

And all the while, leading the inquiry into Layla Martin's death allowed him to indulge in the act every day. It was like slowly and gently pulling back the lid and peering down. Glimpsing every day into that roaring void.

But two years was a long time. And it had become impossible to pretend that reliving Layla's death was enough anymore. It was like the bagel he was chewing on. There was only so many times you could run it under a tap and microwave it back to life. What he really needed was another chance to file away those thoughts and sensations and memories in his mind. Another chance. Another child. *To do this time, what I was afraid of doing to the first one.* He stopped his train of thought, surprised.

Yes, *afraid* was the right word. The shock of the previous day seemed to have shifted something within him. Suddenly he could be honest about that. When Layla had been down there he *had* been afraid. Afraid of the line he had crossed in taking her. Afraid of how he would never be able to go back, to when his fantasies were just that, and only that. He'd even wondered about releasing her, at times. But he knew that was impossible. And who wouldn't be afraid the first time? He felt hot suddenly, embarrassed both by his failure and trying to justify it. But at the same time, a new clarity had dawned on him, with the events of the previous day.

He had been afraid. Of a child. A little girl.

Next time, he promised himself, would be different.

He stood suddenly, keen to move, to push things forward. He lifted the blind and checked outside. The ground-floor part of the unit had small windows that looked out over a second building, in which the farmer himself kept a dilapidated Jaguar car that would never be restored. It was deserted.

Clarke went outside now, breathing in the cool morning air, and walked the entire circumference of his unit. He wasn't sure what he was looking for, but he kept alert, searching for anything he might have overlooked, any way that the Martin boy might have learned of his involvement. But there was nothing. No way out, no way to get a message out. The unit was pretty much soundproof, he thought, especially now he'd added the tiles. He'd tested them by playing music at crazy-high volume and seeing whether he could hear it outside. It was there, like a whisper in the wind, but barely. That was another mistake though, not having it in place for Layla. When he'd first got her there, she'd screamed like a banshee. It was simple luck that no one had heard.

But then it was only natural to refine details over time, to improve his processes. That was what he should expect, if he really planned to be a master of his art. He certainly wouldn't tolerate screaming from the next child.

He went back in and tidied up, getting ready to leave. Allowed his mind to engage gently with the question of what would happen now. Like gingerly slipping the clutch.

How would it work now with the Layla Martin case? There was a chance – a good chance – that he would be off it anyway. What kind of parents would they have to be to still want him? After their own son had accused him of the very crime he was supposed to be investigating? And yet, he didn't really believe it was over. He thought, when it came to it, that the parents would pick him over their son. Especially the mother. The stupid dumb bitch of a mother.

He allowed another thought to filter up in his mind, a nice one. He fancied if he really pushed – and he might one day – it might be possible to break down the professional barrier between them. In the right circumstances, he could probably fuck her. He luxuriated in that thought – where would they do it? Would he tell Jon? Or let him discover the affair by some kind of accident? But then he snapped back.

If they *did* keep him on the case... well, that would be ideal, too. Once he chose his next victim, he could take her in such a way as to link the two cases. That would make his case – the Layla case – even more prestigious, and make sure *he* got to lead the new case as well. Another promotion? He was thrilled at the idea, but why not? It was possible. It was more than possible – it was the most likely outcome. He just had to arrange the pieces the right way.

Of course, with *two* girls dead, he might need to actually get a result, to close in on a suspect. But then he had a plan for that. He already had a shortlist of names, men with histories, so that it wouldn't be difficult to convince a jury of their guilt, regardless of their insistence of innocence. After all, he would have the forensic evidence, carefully planted. He could even fake a confession – even if they later claimed it was false, who would the jury believe?

And if he *was* taken off the Layla Martin case? Well, no matter. He would accept the Martins' decision magnanimously, holding no grudge against them, despite the clearly outrageous slur made against him. That would only further his reputation as an honest copper – a genuinely nice guy. The sort of man you could rely upon.

And in that scenario, he could go hunting for his next victim, freed of the pressures of running the investigation. Which he longed to do. And for which he needed time. For example, he had already bought a van from a small garage in Scotland. The trip up and back had been a pain, but any search for the vehicle would focus on a more local area. Now he had to source false number plates, and there was the question of whether he should respray it a different colour, or have it sign-written – something generic and forgettable?

And yet... *And yet... How did the Martin kid know?* And why did he lie about being approached at the swimming pool? *Why* did the kid follow him to his house? Was it all because he had made some awful, terrible mistake? And if so, what was the mistake?

He felt like the question was driving him insane – genuinely insane – but then, all at once, the shape of a solution suddenly appeared in his mind. It was like a range of mountains on the horizon, on a hazy day. Almost not there at all. But there. He stopped what he was doing to try and bring it into focus. It didn't come. Yet a second idea did; a smaller lump in front of the range, not as impressive or exhilarating, but easier. A movement in the right direction. He could get closer to Gale. Speak with him. Find out how he knew. Once he knew that, he could work out what to do.

The real question was, how to do that?

THIRTY-SIX

The next day Clarke arrived early at the station. Had his work on the Layla Martin case not been put on hold, awaiting the family's decision on whether he should continue to lead it, he would have been busy liaising with the *Crimebusters* production team about the reconstruction of Layla's abduction.

As it was, he pretended to tidy up some paperwork on other cases, while really thinking about what he could do to get close to the boy. He had ideas, but nothing concrete yet. But that was OK. One thing he had learned was the value of patience. Things in his life had followed a habit of falling into place.

Take the death of his parents, for example. To most people, becoming orphaned by a plane crash might seem one of the harshest blows life could deal you. But Clarke hadn't seen it that way. By the time they died, he had already grown independent enough that his relationship with them was more financial than emotional. In fact, just before their death he had argued with his father that he needed more money, so that he could live apart from his college flatmates, who irritated him with their childish ways and nosiness into his affairs. So when their plane went down and he inherited the house, and then received the pay-off from the airline... well, it was certainly convenient.

Luck came again that morning with a call from the super. The ever-stupid Starling.

"Come in. Sit down." Starling's secretary wasn't there that day, so the fat fool had needed to poke his own head out of his office door to tell Clarke to wait outside for a few minutes. A pathetic power game. And now he called him in, without leaving his desk.

But Clarke did as he was asked, walking in with just the right look of concern and respect on his face. It was easy to do, this *was* an important moment, and he was genuinely anxious to know which way it would go.

"I've just had Rachel Martin on the phone," Starling got right down to it. "She's very sorry for what happened, and she's told me that she'd like for you to continue to lead the inquiry."

Inwardly Clarke felt a sense of righteous satisfaction. Outwardly he nodded, deepening the look of concern on his face.

"Does she have any explanation for what might have happened?" He might as well use the opportunity to fish for information.

The DS shrugged – he was oafishly ignorant, over-promoted only because he'd gone to the right schools.

"My guess is that it was some sort of displacement error." Starling used the explanation that Clarke himself had thought up – quite brilliantly, given how it had come to him only moments after he'd been hit with the accusation.

"I expect the boy saw you on the TV, associated with the case, and somehow that morphed into thinking you were involved. And you live quite nearby, so maybe he also simply saw you in the street."

"He put two and two together and came up with five,"

Clarke replied, as if considering the wisdom of his superior's words.

"Precisely."

Clarke let a thoughtful look fill his face, then glanced at his boss, expecting Starling to have a similar expression. But to his surprise, he didn't. Instead, he was watching him carefully. Clarke tried to keep his own look, but it felt wrong now, and he let it slide away.

"Well, that's all Kieran. You'd better get on with it."

Clarke was confused by something as he made his way back to his own office. By the time he sat down he'd got it. He had received exactly the news he'd wanted to hear – and yet, instead of feeling good, he felt flat. Confused. A little concerned.

Partly it was the boy. Not knowing how he knew. But there was more to it as well. DS Starling might be gullible enough to put the man who had killed Layla Martin in charge of her murder inquiry, but it would be unwise to dismiss him completely as a fool. And there was no doubt he had been a little cool just then.

The reason was obvious. His boss hadn't been willing to believe what the stupid kid had said – the boy would need better evidence to achieve that – but at the same time, he had sown seeds of doubt. What's more, Starling had been to his *house*. He'd seen his beautiful girls, which meant he knew his officer was capable of keeping certain things private from the rest of the team. Starling had seen that Clarke wore something of a front at work, and had glimpsed behind it. It was no catastrophe, but Clarke knew he would have to be careful.

Back at his desk he sat musing for a long while. He thought about calling Rachel Martin to thank her, but rejected the idea. Better to wait for her to contact him. He thought about his own plans to take another child, which now felt increasingly overdue, and he thought about the *Crimebusters* programme, and how much of his time that was now taking up. He also thought about the problem of Gale Martin.

And then the phone did ring. The young producer from *Crimebusters* wondering why he hadn't replied to her latest emails. He made some excuse about being busy, and got back to work, coordinating the reconstruction.

There was a lot to do prepping for the programme, but it was fascinating to see how policework was blended with the TV side of things. Clarke knew also that this was a high-risk strategy, to focus so much attention on the actual abduction of Layla. After all, he had been the one who took her, and though he'd worn a disguise – a baseball cap pulled low over his eyes, and a pair of mirrored sunglasses, and contact lenses – these would have done little to alter his age, height or body type. But there was also a secondary layer to the disguise. Focussing on the abduction was exactly what any good investigation *would* do, especially one with no other clear leads to follow. If he didn't focus on it, that might look suspicious. And if any sightings of men in their late thirties did come in, with dark hair and a beard, it would be easy enough to guide the investigation towards other suspects he had pre-selected that would fit such a description.

The real problem, he decided, was not Gale at all, nor the *Crimebusters* show, nor how slowly his other plans were able to develop – on their own he was easily able to master each of them, or perhaps two of the three. The problem was one of bandwidth. He simply couldn't juggle the three issues all together.

Towards the end of the week his mobile rang and the caller ID showed it was Rachel Martin on the end of the line. By then he'd almost forgotten that they hadn't spoken since the crazy incident.

"Hello Rachel." His voice was smooth and easy. Compassionate, but not expectant. He readied for the apology. "How can I help?"

"Oh no. You can't— it's not— I've spoken to DS Starling, I know how hard you're working. I didn't want to interrupt."

Clarke wasn't sure what she meant, but he felt happy – her tone was just right. There was a delicious hesitancy in her voice. He waited.

"Listen, all that nonsense with Gale. I just wanted to apologise—"

"Not at all. Rachel, seriously, there's absolutely no need. I'm just glad it got cleared up so easily, so we can get on with things. I'm still really hopeful about the programme."

"Thank you. Thank you, Kieran. For everything you're doing."

Clarke smiled. He wondered again if he should try to fuck her. Was this the moment? If he suggested they go for a drink? He could fill her in on everything to do with *Crimebusters*, and then he could *fill her in*. He rarely slept with women, though he easily could. Plenty of the younger girls in uniform had made their interest clear over the years, staring at him with their dumb bovine eyes... The woman's voice interrupted the thought.

"Listen, you might think this is silly, but after what happened with Gale, Jon and I had an idea..."

Clarke waited.

"Well, I had the idea actually, but Jon agreed."

"Go on?" In his office, Clarke smiled.

"You know how grateful we are for what you're doing to help – and Gale does too, now that we've explained it better. We just thought it might be nice if you could come around for lunch, this weekend? I mean, you might be busy and everything, and it's short notice, but we thought if you *met* Gale it might put his mind at ease and..." She stopped, seemed to lose her nerve. "Is that inappropriate? Is that a bad idea?"

"No, not at all," Clarke intervened. "*Not at all.*"

In that moment, he visualised the table, with him sat opposite the boy and able to interrogate how and why he discovered that Clarke was his sister's killer. What a wonderful opportunity, falling into his lap like that. Might it mean something? Some message from the void, that he should have such luck?

"It's not inappropriate at all. I think it's a wonderful idea. There's a lot to tell you about the reconstruction plans, too. I'd be delighted to accept."

THIRTY-SEVEN

Gale rolled the dial at the back of the alarm clock until the glowing red digits on the front read 3:00, then pushed up the volume as high as he dared. He looked around anxiously – there was no one there to see him, but then you couldn't really tell. Quickly he wrapped the device in a jumper and hid it under his pillow. Then he turned off his light, and lay down, wondering if he might not even sleep at all until it rang.

Gale had barely seen Layla since that day with the police. She'd been there, waiting with him, while his mother went to speak with the police. And there too, when their mother came back, crazy-furious about what had happened, and telling Gale that he had it wrong, that he'd accused the detective who was helping them of being Layla's killer. His sister had been as confused as he was, when that happened, one moment insisting they were right, the next moment not so sure.

And since then, she seemed to have been doing her best to stay away. Gale still glimpsed her occasionally, out of the side of his vision, but when he did so, she seemed to shrink as far away as she could. Making herself almost invisibly transparent, and certainly refusing to reply if he tried to talk to her.

He'd asked her – of course – what was going on? Had they got it wrong? He'd begged her to answer him, pleading with the darker corners of his bedroom. But she hadn't answered him. If she was there at all, she chose those moments to shrink back into the nothingness.

And to Gale that felt like the blanket of sadness which had settled upon him after her death had come back, and was heavier and more suffocating that ever. It only reinforced how happy it had made him feel when she had come back, in the strange way that she had.

Gale hadn't known much about the detective who was leading the case. He had been aware there *was* a detective and he recognised the name from conversations he'd overheard his parents having. But his parents had decided to keep Gale separate from the details of the investigation, and he'd never questioned whether that was right or not. Now, he was. But alone, there was simply no way of knowing. No way to say if he'd got it horribly wrong – or perhaps worse, horribly right.

As the days ground painfully by, he began to suspect that Layla was there most strongly when he slept. He had no idea *how* he knew this, but he just did. Perhaps he saw her, or felt her, in those moments just as he was falling asleep, or waking. But every time he came to full consciousness, all he could catch was her drifting out of it.

Hence the alarm clock plan. Years before, when Layla was alive, they had received a bag of hand-me-down clothes and toys, and in it there had been a radio alarm clock. For a few weeks he had used it, and been jerked out of sleep at seven o'clock precisely, until the novelty had worn off. But he'd kept the clock in the jumble of things at the bottom of his wardrobe. And tonight – actually tomorrow morning, at 3 a.m. – he would be woken again. And he would confront Layla. He would force her to talk to him once more. To tell him what was going on.

. . .

BRRRRRRRRRRRRRRRRRRRRRRRRRR!

It seemed instantaneous, no gap at all between the last thought he'd had and the frantic noise that now drilled into his brain. Sleep-thoughts freewheeled to make sense of it – a fire alarm; a horrible siren he'd heard once while watching a space rocket being launched on TV. Then he grasped what was happening and fumbled beneath the pillow to find where he'd hidden the clock, and turn off the noise before it woke his parents too. Finally there was silence. All around him the room was dark. He felt a film of sweat all over his body.

"Layla? Are you there?"

Silence. Darkness.

"Layla, please be there?"

Finally, she spoke. "What was that?"

"Layla! You're here!"

"Yeah. I'm here. What the heck was that?"

Gale sat up, peering out into the darkness, but he couldn't see her. "It's my alarm. I set it so I could see you again."

"Oh."

Gale quickly felt for the switch to his reading light. He flicked it on, turning the infinite blackness into the familiar space of his bedroom. She was there, in all her see-through brilliance, lifting a hand to shield her eyes from the light.

"You're there."

"Yes."

Gale wanted to get up and hug her, but he knew he'd tried that before and it hadn't really worked.

"Why did you go?"

He watched her ghostly chest rise and fall as she considered this.

"Layla?"

"I got you into trouble," she said in the end. "I didn't want to make things worse."

Gale pulled up his knees and hugged them, giving room for

her to sit on the bed. She seemed to understand, and did so. Gale watched as the covers didn't sink down under her weight, didn't move at all. But it made him feel better – despite everything.

"Mum says we got it wrong. That the man we saw at the house wasn't the killer after all. He's the police officer who's looking for the killer."

Layla swallowed. "I know."

"Is he? Is he the man who's helping Mum and Dad, or is he really the killer?"

She didn't answer him; instead she looked away, and gave a half shrug that could have meant *yes* or *no*.

"I don't understand. Layla, I need to understand. I need to know this."

She shrugged again. And when she spoke there were tears in her eyes. Only they weren't tears of water. Tiny sparkling diamonds seemed to be falling from her eyes, then disappearing into the semi-darkness of the room.

"I don't know. I can't see him. I can't get close enough to see him. And I just don't know."

THIRTY-EIGHT

After that, she was back more often. They still didn't talk much, but something had changed again. This time it wasn't that she was trying to stay away from him, only that, with something so important between them unresolved – and apparently unresolvable – there wasn't much they could say. Nonetheless, Gale drew considerable comfort from her just being there with him. And though she didn't say so, he believed that Layla felt the same way too.

Layla's reappearance also coincided with a softening in their mother's attitude. For much of the week, she had stayed angry, with Gale and with his father, although Gale didn't understand what he'd done wrong. But then, towards the end of the week, she had seemed to decide to not be angry anymore, and instead tried to be happy. But *then* she was too happy, falsely cheerful and pretending that things were all OK, when obviously they weren't. Gale had seen that before, and knew it wouldn't last.

As the days went by over the week, he'd gone to school as expected. Doing his best to stay silent in class, and then in morning break and at lunchtime, taking himself to the edge of the school field, as far away from the other children and the teachers as he could get. He knew he couldn't see Layla there now – she'd explained how hard it was for her to appear anywhere outside the house, but he liked to think there was a hint of her there. A ripple in the soft autumnal air.

When Saturday came around again, he stayed in his room, just being with Layla. They made Lego cars, but it wasn't as good as it used to be, because he had to build both his car and hers, when before she would have been rummaging around in the pile of pieces with him, searching for the best wheels and the matching triangular pieces that could work as wings (because every good car had to have wings). But it was still good. He would build a bit of his car, and then put it down and work on Layla's, following her instructions as to which piece to pick up, and where to put it. But then their mother shouted up the stairs for him to come down. Gale stopped. From the tone in her voice, it was clear he was going to get a lecture about something.

"Go on," Layla said.

"Are you coming?"

She shrugged. "Might do. I'll see what mood she's in."

Gale got up and held open the door for her, and even though she didn't use doors, she rolled her eyes and went through it. And then they both trooped downstairs. It was almost like old times, except that there was only one chair pulled out from the dining table. And their mother only looked at Gale, completely ignoring the semi-transparent apparition of her daughter.

"Gale. There's something I want to tell you," their mother said. Dad was there too, sat silently at the table, arms folded across his chest.

Gale waited. He knew he wasn't supposed to speak at times like this.

"All this mess with the police, you do *know* you were wrong, don't you?"

This again.

Gale bit his lip. Eventually he gave the lightest of shrugs, just enough to allow his parents to interpret it as acquiescence.

"Yes. Well, it actually did a lot of damage – or it could have done – to the chances of catching the man who took Layla away. And your father and I think it's important to put some of that damage right. Don't you agree?"

Gale, who had been watching Layla, had to drag his gaze away to look at his mother. For a moment his eyes were filled with resentment, but then he nodded.

Almost at once his mother softened. "But we also recognise that maybe we haven't done the best of jobs with you. We haven't *involved* you enough." She exchanged a look with Jon. "There's no rule book for parenting, you know that. And when something like this happens... well, all bets are off. It really hasn't been easy."

A memory flared in Gale's mind. The same table. Another 'family meeting', and his mother using the exact same expression: *no rule book for parenting.* That time around Layla had responded that there actually was a rule book, and then gone to the shelf and pulled out a book titled *The Rule Book for Parenting.* He looked to the shelf now, but couldn't see the book.

"Clearly, we haven't kept you up to date with what the police have been working on, and maybe that wasn't the right thing to do. After all, just as Layla was our daughter, she was also your sister."

Gale looked at Layla again, and this time she clearly mouthed three words to him.

I. Still. Am.

"And—" He realised his mother hadn't stopped talking, but he'd missed what she'd said. "We've been extremely fortunate to have someone as dedicated and experienced leading the investigation."

She was talking about the man again.

"We don't want to lose him."

At that exact moment a thought struck Gale's mind. A new thought. If Layla was real and if she was right about everything she'd said about the man with the snakes – and she'd seemed very certain, back when they'd been talking about it – then wasn't it a bit of a *coincidence* that the man who had murdered her was also the man who was investigating the crime? Too big a coincidence to have just happened by chance. Which meant... which meant he must have *planned it like that.* Gale had no idea what to do with this thought, but at the same time felt in no doubt it was somehow significant, something important...

"We've decided it would help if you met him."

His mother's words cut the thought off.

"Met him?"

"Yes."

Gale didn't understand.

"We wanted to keep you out of everything as much as possible in those horrible weeks just after Layla died. That's why you never met him. And I do think it helped, back then. But now we've decided you would probably benefit from meeting him. And perhaps hearing a little about what's actually going on – like with the *Crimebusters* programme. They're going to feature Layla's case on a television show. And I expect some of the children at school might get to see it. So you should know about it."

Gale didn't know what she was talking about. He had no idea what *Crimebusters* was. And at this point he didn't much care. There was only room in his mind for one, horrible idea.

"You want me to meet him?"

For a second he envisaged being led into a police interview

room by the killer, who would then lock the door behind him. Pull off his human mask, to reveal the monster underneath.

"No—" he began.

"*Yes* Gale. There's nothing at all to be scared about. He's very nice, and he's helping us. We've invited him here to lunch tomorrow. I probably should have mentioned it earlier, but I wasn't quite sure how to tell you." She put a goofy look on her face, like this was some understandable oversight, but Gale ignored her, staring at Layla.

"So," his mother went on. "I expect you to be on your best behaviour."

Gale turned to look at her, and then their father, who was stern-faced, and still hadn't said a word. Gale glanced at Layla again. And this time she looked back at him.

And the look on her face was pure, cold terror.

THIRTY-NINE

Clarke picked up the flowers – expensive ones, from the florists – and the bottle of decent but not too-expensive wine, and went to his front door. Then he stopped, walked backwards and managed to hook his hand through the carrier bag he'd placed on the kitchen table earlier. It was a struggle to juggle all three as he locked up the house behind him, but he managed to get everything into the Škoda without anything breaking.

You could plan for every eventuality, he thought to himself, and he pressed the starter, revving the engine harder than he needed to, but something unexpected would always come up, and you just had to roll with it.

But that was what made the whole thing fun.

It was a short drive to the Martins' home, close enough that he could have walked it, but he had a sense it wouldn't be helpful to draw attention to how close the two houses were to one another. Not until he knew how the kid had found out about him.

He hadn't quite known what to wear either. How exactly does one dress for Sunday lunch with the family of the girl one has abducted and murdered? He decided in the end on dressing down a little, more casual than the smart suits he wore for work. He would look more approachable that way, and the stated purpose of the visit was to help Gale feel more relaxed about him. That was fitting too, given how Clarke's main purpose was to feel more relaxed about Gale.

He arrived right on time, and parked outside the house, hoping they might notice the car. Then he walked up to the front door and rang the bell.

It was Jon Martin who opened the door.

The two men locked eyes. A fraction of a second later Jon smiled. But there was something about the way he did it that stood out to Clarke. *Be aware.* Another one who didn't quite trust him after what had happened? Or was this something else? Had it maybe begun to occur to the husband that the handsome detective might be fucking his wife – or thinking about it?

"I hope I'm not late?"

"Not at all, come in."

Clarke stepped into the hallway, which was large and bright, just as Rachel Martin hurried out of the kitchen, wearing an apron that had photographs of babies on it – presumably Gale and Layla when they were smaller.

"Kieran, thank you *so* much for coming." She smiled, but was clearly nervous. So she should be, after what she'd put him through. If Clarke himself was nervous, he was using it, mining the energy to fuel his performance.

"Thank *you* so much for inviting me." He held out the flowers and the wine. "It's really kind of you."

"Oh you shouldn't." She actually blushed. "That's very kind. Thank you." She took the flowers but handed the bottle to her husband. "Jon, why don't you open this?"

Rachel ushered him into the living room. "Please. Lunch will be ready in twenty minutes, but come through and we can all chat." If she'd noticed the plastic bag he was still carrying, she said nothing.

The house was spacious, open-plan in layout, the dining table already laid. But the kitchen was quite a mess. There were saucepans and oven trays piled up in the sink, as if this meal was an unusual event. Then again, since Clarke never entertained, he wasn't sure if the number of pans used was just normal. Either way, the smell was delicious. Meat of some kind roasting in the oven.

"It certainly smells good."

"Well, I hope so. And I hope you're hungry."

"Oh yes." He smiled, noticing her top, how the apron tied around her back pulled it taut against her breasts. He preferred them more flat-chested, but he could make an exception.

"Shall I open the wine, or do you prefer beer?" Jon's voice interrupted his thoughts.

Careful Kieran. Remember the husband.

Jon Martin was standing by the fridge, which seemed to suddenly match his coldness. "We've got lager or ale."

Clarke examined his tone for anything hidden, but found nothing. Still, he flashed an apologetic smile.

"Actually, I'd better not. I'm driving." The truth was, there was no way he was going to dull his senses at this moment. There was too much riding on it. Too much to take in.

"Oh yes. I suppose you can't really break your own rules can you?" Rachel agreed, and he smiled, as if he gave a damn about drink-driving. "We have mineral water, though?"

"That would be lovely. Thank you."

Clarke glanced around the room as Jon opened the bottle and poured a glass, adding ice from the port on the front of the refrigerator. The table was set for four, but there was no sign of Gale in the room.

"Do sit down, please," Rachel said, indicating one of the stools by the breakfast bar. She busied herself putting the flowers into a vase.

Clarke entertained himself by chatting, asking about her

job, about how she was, and throwing in just enough about Jon Martin's exercise habits to keep her husband happy. The prick was a fitness freak, always training for some run or bike ride somewhere. But all the while Clarke was thinking, *come on. Come on. Where's the star of this little show?*

Where's the boy?

Clarke was just running out of small talk – there was only so much one could make in the circumstances – when the meal was finally declared ready and Jon Martin was sent upstairs to get Gale. And then, finally, a minute or so later...

There he was.

"Gale, love, this is Detective Inspector Kieran Clarke," Rachel Martin spoke clearly and slowly, as if the boy were stupid. "He's come so that the two of you can meet properly for the first time."

Gale stopped in the doorway. For a long time he didn't seem able or willing to look at Clarke, but finally he risked a quick glance. It seemed all he could do. He nodded.

"Hello Gale," Clarke said, feeling his heart beat harder.

The boy didn't respond, but then Clarke didn't know what to expect. So, he reached into the bag, which he had placed on the floor beside his seat. Neither Jon nor Rachel Martin had asked him about it.

"I hope this is OK." He kept his eyes on Gale. "But I actually bought you a gift." He pulled out a box, which he'd wrapped earlier that day, and held it out.

"What is it?" Rachel asked.

For a second Clarke ignored her, his eyes fixed on Gale, but then he remembered himself and turned to look at the mother. He gave her a smile, then he turned back to Gale.

"It's just a little something to say there's no hard feelings on my part. I know how much you've all been through over the last two years, and I know that mistakes can happen."

The boy hadn't taken the gift, so Clarke held it out a little closer, encouraging him.

"Oh, that's very kind," Rachel said now. "There was really no need..." Her voice faded out, then she spoke again, addressing the boy this time.

"Why don't you open it? Come on honey, you can take it."

And then, a little sulkily, the boy stepped forward and took it.

Clarke had chosen the gift carelessly, picking the most expensive thing he saw after a search on Amazon for *'awesome gifts for ten-year-olds'*, but he'd wrapped it carefully, so that the paper would come off quickly and easily. He wanted a dramatic reveal, not a long and painful struggle with Sellotape. When the paper came off, he saw the boy's eyes widen.

"What is it, Gale?" Jon Martin asked. He couldn't see well from where he stood.

"It's a plane." Gale said flatly. "A remote control plane."

"I hope it's OK?" Clarke spun around to speak directly to Rachel now. "It's designed for slightly older children, but I wanted to get something he wouldn't have already... and I... I thought he and Jon could play with it in the park."

"But that must have been ever-so expensive." From the tone of her voice, he might have thought he'd gone too far, but the look on her face said otherwise. Clarke waved away the objection with just the right amount of casual concern.

"Like I say, I really wanted to show that I understand about what happened."

Clarke turned back to Gale, a wide, easy smile on his lips, but what he saw confused him. He hadn't imagined that receiving the gift would be enough to win the kid over, not if he really thought that Clarke was his sister's killer. But he had thought the moment might reveal something. He had thought, if the boy really believed Clarke was in some way involved, there would be a tension – between the kid wanting the toy, and not wanting to accept it from Clarke.

And yet the boy wasn't even looking at the plane. Nor was he looking at Clarke. Instead, he was staring at the wall in a weird, almost – Clarke couldn't interpret it – *animated* fashion. Like there was something there, when clearly there wasn't.

"Say thank you Gale," Rachel Martin said. But the boy simply ignored her.

"I said *say thank you*." Rachel's voice had a sudden edge. Gale's eyes flicked onto his mother for a moment, then he looked back, at the nothing on the wall. A moment later he dropped the present on the side table near where he was standing, without even finishing the job of removing the wrapping paper.

"Thanks." He spoke with barely concealed contempt. Then he went to sit down.

Clarke felt ruffled. Insulted even. He hadn't *had* to bring a gift – much less such an expensive one. The plane had cost over a hundred pounds, and yet the little shit couldn't have been more ungrateful. What the hell was his problem?

Clarke reflected on this as he accepted Rachel's invitation to sit down, opposite Gale. When he was a boy, he'd have been thrilled beyond words to receive such a gift. And yet there it was, conspicuous on the side table, still half in its wrapping. He tried to put it out of mind, to smile again at the boy, but Gale kept his eyes away. After a moment, Clarke realised he was looking away again, not at the same spot on the wall as before, but the gap between the entrance to the kitchen and the end of the table. Clarke narrowed his own eyes, still not understanding.

The meat turned out to be beef, cooked well so that it was still red and juicy in the middle. It tasted good, and Clarke let himself enjoy it. With only himself to feed, he didn't cook much. Food that didn't come from a takeaway was something of a rarity.

"Thank you for sending through the scripts for the TV reconstruction," Jon said, after a while. Clarke swallowed what was in his mouth before answering. He hadn't known whether the parents would bring up the topic of Layla or the TV programme in front of the boy. It turned out they would.

"That's no problem. I wanted to give you the chance to see it before they start filming." He waited a beat. "What did you think?"

"I think it's good. I just hope they do a good job," Jon said. This seemed to be his topic, since Rachel was quiet. "The actors I mean. The girl who's playing Layla, she looks... she looks a lot like her."

"Yes. Yes, I thought so too. She's a talented young lady."

"You've met her?"

"Yes. We interviewed quite a few possible actresses. I wanted to sit in on the casting to make sure the key details were right."

Jon gave a blank smile. "A bit like shooting a movie."

"Exactly that."

Clarke glanced at Gale. He was paying no attention.

"Do you really believe it will help?" Jon asked.

Reluctantly Clarke pulled his attention from the boy, and gave a reassuring look to the father.

"It's impossible to say for sure. But I certainly believe there's a good chance. Someone will have seen something that day, we just need to prompt them to come forward."

"What happens next?" This was Rachel. Clarke preferred talking to her.

He set down his cutlery.

"Well, with the good weather forecast, they're going to try and get all the filming done next week. Then it'll go out the week after that. A very quick turnaround. And then we'll ask for anyone who was there that day, and hasn't yet contacted us, to come forward. We're expecting a lot of leads, so hopefully we'll be busy following them all up. But..." He spread open his hands. "We've got a good team. A small team, but they're all dedicated and experienced officers. Hopefully we'll get something that will make a difference."

The conversation dragged on. Jon Martin seemed fascinated by the mechanics of how they were going to film – would they have to close the beach? What would happen if it did rain? How many extras they needed. Bullshit questions that Clarke couldn't have cared less about, but which he was able to answer in detail, because he'd been working on it all week.

In the end Jon Martin's naivety was exhausted, but by that time all their plates were cleared, and Clarke sensed that as soon as lunch was done, the kid would disappear back upstairs. He wasn't happy for that to happen. He'd come here for answers, and so far he only had more questions.

"Since we're talking about the reconstruction," he said, when it seemed Jon Martin was really out of questions. "And this is a bit of a delicate topic I know – I was wondering how you feel about me showing Gale the plans for the filming? It would be helpful to know if he feels it's as accurate as it can be, in case we need to make changes?" He smiled. The truth was it was now too late to make any changes, but who cared about the truth?

The two parents looked at each other, then Rachel looked at him. "OK. We haven't talked about that, but if you think it's a good idea?"

"I think it could help," Clarke said, nodding seriously, and watching Gale as he spoke. "Gale was there that day, and he was with Layla right before she went missing. If there's anything we haven't got quite right, he might be able to tell us."

"I don't want to." The boy spoke so quietly that Clarke only just heard him. But he did hear.

"What was that, honey?" Rachel Martin asked, a new nervousness in her voice, like she knew what was coming, and feared it. Clarke almost wished she hadn't spoken at all. There was something awful in the boy's tone.

"I said I don't want to see it. There's no point doing the TV show. Not when we already know who killed her."

There was a silence. And then the boy turned, his eyes boring directly into Clarke's face, like a pair of drills.

"Darling?" Rachel began. "We've been through this…"

But the boy ignored her. For a long while he kept his eyes on Clarke's, but then when he looked away, he didn't look anywhere, just stared at the wall. Then, weirdly, he nodded. At nothing.

"Gale, you can't say things like that, you just can't…" Rachel Martin was still talking, even though no one appeared to be listening to her. Except apparently the boy was.

"OK then, ask him if he's got an alibi? Where was he when Layla was taken?"

FORTY

"Ask him where he was," Layla almost spat the words from where she stood against the wall. "If he says it wasn't him, ask him if he has an alibi?"

Gale had waited upstairs with Layla, the two of them anxiously counting down the minutes until the detective arrived. They hadn't discussed it, but it was obvious how important it was. If this really was the man who had kept Layla locked up in his basement, who had spent hours down there with her, then there was no way she wouldn't recognise him. It was the moment of truth.

And then, as soon as the detective had walked through the door, Layla had known. And Gale had known it too. From her reaction. From the way she'd faded, almost to nothing, at the first sight of him from the top of the stairs. And then the way she'd been too shocked to speak, unwilling to look at him, as Gale continued to wait upstairs for as long as he could.

And then, when their father had come up to get him, and he couldn't put it off any longer, Gale had known it from the way she had pushed through him, to be the first down the stairs, as if that might somehow protect him.

Then he'd given him the present, a remote-control plane, and though it was pretty cool, he hadn't wanted it, hadn't even wanted to touch it. And all the while she'd been there, staring. Trembling. Literally shivering with fear.

"Ask him if he has an alibi." She spat the words again. Her chest was heaving up and down from the emotion and stress of seeing him there. "For when I was taken."

"Where were you?" Gale directed the words angrily at the evil man who sat at *his* table, being served by *his* parents. "Do you have an alibi?"

It was weird, how Layla had slowly regained her colour, and solidity, as she seemed to grow in confidence. When the detective had suggested that Gale watch the stupid TV show they'd been discussing, she'd suddenly let fly. She'd leapt upon him, clawing at his face with her hands, kicking and punching. But of course he didn't feel a thing. No one but Gale had the slightest idea she was there.

There was another silence. Gale's hatred of the detective prevented him from even looking at him. Thankfully Layla had calmed a little. She was back next to Gale, her chest rising and falling with the effort of her outburst.

"Gale..." His mother was still protesting, but everyone ignored her – at least, the only people in the room who mattered ignored her. *Gale, Layla, her killer...*

When Clarke replied, his voice was still so even, so reasonable-sounding that Gale hated him even more.

"Actually I do—" he began.

"Gale, this *just isn't on*." His mother again. "Kieran, I am *so* sorry..." But Clarke silenced her by lifting a hand.

"No, it's fine. It really is." He flashed a sympathetic looking smile again, then turned to Gale. "That's a very good and important question. And you're quite right to ask it. But yes, I do have an alibi, as it happens. For when poor Layla was taken."

Gale was flummoxed. There was no way Layla was

mistaken. She hadn't actually *told* him this was the man, but it was obvious from the way she'd reacted...

"Kieran, there's really no need, this is just—" Rachel kept trying, but Clarke turned to her this time.

"Please, Rachel, let me answer. I can clear this up. Please."

There was another silence, but it had a different character this time. Gale turned to his sister, and she'd changed too, her face a picture of utter confusion. He couldn't look for long – the detective was already starting to explain.

"I was on annual leave at the time that Layla was taken. I like to walk, up in the hills, and I'd rented a cottage in the Lake District that week. Which puts me, I don't know, six or seven hundred miles away. Not to mention halfway up a mountain."

On the detective's face there was the merest hint of a smile, but not a happy one. He looked sad, sorry that he was having to say this, but understanding too. Compassionate.

Gale looked to his sister – she was frowning and shaking her head. But try as he might to catch her eye, she wouldn't look at him. Which didn't make sense.

Could this be wrong? Could Layla have got things wrong?

FORTY-ONE

Clarke had never expected to need the alibi, never planned to use it. At the time he'd suspected his setting it all up was more about delaying the actual abduction than the valuable backstop he told himself it represented. A complicated charade to put things off until he summoned the courage.

At the time it had definitely seemed ridiculous, the lengths he had gone to. He'd had to drive all the way up there, check into the rental cottage – making sure that the owner got a good look at his face *and* being sure to mention that he might spend a night or two camping up in the hills. And then the long drive back, before he'd actually done it. Capturing Layla, and taking her to the bunker, with his heart hammering so hard he thought it might just explode, and then having to leave her there, with just enough food and drink that she would survive long enough for him to drive all the way back up the lakes again, check out of the damn holiday cottage, and drive back down.

But that's what commitment looked like. Preparation. Absolute dedication. The willingness to go every single extra mile. Literally.

And *now* look. Now, far from some sort of procrastinating

cowardice, it seemed it was a masterstroke after all. Clarke watched as the doubt, which had begun to show on the faces of Jon and Rachel Martin, slid away.

"You're very welcome to check, Gale," he said, his voice heavily layered with compassion, getting the tone *just right*. "I really mean that. I feared you might not yet be quite sure that you can believe in me, and I want you to have faith. So, I looked up the name of the apartment I stayed in. You can speak to the owner – I haven't done so, because it wouldn't be right for me to enquire about myself. But I expect the lady there will remember me – we got on quite well. But even if not, there are records."

He reached into the pocket of his jacket and pulled out a piece of paper. The email receipt from the cottage. Stapled to it was the receipt from an Indian restaurant – he'd just managed to get there the same day he'd taken Layla. Lamb vindaloo, table for one.

The boy was silent. *Silenced.*

"You can ask your mother or father to check what it all means? I'm sure they will?" He looked at Rachel Martin, a perfectly judged sad smile on his good-looking face, giving her no choice but to nod and agree with him. And she bought it.

But the weird thing was – the really crazy thing – was that the kid *wasn't*. For all his efforts – and he was putting in a stellar performance, for Christ's sake he deserved an Oscar for the work he was doing here – the little shit *still wasn't buying it*. He seemed somehow to know that he was lying, even now. Yet that wasn't possible. Because no one knew. No one *could* know.

For a split second Clarke's expression cracked, the real frustration and hatred and fear showing through underneath. He glimpsed the void.

And then he got it. Perhaps that roaring blackness of hate found a way to inspire him, because the solution came almost fully formed. And a new smile graced his lips, out of sheer appreciation for his own near-limitless creative capacity. If one placed no limits on oneself, then there were no limits.

As the parents simpered and made their pig-like squeals about how sorry they were about the situation, and how it wouldn't change anything, and he still had their *full support* – he simply sat there examining his idea, seeing that it was flawless, and letting the details of how to do it spin into being, like eddies off the main stream of a river.

It was so obvious, so symmetrical, so perfect. And what better place to arrive at the solution to a problem, when the source of that problem was actually sitting across the table from him.

He was going to solve his Gale Martin problem in the most delicious of manners.

FORTY-TWO

There was no question whether Gale would watch it. He might have been kept away from the TV during the awful days following Layla's disappearance, but he was eight then. Now he was ten years old, and like it or not, he had a view on who had killed his sister.

What Rachel and Jon Martin didn't know, of course, was that Layla herself was there too, at least from the perspective of one person in the room. She floated behind where Gale sat on the sofa, as the family waited for the adverts to finish. She would watch the reconstruction of her abduction too. She would see how closely it matched what actually happened, and how successfully the man who prepared the script and oversaw the filming had directed its focus away from his own involvement.

The last ad was a soap powder commercial. It showed a housewife and her daughter arguing in a good-natured way over which of them should fold a pile of freshly laundered clothes, the twist was that the clothes now smelt so good they both wanted to do it. Or, at least that's what the mother pretended. The ad somehow managed to fit a second twist at the end of the one-minute-long story, with the older woman winking at the camera, having outsmarted her young teenage daughter.

If she'd lived, Layla Martin would have been nearly thirteen years old.

An announcer's voice introduced the next programme as *Crimebusters*, and the theme music began.

"Here we go," Jon Martin said, more to himself than anyone else. His wife sat stiffly, not touching him. She had a box of tissues ready.

As for Gale, he was sitting on the sofa, with his knees pulled up tight into his chest. He didn't want to miss the programme, but he wasn't sure he could bear to watch it either. Even with Layla still in it, his world now felt a bleak and hopeless place.

The Layla Martin case was the lead story in the programme – DI Clarke had at least been honest about that – but it was still trailed by a couple of smaller cases. In the first, a gang of con artists had been tricking older people out of large sums of money by convincing them that there was such a thing as invisible subsidence, and that their houses were at risk of collapse from the problem. The other was simpler: a man caught on CCTV robbing several jewellery stores. And then, there he was: Detective Inspector Kieran Clarke. Dressed in a sober grey suit, and looking at home on the TV. He was introduced by the presenter and gave a sad smile. The image changed, to the most famous image of a smiling Layla. The presenter's voice:

"It's just over two years now since ten-year-old Layla Martin was abducted from a popular beach in broad daylight. Her body was sadly found fourteen days later, abandoned in a nearby wooded area. Tonight we feature a full reconstruction of what happened on the day she was taken, in the hope that it will trigger the memory of somebody watching. And that it will lead to whoever committed this horrible crime being brought to justice."

The shot changed back to the studio, the presenter, still talking.

"I'm here with Detective Inspector Kieran Clarke, who has led this investigation from the very beginning, and he's hopeful that tonight – with your help – there could be a breakthrough in the case. Detective—"

The camera closed in on Clarke's face. He looked calm, composed. Handsome even, they'd done something to his hair in make-up, and the beard had been trimmed.

"Thank you."

There were no nerves on show. He looked entirely comfortable. A TV natural. He layered compassion and determination into the tone of his voice, edged with hope.

"We've put a huge amount of work into finding out what happened on the day that poor Layla went missing, and we've spoken to over two hundred people who were there that day. With their help we've been able to produce a reconstruction which you're about to see, and which we think is incredibly accurate.

"However, we also know there were people on the
beach that day, and in the general area, that we haven't
yet been able to speak to. It's those people that this
reconstruction is aimed at. We believe it can, and that it
will, help somebody out there to remember something
that proves to be crucial to this case. So please understand, even if you don't think you know anything, if you
don't think you saw anything relevant, let us be the
judge of that. If you were there, or if you know someone
who was, please, please come forward. Or if you know
anything at all about what happened to Layla, or who
took her. Please come forward."

"I thought DS Starling was supposed to be the one on
camera?" Jon Martin commented as Clarke – onscreen –
paused for a moment. His wife glanced back at him, and had
seemed about to answer, when the TV continued:

"Layla Martin was an exceptional girl, beautiful and
intelligent. She didn't deserve what happened to her.
But it's not just justice we're seeking tonight. Whoever
did this to Layla is still out there, and could potentially
be a threat to other children. I want you to think about
that, to think about the child you have upstairs, sleeping
in their bed. We need your help to catch the person
responsible for this awful crime. We need your help to
make sure it can never happen again. Thank you."

There was just a fraction of a second where the camera
caught the look on Clarke's face, concerned, compassionate. Yet
filled with sad hope. The reconstruction played.

. . .

It began with a family of three playing on the sand. It took Gale a few moments to register it was supposed to be *them*, just a few minutes before Layla vanished.

They showed just enough to establish that the family had been there a while. They had buckets and spades, and the sand-castle they were building was quite substantial, certainly bigger than the actual one that day, and an entirely different design, Gale noticed. The mother was shown reading a paperback novel – that was wrong too, since actually she'd been browsing through Facebook on her phone.

All around them the beach had been made to look busy. Swimmers splashed around, while paddleboarders wobbled and fell in from the wake of speedboats that buzzed by in the distance. And yet, while the TV company had presumably done their best, there was still something odd about the footage, as if everyone on the screen was aware of the cameras watching them. The whole thing looked and felt fake.

After the few opening shots, the camera began to focus more closely on the girl who was playing Layla.

"That doesn't look anything like me," the real Layla objected. It was the first thing she'd said since the build-up to the programme, and the extended speech from her killer on the screen.

Gale didn't answer for a second – he was accustomed now to not replying when his parents were around, but he thought of a way.

"She's got the same swimsuit."

His mother answered that, unaware he'd actually been speaking to his sister. "They want to make it as accurate as possible, sweetheart." She looked tense, her whole body taught. Gale had a sense that she couldn't go on much longer like this – it added to his own sense of foreboding.

"Can we get an ice cream, Mum?" on-screen Layla asked, filling the frame so that her freckles were visible. The boy playing Gale was seen wiping the sweat from his brow, a none-too-subtle reminder to the watching public that it was hot that day.

The on-screen mother looked around sharply – here the message to the viewer was clear too – this was a woman assessing the risks like any good parent would. And yes, the beach was busy, but the ice-cream kiosk was shown as less than fifty metres away on the promenade, clearly visible from where the family was based. There was a queue, but formed mostly of other children.

This had been a delicate matter for the *Crimebusters* production team. There had been some pushback against the parents following Layla's murder, internet trolls putting the blame on Rachel Martin for letting her daughter out of her sight, but also on Jon Martin, for not being there that day, as if there was something outrageous about parents who didn't spend every hour of every day monitoring their children. The producers of *Crimebusters* had wanted to avoid that with their reconstruction.

On-screen Rachel reached into her bag for her purse.

"OK, but you have to go together." A kindly smile, and then fake-Layla replied.

"Thanks, Mum."

The last words Rachel Martin would ever hear her daughter speak.

Then there was a lingering shot of the woman playing Rachel Martin watching attentively, as the two children ran up the beach, zig-zagging around the other encampments of families enjoying the sun and sand. The viewer got to see the pair now from those perspectives, clearly people who had spoken to the police, given how the soundtrack was then cut with excerpts from their interviews.

"It was a hot day, we'd been there for a few hours, when I remember these two children running past. They were having some sort of an argument, about some game."

Gale shot an immediate and alarmed glance to his sister. He still hadn't told anyone about the S-Game, and clearly Layla couldn't.

"They must have overheard us," Layla replied. Her eyes didn't leave the screen. "We were arguing about it."

Another shot, of a large Indian family, who had set up a pop-up shelter at the head of the beach and were cooking on a portable BBQ.

"I remember seeing them both join the queue. I was watching because I was going to get an ice cream myself," a dark-skinned teenager said, who had the beginnings of a moustache. "But I was waiting for the line to go down."

The action changed suddenly to show the scene a hundred yards up the beach. Here, there was a short-cut from a clifftop car park, one which required a short scramble down the upper section of the gently sloping cliff. The camera followed a lady carefully working her way down, but struggling with a plastic cool box. Suddenly a close up of her feet showed her slipping, and then a clip showed her disappearing from view with a shriek. It had the feel of a low-budget disaster movie, with music to match. The next shot was the cool box, its handle now broken, while a voiceover explained how the lady had slipped, and become trapped on a ledge on a steeper section of the cliff.

Then there were close-up scenes of what was supposed to be near chaos. People running towards the woman, who was now shown waving for help. Across the beach people stood up, shielding their eyes as they peered towards the accident. Several people pulled out their phones to call 999, while two teenagers climbed up to the woman, crouching down to help her.

Slowly the beach regained a new sort of calm, the immediate panic over, but most people still watching what was unfolding on the cliff.

"We don't know exactly what happened to Layla and Gale in the queue, but we believe they had some sort of disagreement." Clarke's voice cut in. "It seems Gale decided to go back to his mother, leaving Layla to continue to wait alone."

This was shown visually, but again the acting wasn't convincing. Fake Layla laid a hand on fake Gale's shoulder as they parted, and in the room where the real Gale was watching, he almost burst into tears when the real Layla let her real, translucent hand hover upon his real shoulder.

And then the ambulance turned up. The blue flashing lights only just visible against the bright summer glare, but the siren fired in bursts, to clear a path along the busy promenade. There was a clip of the paramedics helping the woman further down the cliff, stabilising her, and then the camera swung back to the ice cream queue. Only this time, Layla was gone.

"Were you there?" The programme's regular presenter came back on the screen now. A man in his forties, earnest and good looking, his fake tan and dyed hair the subtle marks that distinguished him as a celebrity.

Next to him DI Clarke was still looking earnest. He took off his glasses and cleaned them, before putting them back on.

"Were you perhaps parked up in the car parks above the

cliff? Did you see anyone with this girl?" The image of the real Layla filled the screen again. The famous image. "If you did, you *must* call."

And then the number for people to call flashed large on the screen. The presenter read it out, twice, and it hung there for a while. Gale suddenly realised who the people in the background of the shot were. They actually were the call-centre people, waiting to take the calls from the public.

"That's it." Jon Martin seemed determined to bookend the programme. Gale ignored him, but he noticed his mother stiffen, as if the two words had annoyed her.

"What happens now?" Gale asked. He didn't know who he had directed the question to, but it was his mother who answered.

"Well, hopefully now a lot of people will call in with things they might have seen or heard, and it'll be up to the police to sort through them to find something that helps them catch the man who did it."

Gale didn't tell her again that they already knew who did it, and it was the man who had narrated the story. Instead, he turned to his sister.

"Maybe someone saw him," she said, unheard by everyone in the room except Gale. This time when Gale spoke, it was only for her.

"Yeah." He said sadly, and without much hope. "Maybe someone saw him."

FORTY-THREE

The reconstructions for the *Crimebusters* show were pre-recorded, but the actual show went out live – giving it an air of dynamism for the viewers, which also helped encourage them to phone up and take part. It meant Clarke got to sample first-hand the tension and excitement on set, as the time ticked down to its airtime of seven thirty. And despite his careful planning, there was a much more personal element to the excitement and tension.

Clarke had arrived at the TV studio before midday. There should have been very little for him to do – the reconstruction had been signed off days before, and he'd written the script for DS Starling's starring role. The old fool had insisted on receiving it a few days before, no doubt so he could practise in front of the bathroom mirror.

But then, just before the lunchtime production meeting, Starling had phoned to say he'd woken with a head cold, and wouldn't be able to do it after all. The production crew had flapped their clipboards in a terrible panic – as if the show didn't have its own presenters – until one of them had sidled up to Clarke and asked if he could do it.

She'd flattered him, telling Clarke he had the right sort of face for TV – by which she meant he was a good-looking man, but it was more than that. He knew the case like no one else, as the detective actually leading it. From her point of view, it seemed perfect. From Clarke's, less so – since there was a clear risk in him appearing on the show. But he didn't feel it was a big risk, and put on the spot like he had been, it wasn't easy to refuse. Besides, a part of him had rather embraced the thrill of it.

And from the moment he had agreed, he was suddenly roped into a whirlwind of pony-tailed twenty-somethings telling him where he would be standing, which camera he should look into, which hand signals to look out for. Then he was sent to wardrobe, where his suit jacket was swapped for one that wouldn't cause lines on the viewer's screen – whatever that meant.

Hair and make-up was with a gobby woman from Newcastle who spent forty-five minutes explaining what she would like to do to the bastard that took poor Layla Martin, all the while flitting around his neck and throat with her sharp scissors. It had been alarming when she began, but he soon realised she sensed nothing – not even while he replayed in his mind how he'd carried Layla's body up the steps of the bunker and into his car, before driving it to the woods and dumping it in the ditch. He had almost lost track of time, but then she was done, and he was whisked back into the studio, placed in position, and given his speech for one more read-through.

"It'll be on the autocue too, just in case you forget something," the producer-girl had told him. She flashed a good luck smile, while a countdown from ten rang out. Then the lights had gone down, and the famous *Crimebusters* theme music began playing.

The actual show flew by, and judging by how many people congratulated him afterwards, it went well. At first, he had been too exhilarated to respond properly, but when he calmed down, he was able to thank them warmly, and pretend that what really mattered was what came next.

And in a way, it wasn't pretending. Now that *Crimebusters* was done, the real work would begin. Already the call-centre staff were busy taking calls. Clarke was interested in what the callers had to say, but Starling called and told him – through hacking coughs – to go home, there would be plenty to do in the days to come. Clarke did what he was told. After all, there was one more thing he wanted to do before he could rest.

Clarke was no specialist in computer crimes, but he was expected to have a working knowledge of the intersections between crime and technology, and he'd attended many training courses on the subject. As such he'd been trained about the dark web, and how criminals would access it via VPNs – Virtual Private Networks – and using software such as the TOR browser to further disguise where they were accessing it from. He also knew about the use of encryption software PGP, which stood for Pretty Good Privacy. It was poorly named, since it was actually strong enough to keep online messages so well hidden that no police force on the planet would be able to read what they'd said.

But unlike his fellow officers, Clarke's interest had been more than professional; he'd taken close notes. And in the privacy of his own home, he'd practised. It was all there, once you knew where to look. The usual suspects of drugs, porn and even guns, but also clever little devices like virtual sim cards, and voice modifiers, all of which could be purchased with anonymous cryptocurrency, and then sent to dud addresses – empty houses where they could easily be picked up with no possible link back to him. He'd practised with those too, testing and checking that they worked.

So he was confident when he set everything up that night, late enough that his own team would have finished, but leaving the civilian *Crimebusters* call handers to work through the night, that nothing could go wrong. But he was nervous too. A mistake now would be a disaster.

He double-checked all the protection was in place. Then he triple-checked. And then he wound back the logic in his mind, and ran through it one more time. He knew the team who would forensically examine what he did over the next few minutes – he was familiar with their counter-security technology. And while they were good at what they did, he knew the gaps in their defences.

A long, slow deep breath. Everything was in place. Everything was ready. Another breath. Connect with the moment. This was necessary. This had to be done. And while there was danger, he was able to handle it. To control it. He was unstoppable now, and this would prove it. He hit the call button.

There was a dial tone. Then the almost musical tones of the computer making the call. It rang twice before the note changed. A woman's voice:

"Good evening. You've reached the secure contact line for *Crimebusters*, which investigation are you ringing about, please?"

Clarke spoke into the microphone. His normal voice was corrupted and distorted, but not so much that the words were lost.

"Layla Martin."

"Layla Martin? Thank you, may I take a name before we go on?"

"I don't think so."

A pause. "OK. That's no problem – we can continue the call, but it will help us if you're able to give us your name. Are you sure you're not able to give it?"

"Quite sure."

"OK. Now, your number is coming up as unrecognised, can I take a number so we can get back to you in the event we're cut off?"

"Again, I don't think that will be necessary."

Clarke knew the line was being traced, and that the software would pick up that the call was being routed, in the first instance via Belarus and Finland, and a dozen other countries after that. You had to marvel at the tech.

"OK, sir." The voice on the other end was stiffer now, tension kicking in for the operator. This would probably be the first call she'd taken that wasn't showing a location blinking on her screen. Her adrenaline would be spiking. "What was it you wanted to say?"

"I liked it."

"I'm sorry sir, did I hear you right? Did you say you liked it?"

"Yes."

Another pause. "You liked what, sir?"

"Your little programme. I liked the girl who played her. Of course the real Layla was cuter. And cleverer, I thought."

There was another moment of silence. There would be two telephone operators on the night shift, Clarke knew, and he imagined the other woman would be standing over her colleague now. He could hear the anxiety in the words of the one speaking.

"Sir, do you have any information for the police regarding the abduction and murder of Layla Martin?"

"You could say so. But it's nothing I'm going to share."

"How do you mean, sir?"

"What do you think I mean?"

"I don't know, sir."

"I think you do know. I think you're beginning to suspect."

The toying was fun, but there was a danger of enjoying oneself too much, and inadvertently revealing more than he should. After all, he would have to send the recording and transcript from this call to the psych profilers, and they sometimes came back with explanations that cut a little close to the bone. What's more, once he hung up the phone, it wouldn't be long before his *other* phone would be ringing. And he needed time to prepare for that. His eyes focussed back on the script he'd prepared.

"I bit her ear."

He waited. As soon as Layla's body had been found, the fact that part of her ear was missing had been spotted, but the information had been deliberately kept out of the press. It was a common tactic, giving the investigation an easy way to check if any subsequent confessions were credible. Of course that wasn't why Clarke had done it – he'd simply got carried away – but it was helpful now. You had to ride your luck in these things, make use of what fate threw up.

"I bit her ear. That's why I cut it off."

He could picture the woman now, sitting up rigid in her chair. From her voice he'd recognised which one it was – he'd spoken to her earlier that day, when he'd given his briefing. She'd seemed capable and professional, but had worn too much perfume, so that she stank like the duty-free hall in an airport.

"Are you identifying yourself as the individual who abducted Layla Martin?"

Clarke ignored her. "Would you like to know what I'm going to do next?"

"I need to be clear on what you're saying, sir—" The woman was following the lines she'd been given in training. *Boring.*

"Shut your stupid mouth and listen up. What I'm going to do now is kill someone else, and do you know who?" He laughed. It wasn't on the script, but he couldn't help it.

"The person I'm going to kill next is Gale Martin. Layla's brother. He's *marked*. He's doomed."

More silence. Clarke forgot all of his precautions, surrendering fully to the waves of fury and power that were surging up from the void below.

"I'm going to kill Gale Martin. I'm going to rip out his eyes. I'm going to tear out his organs. I'm going to *butcher* Gale Martin."

FORTY-FOUR

Clarke was shaking as he disconnected the phone, but he'd prepared for the eventuality that he might suffer a slight loss of control, and he followed the protocol he'd written earlier. He deleted the files he had used, writing over them so that a forensic IT team wouldn't be able to recover anything. It was overcautious, but that was a good habit to have, and it helped calm him.

He was a little shocked by how real the anger had been. It was like a dam bursting, and within it he'd almost made a mistake: he'd almost mentioned how the call handler he'd spoken to wore too much perfume. That would have been quite the giveaway.

That done, and since his standard phone still hadn't rung, he went to the kitchen, and made himself a herbal tea. He took it to see his girls. They were more active at night. He sat with them drinking the tea and waiting. Still his phone didn't ring.

Twenty-five minutes later – *twenty-five minutes, what the hell were they doing with that time?* – his mobile finally rang out. He left it for a few moments, as if he might be asleep, and then injected a drowsy note to his voice. He was pleased at how easily it came. He was back in control again.

"I'm sorry if I've woken you sir, but I think you'd better come back in." He recognised the East London vowels of Detective Sergeant Reynolds.

He pulled back on the dozy tone, dialled up the alarm. "Why, what's happened?"

"Um. We've had a call come in. We think it's credible that it might have been from the killer himself."

"From the killer?" To put the correct note in his voice now he visualised struggling to sit up in bed. "You're *kidding*? Please tell me it's traced?"

"Um, no. Afraid not. Whoever made it seems to have gone to some lengths to throw us off. It's tracked as far as Belarus but—"

"Never mind, it'll all be recorded, we can dig into that," Clarke feigned impatience. With Reynolds it was actually quite easy to do. "Tell me why you think it's real?"

"Whoever it was knew about the cut to the ear."

"*Shit*." Clarke left some space before carrying on. "What else did he say? Anything we can use?"

"I don't know sir..." Reynolds sounded suddenly miserable, or reluctant to go on. Clarke knew why, but then again, he wasn't about to shoot the messenger.

"We have a recording of course... but he made a threat. A very specific threat against the Martins' other child. He said he's going to kill Gale Martin next."

Clarke began to count in his head.

One, two, three, four, five...

"I want someone round there. The Martins' house. *Now*. I want officers stationed outside their door. Check the family is OK but *don't* tell them what's happened. Do you understand? Just say it's..." He put a hand to his brow, as if actually thinking this through now. "Say it's routine following an appearance on *Crimebusters*. Shit..."

Six, seven, eight, nine...

"Then get onto Superintendent Starling – no, scratch that, it's late and you shouldn't be waking him up. I'll call him. But I want a crisis meeting. In half an hour."

"Yes, sir."

Clarke hung up. He was standing in the hallway, and he caught his reflection in the mirror, his eyes wide, and pupils flared. He laid two fingers on the pulse of his wrist, feeling the blood smashing through his veins.

This was living. This was pure excitement.

There's a bonus, Clarke thought, forty-five minutes later, as he was pacing up and down at the front of the meeting room on the third floor of the station. Starling really did have a cold, and the stupid bastard looked terrible, sitting there blowing into his hand-kerchief like some pre-schooler – without the first idea what was really going on here. Right under his stupid, snotty nose.

As for Clarke, he still felt wired, like he was on some sort of drug that made his blood fizz as it surged around his body. He was the only one who hadn't touched the pot of ridiculously strong coffee that someone had placed on the table. There was no need; he felt *fantastic*. It was all he could do to keep the manic grin from his face.

"Have we checked in on the Martins?"

"There's a squad car outside their house. I've told them not to move for anything."

"Have they *checked* on them?"

"Yes sir. They were sleeping, but we woke them. They're all fine."

"Good. Dean, Sarah." He turned to a couple of young

detectives, over-keen, graduate-fast-track types. Thought they were smart – really, they didn't know shit. "I want you to put everything we've got into tracing that call. He might think he's safe, but there's a lot of ways you can screw up online, and if he has made a mistake..." Clarke gripped the pen he was holding in a fist and squeezed it. "We might just be able to nail him."

The two detectives nodded as if they agreed with this thought. Technically it was true, but actually the pair would only waste the next few days trying to untangle the jargon the civilian tech experts would bombard them with.

"What do you think we should tell the parents?" Starling snuffled suddenly. He really did look like shit. For a moment, Clarke enjoyed the moment of the most senior investigative officer in the force asking his advice for how to handle the case. But then he set his face with his most serious, concerned look.

"I think we have to tell them what's happened, I don't see we have a choice. We tell them, but we also tell them we're gonna give them twenty-four-hour protection. Officers stationed outside their house the whole time. Outside the boy's school."

There was a moment's hesitation from Starling. As expected. "That's going to be expensive."

"I know, sir, but Reynolds is right, this is a credible threat."

The man looked uncomfortable. Like he wanted to get back to his cosy bed. "How sure are we that news of the ear didn't get out? Could it have been leaked?"

"I ran a Google search for the words 'Layla Martin' and 'ear' before you got here. There're no hits."

Starling considered this, his face dark. He nodded.

"This isn't something I can agree to indefinitely. I need to know what you intend to do to catch this bastard." He turned back to Clarke.

"I understand, sir. That's why I want to focus on tracing the call," Clarke argued. "Even if we're not able to trace him this time, the more we learn about what technology he's using, the better chance we have if he calls again." He paused, giving them a moment to take in how clever that was.

Time to press the point home.

"I also think this shifts where we look."

"How so?" Starling asked.

"OK." Clarke took a deep breath. "For the last two years we've assumed the killer isn't connected to the Martins, they were just unlucky that he chose their daughter, right? There was no evidence that suggested otherwise, and from the very beginning this looked like a random victim. But *now*, if the killer is going after their son as well, well that strongly suggests this is more personal."

The dumb bastards didn't get it. It was obvious from the looks on their stupid, ugly faces.

"More personal?" Starling managed.

"Yes, sir." He nodded briskly, subtly encouraging body language in the others that would sweep them along with him. "I think we need to take a long hard look at Jon and Rachel Martin's backgrounds. He's what? A financial director? What financial decisions has he made? Who have they impacted? And she was a solicitor – again, that will have impacted people. Is there someone they've pissed off in their past? If so, who? Is there more to Jon and Rachel Martin than we're seeing? I want to know."

Starling looked thoughtful now, his thumb and forefinger scratching at the stubble on his chin. He wasn't convinced, not just yet.

"Look, I admit it's a stretch to imagine that someone would do this *just* because the Martins upset them. This person will also be the right personality type – or the wrong type." Clarke conceded. "But the fact is that *someone* killed Layla Martin, and that same person is now threatening to kill Gale Martin. That's no longer random. We *have* to consider the possibility someone has a massive grudge against the family. We need to check it out."

There was more thought from Starling, but in the end he nodded. "Alright."

The word effectively gave Clarke the authority to do what he liked. Plus, it tied up the remainder of his team to another task he knew would get them nowhere.

"But let's keep monitoring the calls too," the Super went on. "We've just made an appeal to the public for information. And that wasn't cheap. We may yet get something worthwhile so I want someone following up on whatever else comes in."

Clarke forced himself to nod in agreement, though inside he'd already written it off.

"Sure. Good idea. I'll put..." He considered his team for who to assign, but he'd already planned their jobs for the next couple of weeks, so no name came to mind.

"I'll put someone on it."

Starling nodded again, then staggered onto his feet. "Good. Well, I'm going to get some sleep. I suggest the two of us go and see the Martins to explain what's happened." He stood to leave and walked to the door. But as he put his hand out to open it, he stopped and turned around again.

"Oh. One thing. I don't want the boy to know. Poor kid's been through enough without knowing he's on this psycho's hitlist."

FORTY-FIVE

"What's going on? Where is everyone?" Police Constable Ellen Cross had arrived for her shift to find the station nearly empty, the atmosphere oddly lacking. There was no one in the kitchen, where she'd made a cuppa for the desk sergeant, automatically selecting his special mug.

"You caught DI Clarke's big moment last night on *Crimebusters*?" He took the tea, turning the mug so the design faced him, a photo of his baby granddaughter with the words: *Thank you to the thick end of the thin blue line.* He took a slurping sip.

"Yeah. I watched it with Joe."

"Well, he only went and hit the jackpot didn't he? The killer called in."

"Noooo..." Cross felt her eyes go wide. "What did he say? Enough for them to catch him?"

"No one's saying, least not to me. But upstairs they're running around like the proverbial blue-arsed flies." He took another sip. "Did you put sugar in this?"

"No, I did not put sugar in. I put one sweetener, which is all you're getting."

"Hmmm. How about the biccie cupboard?" The desk sergeant asked. "Is it as bare as the Super's soul?"

"I didn't look, and unless you've made a miraculous recovery from diabetes you shouldn't either." Cross gave him a motherly look until he raised his hands in defeat.

"Alright, alright. I'll have a tasteless rusk. Would you like one?" He picked up a packet of low-glucose biscuits, and offered one to Cross.

She wrinkled her nose and shook her head.

"Actually, you might get to find out what's going on," the desk sergeant continued. "DI Clarke asked me to send you up, when you get in."

This was a surprise.

"Why?"

"Didn't say. You know what they're like. Information up there is released on a strictly *need-to-know* basis." He seemed to be debating internally whether he should dunk or not dunk.

"Alright." Cross was puzzled still, but she shrugged. "I'll just get changed and go up."

"Uh huh..." Her boss nodded, and dunked. But then he stopped. "Actually no, he said to send you up the moment you got in. Apparently it's that important." He rolled his eyes.

"OK." Cross felt a flutter as she moved towards the stairs.

"Don't forget your tea," the sergeant called out, before she could get too far.

The tea ended up cold. Upstairs, the investigation suite had the hum of close concentration and stress. Several officers were speaking on the telephones, but they were sat alert at their desks, not sprawling as was typical when on routine work. Whenever anyone got up, they crossed the room quickly, with heads bowed. Clarke was in his room, speaking with two other detectives, but the door was open. He saw Cross right away and called her in.

"I need someone to get up to the *Crimebusters* studio and sit in with the girls taking the calls. Normally we'd have a detective in there, but we're all hands on deck – you've heard what's happened?"

Cross nodded, but then shook her head. "Not exactly, I heard the killer called in. Was it definitely him?"

He half-nodded, then shrugged. "Could be. We can't say yet for sure." For a second he looked blank, as if totally exhausted. Then he seemed to come back to his senses.

"If it is, he made a threat against the Martins' other child. The boy, Gale."

Cross was shocked. She felt her mouth drop open.

"Yeah." Clarke gave her a look. "Well, can you get up there? It's about an hour's drive. Take one of the pool cars."

"Um, yeah I mean... why me? I'm not part of the investigation?"

Clarke had already partly turned back to the previous conversation, and he gave the appearance of having to refocus on this one. He held out a hand.

"I know. Look, the truth is Starling wants someone in there, and with everything going to shit, I've used all my guys. You did a good job uncovering that CCTV the other week, so I thought of you. Is that OK?"

Cross blinked, then nodded. "Yeah. Of course." Then she added. "But what exactly do you want me to do?" She was aware, as she asked, that it wasn't really a very detective-y question to ask, and felt a little awkward asking it, in front of three proper detectives. But at the same time, she kinda needed to know.

Clarke turned back to her a second time. He gave a sigh.

"Probably nothing, in truth. They're getting a high volume of calls, and they've said they could do with some help knowing whether any should be prioritised. So get up there and have a read through. Anything important, bring it back to me ASAP. OK?"

"OK." Cross waited, expecting him to go on, but he didn't.

"Erm..." She bit her lip. "How will I know if it's important, if I don't know the case?"

She didn't expect it, but he flashed a smile, as if this was a fair question.

"If it looks important, I want to see it."

An hour later she was driving up the motorway to the TV studios just outside London. She didn't drive much – there was no parking space at the flat, and it was central enough that she could walk to work and Joe's school – so she had to concentrate as she hugged the inside lane. She didn't know how to get Radio Two on the stereo system either, which might have quietened her mind, but it did give her the space to think.

It was weird. Having almost given up any thoughts about joining the ranks of the detectives, suddenly she had found herself asked to carry out tasks normally assigned to the investigative branch of the force. She couldn't quite understand why.

Cross knew how she was viewed – reliable and, in a way, valued – but definitely at the lower end. She was the one sent out to have a word with drunks making a nuisance of themselves in the town centre. Or if a teenager got themselves caught shoplifting. So why had Clarke sent her? It kind of made sense – the way he'd put it. But then it kind of didn't, too.

She considered him now, DI Clarke. She'd known him since he was a detective Constable, when he was in uniform, though he hadn't worked out of the same station then. He was nice enough, she thought. Yet, there was something about him too. Something she couldn't put her finger on. Clearly he was smart, and well-liked – though since his promotion to DI, she would have said a little less so, from the gossip in the canteen. But that was normal.

Cross almost never missed a chance for drinks after work (sometimes taking Joe with her, and parking him in the corner with his games console). And a few years ago, Clarke would have been a semi-regular fixture too, but she didn't remember ever having a good natter with him. He never seemed to let his hair down. But again, that wasn't exactly a bad thing...

She glanced at the car's in-built GPS. She'd got someone to programme it for her when she took the car, and was grateful she had, since she was terrible at map reading. Now the destination was shown on the little screen, just a few minutes away. It interrupted her thoughts for a while as she followed the little line it showed.

Moments later she was parking the car with some difficulty outside the TV studio. It was less impressive than she'd hoped, perhaps expecting something similar to the Hollywood Studios Tour you sometimes saw on TV.

At the reception area inside, Cross introduced herself to a very pretty girl who didn't look old enough to be working there, and who interrupted buffing her nails to give directions to a small office were women sat behind computers, with headsets. Cross knocked on the door, and one of the women stood up and came to open it.

"Detective Cross? I'm Jane Smith, senior manager here."

"Actually, it's just Constable." Cross gave a slightly apologetic smile. "But maybe just call me Ellen." Cross held out a hand.

Smith hesitated for just a second, but then shook it. "I'm sorry, I got the message they were sending one of the detectives."

"I think they were, but something's come up. I'm all they had."

For a second the manager hesitated, but then she nodded, as if this made sense.

"Well, come in, any help is appreciated with this one."

Cross came into the little room and looked around, unable to keep the look of slight disappointment off her own face.

"I thought the call centre was actually in the TV studio? You can see it in the background of the show?"

"Everyone says that." Smith nodded, showing her where to hang her coat and bag. There was a small kitchenette too, and Smith held up the kettle questioningly.

"Sure." Cross smiled.

"We're moved up there for the show, but the studio is used for other programmes too, so once it's all over we get shipped back down to our windowless room here. Glamorous, no?"

"Very." Cross gave a knowing look.

"Tea or coffee?" Smith asked.

"A tea would be great, thanks Jane."

With a mug of tea installed in her hand, Cross was given the tour.

"This is Agnes, Susan, and on the call there is Gemma." The two women who weren't actively answering calls at that moment said hello, while Gemma nodded her head, hands flying on her keyboard.

"You probably know," Jane went on. "We take all the calls that *Crimebusters* generates, so this week it's not just the Layla Martin murder, but all the other featured inquiries. On top of that, because we're a public-facing point of contact, we tend to get a fair few tips about crimes that aren't even on the show, and we try to pass those along too."

Cross nodded, and sipped the tea.

"Have you had many about Layla so far?"

"About a hundred."

"Wow!" Cross said, then thought about it. "Is that a lot?"

"Quite a lot. But it all depends on how the inquiry is presented. Often it'll be quite focussed, asking people if they saw someone matching a certain description, or whatever. But for the Layla murder, they just asked for anyone who was there to call in. Hence..." she held out her hands. "We get swamped."

"Oh dear."

"Yeah. And we can't let any calls go unanswered, because you could end up missing the critical call."

"I can see that." Cross took another sip. "What can I do to help?"

"Well... This pile here," she patted a tall stack of paper, "is the print-outs for all the calls we've received so far. DI Clarke has asked us to send over the ones that are most likely to be relevant first. But it's difficult for us to know which they are. If you could go through them and see if there's anything we ought to be prioritising."

"OK." Cross nodded. The manager went on.

"Since there isn't anything specific we've been looking for, we've tried to get as much detail as possible from every caller, obviously along with their contact details, so that someone can follow it up if necessary." She grabbed the top paper to show Cross. It was a report from a woman who said she was sitting on the beach that day with her two sons. Cross read it until she found the bit where the operator had asked if she'd seen anything suspicious.

The caller indicated she didn't think she had seen anything suspicious, but heard about the abduction on the news later on that week.

"If you could go through them and see if there's anything that we should prioritise, that would be a big help."

"Sure." Cross accepted the pile of papers, fixing a look of confidence on her face that she didn't really feel.

. . .

For the next two hours she read through the call transcripts, getting a sense of the types of calls that came in. They seemed to represent a broad cross section of people who had been on the beach that day. There were people who were renting beach huts; people picnicking in the car park above the cliffs; the mother of a teenager, who thought her son might have been working that day as a lifeguard on the beach. None of them said they had seen anything suspicious – but all had called in because it said on *Crimebusters* that everyone who was there should call.

It was impossible for Cross to know if any of the tips were indeed significant, even if the caller hadn't realised it. She read a few more, always hoping to find something where someone witnessed a child being taken – but of course there were none, because if that had happened the call operators would have flagged it already. She began to suspect that all she could really do was to courier this pile of paperwork back to DI Clarke's office. Perhaps that explained why he had seemed to suggest this wasn't the most important of jobs.

She was distracted by a hand brandishing an empty mug in front of her. One of the other women was offering her a top up. She remembered her name: Gemma. Cross smiled and nodded an enthusiastic yes, then looked around. Jane's desk was empty, as was the other telephone operators, they must have stepped out of the room. And then the phone on the desk next to her began to ring. She'd noticed how they did it by now, and not wanting to let a call go unanswered, she moved across and picked it up.

"Hello, *Crimebusters* hotline, how can I help?" As Cross spoke a prompt popped up on the computer screen in front of her: the words she was supposed to say.

Good morning/evening – You've reached the secure contact line for Crimebusters, which investigation are you ringing about please?

She winced, but a voice came on before she could correct herself. It was a woman. She sounded elderly, but with a forthright edge.

"It's not me that needs help. It's about that poor, poor girl. Layla Martin."

"Yes, absolutely," Cross searched around for a pen. She wasn't about to do keyboards. When she found one, she went on. "What was it you wanted to say?"

"Well it's a bit..." The woman stopped. "It's a bit strange, actually. And I hope you won't think I'm strange in saying it?"

"Of course not." Cross turned away from the screen, which was now prompting her to get the woman's name. She let herself focus on the voice at the other end of the line.

"What is it you wanted to say?"

Suddenly the caller sounded reluctant.

"Ma'am. Are you still there? Were you there that day? When she went missing?"

"Oh yes."

Cross waited.

"Yes. We have a beach hut, my husband and I, a little way along from the kiosk. Where she was supposed to have been buying ice cream. The girl, I mean."

"OK."

"We *had* a hut, I meant to say. Henry, my husband, he unfortunately passed last year, and we had to let it go." The woman stopped.

"Oh, I'm so sorry to hear that. Really sorry."

"Thank you, dear. Thank you."

Gemma was back now, the mug now filled with more tea. She saw that Cross was taking a call, and had leaned into the computer, checking it was recording. Then she gave a thumbs up, which Cross took to mean that she should carry on.

"My name is Ellen. Ellen Cross. I'm a police officer. I'm assisting with the Layla Martin inquiry. Can I take your name?"

"Oh. Yes. It's Mrs Rolands. Margaret Rolands."

"Hello Margaret. And thank you for calling. Can I ask if you saw something? Something that made you think you should call?"

"Yes. Yes, I did. But I can't quite make sense of it. I'm sure if Henry was still around he would have a rational explanation. He did love his rational explanations."

"What was it you saw, Margaret?"

There was a long pause.

"Well, I knew the case of course. It's been in the news what happened to that poor girl, but I didn't think I'd seen anything important, except for last night when that detective was on the television. Detective Inspector Clarke was his name."

Cross felt a strange sensation on the skin of her neck, as if a number of insects were suddenly crawling on her.

"What about him, Margaret?"

"Well, the thing I don't understand... the thing they didn't say on the television... the thing I don't get is, why they don't say he was *there*? At the beach. On the day it happened."

FORTY-SIX

"Could you say that again, Margaret?" Cross was sitting upright in the chair. The room around her seemed to have faded into near black, all her attention was on the voice at the end of the phone line. "Did you say DI Clarke was there? The day Layla went missing?"

"That's right. He didn't look quite the same because he was wearing summer clothes. A baseball cap, and fancy silver sunglasses – you know, with the lenses that are like mirrors."

Cross was silent.

"With those sunglasses on, I'm not sure I would have recognised him, least not if he hadn't taken them off to clean them – just like he did on the TV last night. He was standing right in front of me when he did it. Right in front of the hut. And me – I never forget a face."

Cross took as many details as she could, but there wasn't much more to take. Margaret Rolands had been sitting in a deck chair outside her hut – number 347 – about four hundred yards to the west from the kiosk where Layla Martin was taken from. She was reading a novel by Jeffrey Archer, but wasn't much of a fan, and really using it as an excuse to watch the people passing in front of the hut.

She didn't particularly like days that hot and busy, but she felt the hut had to be used to justify the cost of it. About an hour before Layla's disappearance, she had watched a man in his thirties walking alone along the promenade – and thought very little of it, until last night, when she believed she saw the same man identified as DI Clarke leading the investigation.

Once Cross had gone over everything twice, and checked the contact details the computer had automatically pulled up, she let Margaret go, promising that someone would come to see her soon. Then she hung up, and sat back in her chair.

On the trip back down the motorway, the pile of call logs occupied the passenger seat next to Cross – destined for DI Clarke's desk. But there was one that wouldn't get there, at least not yet. Cross didn't believe that Clarke had done anything wrong – Margaret Rolands could have got mixed up, and even if not, it was possible the investigation team already knew that Clarke was on the beach that day. After all, he lived nearby, thousands of people were on the beach, and there was nothing wrong with it. Yet it was the *second* strange anomaly that the case had thrown up. And in those circumstances, Cross thought it was safer to bring that to the attention of the Super without alerting Clarke to the matter.

Of course, this didn't mean that Clarke was actually involved. That would be crazy. This was just about being on the safe side.

FORTY-SEVEN

The doorbell rang. Layla drifted over to the bedroom window, which overlooked the front of the house, to see a black Jaguar car parked outside the house.

"Who is it?" her brother asked.

"I can't see," she replied. The tops of two male heads were just visible, standing outside the porch below.

It was the morning after the *Crimebusters* programme had gone out, a school day, but their parents hadn't sent Gale in. Indeed, the night had been weirdly interrupted by a knock on the door around midnight, and then Layla had watched their mother creep into Gale's room in the middle of the night. She'd checked him carefully, as if expecting that he might not be breathing, and when she was reassured that he was, she had settled down to sleep on the floor beside his bed.

It was obvious that something was wrong, but their mum had waited until Gale woke, the next morning, before he could ask what. And then she had refused to say. She would only tell him he had to stay home, and then neither her nor their father would say why. They had only repeated over and over that nothing was wrong. When clearly that wasn't true.

"Is the other police car still there? Across the road?" Gale asked.

"Yeah. It's still there."

They heard the front door opening, and then their father's deep voice. Too quiet to be overheard. Layla turned around, to find Gale at her shoulder, by the window.

"Do you want to try to listen? Gale asked.

Layla thought about it a moment. "Yeah."

Gale opened his bedroom door and crept along the landing, and Layla drifted beside him, edging towards the top of the stairs where they could peek downstairs into the hallway. But they were too late. Whoever it was had already been shown into the sitting room, with both their mother and father.

"Can you hear anything?" Gale asked.

"No. They're speaking too quietly."

"We need to go downstairs. We can listen from the hall-way." Gale said. "Or you could go in there?"

After a while Layla nodded, and began to drift, like smoke, down the stairs.

"This is a very difficult thing to say..." The man who spoke wore a police uniform with lots of buttons and patches. He was big, and he looked like he had a cold. Even so, Layla might have said he looked trustworthy, had it not been for his companion. The second man in the room was perched on the sofa and nodding seriously, and he was the man who had killed her.

"As you know, the episode of *Crimebusters* went out last night, and it seems it may have flushed out the man who killed Layla," the man went on. Layla's mother gasped, her hand flying to her face.

"It's not... it's not necessarily good news, I'm afraid."

"How do you mean?" This was her dad. "Surely that was

the point of doing the programme? To get him to come forward, or someone who knows who he is?"

The two policemen – the killer and the other one – exchanged a look.

"What do you mean?" Rachel Martin asked. "What's going on?"

The evil one, her killer, tried to speak, but the other man lifted a hand to stop him. He seemed to be in charge.

"Late last night, after the programme aired, we received a call from a man who claimed to be Layla's killer. When that happens, we typically ask for some piece of evidence that only the real killer would know, in order to weed out false confessions – I'm afraid some people will do anything for notoriety. In this case the man appeared to know about the missing part of Layla's ear."

Instinctively, Layla lifted a hand to the side of her head. She didn't feel herself exactly, not like before, yet she was aware that there was something missing there.

"As a result, we have to take it seriously, which makes what he said next all the more concerning."

He paused, and Layla looked from her mother to her father, both of whom were speaking now.

"What? What did he say next?"

"As I say, there's no easy way to say this, but this man then went on to claim that he had identified his next victim. And then he gave your son's name."

There was a silence.

"Sorry – what?" Rachel asked. Layla looked at her father, his face had gone whiter than hers.

"Gale?" her father said. "He wants to... he said he wants *Gale*?"

"The threat came in late last night, and we had a police protection team outside the house within minutes. Since then we've had regular patrols from marked vehicles – I'm sure you've seen them – but we wanted to explain this to you in person." The man said. "We think it's highly unlikely that he's actually going to try anything, but if he did want to, it would be impossible for him to get at Gale with the protection we've put in place."

"But *Gale?*" her dad said a second time. "Why would he want Gale? What is this?"

Next Layla watched as her mother seemed to shrink in front of her eyes. She contracted into a silent sob, but then it found voice. A quiet, broken weeping. For a few moments it was the only sound in the room, until her father moved across to comfort her, but he seemed dazed himself.

For a while Layla lost it too, she let herself slip back into the fuzz of the whiteness that surrounded her. None of this made sense. It was all too much, too hard to understand, simply too hard to bear. For a long time she stared at the man who murdered her. Who was somehow sitting in her house, nodding his head as her parents talked about how Gale would be next, that the very same man was going to kill Gale next.

How was this happening? Why couldn't she stop it?

"Why would he want Gale?" Her father managed.

"That's a very good question," her killer replied. He leaned forward on the sofa, then clasped his hands together. The same hands that had tried to squeeze Layla's life from her neck.

"At some point I'm going to need to speak to both of you again in detail. It could be that there's someone from your past who has developed a grudge against you. But that might take some time. For now, is there anyone you can think of who might have some reason to attack your family like this?"

Her father looked bewildered. Her mother too. And then Layla saw a look on her mother's face she recognised, sudden distrust in her eyes. And Layla knew this could yet get worse.

"No. *No*. That's... ridiculous." Her father replied to her killer. But now he turned to look at her mother, and there was suspicion on his face too.

There was a pen on the coffee table, just in front of where her killer sat, and Layla found herself staring at it, wishing it were possible to grab it and stab him with it. To stick it in his eyes, to stop what he was doing, ripping apart what was left of her family, and so calmly, with such false concern. She focussed on it, misery filling her up.

But the moment she reached out to grasp the pen, her hand simply flowed into it, as she knew it would. For once she concentrated, willing herself the ability to influence it, but it was impossible. It felt as though she could touch the molecules that made up the plastic of the pen, billions of them, spinning in space. It was like dipping her hand into the ball-pool pit at the soft play centre she'd gone to when she was younger. But though she could stir her hand through the material, it simply wasn't there to hold – like clutching at smoke. Everything she had ever known now inhabited a different dimension to where she found herself. She may as well have tried to reach up and pull down a star.

There was a vase on the sideboard. Layla stared at that too, wishing she could grab it and smash it across her killer's head. Yearning for the ability to simply walk up to her mother and scream the truth to her face. Explain how they were being conned by a monster in their midst.

But she couldn't do it. Any of it. Because she didn't exist. She wasn't real. At least not for them. They couldn't see her, they couldn't hear her, they couldn't feel her. It was only Gale who could do any of those things. Without Gale she was nothing. Without Gale she didn't exist.

And now the monster was going to kill Gale.

. . .

When Layla could take no more, she drifted back upstairs, ignoring Gale's urgently whispered questions from outside the room. Instead, she led him back to his bedroom.

"What? *Who* is it?" He read her face. "It's *him*, isn't it? He's back."

Layla nodded, not trusting her voice for a few seconds. "Him and another police officer. I don't know his name."

"What do they want?"

Layla didn't answer this. Instead, she looked around the room, and then back at her brother. His face, small and smooth, had changed in the two years since she'd died. He'd finally lost some teeth, and his face had lengthened. But he still looked so fragile compared to the man downstairs. The man whose hands she knew were so strong, and whose heart so black.

"What? What did they say? Why are they here?"

This wasn't fair. How did *he* have so much power, when she had so little? How was it that he could not only take her and kill her, but then come to their house, and threaten to do the same to her brother as well? And how was it that she could do nothing about it? How could that be fair?

"Layla? What is it? What did they say? Why won't you tell me?"

It was too much. Too painful for her to deal with. And anyway, the white mists of her reality were closing in, like they did sometimes. And when that happened there was nothing she could do.

"I have to go. I'm sorry, Gale."

"What? What did they say. What did he want? What's going on?"

Layla began to slip away, into the whiteness that was both so filled with pain and yet so much easier than the space she was in right now. Gale's pleas grew weaker and weaker, and even though she knew she should remain with her brother – he was shouting so loud they would surely hear him from downstairs – but she couldn't.

"I have to go," she said again.

She didn't know if she'd already gone, before the words came out.

FORTY-EIGHT

"Hello, Sue." Cross sent a quick smile towards Starling's secretary, who occupied a desk in the lobby area outside his office. "I need to speak with DS Starling."

The woman smiled back, but looked confused. "Oh, hello Ellen." She checked her screen. "I don't have you down for a meeting? I thought I'd cancelled everything that wasn't urgent. On account of his cold—"

"No. I haven't got one." Cross' mind was still racing. She'd taken the call logs to Clarke's office, but thankfully he wasn't there. Then she'd taken the lift up to the fourth floor. "I need to see him. I think it's really urgent."

"OK, I can try him." The secretary picked up her phone. Moments later, she began speaking.

"I have Constable Cross here to see you, sir." She listened, and a few seconds later she looked up at Cross.

"What's it about?"

"I think I need to say that to the Super himself."

The secretary made a disapproving sound before she repeated this down the line, and then put the phone down.

"He says you can go in, but I wouldn't get too close."

. . .

Starling was hunched over his desk, paperwork on one side and an almost equal-sized pile of used tissues on the other. A mug of something lemony steamed in front of him. When he sat back his eyes and nose were red.

"What?"

For a second Cross wondered if she really should be here, bothering him with this. The poor man was ill, and what she was suggesting was... crazy. But then, she couldn't just ignore it, and it made no sense to go back to Clarke himself with what she'd discovered.

"It's just a cold, Constable Cross. Are you here to tell me to go home as well? I've had that all morning from Sue, and I don't have time." He took another tissue from a box on his desk and blew his nose loudly, then spent several moments wiping it, before swivelling around on his chair and picking up his wastepaper basket and dumping the pile of tissues in it. "There. Better?"

"Um. I guess."

He nodded, then held out a hand to the chair in front of the desk. "Have a seat, Constable. Tell me what's on your mind? Or would you like a Lemsip?" He picked up his mug, and took a sip.

Cross sat and took a deep breath before she began.

"DI Clarke sent me to help out with call logs from the TV show. From *Crimebusters*."

"Uh huh. Go on."

"And he asked me to bring them all back for follow-ups, and to tell him if there was anything that looked urgent."

"OK." Starling took another sip.

"But there was one call that I thought I better not show to him, that I should let you see first."

Starling sat looking ill for a moment, then he drew in a deep breath. "OK. Well, let's see it."

Cross nodded, and pulled out the folded A4 sheet from her pocket. She quickly opened it up, then handed it across. Then she sat waiting while he looked it over. He made noises as he read. Loud breathing, but he didn't bother to blow his nose again.

"Talk me through this please, Constable. What are you showing me here?"

"I'm not exactly sure. I mean it could be this woman's a bit crazy, or just got mixed up. But I thought it was a strange coincidence. First, the girl's mother comes in, saying she thinks the killer lives at DI Clarke's address, now this – someone says they saw DI Clarke there, on the day Layla went missing."

Starling's only response was to read the transcript a second time, in complete silence this time.

"OK." He said when he was finished. His large hand began to tap out a rhythm on the wooden top of the desk. "Anyone else seen this?"

Cross thought for a second. "Nobody, sir. Just me, and now you."

"How about the telephone operators?"

"No. I took the call. I didn't share it with them. You said before about mud sticking, and I thought... well I wasn't sure what to think. I thought I should talk to you."

Starling seemed to take a long time considering this, before he responded.

"The Martin family were very keen to have DI Clarke continue on the case. After the misunderstanding of the other child."

It wasn't a question, so Cross didn't answer it.

"And it was a *misunderstanding*, correct?" He went on. "All the accusations that were levelled at Clarke were baseless?"

"I... I think so. I thought so."

Starling stayed quiet.

"I wasn't sure what this call meant," Cross tried to explain. "I mean... I thought it was possible that he *was* there that day, but that it was already known – the investigation team were aware, I mean. I expect that's what's going on here. They already know Clarke was there on the beach that day, and it's just a coincidence..."

"That's quite the coincidence," Starling cut in sharply. "And if Clarke was there, it's the first I've heard of it. And I've reviewed the case in detail several times."

Cross was quiet. The explanation she had been hoping for dashed.

Neither of them spoke for a while, then Starling blew his nose again.

"Look, Constable. You're going to have to imagine that my head is filled with gunk and I can't think straight. Lay out to me exactly what you're suggesting here."

After a very long while, Cross spoke again. "OK. I suppose the chances of this woman, Mrs Rolands, being correct must be really small. She probably made a mistake, and just saw someone that looks similar to DI Clarke. But if she is right, then the implication is... well, it's horrible. That's why I came to you, because I'm not sure what ought to happen."

He stared at her without expression.

"No. I need it clearer. What is the implication exactly?"

Cross stayed quiet this time, blinking at him.

"Are you saying you think DI Clarke, the investigating officer in charge of the Layla Martin case, could actually be the person responsible for the death of Layla Martin?"

"Well, yes sir. I suppose I am."

Starling went quiet again. He turned to the window, stared out of it for a while, then shook his head. Then he got up, went to the door and opened it. He looked in both directions, then drew it shut again. When he sat down he spoke, but his voice was quieter.

"If that's true, it will be the biggest scandal this force has ever faced." He stopped, and simply stared at her.

"Um, I don't know, sir," Cross said after a while. "I guess it's kind of crazy."

Suddenly, Starling leaned back, and pulled open his desk drawer. He took out a blister pack of paracetamol and popped two tablets out. Then he got up again and walked to a side table, where Sue had placed a jug of water and a tray of glasses. He filled a glass and took it back, then swallowed the tablets. Cross got the idea he was doing so mostly out a desire to buy some thinking time.

"It certainly would be crazy, *if* it were true. But it's far more likely to not be true. Furthermore, should news of this get out it would be disastrous. A rumour like this would destroy his career, and should the press get hold of it..." He actually shuddered at the idea. "That doesn't really bear thinking about."

Cross was silent.

"I suppose I'll need to ask him, if he was on the beach that day, or if he has an alibi—"

"Actually sir, I don't know if that's the best idea." Cross interrupted, then bit her lip.

"Excuse me?"

She took another deep breath. "I've been thinking about this, as I was driving back. You see, I know this is all really unlikely, but if there *is* any truth in this, then he's way ahead of us. He's been running your investigation for the last two years. If he's done all that while actually *being* the man you're looking for, then... well, then surely he'll have planned out what to do if something like this comes up?"

Starling had already looked pale. Now he looked whiter.

"I appreciate your logic, Constable. The implications, not so much. But I like your logic."

"Thank you, sir."

Cross waited for her boss to go on, but in the end, she ended up speaking again. "What are you going to do?"

Starling shook his head. "Honestly, I don't know. I'm going to have to give this some thought. In the meantime, I need you to not tell anybody about this. Can I have your word on that?"

"Yes, sir."

Starling thought again.

"Christ," he said in the end. "I thought I was already having a bad week. Thank you for making it so much worse."

FORTY-NINE

The next night Layla forced herself back into her brother's bedroom. It hurt to be there now, acute pain. It seemed so cruel that of all the senses which had been taken away, the one that remained was this capacity to feel such intense pain. It was there now, it was always there now, a raw rasping flavour to it, as though the white mists that swirled around her were filled with invisible cheese graters that scraped and scratched at her skin every moment she existed. They only penetrated a little way yet, but they were getting deeper. Eventually they would cut right through her. And all she would be was pain. Nothing more. Nothing less.

With an effort she pushed the thought away, and watched her brother sleeping. His pyjamas were rucked up and twisted, the thin single duvet half on the floor and half on the bed. His narrow chest rose and fell with his breathing. She knew that his dream was her pain. In that way, she could see into his mind, as he slept. And she watched him now, watching her, watching him, watching her, watching him – all the way down, and all the way up. She wished that her situation might be simpler, easier to understand. She wished for many things. She wished for her touch back, so that she might brush the strands of hair from where they rested against his closed eyes.

And she wished she didn't have to do what she was about to do.

She watched, as Gale woke with a start. Confusion seemed to drain off him, but then fill again, as his dream about his dead sister faded, replaced by a reality where she floated beside him, love and pain written in her eyes.

"What did Mum and Dad say?" Gale asked, stubbornly, as if they hadn't been apart since when the police officers had come to the house.

"Shhhh."

They hadn't told him – Mum and Dad – Layla had been there enough to know this, barely present in the background. They hadn't told him what the killer had threatened. And they wouldn't tell him either.

Layla felt a strange dryness in her mouth, just as Gale struggled upright and grabbed his water bottle from his bedside table. As he did so. he seemed to notice the time, three in the morning. He frowned at his sister, questioningly.

Layla shook her head. "Shhhh." She said again.

Gale bumped the bottle back down, sitting up straighter again. "When I went to sleep the police car was still there, waiting outside the house. They're there all the time. And no one will tell me why."

"Shhh. I know."

"Dad won't tell me. Mum just keeps hugging me and crying. And now you won't tell me. I want to know what's going on."

"We need to do something." Layla reached out a hand, even though he couldn't touch it. "We need to go downstairs. Bring your duvet."

"Why?"

"Because it's cold, silly."

For a moment it seemed like Gale might refuse her. But then he pushed himself out of the bed, standing in his bare feet. He rolled the covers into a loose ball, then took them as he followed her out of the door and down the stairs.

"What are we doing?"

"Downstairs."

Layla led them down to the living room, where a large L-shaped sofa faced the TV and the window. Gale went to switch on a lamp, but Layla warned him not to.

"The police are out there. They'll see the light."

"But *why* are the police there?"

"Please..." Layla shook her head.

He went to the window, and Layla thought he was going to open the curtains to look, but instead he tucked them better around the edge of the window, and then he placed the lamp onto the floor, and half covered it with the duvet. When he turned it on, there was just a glow from inside the covers.

"I don't like the dark," he explained, and Layla nodded.

For a long time, she didn't say anything. She just drifted up and down, the ghostly equivalent of pacing. All the while Gale waited, trusting that there was some point to this. Something she was going to explain.

"We need to make Mum understand," Layla said eventually. "We have to find a way."

"We tried already with Becky," Gale replied. "Nothing worked. There's no way an adult is going to believe us."

"We have to. We don't have a choice."

"Why?"

Layla was quiet.

"Layla? Why are there police outside? What's going on?"

Layla moved to her brother, and lifted her arms, so that they flanked his body – not touching, because they couldn't touch. But she held his eyes with hers. And then she blinked.

At once everything she knew, everything she had seen the day before in this same room, when the man investigating her murder had calmly explained how her killer was going to kill Gale next – even though he was one and the same person – it was all transferred to Gale. A package of knowledge passing in a moment. It hit him like a physical blow, pushing him backwards.

His face, already pale and stretched, took on an expression she had never seen before. Layla understood why; few people got to be so confronted with the idea of their own death, as Gale just had. But she had. She knew it well. It took him a while, to speak again.

"Will I be with you? When it happens?" Gale asked quietly, almost calmly. His eyes glowed white in the half light, staring into the empty space of her own.

"I don't know," Layla replied, equally quiet.

"But do you think I might be? Do you think we might be together?"

Layla bit her lip, considering the question. She glanced around, at the whiteness around her, filled with nobody, nothing, except the pain ever-searching for ways to embed itself deeper into her soul.

"I'm sorry Gale, I just don't know."

He surprised her then by crying. Not out-of-control sobbing, but quiet, heavy tears that dropped to the carpet and plopped on the table. She wished she could wipe them away.

They both sat in silence for a long while, before Gale spoke again. He'd stopped crying now.

"*How* is it going to happen? There's no way I'm going to get into his car. Not in a million years."

There might have been, between two other people, an element of criticism of Layla in this comment – after all, they both knew she had done so. But there was none intended, and not for a moment did Layla consider that any was implied.

"I don't know. I think he must have a plan. Otherwise, he wouldn't have done it. He must have planned it all out, that's why he's the top detective on the case. That's why I told you too, you have to protect yourself."

Gale nodded, then swallowed.

"What about the police outside? Are they good or bad?"

She hesitated. "I think they're good. I think they'd stop him, if they knew. Or if they believed you."

"But no one will ever believe me," Gale said. "Because I'd have to tell them I was told by a ghost, and that's totally mental."

"But they might believe Mum," Layla added. "And I think that maybe we can convince her. If we really try. If we really, *really* try." She paused, and wished again she didn't have to do this.

"Will you go and get her for me?"

FIFTY

"Mum!"

Rachel Martin woke with a jump, jerked out of a dream.

"What is it, darling?"

"We need to speak to you," Gale said.

"Are you OK? Did you hear something?"

As she spoke she reached for her phone, which was plugged in, charging on the bedside table. No missed calls, no messages. If there was a threat, it was closer.

"Did something wake you?"

"No. We just need to speak to you."

"You didn't hear anything?"

"No."

As the fear of a possible threat faded, the reality of the moment replaced it.

"Honey, it's three o'clock in the morning."

"We need to speak to you," Gale said a third time. "*Now*. We need you to come downstairs."

For a moment Rachel thought about saying no, telling Gale that whatever it was would have to wait until the morning, but that insistent "we" cut into synapses both sluggish with sleep and wired from constant tension. And Gale had spoken with a weird intensity, that Rachel found oddly compelling, as if the easiest thing was simply to obey. Automatically she swung out of the bed, slipped on a gown, and followed her son downstairs.

"What is this, Gale?" Rachel asked, as they descended, and then when he didn't answer, she asked again, this time looking in confusion at the duvet covering the table lamp, which was placed on the floor. "What do you need to tell me?"

But he ignored her. Instead, he took a candle and box of matches from a drawer. He lit a match and melted the bottom of a candle so that it would stick to a saucer that he must have got from the kitchen. When it was secure, he lit the candle, too, then put it in the middle of the table. Then he went and turned off the lamp, so that the candle was the only source of light illuminating the room.

"Sit down," Gale said, when he was done. He took a seat himself, but there was something weird about how he did so; the movement was wrong, it wasn't how Gale moved.

"*Darling?* What's going on?"

"Sit down," Layla repeated – no, *Gale* repeated. Rachel blinked at her mistake. Her eyes focussed on the flickering candle. She was going mad. For a second, it was as if she'd heard her daughter's voice.

"What it is Gale? What's going on?"

"Sit down, Mum," came his voice. More obviously Gale this time. Of course it was Gale.

"*Sit.*" This third time Rachel did as she was told, taking the seat opposite her son, the candle lighting the space between them.

"Take my hands," Gale said. He held his own arms out either side of the candle. Palm upright. She did what he asked.

"Hold me. Don't let go."

"Oh, honey..."

Gale was silent, waiting. Across from him, Rachel saw his eyes watching her, then lose their focus, and then, for the tiniest moment of time, almost too quick for her to register, his eyes seemed to almost dissolve away to blackness. It was alarming. She tried to pull her hands back, but he was too quick. He stopped her.

"Gale, this is... you're actually scaring me—"

"Hello, Mum."

"Gale? This is frightening, what's—"

"Please just say hello."

Rachel opened her mouth, then closed it. "Hello."

Gale smiled. No, *Layla* smiled. Rachel shook her head. It was Gale's face, but somehow it was Layla's smile. What had just happened? What on earth was going on?

"It's me. It's Layla."

"*What?*"

"It's *me*, Mum."

What?

"I can see it's you, Gale." Like air rushing into a vacuum, rationality flooded back into Rachel's mind. Comforting, soothing reality, even though her reality was anything but soothing. "What I'm wondering is why you've brought me down here in the middle of the night."

Gale smiled. *Layla* smiled.

"What—?"

"I need you to believe me, Mum," Gale said. In Gale's voice, the words coming from Gale's lips, but speaking as if he wasn't Gale, but his dead sister.

"I know the man who killed me wants to kill Gale next. And I don't want that to happen. I can't let that happen."

Rachel tried to twist away again, to deny what she'd just heard, but her son's hands were holding her too tight. She was left staring at him – *somehow at her* – it was... it wasn't real. It couldn't be.

"Gale, you're scaring me—"

"Mum, please. Just try to believe. Just let yourself believe. For a moment. Then you'll understand."

She didn't take the instruction, not as he – or she – had asked, to accept the impossible. But she took her own version of it, where she would play along with whatever game this was that Gale wanted to play. Needed to play.

"How did she...?" Rachel stopped. She felt her heart thumping. This was insanity. Her, or Gale, or somehow the both of them together were going insane. As if things couldn't get any worse, they were actually losing their minds. But she went with it.

"How did *you* know about... about the man wanting to take..." She seemed reluctant to submit to it fully, even to her playing-along version of whatever this was. But eventually she did. "To take... Gale?"

"I was there. Yesterday," Gale replied. "I was with you in the room when they came to see you."

Rachel was silent.

"I saw the two of them, the man in the uniform, who did most of the talking, and then *him*. The one who killed me."

It was too much. Rachel jerked again, breaking one of her hands loose, and then using it to prise Gale's fingers off her other hand. "Oh, come now, Gale." She rubbed her eyes. "This is just silly. Everything you told me about Kieran proved to be wrong. He's trying to *help* us, and it doesn't help—"

"I'm going to tell you how he killed me."

Gale seemed to have stayed in his trance. His hands hadn't moved, just fallen onto the tabletop where her own hands had left them. Now, as if they had a spirit of their own, each of them seemed to jerk and twitch, as if seeking the contact Rachel had just taken away. She watched them a second, like wounded animals, then she reached out again. As her son's hands found hers again, and gripped her tight, she felt the power, the importance of their touch. She swallowed.

"Please listen," Gale said. His head was bowed now. Rachel couldn't see his face in darkness, but she knew if she could it wouldn't be his face at all. It would be Layla's.

Rachel took a long, deep breath, then nodded. She squeezed her son's hands as she listened to her daughter.

"OK."

"He drugged me, once he got me in the car. I don't know what it was, but it smelt like cherries, and it hurt my throat. Then he left me. For a long time. More than a day. I didn't know where I was. There were steps up the walls, like a basement—"

"There is no basement in that house." Again, rationality forced Rachel to interrupt. "The police—"

"Then it's another house. It's somewhere else."

She was silenced. He was so firm, so sure. *She* was so sure.

"At first, I was alone. But I couldn't get out. There was only one door and it was locked. But then he came back, and I thought he might let me go. But he didn't. He wouldn't."

Rachel looked down at her hands, once again being gripped tightly by her son, but she didn't speak. It was incredible. Gale's voice, his intonation, the tone he had taken, it was unmistakable now. Unmistakably Layla.

"Some of the time it was like he wanted to be friends with me. Sometimes it was like he was scared of me. And sometimes, it was like – he wanted to do things to me, like the way you warned me. Do you remember?" Suddenly Gale's head snapped up again, and he looked at her.

Instantly Rachel's mind exploded into another moment, as if some impossible force had punched her backwards in time.

In an instant she was sitting on her daughter's bed, some years before, explaining the need to watch out for the very, very rare chance that someone might want to touch her, in a way they shouldn't. She remembered the moment – in a way it tortured her, that she hadn't said enough – but this *wasn't* a memory, she could see which of her daughter's duvet covers was on the bed at the time, a detail that wasn't *in* her memory, her school bag was on the desk, books spilling out...

She was pulled away from thought now by the intensity in Gale's eyes as he stared across the table at her.

"You remember."

"Of course I remember, but you..." Rachel felt her face crumple from the confusion of it. He hadn't been there. Gale had been away – that was why she'd chosen that night to have the talk. And it was unthinkable she would tell him.

"You weren't... Gale wasn't there." And then she watched as her daughter nodded sadly back at her.

"Did he? Did he... do things to you?" Rachel knew the answer to this, Kieran Clarke had sat them down to tell that terrible truth, which had been confirmed by the pathologist's examination.

"A little," Gale said. *Layla said.*

Rachel felt her throat constrict. It was so Layla to make light of it. She never liked to make a fuss. They used to joke, when Layla had been tiny, that she could go days without eating, and only then would she say she was a 'little bit hungry'.

"Oh, darling. *Oh honey.*"

"I sort of fought him off, like you told me. So, he couldn't..." Gale was quiet a moment. His mouth open, his breath making the flame flicker.

"But then he brought the snakes."

Rachel swallowed again. "What about the snakes?"

"He first told me about them in the car. I didn't really understand then. I didn't think he actually had snakes. But then he told me again, in the basement, where he kept me. And then one day he said he'd brought them to see me. Then he went away for a while, and when he came back, he had an actual snake wrapped around his arms. He held its head funny, so it couldn't twist around. He said it was really poisonous, and if it bit me, I would die, and I would never go home to see you."

"Oh, honey..."

"He said if I didn't do what he wanted, he'd let it bite me. So I let him do it. What you said I shouldn't do."

"Oh God. Layla. *Gale*. I'm so sorry. It's not your fault—"

"I don't need you to be sorry Mum. It's too late." Gale was squeezing her hands now. "And it's not your fault. But you *need* to stop him. You need to believe me. You need to believe *Gale*. We need to stop this man before he does the same to Gale. We need to stop him before he kills him."

Gale squeezed harder, and his head snapped back upwards. For a second he stayed staring into Rachel's eyes. Imploring, pleading. And for a moment it was like watching one of those 3D pictures that were two images in one, when you changed the angle you viewed them from. One moment they were Layla's eyes, the next they were Gale's, and then they changed again. And then Rachel watched her daughter fall away backwards, as if dropping down a bottomless well, but not tumbling, not even moving, but staring straight back at her, as she grew smaller and smaller and smaller. Until she was no longer there at all.

Moments later a thin line of drool appeared in the corner of Gale's mouth, as if a spider was dropping down a line of silk. Rachel stared at it, like a tiny diamond in the reflected light. Finally, she realised his grip on her hands had relaxed, and she let go, brushed the thread away with her thumb. Then she took his hand once more.

"And you know who this was, darling? The man who did all this to you? You know who it was?"

Gale was silent.

"Was it DI Clarke? The man you're talking about? Was it Kieran Clarke?"

But then she realised that her son wouldn't answer her, couldn't do so, even though he was still sat at the dining table, opposite her.

Because Gale was fast asleep.

FIFTY-ONE

When Rachel awoke the next morning, the adventures of the night were like a too-real dream. Visions of it burst into her mind, too vivid to be imagined, and yet too crazy to be true. She turned to see her husband sitting up in bed and scrolling through his phone, as if nothing were amiss in the world.

The sight of this somehow offended her, and she got up, wrapping herself with her robe before going to the window. Outside, she saw the police car parked opposite. It was just possible to see the two figures in it. They'd been there all night.

"Have you checked on Gale?" she asked. Jon stopped what he was doing.

"Asleep. I looked in on him when I woke up."

She saw his slippers, which hadn't been there earlier, on the floor, so she knew he was telling the truth. She nodded, reassured, but got up to check herself anyway. And then when she got there, and saw her son's bed was empty, the duvet turned back, she yelled out in panic.

"He's not here!"

She felt the fear rise in her, only half-hearing her husband's response, leaping out of bed and coming to check for himself.

She glanced around the rest of the room, but there was nowhere to hide – no reason for him to hide. Then she rushed down the stairs. Almost at once she saw him, buttering toast at the kitchen worktop.

"Darling. Are you OK?"

He looked sad, lonely – like he usually did these days – but surprised too, at the intensity of his mother.

"Yeah. I'm OK."

She stared at him, baffled for a moment, as the events of the night before – the dream she'd had, for surely that was the explanation for it – filtered back into her mind, like gently falling snow. She'd carried him upstairs, all thirty kilograms of him, after he'd fallen asleep at the table. She shook her head, shaking away the impossibility of it all, not least the unlikeliness of her son being so talkative.

And then, out of the edge of her vision, she saw the dining table, where they had sat in her dream. And slowly as if not quite daring to do so, she turned her head. She didn't know what she expected to see, certainly not Layla floating there. Nothing, she supposed, since there should have been nothing to see. But there *was* something.

The candle itself had almost disappeared, burnt away, but the saucer that Gale had placed it in was still there, a small puddle of melted wax cooled in the bottom. She went closer. She touched it with her finger, feeling the soft wax, warm but not hot.

"Gale, do you remember anything about last night?" she asked, swinging back to face him. He had the toast in his hand now, about to take a bite.

"What?" She saw the confusion. He wouldn't hold her gaze, but because he was being evasive? Or because of his misery?

"Do you remember putting the candle here? Talking to me?"

He gave her a look. Genuinely confused. "When last night?"

"Nothing," she said, quickly, turning away. This was insane. She was going insane, but that wasn't something she was going to inflict upon him.

Poor Gale already has enough going on, she thought to herself. And like a dam bursting, it all suddenly started swirling into her thoughts: Layla's death, of course, but then the arguments she and Jon were having, the TV show. And now the horrible, terrifying threat against Gale himself. She stopped, feeling the breathlessness approaching. The panic welling up. She forced herself to count slowly.

Kieran Clarke. Detective Inspector Kieran Clarke. *He* wanted to kill Gale. Layla had told her. Kieran Clarke was leading the investigation of Layla's murder. But Kieran Clarke was *also* the monster who had killed her.

No. She touched her hands to either side of her head, as if physically trying to keep it fixed in a straight line. Aligned with the reality shared by the rest of the world. This was just crazy. It was insane. And even if it *wasn't* insane, there was no way that anyone would ever believe her if she tried to explain it.

And yet...

She went to the window again, checking the police car was still there, protecting them. *That* was real, wasn't it? The threat that *had* been made. Or had it? Perhaps that wasn't real, not really real. What if that was the answer? She was going crazy, and this was just another part of it. Another step down to madness. Perhaps those ideas you sometimes heard – about how we all lived in a simulation of reality, and not in real life at all – perhaps they were right. If that were true, then why would there be any limit to how crazy things could get?

Terrified at the thoughts circling inside her head, she went to make coffee, almost expecting the machine might grow wings and start circling around the kitchen.

But it didn't. It behaved. She tried to refocus.

What could she do? What *should* she do? Her mind scrolled through the options, as if on an internal Facebook feed. She dismissed each one as soon as it appeared in view. *Tell Jon what had happened.* There was no way he would believe her. *Tell Gale, try to get him to remember.* It was horribly cruel, she would have to tell him about the killer's threat to target him next. And what would be the point? He already believed Clarke was the killer. *Tell the police – but who?* Certainly not Clarke himself. She recoiled at the very thought, literally stepping back from the work-surface, as if it had just pushed her away. Tell someone *else* in the police? *Who?*

For a moment she contemplated how it would be to try to speak with DS Starling. They had met several times, and more than once he had told her to contact him if she needed anything. But they had never really gelled. For one thing, he'd always seemed to be trying to cut down the number of officers working on the case. She'd resented him for that, and he seemed to resent her back. And anyway, what could she say? That she wanted Clarke off the case after all? She'd only just confirmed she wanted him to carry on. And did she want him off? No one had been a greater champion of the case than Kieran Clarke.

He'd killed her daughter! Of course she wanted him off the damned case.

Her eye was drawn to Gale, who was sitting on the sofa by the window, feet pulled up underneath him, and staring out into the garden. Had Clarke killed Layla? She'd accused him once – when she'd gone charging down there with the picture of the house that Gale thought the killer lived at – and look where that got her. And when Gale had accused him a second time, when they'd invited him for a meal, he'd had an alibi. He couldn't have done it. Reality was *real*.

She breathed hard, ignored the coffee she'd made, and forced down a glass of water instead.

Oh God. They'd invited him for a meal. The man who had killed their daughter. *They'd invited him into their house.*

Suddenly, she didn't care if this was real or not, it was enough that Gale so passionately believed it was real. Allowing Clarke to continue to lead the case – to have anything to do with the case – that was a betrayal of her son, even if last night wasn't true.

She held out a hand to steady herself against the work surface, unable to believe how she hadn't seen this before. And then an idea came to her.

Maybe there was one person in the police that she could speak to.

FIFTY-TWO

"Here, boy. Come on. Come 'ere." Ellen Cross dropped into a low crouch and held out her hand. The dog – a brown misfit of breeds – kept away warily. It couldn't have been more than six months old, and it looked reasonably well cared for, but it was scared. The call had come in from a member of the public, an elderly lady who reported seeing some 'youths' taunting a dog in the town square. Several other Constables had declared themselves too busy before Cross was dispatched to investigate.

It had been two days since she had given Starling the transcript from the call with Margaret Rolands, and still she'd heard nothing from him, but in that time she'd thought of little else. And the conclusion she'd come to – the only conclusion that made a scrap of sense – was that there'd been some mistake. Either Margaret Rolands had seen Clarke on the beach on a different day, which was quite possible, or she was wrong about never forgetting a face, and the man she had seen hadn't been Clarke at all.

"Come on, darling, it's alright." When she'd arrived, the elderly lady was still there, the youths long gone (if they'd ever existed). The animal was now trapped in a corner between two buildings, which seemed to be adding to its anxiety.

"It's got no collar on," the lady said from behind Cross. "Perhaps it got lost, or perhaps the owners threw it out. It's terrible what people do these days."

"Isn't it." Cross didn't look around, but continued to speak reassuringly to the animal. And there was something in her tone that seemed to work. Or perhaps it was just ready to give up, because as she moved slowly and gently closer, this time it didn't back away. She made no effort to grab it, instead letting it sniff at her hand.

"That's it. I'm not going to hurt you."

Calmly, Cross moved a hand around the animal's abdomen, and drew it nearer. It seemed to think about running again, but didn't, and moments later she was able to pick it up. She stroked its coat flat along its back. It was light – there was more fur than dog.

"Oh, well done. It likes you."

Cross considered her options. She could call the dog patrol – the council operated a two-person team, who drove around the town in a van, and would be able to secure the dog, beginning the process of trying to have it re-homed. But once that process started, it was a ticking clock. If no home could be found, it would likely be destroyed. On the other hand – she felt the animal's ribs – discernible, but well-padded with flesh. She felt confident this wasn't a stray. So instead, she carried it a short way to where she knew there was a veterinary practice. The old lady followed, enjoying the ongoing drama.

"Hiya Jane." Cross smiled at the receptionist as she went inside. Years of patrolling the town centre meant she was on first name terms with many of the people who worked there. "We found this little fella in the square and we're wondering if he might be lost. You wouldn't be able to scan him for a chip, would you? Maybe we can get him back to his family?"

The vet – who was also well-known to Cross – came out now from the consulting room. In moments, the dog was on the examination table being checked over.

"He looks a little nervous still, but otherwise in good health..." The vet took a device from his desk, switched it on, and began running it around the dog's shoulders. After a moment it beeped, and the vet showed the result to his receptionist, a number on the screen's device.

"Aha. We have a hit."

There was a computer in the consulting room, and the receptionist typed the number from the device in. Seconds later the screen flashed up with an address and a phone number. Cross and the old lady waited while she phoned it.

"Hello, this is Langham's Veterinary Practice, I'm just calling to see if you've lost—" She didn't get any further before the voice on the other end interrupted her. Jane smiled as she listened. A few minutes later she put the phone down.

"They're coming down right now, he escaped from the garden this morning. I think that's case closed for you!"

Cross left the vet's with the old lady still tailing her, as if expecting to be asked to give a full statement. She was beginning to wonder what it would take to shake her off, when an excuse appeared. Her radio crackled with static, then the control room asked for her directly.

"PC Cross, come in please. Request for you back at the station."

"Excuse me," Cross told the old lady, and replied. "What is it?" They were speaking on a private frequency, but it was normal to keep details to a minimum.

"Lady's come in to see you. Wouldn't give her name, but I recognised her."

Cross was confused, and about to radio back, when the voice went on.

"It's Rachel Martin, mother of Layla Martin."

"OK. Tell her I'll be there in five."

FIFTY-THREE

Cross hurried back to the station, then made her way to the front desk, where she was directed to interview room four – one of the less comfortable ones. For a second she didn't recognise the thin, nervous looking woman who sat there for a few moments, fiddling with the handle of her handbag. She'd lost weight, looked ill.

"Mrs Martin?"

"Hello!" A flash of a smile, teeth flecked red by poorly applied lipstick. Cross closed the door and ignored the chair that was placed opposite the woman. Instead, she came closer, crouching down, a hand on the woman's shoulder.

"It's Rachel, isn't it? Are you OK? How can I help?"

Rachel Martin burst into tears.

It took a while to calm her, but Rachel Martin seemed determined to speak.

"After we met before, you said if you could ever help, I should call you. I hope that's OK, that you meant it?"

"Of course I meant it. What's the problem? Is Gale OK?" Cross knew about the guard that had been placed outside the family home; if it had been breached, the mother would come to see her.

"Yes... no. He's with my husband. And the police are outside, so he's OK for now. But you know about the threat that was made against him?"

"Yes. Half the station is working to catch whoever it is."

"But not you?"

"No. I'm... I'm not a detective. I've just been asked to help out a few times. I was happy to do so." Cross waited. The woman across from her was clearly preparing herself to say something. Something that wasn't easy to say.

"You were there, when I came in before, with the picture of Detective Clarke's house? You were there at the interview?"

Cross nodded again. "Yes."

"And you got the CCTV? From the swimming pool? You told me that it was just luck that I was late that week? Because, had it been any other week, they wouldn't have had the two systems running at once. Do you remember?"

"Yes."

"Well, I realised something that scared me. I realised the date I gave you was wrong. I *was* late the day I told you, but there was another day too, a couple of weeks after, when I had *another* meeting. And I think that's the one that Gale was talking about. *That's* the time when he and Layla were approached by the man. And so... I'm not sure now. About whether it was DI Clarke or not. The man who approached them that day. I think it might have been Clarke. And I don't know what to do."

Somehow Cross knew she was lying. She'd heard talk – drinks after work – about how you could tell by the way someone looked up and to the right, if they were accessing the creative side of their brain, and to the left it was the memory part – or was it the other way around? She could never remember. But then she'd heard too that this was nonsense, and you never could really tell, not if someone was a good liar. But she'd been around liars a lot. Terrible ones. Full-on street alcoholics and drug addicts too out of their minds to stand up, but would swear to her face that they hadn't touched a drop, or taken anything. Even sometimes when the needle was still sticking out of their arms.

She'd developed an eye for it, spotting the liars, even if she couldn't say how she knew. But she knew Rachel Martin was lying now.

"I know he doesn't have a basement," Rachel Martin was still speaking, as if she hadn't noticed Cross's reaction, "but couldn't he have taken her elsewhere? Might he not have another property? Somewhere you didn't check? Maybe he could have taken her there?"

"Are you talking about DI Clarke?" Cross stopped her.

"Yes. Kieran Clarke. The man Gale says approached him and Layla, at the swimming pool."

Cross shook her head. And yet, combined with what Margaret Rolands had told her...

"Have you told anyone else about this? DS Starling?"

Rachel Martin shook her head. "No. I wanted to speak to you first. I don't know why. I wanted to see your reaction to it..." She squeezed her eyes closed. When she opened them again, she fixed Cross with an imploring look.

"Listen, I know this seems crazy, so improbable it can't be true. But then I remembered that you were *there*. You saw the look on his face when I showed him the picture. When I talked about the snakes. Gale told me about the snakes. That's the only reason I knew. And you saw how he reacted. I was so shocked and confused myself that I got the date wrong, that I wasn't sure what it all meant, but thinking back, I believe Gale was right. There was something about Clarke's face that wasn't right."

Cross did think back. Letting DI Clarke's reaction come to

her mind when Rachel had given him the print-out of his house. Her stomach knotted.

"I need you to wait here a moment. I need to see if DS Starling is here."

Cross stepped outside to call his number, and told Sue she needed him at once. Five minutes later he was downstairs and Rachel Martin was recounting the same story a second time to both of them. The funny thing was, this time Cross wasn't sure if the woman was lying or not.

"You're sure?" Starling was checking the facts. "There was a second time when you were late? And you didn't remember that when we spoke before?"

"That's right."

"And you think it's this second time that the children were approached?"

"Yes."

Eventually, Starling turned to Cross.

"Constable, could you get onto the pool, right now. Find out if they do have any footage for this other date?"

Starling sent a bleak look towards the mother. He looked shocked still, a man whose worst nightmare seemed to be coming true, but then he forced a smile, as if reassuring her it wasn't really.

It took less than twenty minutes to confirm from the swimming pool security man that the old system had definitely been switched off by the second date Rachel Martin had given, and that the new system had definitely recorded over the data in the months since, and that there was categorically no chance there were any other tapes they could look at, nor any other camera that covered the area.

Cross then found out who would have been staffing the front desk, and managed to speak to her as well. But she had no memory of the incident the boy had described. Cross then came back to the station and Starling's office to report what she'd learned. To her surprise Rachel Martin was there, too, white faced and drinking coffee.

And then Starling told Rachel everything.

"I have some disturbing news to tell you," Starling began. She could see the sandy hairs on the back of his neck standing up, as if electrified. "This is something that has only very recently come up, and we're still considering how to handle it."

Rachel waited, her face drawn. She looked broken.

"Following your daughter's case featuring on *Crimebusters,* we did receive one other call, which hasn't been shared with DI Clarke."

Rachel's eyes flicked from the DS to Cross, and back again. "What call?"

"Without any supporting evidence – and given how incredibly unlikely it seemed that there was any truth to it – I've not yet acted. But it seems you now might be sharing some supporting evidence."

"What? I don't understand."

"I took a call." Cross herself stepped in to answer, noting how Starling quietly nodded his approval. "A member of the public believes they remember seeing Clarke at the beach when Layla went missing."

There was a silence in the room.

"Oh my god," Rachel said. Her hand went to cover her mouth. Then she suddenly buried her face in both her hands. It was a while later before she went on, showing her face again. "Oh my god. It's real. It's really true."

"We don't know that." Starling's voice was surprisingly sharp. "We are nowhere near able to say that. And I don't believe we even have the level of evidence we would require to even launch an investigation." He pulled two large thick fingers across his chin.

"So far, we only have Gale's word against him, and the statement from the person who phoned in. There isn't a defence lawyer on the circuit who wouldn't get both thrown out before they got to a jury. And there's another problem."

Neither Cross nor Rachel answered, but Starling didn't seem to want them to.

"As Constable Cross reasoned previously, *if* this is true, then Clarke has had plenty of time to destroy any evidence of what he's done, and possibly to plant other evidence to defend himself should he ever be accused."

"He did!" Rachel gasped. "He came to our house. For dinner!" She looked almost apologetic, but went on. "I thought it might help Gale to meet him, but Gale accused him again and it was *awful*." She paused a second, but was impatient to get to her point. "Only Clarke said he had an alibi. He said he was walking in the Lake District! He gave us proof, a receipt from the Airbnb he used."

Starling considered this. "Do you still have it?"

She was blank a moment. "Yeah, it was just a print-out from his email, with the name of the place he stayed and when he was there, but it was when Layla was taken. The dates matched. I have it at home still... I... I didn't think—"

"That's OK." He looked pointedly at Cross. "We'll get them, have them checked out, without him knowing." Then he changed tack.

"I take it you want him removed from the case?"

"*What?* What kind of a question is that? If he killed—"

"I understand." He held up a hand for her to stop, and looked grateful when she did so. But then he paused for a long time. "I'm sorry. I do understand. At least, I can imagine how difficult and painful this must be. But we need to consider this from a policing perspective as well. If we do remove him from the case at this point, it will alert him to the fact that we have suspicions. And if he is involved, that would remove the only advantage we currently have. What's more, we don't know it *is* him. And I have to say that aside from these concerns, he's been conducting an exemplary investigation to this point—"

"Except that he hasn't caught anyone," Cross interrupted.

Starling looked surprised by her intervention.

"Yes." Starling touched his glasses. They were titanium rimmed, and held lenses so light there couldn't have been much wrong with his eyes. "Perhaps. Either way. We have twenty-four-hour protection on your son, following the *Crimebusters* threat. And so, whether the threat comes from an unknown person, or from DI Clarke – however unlikely that is – your son is *safe*. You are safe, which gives us some time to work out how to handle this."

Again he seemed to sink into thought, before speaking again.

"Mrs Martin, I'm going to ask that we keep the details of this meeting strictly between ourselves at the moment. Any leaks from this room could get back to DI Clarke – and if he is responsible for this crime, it will greatly increase his chances of escaping prosecution." He fixed her with a firm stare, until she nodded.

"What are you going to do?"

"In the short term I'm going to review the case myself – with the help of Constable Cross here – and including the documents you mentioned from his supposed alibi. Cross will accompany you home to fetch the photographs. It's possible that will clear this up, one way or another. In the meantime, please bear with us."

FIFTY-FOUR

By the time that Cross returned to Starling's office, he'd printed out the entire case file. There was nothing unusual in him doing so, and it wouldn't be recorded on the file itself, so that Clarke would have no idea his boss, along with Constable Cross, were sat in the office upstairs poring over the logged details of his nearly two years' work.

For Cross it was the first time she had examined the paperwork of a murder case in close detail, and although she knew the rough outlines of the case – almost everyone in the station did – there was a huge amount that was new to her.

Clarke, along with his team of detectives, had interviewed over four hundred people who were on the beach that day, and followed up on scores of potential leads. They had identified dozens of previous offenders, both locally and further away, and established their whereabouts when Layla was taken. The area where Layla's body had been dumped, a small wooded area a few miles out of town, had received three full forensic sweeps, and there were reports included on objects found there, none of which appeared relevant.

The entire pathologist report was included, detailing the

strangulation marks – not considered forceful enough to even cause unconsciousness, and the missing portion of ear, and a second section of skin around the girl's waist that had been cut away. And then there had been the appeals for information, culminating in the largest of all – the *Crimebusters* programme.

For several hours, they read through the documents together, and when Starling had finished, and Cross hadn't, he picked up the telephone to check out the Airbnb address that Rachel Martin had provided.

Four hours after they had begun, Starling sat back in his chair. He looked pensive.

"I have to say I can't see anything out of place here. Everything looks about as solid as it could be. It's almost a textbook inquiry." He drummed his fingers on his desk for a while. "Except for the fact there's no arrest and no credible suspect."

Cross said nothing. She set down the sheet she had been reading – the conclusions from the pathologist's report – and waited.

"And, of course, in many cases similar to this, the evidence simply doesn't turn up a suspect. At least not until a thorough inquiry like this happens upon the right stone to turn over."

"Unless he is the stone, and he's deliberately leaving it in place."

"That is the dilemma." Starling shrugged. He pulled open his desk drawer and took out a packet of tissues, then blew his nose lightly, his cold was almost gone now.

"What about the alibi?" Cross asked. Starling came to sit back down, pouring them both more water.

"He was on annual leave over the time Layla went missing and her body dumped. And he did book an Airbnb in a village called Keswick." He turned the screen on his laptop, which was already showing a Google Maps route from the South Coast up to the Lake District.

"Six hours six minutes. Three hundred and fifty-five miles. The host thinks they remember him turning up, a couple of days before the abduction, and then leaving six nights later. But they're not absolutely sure, nor are they able to say if he was actually there all the time. And why would they be?" He drummed his fingers again.

"Would there be any traffic records?" Cross interrupted him. "If he drove up and down the motorway to get there, would that be held on some database somewhere?"

Starling shook his head. "More than two years after the event? Not a chance." His fingers began their rhythm again. "So where does that leave us?" He sucked in air through his teeth, and seemed to be asking rhetorically, since he continued himself, "There's nothing in the case file that looks out of place; he appears to have at least a partial alibi. On the other hand, we have a possible sighting of him on the beach the day Layla was abducted, and then we have the possible approach to the children outside the swimming pool." He stopped the drumming and looked sharply at Cross.

"Your face was interesting while Mrs Martin explained how she got her dates mixed up. What did you think about that?"

Cross tried to answer as honestly as she could. "When she first told me, I thought she was lying. But the second time, when she told you as well, then I wasn't as sure."

"Why?"

"I don't know. Just a feeling I suppose."

Starling didn't answer this, and stayed silent a long time. After a while he began drumming his fingers again. Finally, when he spoke he seemed to have reached a conclusion.

"I have to say, on balance, this appears to weigh considerably in DI Clarke's favour. We don't have any firm evidence that places him as a suspect, and there's considerable evidence to suggest he was over three hundred miles away when Layla was taken. Altogether, this feels like some sort of crazy—"

"What *don't* we know?" Cross surprised herself by interrupting him. He looked affronted. But then Cross picked up the pathologist's report again.

"Come on, what is it we don't know?" she persisted. "In all this?"

He looked at her, then nodded very lightly. "Well. The obvious thing we don't know is who murdered Layla Martin. My point, if you'd have let me finish, is that I don't think we have any evidence whatsoever that DI Clarke had anything to—"

"There's something else we don't know." She held the paper out to her boss, but he didn't take it, and Cross shook her head.

"We don't know *how* she died."

Finally, Starling leaned forward to look at the report again.

"The cause of death is unknown, right?" Cross went on. "They weren't able to say exactly why she died. Only that it might have been from fright, causing her heart to stop?"

Starling waited, not moving.

"I mean, it's clear it was *murder*. She was abducted, and there are the marks on her neck from where the killer tried to strangle her, and the cut marks on the ear and her waist. But none of those killed her, so something else did."

"It's not as uncommon as it might sound, to be literally scared to death."

"That's what it says here. But it also says that's just a possibility. And the man who phoned through to say he killed Layla, he said he removed the ear because he bit it. Maybe he wanted to avoid leaving teeth marks?"

"Yes."

"And the section around her waist? Did he bite that too?"

"I have no idea. He may have done. He didn't say."

"But what if *he* didn't bite the girl. Not at her waist anyway?"

The idea was still forming in Cross's mind, more a feeling at this point, that something was missing. She fell silent, needing time. Meanwhile Starling made a steeple of his hands and sat back at his desk. He stayed there, waiting, until she was ready.

"OK," Cross continued. "The one thing I don't understand. In this whole file, there's no mention of snakes. Not in the pathologist report, nor anywhere that I've read."

"Correct. But why would there be?"

"Because..." Cross frowned, needing the question to crystalise her feeling into a thought. "Well, if it *is* Clarke we're looking for well... he *has* snakes." Cross looked away a moment, then leaned forward again, eyes widening.

She'd got it.

"What if that was *how* she died? I mean, if you're going to abduct and murder a child, and you keep poisonous snakes as pets, mightn't you combine the two... interests?" At once, the idea felt both insane and yet somehow right. Or possible at least.

A look passed across Starling's face, which went from mild irritation, to mild interest. But he said nothing.

"At least we could see if it's relevant. Now we know that Clarke has snakes, maybe they might explain how she died?" To her own mind, her voice sounded plaintive, more hopeful than convincing.

Starling didn't answer directly, but he kept his eye on her, picked up his desk telephone and pulled it towards him. Then he lifted the receiver, before changing his mind and dropping it back down. He pressed the conference call button instead, so that Cross could hear. Then he began scrolling through the list of saved contacts. Seconds later it was dialling. Starling used the time to speak.

"I'm calling the pathologist who carried out the post-mortem. We go back a bit." There wasn't time to say more before the line was answered.

"George! It's Steven Starling. Have you got a minute?"

"Hello, Steven." The voice that came through the speaker was friendly. "Only if it really is a minute. I've got an post mortem scheduled for four and I haven't had lunch yet."

"I'll be quick. Can't keep the dead waiting."

There was a half-laugh on the line. "What do you need?"

"You carried out the post-mortem on Layla Martin."

A pause. "Yes. I did."

"And you stated the cause of death was impossible to determine?"

Another pause. "Not exactly, as I remember it. The cause of death was relatively easy to establish. Her heart stopped, which meant her brain was starved of oxygen. What we were unable to say with certainty was *why* it stopped."

"But you speculated that it might have been simple fear?"

"I wouldn't call it simple. It's not so much fear itself, but the physical manifestation of fear. The heart is a pump. If the muscles that surround it become too tight, they can crush it, or restrict the flow of blood going in and out. Either will cause it to fail, and it doesn't need to fail for very long before it causes irreversible damage. It's relatively unusual in humans, because we don't tend to lead terrifying lives. But in other animals – those captured for display in zoos for example – it's rather common."

"And that's what happened in this case?"

"Likely yes. There are other possibilities, of course. The victim might have had a weakness in her heart, which made it give out. We can't say for sure. What we were able to determine was that the heart failed, which led to hypoxia of the brain. Excuse me, my sandwich is staring at me and I'm going to give it a bite."

Starling gave him a minute, as a few grunts of satisfaction came through the speaker.

"Did you check the body for the presence of toxins from a snake bite?"

The noises stopped.

"No. I didn't." The voice came back in the end. And then both men began to speak at once. Starling fell quiet, letting the pathologist speak.

"We carry out a range of standard tests, depending upon how the victim presents, and on the instructions of the investigation team. And no one ever mentioned snake venom. Actually, I don't think it's something I've *ever* checked for." The man paused. "Is there something I should be aware of?"

"At this point, it's very unlikely, but I'd appreciate you keeping this conversation confidential."

"Of course. Goes without saying."

Starling considered. "If Layla had been bitten by a snake, *could* that have caused her heart to stop?"

There was another silence.

"I'm not sure I'm qualified to say. Maybe. Maybe not."

"If she had been bitten, and it caused her heart to fail, would that have been picked up?"

Another pause, but when he spoke he sounded more certain. "I find it difficult to believe I would have missed the puncture wounds that would indicate a snake bite. Except..."

"Go on?"

"You'll recall there were two unusual wounds on the body? A portion of the left ear was missing, and there was a small area on the right side of her waist where some tissue was also removed. I speculated at the time that the size, shapes and locations was consistent with it being removed by a small blade of some type, possibly a kitchen knife, but that it wasn't possible to say why it was removed. I suppose it's conceivable it was done to remove puncture wounds. Although I stress, that's pure speculation."

"Of course. *Would* you have been able to tell? At the time of the post-mortem? If you had been told there was the possibility the child died from a snake bite? Would there have been evidence left in the body?"

When he replied to this question, the pathologist sounded circumspect.

"Can you give me twenty minutes? I'm going to have to make a phone call of my own at this point."

Starling rang off and stared at Cross. They didn't speak much as they waited, but in less than ten minutes the phone rang again.

"Starling."

"Steven. I've spoken to a friend of mine in the US. Highly experienced pathologist. Did a number of years in Australia too, which is why I thought they might have something to add."

"And? Does he?"

"She. And yes, but not so much from criminal cases. It seems your average Aussie murderer still prefers a good old-fashioned stabbing. But she's worked on a fair few accidental deaths from snake bites – it's more common out there than I realised."

"OK. Go on."

"It seems there are several ways that snake venom can attack the human body. But the two most common would be causing the kidneys to fail, and – wait for it – causing the heart to fail. And before you ask, yes, the latter would present in an almost identical way to what happened with this victim. However, that's far from conclusive."

"Of course. But you would have been able to check? There are tests?"

"Yes." He sounded cautious now. "But it would help a lot if we knew the species of snake."

"We can check what species of snake Clarke has," Cross muttered, more to herself than the Super. But that wasn't the question he wanted to ask.

"OK. Now for the sixty-four-million-dollar question. Would you be able to tell *now*? If we exhumed the body?"

A hesitation. "I have to say you've really put me off my lunch. An exhumation. It's been, what? Two years?" Another pause. "OK. In theory, certainly possible, but it would depend upon what state the body is in. In turn, that would depend on a number of factors – what depth it was buried, how well-sealed the casket was, and whether the body was embalmed. I've seen bodies where the facial features are still recognisable after that period of time. And I've seen a kind of human soup with bones in. No way of knowing in advance what we'd get."

A few minutes later Starling pressed the button to end the call. The room fell silent.

"Exhumation?" Cross screwed up her face in distaste.

"Well, you've seen it." Starling waved a hand over the piles of paper that now covered his desk. "There's nothing else here. If it was Clarke, and if he used his damn snakes to kill the girl, I don't see any other way we're going to prove it."

"Even if we did find evidence of... snake venom. It wouldn't show it was Clarke's actual snake, would it? Wouldn't he just argue that it was someone else with another snake, of the same species?"

"He might, but would you believe it, if you were on the jury?"

Cross didn't answer.

"Alternatively, he might recognise that we knew, and confess. But even if not, we'd know for sure it was him, and likely it would prise apart any defences he's laid to protect himself. We could launch a full-scale investigation. He'd be finished, either way."

She nodded, her face still twisted with the idea of it.

"There is another problem, though," Starling went on.

"What?"

"If we tell him we're exhuming the body to look for

evidence of snake venom, then he's going to know damn well we suspect his involvement. And that will give him plenty of time to destroy any remaining evidence that might still exist." Starling stared off into the distance. His office overlooked the car park, but there was a good-sized patch of sky still visible.

"So, what do we do?"

"I don't have the faintest idea. Basically, we need a false reason to exhume. Something that he'll go along with because he knows it doesn't implicate him, but which allows us to carry out the tests we need to do, on the quiet."

He stared at her, looking blank. And as he did, an idea came to Cross.

"There is one thing we could do," she began. "It's a bit weird but..."

FIFTY-FIVE

Clarke surveyed his world. His team – expanded again so that he now had fifteen officers reporting directly to him. All were hard at work on tasks that would get them precisely nowhere. Further afield, he knew that a squad car was currently stationed on the road outside Rachel and Jon Martin's house, where two more officers were wasting their time. Or perhaps not completely. Perhaps it would reassure the parents to see it there. Or maybe it would keep their minds on the threat against their son.

Gale.

Just the thought of him sent sparks fizzing and buzzing around his mind. He would be a kind of recompense, Clarke felt now. For the mistakes Clarke had made, and the failure of courage that his sister had represented at her death. This time around there would be no fear, no hesitation. His plan now was complete. He had assessed and refined every detail until he was certain it couldn't be improved any further. There was still some room for risk, some space for something to go wrong, but he had complete faith in his ability to improvise under pressure

– recent events had proven that. Now it was just a matter of choosing the moment.

"Sir." Clarke's musings were interrupted by one of his junior detectives. She'd just gotten off the phone.

"What is it?"

"Something a bit strange. We've had another call come in from the *Crimebusters* team." Clarke almost lost all interest – he hadn't made his second call yet, so this had to be either fake or a mistake. But then again, he couldn't show that he knew that. So he made himself look sharp.

"He's called again?"

"No. At least, it doesn't seem so. The number traced back to a pay-as-you-go mobile, and it was a woman's voice. She didn't give a name."

"Well, what did she say?" Clarke struggled to disguise the irritation in his voice. Whatever this was, it was a distraction to his grand plans, and he wished he could simply send this woman back to her desk.

"Not very much. She just said this would help us find who killed Layla Martin, and she gave us a bunch of letters and numbers."

Clarke waited, then when the woman didn't go on, he snapped. "Letters and numbers?"

"Yeah. Bo9DK4TZ2D. Six letters, four numbers. B, zero, nine, D, K, T—"

"OK, OK. Nothing else? Just some code?"

"She repeated it twice, and said it would tell us all we need to know. Then she rings off." The young detective waited, while Clarke fought to concentrate.

"Well, what does it mean?"

"I've no idea sir."

"Show me the whole code," Clarke demanded, then he thought while she slipped the handwritten digits in front of him. He had no idea what they meant, and barely cared. It was some nutter trying to make this about themselves, trying to piggyback onto his – Clarke's – brilliance, and now *he* had to deal with it.

And then, as if the timing hadn't already been irritating, Starling came slobbing down through the office in his ill-fitting uniform.

"Something up?" Starling asked, dumb-ass smile fixed into place. Before Clarke could do anything to stop her, the young detective was telling him about the mysterious code, as if it might actually be something.

"It's probably nothing," Clarke interrupted them. "Highly likely to be a hoax, appeals like this often bring the crazies out of the woodwork."

He regretted the comment as Starling turned his eyes onto him. "It could be. Have you looked into it?"

"Looked into...?"

"Have you tried to find out what it's referring to? I'd be reluctant to dismiss it without at least trying to find out that."

As Starling spoke, Clarke could already see another of his team pulling up the Google home screen and typing the digits in one by one. He frowned, anxious now.

What the hell was this?

Starling and the young woman detective gathered around the screen, as it returned a list of results. But after a couple of seconds, it was clear they all led to the same thing.

"What is that?" the woman detective asked.

The man who'd typed the search answered, he was close enough to read the text.

"It's a page for a pet microchip reader."

Twenty minutes later and combined knowledge in the room about animal microchip technology and practices had gone from practically none, to near-expert level. The chips them-

selves were about the size of a grain of rice, and used radio
frequency identification technology, known as RFID, to store a
unique identifying code inside the body of an animal. It was
harmless and almost painless to insert, and was typically used in
pets, but the devices were also used in livestock farming. The
code that the tip-off had revealed was not an actual code from a
pet microchip, but rather the Amazon product number that
brought up the sales page for a machine that read them.

By the time this was known, almost everyone in the room
had stopped doing the work Clarke had asked them to do, and
was joining in, asking variations on the same question.

*Why would someone send a hint about a pet microchip
reader?*

And the team – which comprised skilled and experienced
detectives – didn't hesitate in trying to speculate, and search
what they knew for links. In minutes, they'd identified that their
list of possible suspects – a man long since eliminated – had
included a man who had trained as a vet, and another who
worked on a farm.

Clarke listened, his irritation and frustration beginning to
evaporate, as he saw the possible advantages of this – *bizarre* –
twist of fate. After a half hour of this, with Starling still there, he
indicated Clarke's little office with a tilt of his head.

"A word, if I might, DI Clarke?" Starling began walking
towards the room without waiting.

Clarke felt his brow furrowing again, but he followed.

"Are you thinking what I'm thinking?" Starling asked, once
he'd closed the door behind Clarke. He sat easily on the edge of
Clarke's desk, leaving Clarke himself nowhere comfortable to
put himself. He ended up standing uneasily beside the door.

I sincerely doubt it.

"What are you thinking, sir?"

Starling looked serious for a moment. "I'm thinking that any
moment now you're going to be asking me what the options are

for using one of these scanner things over whatever's left of Layla Martin, but I want to urge the greatest possible caution."

"I wasn't—" Clarke stopped himself. He didn't have time for this. He needed to go over his plan; it was almost ready to go, but it was complicated, and he didn't have the bandwidth for anything else. Clarke had a very high opinion of his own intellect, and in reality he was clever enough to know there was a limit. If he had to divide his attention between too many disparate strands of thought, that's when mistakes could creep in. He fixed a neutral look on his face and tried to think.

What would a detective in his position do, if he wasn't also the killer? How should he act right now?

He didn't want to face the answer – and not just because it was a massive waste of time. Some bullshit hoax cooked up by some weirdo. There was another reason too. Layla's body was in the ground. When the remains were released back to the family, he'd done his best to point them in the direction of cremation. But they'd insisted on a burial. It turned out he'd had the poor fortune to pick a family who owned their own plot in a cemetery – who the hell still had one of those? But it didn't matter, she was under the ground and forgotten. The very last thing he wanted to do was dig her back up again.

He stared at his boss, sitting there, waiting for an answer. Starling suspected nothing, but if Clarke wasn't interested in this stupid microchip, he might become suspicious. And if they wanted to dig her up and scan her like a rabid dog, well... where was any harm, really?

"What are the options, sir?"

Starling shook his head. "I've been involved in a couple of exhumations and it's not good. We'd need agreement from the Home Office and oversight from Environmental Health. It's expensive, too. Not just the cost of a couple of shovels." He paused. "And it's traumatic for the family. I'd need assurances from you that there aren't other areas which are more promising for the inquiry. Have you come across anything looking at the family history?"

The direct question jolted Clarke. The truth was, he hadn't had the time to pay it much attention; his own plans had taken priority.

"Nothing yet, sir." He hesitated, but knew he had to go on. In order to look convincing in his act of wanting to find Layla's killer, he had no choice but to appear keen to follow this new lead. "I think we have to do it." He felt disgusted at himself for saying the words.

"So do I, Kieran. So do I."

Clarke sighed inwardly, knowing a new task had just landed in his lap. He would need to work through a ton of paperwork to set up an exhumation, and it would find nothing. It was simply an expensive, bizarre, but largely irrelevant distraction.

But it wouldn't put his plans back for long.

FIFTY-SIX

Three days later, Clarke made it known that he wasn't to be disturbed. It gave him the space to doze lightly in his office. He did so easily, knowing he would need to be as alert as possible later on. He preferred to work at night – the dark held few fears, and most people would be asleep in their beds, leaving the world to the hunters.

The nonsense of organising the exhumation was out of the way, at least. It still had to be authorised, but that was a formality, with Starling's approval already given. And once the rubber had been stamped there was nothing for Clarke to do. He might not even attend when they actually dug her up – that all depended upon how things turned out after tonight. He wet his lips with his tongue, tasting the air.

He left the office early, going first to the lock-up to make his final preparations there. He'd installed a small fridge downstairs, and he had stocked it with food. Then he checked the shackles were secure. It felt strange touching them, knowing they would soon be filled with the child. *Gale.* Clarke returned home to wait, impatient for the drama to begin.

He didn't cook, but picked up a take-out from the local

curry house, eating it in the kitchen, with the TV and radio off. He fed his girls. He showered. He paced.

At midnight he fired up his laptop computer, and set up the programmes that would route the call from his second mobile phone in another complicated and circuitous route. As he did so, he thought briefly of the call they'd received about the microchip – it had come from a simple burner phone. He could have used the same technique, but had chosen not to, since it could still be tracked, even though the number wouldn't be listed anywhere. That call had come from somewhere in south London. He wondered who had made it, and what their intention was. But he shook the thought away, he had to focus. Everything now depended upon his focus.

With the threat made against Gale Martin, certain procedures had kicked in, and others had been adapted to the particular situation. Adapted with the help of the lead investigator, DI Clarke. One of these was that there would be two uniformed officers stationed in a squad car outside the Martins' home whenever Gale was there. A second was that, should a renewed or live threat be transmitted to these officers, they should either go into the house to increase the level of direct protection, or that they should move Gale Martin out of the property, to a secure location where he would be safe.

At 1 a.m., Clarke made the call, connecting his second phone to his laptop so that it was routed through the software. He'd pre-recorded what he wanted it to say, so that when his own police mobile phone rang, he would be able to answer it as normal. He listened as the file began to play, coming from his secret phone, to his normal phone. A few seconds later he hit start on a recorded app he'd installed, and then began talking, demanding to know who was speaking, and where they were. The effect he wanted to create was that the call had woken him, but he'd quickly understood its significance, and tried to secure it as evidence.

Then he ended the call on the first phone, but kept talking on the second, as if unaware the caller had hung up. Afterwards he hung up on his regular mobile too.

His heart was thudding in his chest. There was no turning back now. In the days to come, the telephone records and the timings of the calls would all be studied with great care, and perhaps a little suspicion. But if everything looked just right, he would be beyond suspicion.

He removed the SIM and battery from the burner phone, and placed all three in his blender, then turned it on. The noise was horrible, a furious grating as the blades attacked the metal and plastic, but the device was destroyed in seconds, well beyond the state where any information could be recovered from it. He carefully emptied the remains into a plastic bag, washed the blender, and left it to drain. Then he made a second call.

"This is Detective Inspector Clarke, are you in position outside the Martin house?" he asked, as soon as the line connected. "Is anything going on?"

It was a man who answered, PC Paul Johnson. Clarke knew him well. Indeed, he'd specifically selected him for this role.

"Uh, yes sir, we're here. There's nothing."

"You're sure? I've just had a call. Sounds like the same guy who threatened the boy before."

There was a pause. Clarke could imagine the man blinking in the darkness. Could almost see his barrel-chest puffing out as the disappointment of spending another boring shift was replaced with the hope that something dramatic might yet happen.

If only he knew.

"Negative, sir. They've all gone to bed. Lights went off about an hour ago."

"OK. I need you to get in there." Clarke waited a beat. "*Right now.* From what he's just said, there's a chance he may actually be inside the house now." There was no need to pass on exactly the message he'd just sent – he wouldn't be expected to do so, and he had to act exactly like a senior officer would do, in these circumstances. He heard Johnson stammering, not keeping up.

"I... er..."

"You still there?"

"Yes sir."

"Why?! Get in there, now. The pair of you. I've received credible information that the suspect may be inside the Martin house, right now."

Still the dumb shit seemed unable to act. Had he been the right choice, after all?

"Er, how sir? They're all asleep."

Jesus.

"Then wake them the hell up. Get your eyes on Gale Martin and call me back the second you do so. I'm on my way there right now." With that, Clarke ended the call and grabbed his car keys. He took a moment to draw in some deep breaths, to revel in how his head was almost fizzing with excitement. Then he headed for the door. He picked up the bag of broken mobile phone as he went.

The route he drove took him past a public bin he'd identified earlier, at the entrance to a park. It was used every day by dog walkers to deposit the bagged waste from their dogs. His own bag, when tossed in with them, looked similar enough that it would never raise suspicion. And no one would want to rummage around, investigating its real contents. As he got back into the car, his regular work mobile rang again.

"Uh, sir?" It was Johnson.

"Can you see him? The boy?"

"He's asleep – well, he was asleep. We've woken him up, and the parents."

"Can you see him? Is the boy OK?"

"Yes sir. Affirmative sir. I'm in the doorway of his bedroom. He's in bed, with the mother."

"OK. Good." Clarke pretended to sound relieved. "I need you to go downstairs. Check for any signs of forced entry. Someone needs to stay with the boy, too."

"Sure." Johnson sounded dazed. Out of his depth. *Good.*

"Stay on the line with me. I'm nearly there."

Clarke had the house in view now. This had to happen fast. He kept speaking, on the car's hand-free system.

"Sir, I've checked all the windows and doors. No signs of a break in."

"Good. Thank you, Johnson." Clarke was quiet for a few seconds, but then carried on. "OK. There's one other possibility to explain the message I've received," he said, as if thinking aloud.

"Uh, OK. What's that sir?"

Clarke hesitated, as if he didn't want to voice this. "If someone in that house has just sent me a threat against Gale, and there's no intruders, then we might be looking at one of the parents." He tapped his thumb rapidly against the steering wheel, as if he was thinking hard on the spot. "Or maybe both of them. Until we know for sure, I need to you to get Gale away." He spoke as if he'd just made the decision, but now it was made, it needed acting on. "Get him out of there. We'll pull him back to the station where we can be sure, and until we figure out what the hell is going on."

"Um..." Johnson sounded anxious. "I don't know how easy that's gonna be, sir. The mum's pretty protective."

"I need you to do this, Johnson. Whatever it takes. If you have to arrest her to get the boy out of there, you do it? You understand?"

"Yes, sir."

"Can you do this?"

"Yes, sir."

"Good man."

Clarke had said enough. He hung up the phone.

———

Inside the Martin house there was a sense of chaotic shock. It was Jon Martin who had gone downstairs in his dressing gown, to answer the door, but when the officers had gone upstairs they'd found Rachel Martin awake, too, in the boy's bedroom. She'd stayed there. She seemed unwilling to let her son out of her sight.

Now, Johnson came back upstairs, standing in the doorway. "Ma'am, I'm afraid we've..." Johnson stopped, seeing the look of terror on the boy's face. "Perhaps I could I have a word outside?"

They went into the hallway, and Rachel Martin closed the door, telling her son again that there was nothing to be scared about. Johnson spoke in a low voice.

"Ma'am, we've received what appears to be a credible and imminent threat against your son. As a result, we need to take him to a secure location where we can guarantee his safety." Johnson cleared his throat.

The woman was breathing hard, obvious terror written on her face. But she nodded, as if working hard to keep control of herself. "OK. I'll come with him."

Johnson almost nodded too, but then he shook his head. "No. That's not going to be possible."

"What do you mean, not possible?" Rachel Martin's voice rose in pitch. "I'm not leaving him."

Clarke's words rang loud in Johnson's head. From some-where he found the right words. "I'm sorry ma'am, but you're going to have to. The nature of the threat... I can't go into details for security reasons..." He thought. "But if you don't do *exactly* what I say, you may be putting your son in danger."

"Why?" Rachel looked newly terrified. "What are you saying? He's safe with me. He's *only* safe with me."

After what Clarke had just told him, the mother's words sounded suspiciously like a threat, even more so when she went on.

"No. I'm not letting you take him," Rachel insisted.

"Ma'am, you're going to have to." Johnson's voice hardened.

"*No.* Absolutely not. I'm not leaving him."

Johnson stared at her, wondering what to do. He loved everything about being a cop. His favourite role was sorting out the drunks, fighting outside the clubs. You could throw them around – within reason, since everyone wore body cameras these days, and people had mobile phones. But you could be pretty forceful when you chucked them in the van and get away with it. And he'd been excited at first to be sent to guard the Martins' house from a psychopathic killer. Until it had proved to be incredibly dull. But this was anything but dull. He was almost overwhelmed by the moment. The intensity of it.

"Ma'am, the nature of the threat—"

"No. No way am I leaving him."

"You don't have a choice." Automatically Johnson's hand reached for his handcuffs, which he always wore clipped to his belt.

"What are you *doing*?" Rachel Martin must have seen the movement. "Are you going to arrest me?" The tone of her voice made him pause, and she went on. "This is crazy!"

Johnson realised she was talking to her husband now, who had arrived at the top of the stairs. Johnson swallowed, glanced at the father. Another threat. Two against one. But he'd been trained for this. *Take control of the situation, demonstrate authority.*

"That's exactly what I've been ordered to do. If you don't comply."

"Comply? What's going on?" Jon Martin interrupted.

"This officer wants to take Gale."

"Take Gale where? Why?"

"Stay right where you are, sir. I need to remove your son to a safe place. I cannot reveal where that is at this time. Nor can I reveal the nature of the threat, but I can assure you it's highly credible." Now the words were flowing like water to Johnson. His training combining easily, dangerously, with the thousand cops shows he'd watched on TV. "I need you both to step aside and let me do my job."

Rachel looked at her husband for a while, then she turned back to Johnson. "No way." She said again. And then she made to move.

Almost without thought, Johnson had positioned himself so as to block Rachel's path back to the boy's bedroom door, and as she tried to push past him now, he moved fast. He caught her arm, rolled it around her back and lifted. Hard. Immediately she screamed, and he backed off a little. But he held her arm there, pinning her in place.

"Mrs Martin, I'm not letting you go in there. And if you don't back off I'll arrest you for assaulting a police officer."

"Assaulting?"

The other officer had joined them now, younger then Johnson, and less experienced. He'd spent his last few shifts enthralled by Johnson's stories about how real policing happened. Johnson tried to signal with his eyes what he needed his colleague to do.

"What's going on, Paul?"

"I need to get the boy to safety," Johnson ordered. They were the same rank, but there was no doubt who was senior. "You need to stay with the parents until back-up gets here. It's on its way."

The second officer came over, eyes wide, as Rachel continued to struggle. But with the grip Johnson used, it was easy for him to keep her fixed in place. He lifted her arm higher again, aiming to quieten her down.

"Get. Off. Me!" She managed to say, through panted breaths. But Johnson expertly transferred Rachel's arm to the younger man, checking he too had the correct grip.

"What are you doing?" Rachel said again, but Johnson ignored her.

"Get her into the bedroom there," Johnson was committed now. He cocked his head towards the master bedroom. "I'll get the boy somewhere safe." His colleague did what he was told, Rachel's struggles now useless. But her last call was to her husband.

"Jon, do something!"

He took a hesitant step closer to the action. "Is this really necessary?" Jon Martin asked.

"Yes, sir. It is." Johnson told him. "And if you don't want to be arrested, you'll accompany my colleague into the other room right now."

"No!" Rachel called out. "Don't do it, Jon. Stay with Gale."

Jon Martin hesitated, and Johnson willed him to move. The father looked like he took care of himself, yet Johnson had zero doubt he could handle him. But that would leave no one to move the child.

"Don't do it, Jon. *Don't you dare* leave Gale."

"Jesus Christ, Rachel," Jon Martin seemed to crack from the pressure. He took another step nearer the boy's door, but then stopped as Johnson tensed. He turned to his wife.

"Look, I don't know what's going on here, but us getting arrested isn't going to help. I think we need to trust the officer."

"That's right, sir." Johnson growled.

Rachel struggled again, but the other officer tightened his grip, telling her to stay still.

"Where are you taking Gale?" Jon Martin turned back to Johnson. But the big man wasn't listening now. He had his opportunity and he was going to use it. He banged open the door to the boy's room and looked around. The boy was safe still, lying in a foetal position on the bed, shaking with fear.

"Don't worry, son. I'm going to get you to safety. Alright?"

Johnson could bench-press twice his bodyweight, and the child weighed nothing. Or maybe that was just because Johnson was so damn fired up from the excitement of it.

"He'll be somewhere safe. And back-up will be here to keep you informed." He nodded to the father as he pressed him out the way with one arm, the other easily carrying the boy. Then he moved quickly down the stairs. And out the house.

Clarke watched from up the street as Johnson exited the house, the boy under one arm. The parents nowhere in sight. *Perfect.* He made a fist as he floored the car, wheel-spinning as it accelerated. Then he braked hard to come to stop behind Johnson's marked police car, just as Johnson was shutting the rear door, with Gale Martin inside.

Clarke leapt out, and started talking at once, not wanting to give Johnson any time to think. "The parents are inside still?"

"Yes, sir."

"Anything suspicious?"

"No. We have the mother restrained upstairs."

Clarke's eyes flared wide for a second. It wouldn't have mattered had Johnson not been up to his role, Clarke had a back-up plan – which involved going in and getting Gale himself – but the big man had excelled himself.

"Good job. This is probably a false alarm, but you've done well. Now stay by the front door until back-up gets here. I'll take the boy to the station."

"Sir..." Johnson hesitated. Something about the change of plan clearly registering as odd. He rolled the keys to the car around in his hand, but didn't pass them across.

"Give me the damn keys." Clarke held out his hand.

There was a moment's further hesitation, then Johnson passed them across.

"Good. Now go. *Guard the door.*"

Johnson went back towards the front door, looking around at the night with alarm, as Clarke got into the car.

He was unable to resist a smile as he spied Gale's terrified look in the back seat, the way the boy was desperately trying to open the doors, but this was a police car, the rear specially adapted for the doors not to open from the inside, a metal grille separating the rear from the front. He fired the engine.

Don't get complacent. Not out of the woods yet. Not even into them.

Clarke could see the fear in the boy's eyes as he barrelled off down the street, but it didn't matter. He drove fast, following a route he'd studied and pored over through long nights of planning. The first part took him in view of several CCTV cameras. It would help if other cars were captured at the same time – but even if not, it didn't matter. Rather than proceed directly towards the station, he then turned off, going a more circuitous route. The explanation he would later give was that he was avoiding taking a route that might be predicted.

Finally, he slowed. Lining up his approach. The location he'd chosen was quiet, no houses in view, and almost zero chance of other traffic interrupting him at this time of night. The kid was screaming now, crying in the back of the car. Clarke was so focussed he almost hadn't noticed.

Now.

He veered hard to the left, keeping the vehicle in control

through the slight skid as it left the road, then aimed to break through the initial line of bushy brambles. They slapped against the car as it bumped off the road. Just beyond were two small trees. He aimed at the larger of them, looking to hit it on the left-hand side of the car's bonnet. There was a roaring bang on impact, then the airbag fired. Clarke slammed into it, harder than he'd imagined it would be, but not so much that he felt injured. In fact, he felt nothing. Only a rigid, laser focus. Breathing hard, he paused for only a few seconds before it had deflated enough that he could move. He unclipped his seatbelt and pushed at the door. He was ready to beat it open if he needed to, but luckily it was undamaged and swung open easily.

He stumbled out, and pulled his mobile phone from his pocket. He threw it into the undergrowth, a few metres from the vehicle. Then he reached into his jacket pocket and grabbed two more items. The first was a small emergency vehicle-glass hammer, and he used this to smash the corner of the driver's window. It shattered on the first blow, and on the second he was able to knock out a hole.

Ignoring the kid, who was more moaning than screaming now, he took the other item, a small canister of tear gas. He could have got some from the station, but it was easily available on the dark web. He ripped off the safety, and aimed it inside the car, pointing at the kid's face. He pressed the trigger and poured the whole contents inside, still ignoring the screams. Within seconds the whole car was filled with clouds of the stuff.

Clarke gave it thirty seconds, then pulled open the rear door. Gale Martin was slumped sideways on the seat, his eyes rolled back in his head. Clarke felt a beat of fear that it might actually have killed him, despite his research. Still, he leaned in, binding the boy and taping his mouth. Then he grabbed at the kid's feet and pulled him outside, not caring that the boy's head thwacked on the ground as he did so. Then he scooped him up into his arms and started moving.

It was fifty metres to the van. The boy was heavy – and not quite unconscious – and Clarke had been in an accident, but he could have run ten times the distance, such was the effect of the adrenaline in his system. He got there and tore open the back door, then dumped the child inside. He shut the door and locked it, then ran around to the driver's door. Inside the cab he got his first glimpse at his own face, eyes white in a mess of fresh blood.

It was an eleven-minute drive from where he'd abandoned the police car to the lock-up – as close as he'd dared. Once he got there, he opened up, and then once again heaved the still-dazed, blubbering child onto his shoulders. He got Gale inside the unit and down the steps into his pre-prepared dungeon and, working quickly, he got the ankle and wrist restraints secured to the shackles he'd concreted into the floor.

Clarke noticed how much his own hands were shaking as he worked, but instead of making him anxious it thrilled him. This was no fantasy: *he was doing this*. No. He had done it. After two years of inactivity, he was all-powerful again. He had a child. He shook the thought away. Regained his focus.

Not yet. Don't celebrate yet.

He checked the room, double-checked it, but was satisfied. The boy looked terrible, but he shouldn't die from the effects of the gas, and he had water. Furthermore, Clarke needed to get back. Outside, he locked everything up, moved the van around the corner and left on the motorbike. He parked that a two-minute jog from where the stricken police car was still hidden in the bushes beside the road. Even though he'd planned for it to be almost invisible had any traffic gone past, he was still hugely relieved to find it looked exactly as he'd left it.

Again, he checked around himself quickly, to make sure there was nothing he had missed. The weather had been dry and though the ground was scuffed, vegetation trampled down, there were no footprints – one less worry.

He got back into the car, strapped himself into the seatbelt, and then pulled a set of handcuffs from his pocket – not his police-issued set, but another purchase from the online merchant sites of the dark web. He snapped one end around the steering wheel, and the other around his right wrist, then before he had time to consider the pain, he wrenched his hand – once, twice, three times – as if trying to break free. Finally he pulled the second tear-gas canister from his pocket. He pointed it at his face, took in a few final breaths of air, then pulled the tab.

For the second time in half an hour, the car filled almost at once with the chemical fumes. Within moments, Clarke was screaming in pain.

FIFTY-SEVEN

The dawn chorus started early and gently. But soon it gathered in pace so that – to Clarke's sparkling senses – it became incredibly beautiful. It almost appeared to him that the birds had gathered solely to perform their songs for him – a private concert in honour of the wonderful thing he had done. As it reached its crescendo, he bathed in it, marvelling in its exquisite beauty, its brilliance mirroring his own.

But there was one small problem. In the adrenaline-pumping rush of the previous night, to secure the child and ensure that neither suspicion nor blame would fall on him, he had neglected one element. Before handcuffing himself to the car's steering wheel, he hadn't considered when he would next use the toilet. In his planning phase, he'd actually expected to be discovered sooner – he'd imagined helicopters flying overhead, teams of men beating their way through the undergrowth, until they came across him. It was an unexpected bonus to hear the birds literally singing his praises. But all the same, he'd underestimated how inept his colleagues really were, and it was making him uncomfortable now.

Clarke considered his options. He might be able to free

himself enough, one-handed, to get the car door open, and relieve himself outside. It would be awkward, but soon he was going to need to try. But as he thought about that, another idea occurred to him. What better way to cement the impression that he was a victim in whatever had happened, just as much as the boy, than to be forced to relieve himself right here? In the seat. It would be embarrassing, but that was the point. He liked the idea.

But just then, there was the sound of an engine, not passing on the road, as others had that morning, but slowing and then stopping. Then shouts. The pressure on his bladder was still there, and suddenly he released it, feeling the hot liquid pooling in the seat, and running down his leg. The acrid smell steaming in the cool morning air. He breathed in deeply. A few moments later he tried a weak cry.

"Help, I'm in here!"

Then there was a face at the window, a copper – no one he knew – pale with fear. The door pulled open, Clarke jerked, so that he almost fell out sideways. The man had to catch him, before the handcuff on his wrist stopped him.

"Oh my—!" The officer recoiled in a horror that sent a pulse of excitement through Clarke.

"The kid, they took the kid."

"Sir, you're hurt. Don't move, There's an ambulance on its way."

Clarke did what he was told, leaning in to the fatigue he felt, the hangover from the adrenaline of the night before. The handcuffs were taken off first – he'd used a set that took the same key as his own standard-issue cuffs. But he wasn't allowed out of the car until the paramedics were content his neck was undamaged. All the while, he drew in sweet breaths of bottled oxygen that tasted like nectar after the tear gas.

Then they got him on a stretcher and carried him to an ambulance. By then it was just one of a dozen emergency vehicles that now crowded the scene. He spotted the Jaguar of DS Starling there, just before the man himself talked his way past the medics.

"Clarke – what the *hell* happened?"

Clarke explained as best he could with a voice that croaked and broke. The message he'd received, a man's voice, who claimed to be watching Gale as he slept. His own uncertainty over whether the perpetrator could actually be one of the parents, most likely Jon Martin. And then the rush to get Gale to the safety of the police station, following the protocol put in place and agreed by the Super himself. But on the way, Clarke's sense that he was being followed, and his subsequent decision to not take the predictable route, but to try and evade anyone who might be following. And then, run off the road by a black saloon car – maybe a BMW or an Audi, lights off so he didn't get the number plate – the impact of the crash, and seconds later, just as Clarke was checking Gale for possible injuries, two balaclava-clad men outside. One began hacking at the window with an axe of some sort. There was no time to react, before the glass gave way and the spray fired into his face. He'd managed to turn his head away just enough to protect his eyes, but still, instantly his whole face had lit up on fire. Then, when he'd come to, the rear door open, the kid gone, Clarke handcuffed to the wheel, unable to react.

"Shit." Starling looked utterly shell-shocked, giving Clarke the slight concern he might have overdone things, but it was clear from his next comment he'd bought it. Bought it all.

"You said *them*? There were two of them?"

"I think so. I can't be sure, but there must have been. One that was following me, another that ran me off the road."

He let himself pant, thinking now that the bastard should really let him get back on the oxygen. Quit the questions. But they kept coming. *Did he see their faces?* No – the balaclavas. *Age? Race?* Unknown. Finally, the questions ceased, and he interjected with his own.

"Do we know where he is? The kid?"

Starling answered with just the smallest movement of his head. "No."

Clarke had to imagine the scenes of chaos at the station, since the doctors refused his repeated requests to discharge him. His face hurt. He had significant abrasions on his face and neck, along with burns from the deployment of the airbag. His eyes were still swollen and puffy, despite the fact that he'd only sprayed a small amount of the pepper spray into his own face. Furthermore, he was told he was lucky not to have suffered any further injury from either the crash, or the firing of the airbag. In truth that wasn't quite the case, he had researched how modern cars vary the speed and strength at which the bags are deployed, and knew in advance what injuries he was likely to suffer.

Still, when he saw himself in the mirror he was thrilled with what he saw. No one was talking about whether he had in some way contributed to the abduction of the boy, and no one would – it was preposterous to imagine he might have left the car, even without the handcuffs.

On the contrary, he was being treated as a brave hero, who had done everything possible to thwart a bizarre and unexplained, but clearly highly professional operation to take the child. Every theory under the sun would be discussed, right up to the possibility that government agencies had been involved.

By the time Clarke came to give his statement, his mind was fully clear, and the delivery of lies, half-truths and false leads couldn't have gone better. Every answer was vague enough to send his team chasing ghosts. And while he would eventually come back to lead them – in perhaps the most high-profile investigation in modern policing history – that would have to wait. What was also clear was that he would need time off to recover from what had happened.

And so, less than twenty-four hours after kidnapping the child, he was finally discharged from the hospital and sent home. Not expected back at work.

He had time on his hands.

FIFTY-EIGHT

It was so easy, it was so wonderfully easy. As long as you were prepared to dedicate yourself to a cause, to put in the work, thinking and preparing. If you were willing to simply consider what *they* considered unconscionable, then it was child's play to outwit the ranks of oafs and goons that made up the personnel of the British police force. Clarke wondered, as he left his house and drove out to the unit, looking in his rear-view mirror every few moments at the gloriously clear road behind him, whether he might do this for his whole life, without ever being caught. Certainly he had got away with it this time.

He stopped outside the unit, alert and cautious now, like a fox coming out of its den when the wind wasn't blowing it its favour. But there were no warning signs. Nothing to show that anyone had visited since he'd deposited the boy the previous day. He went up to the door, listening hard before unlocking it. Nothing.

He just hoped that didn't mean the boy was already dead.

He took a final look around outside, then went in, shutting and locking the door behind him. The blinds on the small window were down, and he lifted them, letting a little natural light in. Then he switched on the PC, pulling up the feed from the monitor in the room below. He eagerly absorbed what it showed him.

The child was still on the bed, curled up like a foetus, which wasn't how he'd left him. If he *was* dead, it had happened after Clarke had brought him here. More likely that the pepper spray had worn off and he was sleeping, or just waiting.

Clarke scanned around the room with the camera. The bucket had been pushed away from the bed, as far as the chain allowed, suggesting it had been used, and adding further weight to the idea the child was fine. Clarke smiled.

As he dressed for the occasion, he imagined the fear the boy must have felt, when he'd woken up there. The tortured dreams he might be having at this very moment. He let the thought expand within him, enjoying the way the excitement swelled inside.

He hit play on the music, took a deep breath, and unlocked the upper door.

FIFTY-NINE

There was no fear exactly, when the car crashed. It was all sound and movement and *consequence*. The impact slammed Gale against the grille that divided the back of the car from the front. He'd had one arm hooked through the seatbelt, which turned him sideways, making it his side that took the brunt. And then in the dizzying moments afterwards, the man had sprayed something into his face, and his eyes had suddenly exploded into a pain so pure it was like nothing he had ever felt before. Gale had clawed at his eyes, with fingers that suddenly felt like fat clumsy sausages, he knew the man was grabbing him, hauling him, slapping tape across his mouth so that it was hard to breathe, pulling his hands behind his back, then binding them there.

He'd been half-carried through the wood – Gale knew the two of them had fallen at least twice, but perhaps many times – before he'd been bundled into another space, suddenly alone. There was cold, ribbed metal on the floor, metal walls. It was only when the noise of an engine rumbled through the space, and it began to move, that he knew it must be a van. He'd rolled into a corner, to stop himself banging into the sides as it bucked and banged. The pain in his eyes was still strong, but lessening now, it had to – such a pain couldn't be sustained.

And then the movement stopped, the door swung open. The man was there again, ordering him out, bundling him into some sort of farm building, and inside, down stone steps. He was thrown on a bed and metal shackles were put around his ankles. His hands were freed now. Clarke growled something Gale didn't hear, and went back up the stairs. He shut and locked the door. Then silence. The beginning of the wait.

That's when the fear had really come.

At first, he'd been too scared to call out, in case the man came back, but eventually the silence and stillness around him convinced him to try. But in the space his voice seemed weak and ineffective. He couldn't understand why. He let himself stop, to look around. To make sense of the place.

It was a large room, with him in the centre of it. The bed was secured to a heavy pillar, that appeared to be holding up the roof. There were other pillars, at different parts of the room. His ankle shackles ran to circles of metal that had been set into the floor; already the bracelets had rubbed off the skin where they touched him.

When he tried to get up, he found the chains would only allow him to reach about halfway across the room. If he lay down, he could just touch the bottom of the steps with his fingertips. Also within his range was a small fridge, the cable running to an electrical socket he couldn't reach. Inside were three bottles of water, and three supermarket sandwiches. Tuna and mayonnaise, cheese and mayonnaise, ham and mayonnaise. Gale didn't like mayonnaise. There was also a metal bucket.

There was nothing else. The room was otherwise bare – except, now he noticed that a camera had been installed at the top of the stairway. Right next to the only door.

He called out again, louder this time, then as loud as he could, a proper yell, but there was something odd about it again, the room itself seemed to swallow the sound.

And then he wanted her. Layla. His big sister. He didn't know if he could summon her, he knew she was the only person he could summon. But should he? Clearly this was the same place Clarke had brought her. The place he had killed her. So could Gale bring her back? Could she even be here?

And would there be any point? There was nothing she could do – he was going to kill Gale, that much was obvious.

I will not bring her here. I won't do that to her.

Gale refused to say her name, to even think her name again, but his courage didn't stop the tears.

As the hours went by, he realised the crying was helping to clean the chemical out of his eyes, and he kept doing it. Then he became thirsty, or perhaps gradually recognised that part of the sensation of pain in his body was a familiar one: extreme thirst. He was flummoxed for a while, until he remembered the fridge. Then he rolled off the bed and took the first two bottles, finishing them both in just a few gulps. He left the sandwiches.

Eventually – *five hours later, ten hours?* Maybe even twenty – he had no way of knowing – he curled up on the bed and let himself sleep.

When he awoke, nothing had changed. The room, the chains, the bed, everything was as it was before. The only thing was that the fear was less, tempered by not boredom certainly, but some absence of stimulation that dampened terror into something less urgent.

His mind turned to what Layla had done when she was here, what thoughts had gone through her head. She'd told him that, at this stage, she hadn't known she was going to die. Was that better or worse? He still refused to say her name, to do anything that might act to summon her.

He drank half of the final bottle of water, and after growing increasingly uncomfortable, used the bucket, then pushed it as far away as he could. He didn't know how long he'd been there, but thought it might be days already. He pulled apart one of the sandwiches, wiped away the mayonnaise, and ate it as best he could. Then he devoured a second, mayonnaise included, suddenly finding himself famished.

He wondered if he should have done more to ration what he had. But then, what was the point? He was going to die soon enough. That brought back the fear, a return of the tears – for himself, for his sister, for his mother and father, who would be even sadder this time around, because now they had lost both of their children. He wondered if they would believe him now. Would they catch Kieran Clarke? Gale did not consider for a moment whether they might catch him in time – before he came to kill him. He only thought about what might come after.

He had to use the bucket again, and then, to his horror, realised it wasn't going to be just a wee. For a long while, the smell had lingered in the room.

He wished he had a clock, or some way of checking how much time was passing. It seemed endless, the waiting. There was hardly any water left, and though he felt thirsty, he thought he should ration it now. He wondered if there was anything he could do with the empty bottles, any sort of weapon he could fashion. Eventually, he felt it must be late again, possibly the next day, or the one after that. He curled up on the bed. Tried to sleep.

And then there were noises again. Footsteps overhead. For a second he considered they might be rescuers. Maybe. But never really. He knew. He heard it in the tuneless whistling, the strange laughing. He got up. He considered trying to hide, but there was nowhere. Nothing to do but wait and see what happened next.

And what happened next was extraordinary.

SIXTY

Gale couldn't see what the man was wearing, or whether it was supposed to be serious, or some sort of joke. First of all, a pair of black tights descended into the room, then a tight black long-sleeve T-shirt, and finally the man's head, but instead of a human head, he was wearing some sort of huge headpiece. A snake's head, made out of what looked like soft rubber. Gale had similar items in his dressing up box, from when he was younger. He'd sort of grown out of them now.

But it wasn't the costume the man was wearing that most startled Gale. Instead, it was the sudden appearance of Layla. She just dissolved into being on the steps, as if she'd been there all along, but invisible. She rushed towards him.

"Don't speak, don't tell him I'm here," she cautioned at once. "He's been watching you, from upstairs."

Clarke had almost made it down the stairs now. Whether he could see properly in his snake-head outfit, Gale didn't know, but he seemed unsteady on his feet. He stood taller once he reached the ground proper.

"I am *All Powerful*. I am the Great..." Clarke spoke with a strange voice, even allowing for the costume he wore, but Layla ignored him. She pointed at the bucket.

"Use it, Gale. He's a *coward*. Use it."

Gale didn't have time to think, just acted upon his sister's words, without really knowing what they meant. He swung off the bed and reached for the bucket, feeling the weight of its contents swilling about. He lifted it and sloshed it at once in the direction of Clarke. The wetter parts hit on the mask and his neck, the solids struck his chest, where they clung for a moment.

The entire thing seemed to stun Clarke into inaction. Then his hands went up, tugging at the snake mask to remove it, so that he could see what had happened. His hair was sticking up, from the mask, the expression on his face pure disgust.

"You little... You little shit!" His deep voice was gone, now he sounded shrill and whiny. For a second or so, Gale felt a new rush of fear that the man might kill him right now, in punishment, but instead he turned on his heel, and ran back up the stairs. Layla laughed as he did so, and unable to help himself, Gale did too.

"That was disgusting!" Gale said.

"*He's* disgusting." Suddenly serious, Layla fixed her eyes on her brother. "And anyway, I can't smell it!"

Gale bit his lip. "You're actually here. I didn't want to call you. I didn't think..."

"I know. Thank you."

"But you were here anyway?"

Layla shrugged. "Not all the time. I've been... sort of looking for you."

"How? How did you find me?"

Layla shrugged, a little sadly. "I can't... You know I can't explain. How it works."

"Maybe I'll find out soon. He's going to kill me."

Layla didn't answer this, instead she looked around the room, as if inspecting how it had changed.

"He is," Gale insisted. "He'll be back, any minute. I want to know, will I join you? Will we be back together?"

"I don't know. I don't know, honey. I don't..."

"Don't what?"

"It's just, *I'm* the only one here. I haven't seen anyone else. So, I don't know if you'll... Maybe he won't kill you? Maybe we can make him change his mind?"

The door opened, and the man came back down the steps. This time he was without the ridiculous snake head dress, and carried a bucket and mop.

"You'll clean that up," the man said. Cautiously he continued to the bottom of the steps. "You're lucky I have a shower upstairs, but if you know what's good for you, you fucking clean it up."

"What should I do?" Gale whispered the words to his sister, quietly enough that the man couldn't hear him from the other side of the room.

"Ask if he'll let you go."

"Will you let me go?" Gale felt so much better to have Layla with him – his voice was almost normal. "If I clean it up?"

The question appeared to surprise the man, or perhaps it was the confidence Gale was showing. He blinked a few times, then mumbled an answer that Gale didn't hear.

"What?"

"*No.* No, I'm not going to let you go. Don't you understand that? I've captured you. I'm going to do what I want with you, and then I'm going to kill you." The words seemed to partially refill the man's own confidence, but not completely, as if he were trying to paper over doubts. "But only at the end, the very end, will I actually kill you, and by then you'll be begging me to put you out of your misery."

"Look like you don't care," Layla said at once. She moved to stand between the man and Gale. Gale didn't respond, save for a questioning look.

"You need to make him mad. I don't know why, but trust me. It'll help."

Gale adjusted his focus to look through his sister. He saw the mess on the floor. By then he had a clear idea of which bits of the room were impossible to reach with his chains. He thought of the sarcastic arguments he'd had when his mother asked him to clean his room.

"No, I mean, you *have* to let me go if you want me to clean up. I can't reach over there." With a huge effort, he managed a smile, and he tried to twist it ironically. Layla clapped her hands in delight.

The man didn't reply, but his shoulders dropped. He put the bucket on the floor. Then he held out the mop in front of him, like a weapon, and he slowly advanced towards Gale. It seemed he suspected Gale might have some other attack planned; so that now he was measuring where Gale could reach. He stopped well short. It was clear that Gale was right. The contents of the bucket had spread beyond the range of Gale's chains. The man appeared unable to work out what to do.

"Come here."

There was no advice from Layla now, and Gale found himself obeying the command. He was already standing, but stepped forward, heart hammering in his chest. Now he was close enough to smell the man's breath. His chains clanked behind him, and he felt the heavy drag on his feet.

"Closer."

Gale took the final step he could, the tension on the restraints lifting the chain off the floor, hurting his ankle. Then suddenly, without warning, the man pushed the mop in a stab-bing motion towards Gale's stomach, giving him no time to react. Despite the padding of the mop's head, it winded him, and then the man began striking him on the side. Gale slipped, and then he was on the floor with the man standing over him, raining blows with the mop onto his head and chest, and roaring with an awful rage.

The attack went on for minutes, and Gale had no choice but to lay there, his arms and hands protecting his head as the blows kept coming. As a weapon the mop was a terrible choice, but even so, the stick it was attached to was hard, and soon there was blood running down Gale's face. He felt other cuts in his side. Finally, the man stopped, panting from the effort. Gale lay still, crying again now, tears mixing with the blood.

"I will..." the man panted, "not tolerate... insolence. Do you understand me?"

Gale didn't reply.

"*DO YOU UNDERSTAND ME?*"

Without meaning to, Gale found himself nodding his head.

"Good. Now clean up this filth." The man threw the whole mop, aiming again at Gale's head. Then he strode to the bucket and picked it up. It was metal, and heavy, and for a second Gale thought he was going to strike him with that as well. There was time to wonder if that might be the thing that killed him – but perhaps the man had the same thought, and instead he placed it beside him with his own sarcastic smile.

"You know, your sister wasn't so brave."

That made Gale's head go up. He looked around, for Layla, but for a moment she was gone.

"Oh yeah. She begged and screamed the whole time. There wasn't anything she wouldn't do." With these words the smile turned to a nasty grin, and he ran his tongue around his lips. At the same time, he ran his hands down his stomach towards his groin.

"That's why you're so fucking cocky? Isn't it? Because you

think I'm not interested in you in that way? Well, you might just be wrong about that. So, think about that a while."

He turned to go, and this time, climbed the stairs without looking back.

SIXTY-ONE

Upstairs, Clarke went to the window and checked outside. It was nearly an automatic action, he did it so often, but this time he saw how much his hands were shaking as he leaned close to the glass. There was no one around – he already knew there wouldn't be – but his hands still shook. This had never happened before – he didn't even know how it was happening, and feared it might be something medical. How could he continue to go to work, and keep everything under control if his hands were betraying him like this? What if it got worse? What if his whole body was going to shake from now on?

He felt a wave of panic building, just about to wash over him, and fought for solutions to a problem that wasn't even real. Maybe he could blame it on the accident? Post-traumatic stress disorder. He was already on sick leave; surely he'd be believed? But the thought made him remember his mobile, which was on the countertop. It had been found in the bushes near the accident site, and returned to him in the hospital. And then he had asked Starling to keep him up to date with any developments in the search for the boy, or any leads on who might have taken him.

There were a dozen or so messages, and a couple of missed calls from people who hadn't realised he was off work. He ignored the calls but read through the messages. They had no idea. They didn't even know where to begin looking, and the thought calmed him down. He had as long as he needed here, to do whatever he wanted to Gale Martin, and no one would interrupt him.

But what *did* he want to do? That was a different question. Now he had the boy, he knew one fact. The things he had done to the girl, he felt no desire to do with the boy. That was in a way disappointing – but it was also OK, because there would be others, females only from now on.

The boy had been taken for a slightly different purpose, he reasoned. He needed to learn how he had known, and taking him was the only way to find out. He needed to eliminate the threat he had posed. So *that's* what he would do. He would question him, and if the boy refused to tell him, he would torture him. He would force him to tell him the truth. And then he would kill him, and then he would move on.

The final message on his phone was from Starling, informing him that the exhumation of Layla Martin's remains was due to take place that morning and asking if he wanted to attend. Clarke nearly laughed out loud at how much hope they were still pinning on such a crazy theory. It was a sign of just how desperate they were. But as he thought about it, he realised it was also something he hadn't properly planned for. In his mind, he would spend the whole time here, with his prize, but he knew that was wrong. If Starling really thought there was a chance the exhumation might give them a lead, then he also ought to look hopeful. Maybe he should go, put on a disappointed face when there proved not to be a pet tag that somehow revealed the identity of the killer. Show off his nicely bruised face.

He didn't admit it freely to himself, but he knew. There was another reason for wanting to go to the exhumation. The thing with the bucket had freaked him out. He'd expected the boy to be broken, terrified like the girl had been, but he'd been ready, planning an attack. He thought he had now beaten that out of the kid, but he wasn't quite sure.

And something about that didn't feel quite right.

SIXTY-TWO

Clarke pressed the brakes gently as he pulled up behind the half dozen other vehicles parked in the graveyard. He hadn't been there since the funeral, and it was almost as busy as it had been that day, except there was now a blue forensic tent over where they'd buried Layla. Problem was, that was quite a way away, and he didn't feel like walking, not after the injuries he'd sustained in the line of duty. He spotted a better parking space, further up, and even though he had to put two wheels onto the grass to get around a squad car in front of him, he squeezed through, and parked the car closer.

Then he got out, limping the last few metres, just to make the point, to where Starling was talking to a man in a forensic oversuit. Clarke knew the man – he was the pathologist who had carried out the post mortem of Layla's body – but he couldn't remember his name. No matter, the man was useless – the conclusions he'd drawn from Layla's body the first time around were so far off the mark they were laughable. There was little danger he'd do better this time around.

"Afternoon, sir." He nodded a hello to the pathologist,

covering that he didn't know his name, and then gave a painful smile to draw attention again to his injuries.

"DI Clarke," Starling peered at him a little anxiously. "Are you sure you're OK to be here?"

"I'm fine." Clarke lifted a hand modestly. "The painkillers are helping." He turned to the pathologist, wanting to get on with it. "So, where are we? Have you been able to scan the body yet?"

The pathologist held up the small device he was holding in his gloved hand. Clarke had seen it before, or something similar. They'd bought several of the pet microchip scanners from Amazon, covering every possible frequency. As if they really might hold the key to the case. *As if.*

"They're just lifting her out now. Fortunately, she was buried in a good quality casket, which should also mean the remains are relatively intact. Even if not, the chip should have survived. If there is one." He shrugged. "Hopefully we'll get a hit."

Clarke nodded, in a way that was supposed to look pensive. "Let's hope so."

The conversation seemed to fall strangely flat, and Clarke cursed himself for not arriving even later. Turning up here was necessary, but it was still a monumental waste of time, when he should be at his unit, enjoying his prize.

"Is there anything new on the case, sir?" he asked Starling. Partly to break the silence, partly to find out. His boss shook his head.

"I'm afraid not. The family are beside themselves, as you can imagine. We've got a lot of guys looking into how the boy was taken, but at the moment, he seems to have vanished into thin air." He hesitated, then glanced at the pathologist again. "I'm sorry to say that we're putting a lot of hope that this might turn something up."

At that moment Starling's phone rang, and he excused himself to answer it. Clarke was left alone with the pathologist. But just as Clarke was about to say something to him, the man was also called away, this time by a woman whose head had emerged from the tent. The pathologist gave Clarke an apologetic look.

"The moment of truth." He ducked his head out of sight.

"Good luck!" Clarke thought to say, but he said it too late.

Clarke paced up and down for a while, unsure what else to do, and even a little annoyed that there weren't more people here, and that no one who was here appeared to be paying him any attention. He even dropped the limp, since it was difficult to do in a way that felt genuine. After a while, Starling joined him.

"Summary of the forensic report from where the boy was snatched. Pretty thin gruel. No fingerprints or fibres, least not what you wouldn't expect. Ground too hard to get any foot-prints. There could have been one of them, there could have been a dozen, we just don't know."

Clarke winced to show his frustration. Then, when it seemed that Starling was done, he replied, "I think I might wait in the car, I'm feeling a little..." He screwed up his face, to indicate the injuries he'd received, then turned towards where he'd parked the Škoda, but was surprised when Starling dropped a hand on his shoulder.

"Come and sit in mine, you can have a look through the report." And so he had to go and wait in the DS's Jaguar, with its cream leather and the smell of the man's aftershave, while he flicked through the report on Starling's iPad. Thankfully it wasn't long before the pathologist was tapping at the window.

Starling got out of the car, so Clarke was forced to do the same.

"Well?" Starling had looked around, to make sure no one

could overhear them. His voice was expectant. But the pathologist shook his head.

"Nothing. The remains are in a reasonably good state, which meant we were able to turn them to get good access to both sides. We've used three different scanners, set to all frequencies that are used for this sort of thing. We've been up and down the body two dozen times. There are no hits. And these things are virtually indestructible. If she ever was chipped, she isn't now."

Clarke tried to mirror the body language of his boss, letting his shoulders slump a little, but he couldn't match the next thing that Starling did, suddenly slamming his palm against the roof of the car. Starling didn't say anything, but then did it again. Finally, he took a deep breath.

"*Damnit.*"

Clarke didn't know what to say. He was almost amazed the old man had invested so much hope into this – so much so it was difficult not to laugh. But then he looked around, at the scene around him, and he simply wished the stupid bastard would give the order to get the remains back in the ground, before anyone had any other dumb ideas.

"OK." Starling nodded slowly, clearly still recovering from the disappointment. "Well, that's that then." He looked to Clarke, as if hoping his star detective might have some other thought, but Clarke just stood, slowly shaking his head.

Starling turned back the pathologist. "I guess you should put her back."

SIXTY-THREE

Clarke took a detour home on the way back to the unit. It wasn't generally a good idea to move his girls – their tanks were temperature and moisture controlled and it wasn't possible to maintain these things in the car, or at the unit. But he felt that having them there with him would give the boost he needed for what was going to come next. Besides, there was a kind of tradition to it, that he felt he ought to preserve. So he moved them into their smaller travelling cases, and then backed the Škoda into the garage at his home, whereupon he was able to load them comfortably into the boot. Finally, he covered them with a blanket so that they couldn't be seen. Then he drove back to the unit. Here it was deserted so that he could simply carry them inside.

He quickly checked the boy on his monitor. All was well. He was still chained to the floor by the bed. Clarke switched the screen off again, then he fetched his girl, the kingsnake, and stroked her a while.

The animal calmed him, allowed his mind to settle after the irritation of the unnecessary exhumation. He stroked the snake's smooth, cool back, let her slip gracefully over his hands, and coil herself around his wrists. In a way this was all unnecessary too, he considered. This business with the boy – perhaps it was better to get that settled faster too. The snake's tongue flicked in and out, tasting the air in its new environment. Not quite new, they had been here before: the kingsnake and his other girl, the much more venomous viper.

Much calmer now, he contemplated dressing again in his black leggings and skin-tight top. He'd washed them, as disgusting as that was, and they were now dry again. But he decided against it. This would be better done in his detective persona. And this would be quick. Get in. Find out what he wanted to know. Kill the child and get rid of the body. He stayed still for a long time, relishing the calmness transmitted through the snake. Finally, after a long time, he put the animal back into its travel tank, and closed the lid.

He checked again on the monitor that it was safe for him to enter. And he unlocked the door.

SIXTY-FOUR

There wasn't much Gale could do about the cuts to his face except wash the wounds with a little of the remaining water. He drank the rest. The thrill he had felt at being reunited with Layla had taken a battering too. At first it had made his situation a million times better, yet he knew now there was nothing she could actually do to alter the horrific reality. He was going to be murdered by the madman that held him prisoner. She would be there to watch, but helpless to intervene. And then he would never see her again. Nor his mum or dad. His eyes hurt. His face hurt. He had never been so scared.

The door opened, and slowly, casually, the man came down carrying a chair. He set it down on the concrete floor, out of reach of Gale. Gale didn't move, just sat on the bed and watched. Then the man raised a hand to show he was carrying something else: a pair of pliers.

"So, we're going to have a little chat, you and I," the man said.

Gale didn't reply, just lifted his head, and waited.

"And if you don't want to talk, or I think you're not telling me the truth, then I'm not going to piss around asking you nicely." He toyed with the pliers now, opening and closing the jaws with a snapping sound. "I'm going to use these to cut off the ends of your fingers. One by one." He didn't smile, but fitted one of his own fingers between the jaws, as if working out how easy it would be to do what he'd said.

"So I suppose we can do this the nice way, or the not-so-nice way. Which would you prefer?"

There was nowhere for Gale to go. No way to block the man from his mind, and try as he might to tell himself he no longer cared, he felt his fingers curling into his palms, trying to retreat from the threat.

"How did you know? When you came to my house, and then told your stupid bitch of a mother that it was where the killer lived, how did you know? How did you know it was me?"

Gale didn't answer, he just watched as his sister went up to the man, and violently thrust her fingers into his eyes. He didn't even blink. She screamed at him, clawed at his face. Nothing.

Gale watched, grateful but sad. And wishing he didn't feel so terribly scared. His eyes found his hands and he looked at his fingers, in a sort of stupefied wonder that he would soon know what it felt like to have one cut off. It didn't seem real, and yet it felt too real. He was tired, so tired. His sister continued to attack the man, almost out of control with rage, and yet he acted as if she wasn't there at all. In a strange way, that felt almost worse than the thought of what the man was threatening.

"Tell me how you knew."

"*You bastard, you evil bastard,*" Layla screeched.

Suddenly Gale couldn't take it anymore. He had to stop *her*. "I guessed."

The man's eyebrows rose in surprise at Gale's answer, and Layla finally, thankfully, stopped. For a while there was silence.

"You guessed?"

Gale nodded.

"You guessed. OK. Great. Except, there's seven billion

people in the world. And it's not really the thing that people *guess*, is it? So you wanna try again, or shall we take off the first finger. Your choice, kid."

Gale didn't answer. He had no other answer. He looked at his hands again.

The man got up suddenly and came straight towards Gale. "OK. This is your fault, not mine."

Before Gale could react the man had grabbed one of his hands, and was trying to fit the jaws of the pliers around the finger. But now Gale fought back, pulling his arm away. Unseen and unheard, Layla was again beating him around the head with her fist, screaming and spitting in his face, and now Gale didn't want her to stop, but it made no difference. For almost a minute the three of them struggled, until finally the man gained control. He was almost sitting on Gale's body on the bed, pinning one of Gale's hands underneath their two bodies. The other arm was free, both of the man's hands wrapped around it.

The man bent to the floor where the pliers had fallen and picked them up one-handed. He held one of the handles, and let gravity pull the jaws open. Then he fitted them around Gale's smallest finger. The digit looked tiny against the metal, and it was obvious that with almost no pressure at all they would slice through the tissue and crush through the bone. For a second this seemed to give the man pause. He put just enough pressure to hold the pliers in place, but it was enough that Gale cried out.

"That hurt? I haven't even started yet." The man squeezed a little harder.

Gale was stunned at just how much more it hurt than he'd imagined. It was like a bright white light of pain was pulsing directly into his brain.

"Shall we do it? Shall we cut it off? Or you wanna have one last try?"

Do it. Tell him. Just tell him about me. Through the light of the pain, Gale was suddenly aware of Layla, now screaming into his face.

Just tell him.

"OK." Gale managed to nod despite his position, and almost cried in pity that the man released the grip. He didn't let go completely, still keeping the pliers in place around the finger, but the pain was back to normal levels – the sort of pain Gale now knew from having his ribs broken, tear gas sprayed into his eyes. His hand still hurt, but he could breathe through it.

"I knew because... because... Layla told me."

The man seemed perplexed by the words. It was several moments before he replied. "What?"

Gale said it again. "Layla told me."

"Layla told— How the hell did Layla tell you? She's fucking dead."

"I know."

Gale was crying hard and wished he could have his hand back to wipe the tears away, just wished he could have his hand back.

"So if she's dead, how the hell is she gonna tell you? Huh?" The man squeezed again with the pliers, sending a new shock-wave of pain crashing into Gale's brain, but he quickly released it again.

"I don't know how it works. She just told me."

The man's face was screwed up in an incredulous look. "Layla told you?" he asked again. "You mean before she died? You saw her?"

"No."

"But I had never met her before. First time I saw your sister was the day I took her, from the beach."

"No. It was *after*." Gale had nothing left but the truth. There seemed no reason not to say it. "After she died. I started seeing her. I thought it was just in my head. But then she talked to me. She told me how you kept her here. About the snakes."

The man backed off the pressure still further on Gale's finger. Now the look on his face was more like a man who thought he was being pranked, but wasn't quite sure.

"So... your sister told you. But as a ghost?"

Gale nodded, leaving his head drooped down into his chest.

Suddenly the man laughed.

"That's good. You know what? That's really fucking good. You've got a hell of an imagination there, kiddo. So what, she comes floating into your bedroom, dressed in a white sheet?"

Gale's voice was almost too weak to register. "Normal clothes."

"Normal clothes? Well *excuse me*. But she whispers into your ear, does she? *Kieran Clarke*, that's your killer?"

"She didn't know your name."

The man released his grip on Gale's hand and got up off the bed. He began pacing up and down the room. He stopped.

"You're actually serious, aren't you?" He was watching Gale's reaction carefully. "You actually believe this?"

Gale nodded.

"So how does it work? You can just conjure her up, whenever you want?" He waited. Gale didn't want to tell him, but he felt defeated. There was nothing left. It didn't matter anymore.

"She can only come to places where she was in real life. Like home, and school."

"Only places she was in real life?" An idea seemed to hit him. "So, she can come *here*? Right? Because she *was* here. You know that, right? She was right here. This is where she died."

"I know. She told me."

For a second time the man wore a look of amusement, but this time it was edged with something else. A hint of anxiety. "So *is* she? Here, I mean? Right now?"

Layla had been quiet since he'd told him, just watching the two of them. But now she reacted. She stepped forward, getting right into his face, before spitting at him.

"She's here," Gale said. And then, since Layla was now holding up two fingers to the man, waving her hands around his face, added. "I don't think she's very pleased to see you."

Tell him he's evil. Worse than anyone, ever. Tell him he makes Voldemort seem good. Tell him he smells bad. Tell him he's a coward – a coward who wasn't even brave enough to kill me.

―――――――――

"She says you're evil and worse that even Voldemort. He's from *Harry Potter*."

Clarke laughed at this. He make a faux-scared impression, holding his hands out flat and waving the fingers. "Oooo, worse than Voldemort." Then he laughed again. "Wow, this is surreal. You think that your sister has come back to you as a ghost, and is in the room with you right now? That's good. That's funny. Actually, that's hilarious."

He stopped what he was doing, and thought for a while.

"You know what, I'm gonna destroy a few of your illusions before you die," he said at last, then began nodding slowly. "You still believe in Father Christmas?" He didn't wait for an answer. "Well, you shouldn't, it's your parents. Tooth fairy? Same deal. And as for ghosts, well I'm sorry to tell you kid, but they don't exist. It's all in your screwed-up head."

"She said you're a coward who was too afraid to kill her."

The humour that Clarke had felt drained away.

"What'd you say?"

"I didn't say it, she did."

Suddenly Clarke grabbed for Gale's throat, trying to physically push this distinction away. "What the fuck did you say?"

"She said you were too afraid to kill her, that's why you used your snakes."

"How the..." Clarke pulled back, moving away from Gale

again. "You can't... how *the fuck* do you know that?" But now he came close again, bringing his face right up to Gale's. "You *cannot* know that. It's not possible..." Abruptly he pulled away and walked to the wall. He stared at it a long time, then swung around.

"You're gonna tell me." He closed on Gale again now, with surprising speed, and then grabbed his hand again. He forced Gale's thumb into the jaws of the pliers, and pushed them together, already putting considerable pressure, so that Gale yelled out in renewed pain. The first time he had put the child's tiny finger in the pliers he had felt fear, disgust at how fragile it was, how easy it would be to cut it off. Now he wanted to do it.

"I'll do it," Clarke called out, panting from the exertion. He'd never done torture before, though he'd dreamed of it. "Tell me how you knew it was me. The real version this time."

He pressed harder with the pliers, until blood leaked down both sides of the blades, and a kind of elated euphoric terror came over Clarke. He was really going to cut this child's fingers off.

"TELL ME!" he roared.

Then he found the strength to calm a little. He knew, on some animal level, that if he actually removed the digit the boy would pass out, and perhaps he would never know. Or that's what he told himself. And there was awareness too, the child was whimpering something, trying to talk.

"Okay! Okay! I saw you... I saw you before."

"I knew it." Clarke grinned manically. "I knew it." Again he released Gale's hand. "You saw me talking with Layla at the beach. I was wearing sunglasses, but I took them off when I spoke to her. It was one of my mistakes, but I was worried she wouldn't trust me if she couldn't see my eyes. That's it, isn't it? You must have turned around and saw me?"

But Gale shook his head. "Not then. Earlier."

"What?" Clarke frowned at him. "I never saw Layla before,

so how could you...?" Without really thinking, he grabbed for Gale's hand again, to fit it back in the pliers, but he screamed and managed to pull it away.

"Not then. I saw you in the pet shop."

"The pet shop?"

"A year before Layla. I had to do a school project on snakes, and my dad took me to The Reptile Room, to see what they had. And you were in there. You were buying the pit viper, and I asked you about it. You spoke to me."

Clarke had to move away again, to process this. He tried to search his mind; he remembered buying the snake, from the fat guy from the shop, who'd acted like they were friends, but had there been... yes! He *had* spoken with some dumb kid that day, showing off his girl before he took her home. And that was *this* dumb kid?" He spun around.

"So you saw me at The Reptile Room, but how did you know I took Layla?" He waved the pliers threateningly again.

"I don't know. *I really don't know.* I tried to figure it out, but I can't. Please..." Gale cradled his hand in his other arm. He looked pleadingly at the man.

Then, suddenly Clarke let out a laugh. It started as more of a bark, but then he kept it going as a long roar. When he finally stopped he turned back to the boy, an evil look in his eye. "I get it. Now I get it. Maybe you saw me talking with Layla, maybe you didn't, it doesn't even matter. But when you saw my face on TV, or the newspapers, as the DI leading the investigation, and you remembered I had the snakes, you just invented the rest. It was all in your head!" He chucked, then went on. "You put two and two together."

He stopped, breathing hard now.

"Or rather, you didn't. You put two and two together and came up with about five-fucking-thousand, with your bullshit story about seeing your sister's ghost!"

He felt calmed now, the manic energy gone. He sat back on

the chair, rested his head in one hand. "Oh, boy. It's so simple. Once you see it." He smiled a great grin of relief. "But you know what? It proves I was right. I had to take you. And I have to kill you. You're dangerous."

He held up the pliers, enjoying for a moment the renewed look of fear in the boy's face, but then he dropped them to the floor where they landed with a dull thud.

"Guess we won't be needing these anymore." He kicked them away so the boy wouldn't be able to reach them.

"Which is kind of a good thing, because blood is such a drag to clean up." He stopped and studied Gale's face. "And you know how I know that? Because of cleaning up after killing your sister."

Clarke pushed up his sleeves, and advanced towards Gale.

"And now I'm gonna kill you."

SIXTY-FIVE

The wait seemed to go on forever, the hands on the wall clock in Starling's office dragging themselves toward 1 p.m., and then finally past the hour. Quarter-past one. Half past. Still the phone didn't ring.

"Has the car moved?" Cross asked.

"Hmmm?" Starling had been lost in thought. Then he pushed the laptop around, letting her see the map on the screen. A red flashing dot was centred on what Cross now knew was DI Clarke's address. It had moved there directly from the graveyard, where Layla's exhumation had taken place earlier that day. Cross watched the tracker's dot now, reliving the extended trauma of fitting it.

Until the abduction of Gale Martin, there had been no need to track Clarke. He worked long hours, and could usually be found in the investigation suite two floors below Starling's office. If he wasn't there, they knew where he lived. Furthermore, there was no manpower available to put a team out watching him, not while the Martins' house was also being monitored twenty-four hours a day, and certainly not without Clarke himself becoming aware that he was being observed.

That changed with the dramatic kidnapping of Gale, but it didn't change quickly.

Starling first mentioned the idea of placing an electronic tracker on Clarke's Škoda while he was in hospital, but before he could do so, he needed to secure a court order. That finally came through a few hours before the exhumation, which was when Cross had been given the task of fitting it.

And since Starling, Cross and the pathologist were the only people who knew the real reason for the exhumation, and the actual suspect it was designed to expose, she had to fit it without being seen by Clarke, or any of the other police personnel present. And that was made considerably harder when Clarke hadn't left his car where they'd planned, instead driving much closer to the graveside. But she'd done it, crawling mostly, from behind one parked car to the next, her knees in the mud and her heart hammering in her chest. Then the fear had come that she hadn't done it properly, until they'd got back to Starling's office to check if the thing was actually working.

And now the waiting. The two possible versions of the reality she was living seemed to alternate in Cross's mind. In the one, her idea was as crazy as it seemed. DI Clarke was of course entirely innocent, and they had set up this ridiculous exhumation for nothing, all while drawing away vital resources from the investigation, which could well prove to result in the boy's death. If that happened, their actions – hers and Starling's – would be revealed, and while he would be the one held responsible, she wondered how she would live with herself.

In the other version, the phone on Starling's desk would ring at any moment, confirming that the lead investigator of one of the force's largest inquiries was also the perpetrator of the crime, some sort of horrific murdering puppet master. Both thoughts were horrific. Cross felt like she'd aged ten years in the last week.

Starling's desk phone rang, the sound piercing the silence. His hand shot out, picking it up.

"Starling."

There was a silence before he spoke again. "Thank you. I appreciate you putting this through so quickly." Then more silence.

Without saying another word, Starling replaced the receiver. His mouth stayed open, and he breathed with some difficulty for one or two breaths. Then he closed his mouth again, and covered it with one hand. His eyes went back to Cross. He nodded as he found his voice.

"The lab report has found residues of certain chemicals consistent with coming from the venom of a specific species of snake, notably something called a pit viper." He swallowed. "The same species registered to Kieran Clarke. It's him." He closed his eyes.

Cross was on her feet, thoughts flooding into her brain faster than she could process them. "We need to go. We need to get him now." She felt a combination of exhilaration and deep sickness. For a second she thought she might actually be sick; her eyes found Starling's wastepaper basket.

Starling himself seemed fixed in place, unable to move.

"Sir, we need to get Clarke. The girl was kept alive for nearly two weeks. There's a chance Gale will be alive too, we need to get him to tell us where he is."

Slowly Starling nodded. "I know. We have the armed response unit on standby to pick him up. I'll give the go ahead now." He picked up his mobile, but before he could make the call, the screen of his laptop changed. The flashing red dot, which was the location of the tracker, turned orange, indicating a change of status.

"Shit," Starling muttered. "He's moving."

SIXTY-SIX

With the confirmation of the cause of Layla's death, the need for secrecy in investigating Clarke was removed, but the problems of secrecy were replaced with those of urgency. The tracking device showed Clarke's Škoda had moved to a set of buildings on farmland, not far from where he lived. A map search had listed the largest as being an underground bunker. The plan to arrest him was quickly adapted.

All told, it took just over an hour before the three cars, each occupied with four officers, all wearing bulletproof vests and helmets, were crashing down the unmade road to the unit. Some carried handguns, more were armed with Heckler & Koch MP5 submachine guns, held across the officer's chests. The vehicles were travelling so fast the wheels weren't bottoming out in the rain-filled potholes, but still sending skirts of dirty water high in the air.

Cross had begged her way into travelling in the final car, Starling being too busy to argue against it. The armourer of the ARU – Armed Response Unit – had thrown her a bulletproof vest, and shown her how to wear it.

BANG! Her head hit the roof of the car as they hit a particularly deep pothole. Cross wondered if this was real. It couldn't be, yet it was.

The first car skidded to a halt in front of the unit, the second and third cars had to change direction fast to avoid hitting it. At once the officers began piling out.

"That's Clarke's car," someone shouted, but Cross already knew that, she and Starling had followed it on the screen, seen where it stopped, and then asked each other what the hell it was doing there. And what kind of a place Clarke was leading them to.

The commander of the ARU took in the scene. Cross barely understood what was happening and just tried to keep back. One of the other officers had brought out a large red battering ram from somewhere. He needed both arms to lift it, and took it to the door, waiting until he was given the order. All the while other officers covered what he did, guns ready.

A moment later they were all in position, and the lead officer nodded his head. The battering ram swung back and cracked into the steel of the door. The metal nearly buckled from the impact, but the lock held, suggesting it was bolted from inside. The device was drawn back again and then once more smashed forward. This time it broke straight through, swinging the door open hard.

"ARMED POLICE. ARMED POLICE|!" Within seconds, eight officers were inside the unit, the rest only waiting outside because there wasn't room inside for more of them to operate safely. Cross had to stay outside too, until she was given the all-clear. It came a moment later, the word shouted from inside.

"Clear!"

Then there was another shout:

"Jesus Christ, there's a fucking snake!"

"I'm going in," Cross said, more to herself than the other officers who were still outside the unit. They didn't stop her, and stepped through the doorway to see a bizarre sight, a small room dominated by a large table, with a kitchenette along one wall. There was a computer set up on the table, along with two small glass tanks. Two officers were frantically trying to put the lid onto one of them, while another brandished his weapon, as if about to shoot through the glass. But three other officers were clustered around a second door.

"There's another doorway here, lights on the other side. It's locked."

It took a few seconds more for the battering ram to be brought to bear, but this door was much weaker, and it crashed open on the first blow. When it did there were steps leading downwards. More cautiously this time, the first officers glanced in, weapons held ready. Then they flowed down the steps one after the other, the lead officer yelling as he descended.

"Down on the floor! Get away from the boy!"

Cross was the fourth person down the steps, the bulletproof vest digging into her waist as she tried to keep up. She almost couldn't believe the sight that greeted her. Clarke was slowly backing away from a bed chained in the centre of the room. He wore an evil, snarling grin, and there was fresh blood on his face. On the bed was a lump, it took her moments to recognise it as human, and when she made out that the appendages draped onto the floor were actually arms and a leg, the shape began to make sense.

One of the officers went to the boy, fingers feeling for the carotid pulse in the neck. He adjusted his hand, waited, then adjusted it again. He leaned his head on its side, close to the boy, to feel if there was any breath. Then he looked around, shaking his head.

"You're too late." Clarke's voice rang out, cutting through the noise and chaos of the room. He seemed to be gloating. His white teeth were showing. He was grinning.

"You're all too late."

SIXTY-SEVEN

Clarke surveyed the scene. He was All Powerful, and this was his moment. The boy watched him back. He looked scared again. Miserable, broken, terrified. This wasn't murder, this was a form of mercy. And for that reason, there was no reason to delay it, certainly no reason to be frightened. He kicked the pliers out of the way – it was possible the boy might make a grab for them, he had surprised him already with the bucket, and the bullshit excuses about his sister. But that was all in the past. Now it was his time. The moment he'd fantasised about.

He stepped forward towards the bed, his arms out in front of him, hands outstretched, reaching for the neck. His hands were gratifyingly still; he felt no fear. He'd done this once before – after the girl was already dead, admittedly, but still, he'd been here. And this time he wanted to watch the life slip away. The boy moved quickly, but only as far as the chains would let him go, the other side of the bed.

"I don't want to play around, boy," Clarke said. He grabbed the nearest chain and tugged at it violently. The foot was pulled out from under the boy, and he fell, his lower half on the bed, upper parts on the floor. "Get up."

The boy didn't obey, instead trying to get himself under the bed, so Clarke pulled harder. Dragging him out, like a snail from its shell. His fingers moved from the chain to the boy's actual leg, feeling the definition of the muscle. They worked their way up, his knee, his thigh. He lingered at the groin, but his heart wasn't in it. Not this time. He gripped onto the pyjama top the boy was still wearing and screwed it into a bunch in his hands. Caught at the boy's nipple, causing a whimper to escape his lips.

He saw nothing of the ghostly figure of Layla Martin, who clawed at his own eyes, bit his face, punched and spat repeatedly. Heard nothing of her desperate cries.

It was pleasing how easily his hands found their way to his neck. *Careful, though.* He was sure to keep his weight on the boy's body, to prevent there being any chance of him getting a kick in. He began to squeeze. But then, a sound. Upstairs there was a whoop-whoop of an electronic alarm.

Clarke froze where he was, unable to make sense of the noise. A false alarm? It must be. He almost ignored it, but then he didn't – leaping off the boy, leaving him gasping, and then sprinting up the steps into the room upstairs. He hammered at the keys on the computer so that it pulled up the video feed from the intruder alarm on the screen. He'd set up a speed trigger on the access road, so that if anyone drove down it too fast, it would trigger an alarm and set a camera running. He watched in horror and disbelief as the screen showed him two police cars – no, three – arriving at speed towards the unit. He blinked, *it couldn't be.* But it was real. There was no doubt, he was caught.

He acted on instinct now. He lashed out at the travel tank of the snakes meaning to break it, but only succeeding in dislodging the top. He breathed, seeing his girl emerge immediately from her nest, tongue flicking with interest. Then he rushed back to the downstairs room. The boy was still there, staring at him, not understanding. Not knowing he was about to be rescued, not knowing he had defeated him. Well no, he hadn't yet. Clarke swung around, grabbing the key from the outside of the door, and fitting it as quickly as his shaking fingers would allow, into the interior. Then he locked it and came running back down the stairs.

There was much less caution this time. He leapt onto the boy, ignoring and smothering his struggles easily. His hands again went around his neck, and a vicious look came onto his face as he squeezed, deeper and harder. It felt like squeezing toffee, like crushing fruit, and it was amazing how instant the effect was on the boy's face.

The boy opened and closed his mouth, like a fish taken out of the water, and the colour changed too, the face going from red to white, and then distinctly blue. All the while the boy's body bucked and twisted below him, subdued by Clark's own weight. Flecks of white spit formed at the boy's mouth and nose, then the bucking changed from being constant, to just now and again, and finally, as Clarke continued to squeeze with every ounce of his strength and twisted and dug his thumbs into the boy's throat, he felt his head go still, felt the fight pass out of him in a moment. The boy went quite limp.

And then the door burst open.

SIXTY-EIGHT

Layla knew the moment was coming, and knew there was nothing she could do to affect it. Every time she tried to shout at the man, or hit him, or take out his eyes, he felt nothing, and her efforts were only exhausting her. But there was nothing else.

When the attack came, the speed with which Clarke launched himself upon her brother took her by surprise. When he had tried to do the same to her, he had hesitated, fought back tears, spent as much time berating himself as he had trying to choke her. And finally he had given up, and then that night, when she had been asleep – or as close to it as she was able to get while imprisoned there – he had returned, and slipped the snake into her bed.

But at the same time, she was ready. She had no idea how she was able to do it, only that at moments like this, of the most extreme stress, she was able to somehow invest herself within her brother's body, switching places, in some way, so that he was in the place where she was stuck, and she was the one within him.

Of the consequences, she knew nothing. Only that it would take away the pain at the moment the man took his life.

She surged all her power now, to flow into Gale, as the man straddled him. She was shocked at how much her brother fought, directing his fury both at the man, and at her, as if he knew what she was doing, and wanted to refuse her – that hadn't happened when she had taken over his body before, speaking to their mother. And then the alarm had sounded. The man had leapt off, as if scalded, had run up the steps where she'd heard him calling out with a yell like a wounded animal, and then the smash of something into the floor.

"What are you doing?" Gale asked, he seemed not to have heard the noises above.

"*Let me.*"

"No."

"Let me, Gale. He can't hurt me anymore."

Fresh tears formed in Gale's eyes, and Layla leaned forward to wipe them away. And something amazing happened, instead of her fingers pushing through the liquid of the tear, through the physical surface of Gale's face, something else happened, the water transferred to her fingers. She drew them away, taking the tear with her, and both of them stared at what had happened.

"When he comes back, don't resist. Just let me take over."

"Will I see you? When it's over?"

"I don't know. I just don't know."

He was back in the room now, locking the door and running down the steps now. Layla had no idea what had happened – what was happening – but she knew what was about to happen, and that this time, there would be no interrupting him. She forced herself to flow into Gale's body, as the man pinned it to the bed and straddled him, those hands going to his neck – to her neck. She felt the constriction, she felt the breath forced out of her, the impossibility of taking in any more. She saw his eyes,

the wild, insanity of his eyes. And she smiled, as she slipped
away.

SIXTY-NINE

"He's dead." The officer who had got first to Gale's body dropped his head. He still had one hand by the boy's neck, as if a pulse might suddenly reappear, but they all knew it wouldn't. Cross sensed the change in the atmosphere of the team – from the highest of tension, laced with the hope that they might save the boy – to this, the worst possible outcome. Arriving moments too late.

Clarke was led away, arms roughly handcuffed behind him. Weapons still trained on him, as if he were still a danger.

"Time of death, fifteen hundred hours," the lead officer of the firearms unit called out, but then someone else spoke. Cross was only dimly aware it was her.

"He was strangling him. We need to restart his heart."

Someone put a hand on her, presumably to calm her down, but she fought them off angrily, then found herself rushing forward towards the bed.

The boy was dressed just in his underpants and pyjama top, his limp body twisted and damaged. There were cuts to his face and arms. As part of her training as a police Constable, expected to patrol a beat, she was trained regularly in emergency first aid, and the training came to her with perfect clarity. Without even thinking she adjusted him into the correct position and began to pump at his chest with her hands. He was frail, just a child, and she was careful with the pressure – she'd practised with both full-size dolls and smaller dolls, to represent children.

Push down five cm, approximately one third of the chest diameter. Release the pressure, then rapidly repeat at a rate of about one hundred compressions a minute.

One time that she'd practised, the teacher had told her to work to the rhythm of the song 'Stayin' Alive', by the Bee Gees. It stuck with her, and filled her head now, in the horror of the basement dungeon.

Thirty compressions – focus – tilt the head, lift the chin, give two effective breaths. Continue compressions and breaths in a ratio of two breaths for every thirty compressions.

At some point, she didn't know when, someone tried to stop her, to tell her it was useless, but again she flung their hand off her, lashing out with her own arm and screaming at them to leave her alone. She didn't care. Her world had reduced to one single aim. To not give up.

It didn't matter that it clearly wasn't working. It didn't matter that the boy was clearly dead. The training was clear. Continue until the patient showed signs of life, or until more qualified help arrived. Or until exhausted.

Both of the last two came at once, when a new hand reached for her, more gently than before. But this one didn't wear the dark blue of the police uniform, but the green overalls of a paramedic. And the voice was softer.

"Let us take over."

Cross finally let herself stop, and rolled away sitting on the hard floor. She stayed there, just sitting in this horrific space, where one of her colleagues, a man she had worked with, drunk with, assumed was a good officer, had stolen children to murder them. She barely heard the paramedic's call of "clear", nor saw the way the boy's limp body bucked under the shock of the portable defibrillator. Only the shakes of the heads of the other officers that now stood transfixed by the final drama of the day.

SEVENTY

"Sit down here, Joe, I shouldn't be too long."

Geoff – Ellen Cross's ex – had let her down again, a last-minute gig in Manchester, so he wasn't able to look after their son as arranged. It meant she was caught between her two worlds, albeit one had been shaken to the core.

"Look, there are magazines if you want." She picked one up from the side table. An old copy of *Top Gear* with a sports car on the cover, partly obscured by a sticker saying *Property of the NHS*. But Joe ignored it, pulling his gaming device from his pocket instead. Cross watched him a second, unable to look at his face without seeing that of Gale Martin. She had to look away.

Further along the corridor she had already noticed DS Starling, deep in conversation with Jon Martin and a doctor, judging by her white coat.

"When I'm done here, maybe we could go get a pizza? Or something?"

Her boy stopped what he was doing and looked up. For the briefest of seconds, a smile passed across his lips. "OK."

"Alright. Just wait here a while. I won't be long."

She left him, once more engrossed in his game, before meeting Starling halfway down the hall, where he'd come striding down to meet her.

"I'm sorry, I couldn't get anyone to look after him at short notice."

He seemed confused for a second, but then realised she meant her son. He glanced at the boy, but said nothing.

"How are you doing? An incident like that, you need to look after yourself, shock can hit at any time."

"Yeah. guess it hasn't really sunk in yet."

"Well, take your time. There's support in place, and you should use it. Take as long as you need."

"Thank you, sir." Cross hesitated. There was something else on her mind.

"What is it?"

"It's just... I wanted to know. He's definitely dead? DI Clarke?"

"Absolutely. It seems he had a knife concealed around his ankle. He went for it as he was being put in the car, and would probably have killed the officer holding him, had he not been shot. The bastard took the coward's route out, which is going to leave a lot of questions unanswered, unfortunately."

Starling hesitated now, as if not sure that this was the time or place to go into this, but perhaps he felt he owed her. "There are a few things we have been able to make sense of though." He offered her a look, as if checking if she wanted to know now, or wait.

"What things?"

"It seems that Clarke recorded everything that took place down there, at least for Gale's abduction. We've found nothing from anything previous. But looking over the footage, it shows him torturing Gale Martin – apparently he was trying to understand how Gale knew about Layla. Which I think we've been wondering too. It seems the boy happened upon him in a pet shop, where Clarke purchased his snakes. They had a conversation, which Gale Martin remembered, but Clarke didn't." He fell silent.

"There's something else. Kind of weird. It shows Gale Martin talking to someone who isn't there. It's as though he was pretending to see his sister with him, while he was being held in the bunker. Having full, one-sided conversations. I'm told it's almost harder to watch than the torture scene."

He shook his head. "I don't know. I'm not sure how this all fits together. Not sure we'll ever know now. But probably you were right about Rachel Martin lying about the second time she was late to the swimming pool. Probably Gale only saw Clarke in the pet shop, and then on the beach that day. And from that he constructed... I'm not sure what he constructed. Maybe this is just what happens when you put a ten-year-old under unbearable pressure."

Cross didn't reply.

"Listen. This isn't the time, but I want to say it anyway. You've done outstanding work on this case. You've made some excellent calls, and shown your instincts are impeccable. I also know the work you do as Constable is valued. Highly valued. But I want to say, if you ever wanted to move into the investigative branch, I'd be more than happy to personally sponsor you. I would give you my full support."

He laid a hand on her shoulder. "Don't say anything now. Think it over. Take as long as you need."

At the opposite end of the hallway, Jon Martin was now standing beside Rachel. They seemed to be waiting.

"Gale's parents would like to have a word too, if that's OK with you?"

"Yes, sir. Sure." Cross drew a breath to compose herself, and expected Starling to move, but hesitated, looking the other way

down the corridor, not towards the Martins, but towards Joe.
Starling spoke again.

"It's Joe, isn't it? Your boy?"

Surprised, she answered.

"Yes, sir."

"Why don't you call him over? I think he should hear this."
Starling waited until Cross nodded a single time, concern at the
idea clear on her face, and then he called out loudly to the boy.

"Joe, would you mind coming over here a moment? There's
something I think you should hear."

Joe looked scared at being addressed by one of his mum's
colleagues, and someone who looked clearly pretty high up too,
but he got to his feet and came meekly towards them. When he
did, Starling turned and led the way back to where Gale's
parents were waiting.

"Jon, this is Constable Ellen Cross, I don't believe you've
met? She was the first person to become suspicious of Kieran
Clarke's activities, and she's been working very closely with me,
in secret, to investigate him. And of course, it's also PC Cross
who saved Gale's life this afternoon by administering CPR." He
stopped, and then glanced at the boy.

"And this is her son, Joe. I wanted him to hear."

Jon Martin started trying to say something in reply, but
his wife stopped him. Instead, she stepped forward and
wrapped her arms around Cross. For a long time, she just
stayed there, not speaking, until she finally let go. Her voice
was hoarse.

"Thank you. Thank you so much. Thank you for everything
you've done."

Cross found that the tears were infectious, and for a few
moments she let herself go, matching Rachel Martin quietly,
sob-for-sob. Then the moment passed, and both of them were
wiping their eyes. Jon Martin took the opportunity to thank her
too, his voice much quieter.

"How is Gale doing?" Cross asked him. "I haven't seen him since the ambulance."

The doctor answered her question. "He's extremely shaken up, as you can imagine, but there are no serious physical injuries. It's quite remarkable really." She paused. "He was actually dead, clinically dead; it's very rare for someone to come back from that. Not unheard of, but rare—"

"He asked to see you," Rachel interrupted. "Will you go and see him?"

All eyes turned to the doctor, as if seeking permission.

"A quick visit."

Rachel's eyes widened as she turned back to Cross.

"Of course. I'd love to see him."

"Your boy, too. He can go in – if he doesn't mind – of course. Gale would like that, I'm sure, he would. After all these grown-ups. He'd love to see someone his own age."

Again, they all looked to the doctor, who nodded that she had no objection.

Rachel Martin led the way, knocking softly on the door, but not waiting for an answer before she pushed it open.

"Hi, honey, I've got someone to see you."

SEVENTY-ONE

Gale Martin was laid flat in the bed, two small bandages on his face, his hair sticking up. He looked over as the entourage filed in, lining up against the wall in the small room.

"Honey, here she is, the lady who saved you."

Gale didn't answer, but Cross smiled anyway. "How are you feeling?"

Gale's neck had come up with deep blue bruises intertwined with angry red marks. He gave a weak smile.

"I'm OK. Thank you for saving me."

"That's alright. It was the paramedics really, they brought you back, but I'm so, so pleased they were able to."

Gale seemed unable to reply, and Cross didn't force him. She went on.

"And I'm so sorry for everything that's happened. I'm sorry you weren't believed earlier."

Gale glanced around the room, for a second his eyes alighted on the other boy, Joe. Then they went back to the Constable.

"That's OK." His eyes went back to Cross's son. "Hi, Joe."

Cross turned to look at each of them.

"You two know each other?"

"His school and my school both have the same Lego club," Gale said. "I had to stop going when Layla died."

"Hi Gale," Joe said. Then he went on. "I'm sorry about everything that happened to you. And to your sister."

"Thanks."

There was a silence, and after a while Rachel broke it.

"Well, the doctor said we have to keep this brief, so we'll let you rest, honey."

Gale nodded, and Jon Martin opened the door for them to file out. But as they did, Joe Cross spoke again. Hesitantly at first, he held out his hand.

"Erm, I don't know if you want it, or how long you'll be in here or anything, but if you want..." He held out his hand, and in it was the device he'd been playing with outside. "It's a Nintendo Switch, and I've got Mario Kart, and also..." he reached into his pocket and brought out another cartridge. "I've also got Animal Crossing, if you prefer?"

Gale smiled, deeper this time. He looked to his mother, who nodded, biting her lip.

"Thanks."

"Maybe you can give it back to me when you get better?"

Cross felt the prickling of tears in her eyes again as her son laid the device on the bed – a device he was usually glued to – then she nodded, ready to leave. She put her hand onto her son's head, tousling the unkempt mess that was his hair.

SEVENTY-TWO

FOUR WEEKS LATER

There was a knock on Gale's door – his new door.

"Who is it?" He glanced at his sister, who sat on her bed, inspecting her fingernails.

"It's me," his dad said, from outside. "Can I come in?"

Layla flashed an 'OK' smile, and Gale replied.

"OK."

The door opened, and Jon stepped inside. He looked around, as if appraising the space.

"How you doing?"

"I'm OK," Gale replied. His lips formed into a quick smile, then he waited, looking expectantly at his father.

"I just wanted to check how you were settling in," Jon Martin gave a light chuckle. "You know, in your new room and everything." He rolled his eyes a little, as if they were sharing a sort of joke. Gale thought about this for a few moments, then smiled a bit.

"I guess it's OK."

His parents had worked together to empty Layla's old room of her things, and then redecorate. A few of her toys had gone to Gale, but most were bagged up and taken to a charity shop, along with most of her clothes. Some had been kept, though, carefully folded by Rachel and stored at the top of her wardrobe. Then they'd gone to the big DIY store, where Gale had been allowed to choose some new wallpaper. It wasn't easy to decide, there was some with planes and cars, which he'd liked, but after discussion with his parents and Layla – it was her old room after all – he'd rejected these in favour of something a bit more subtle and grown-up.

Gale glanced at it now, on the wall by the window. The paper really did make it look there was a giant crack in the wall, and about forty different Minions – from the movie *Despicable Me* – were climbing in, some with ropes and ice axes, some with skateboards, and there was one who'd got too high and was jumping off with a parachute.

His dad considered it now. "You still sure about the walls?"

"Yeah!" Gale answered without waiting to hear what Layla said. But then he glanced at her, and she shrugged.

"It's your room now," she told him.

Suddenly Gale turned back to his father. "Do you know what's going to happen to my old room yet?" he asked. The truth was he'd been wondering, and possibly slightly worrying, since that question had once been the source of considerable tension in the family.

"Actually, yes, I think we do."

Gale's eyebrows went up. This was news.

"I'll have to let your mother tell you the details, but she's going to turn it into a small office."

"She already has an office. At work."

"Yes. But this will be a home office."

"Why does she need a home office?"

Jon smiled as if about to share a secret. "Well, she's had an idea, for what she wants to do, and I think it's a really good one."

"What idea?"

Jon sat down on the bed – Layla had to move quickly out of

the way, to avoid her father's backside passing straight through her. Gale watched, a little amused.

"She's decided to create a charity, in memory of Layla."

Gale's smile turned to puzzlement, and when he glanced at Layla, she seemed to feel the same way. "What sort of charity?"

"Your mother's idea is that it will support people who have lost children in difficult circumstances. Like we did with Layla. It's a way to keep her memory alive, even if she can't be with us herself." Jon offered his son a sad smile.

Gale exchanged a look with his sister, who was tipping her head from one side to the other, as if weighing this up. He looked back at his father.

"How is it going to support people? If they've lost someone, how's it going to help?"

"Well, there's money." Jon's voice became more business-like. "We're lucky because we can afford proper counselling, and we don't have to worry about our day-to-day bills, but there are people who aren't that fortunate. The charity can help with that. But then there's other ideas too. I think your mother wants to..." He paused, bit his lip. "I think she envisages sending people off on retreats, to get some space to grieve properly. I think she might actually lead the retreats herself. Get people together, let them learn from each other." He smiled suddenly. "I had an idea too. For outdoor experiences, as a way to heal from grief."

Gale considered this, and seemed satisfied.

"What's it going to be called?"

Jon gave a short laugh. "Actually that's the tricky part. I don't know. Your mother likes the idea of 'Layla's something', but we're not sure on the 'something'."

Gale thought for a moment, but no ideas came, and then his father was talking again.

"But talking of outdoor experiences, there's another reason I came up here this morning."

"What reason?"

Jon hesitated, then shrugging lightly. "There's a little surprise downstairs."

"What surprise?"

"Come with me, you'll find out."

The three of them went down the stairs together, Jon Martin walking Gale in front of him, Layla drifting down behind.

"What is it?" Gale asked again.

"Hold on and you'll see." Gale felt his father's hands cover his eyes and he was guided into the lounge.

"OK, you can open your eyes now."

He did so, to see his mother sat on the sofa, sheaths of paper on the coffee table in front of her. He peered at them, trying to work out if this was the surprise. He managed to read the words 'Charity Commission' before his father interrupted again.

"That's actually your mother, the surprise is behind you."

Gale turned, to see that Layla had already seen it. His eyes widened.

"Wow!" Leaning up against the wall was a bike, with thick knobbly tyres and cool-looking front suspension forks.

"It's a good one. Decent brand and pretty light," his dad said. "And I've found us a really good route through the forest, and a café that does amazing hot chocolate." He smiled at Rachel. "Your mum's coming too."

She looked up now, and nodded firmly. "Yep. I am. I've even bought some cycling shorts. I literally cannot wait to put them on." The way she said it, Gale knew she meant the opposite. But in a nice way. A funny way.

"I think you look good in them," Jon said, innocently.

"Plus," Rachel ignored her husband, "I heard that getting fresh air is good when you need to solve a creative problem."

"What creative problem?" Gale asked.

A look of pride came over Rachel's face, she waved a hand over the papers. "We're going to start a charity. For Layla. It's going to help other families who lose someone important rebuild their lives." She crossed the room and wrapped an arm around Gale, pulling him closer. With her other arm she also pulled her husband into the same embrace.

"We just need a name." Rachel said.

Gale followed in the tyre tracks of his dad, who seemed to know all the best routes, and even led him over some little jumps out on the common. His mum missed them out, and complained that her legs hurt on the uphills, but she was smiling too. All the while Barney raced alongside, panting and ears flying as he bounded forwards. And right beside him flew Layla, her hair trailing backwards in the wind, a huge grin on her face. The effort of keeping up was such that she seemed to generate an inner glow.

"Come on Gale, there's a really great little downhill over here," Jon Martin called out. "Just feather the back brake, don't use the front, or you might wash out the wheel."

"OK."

An hour later, they arrived at the café. Jon went to order, and then returned with a tray bearing three tall mugs, steaming in the cold air, and two generous slices of cake.

"We've done fifteen kilometres. I think we've earned it," he said, as if thinking Rachel might object, but she just smiled.

"Layla's *Space*?" She said instead, sounding out the name in her mind. They'd been discussing it again on the trail.

"It kind of sounds wrong," Gale replied, sensing his sister agreed. He glanced at her, and she nodded sagely.

"Layla's *Hot Chocolate and carrot cake*?" Jon slipped into his seat. The table had four spaces and one was left empty, except that Layla was hovering there, still glowing from the effort of keeping up with the bikes.

Rachel laughed, as she picked up a fork and dug it into the cake. "Now where did you get that idea from?" She slipped the cake into her mouth.

"I did have a real idea," Jon went on, becoming serious now. "How about Layla's Friends?" Rachel went quiet for a moment.

"Mmmm. I quite like that," Rachel began. "Except," she frowned now, wrinkling her nose. "The problem is, the people the charity will help *aren't* Layla's friends, she never got to meet them and, I'm not sure we want to be reminded of that." Gale bit his lip, as he sensed his mother's mood shifting.

"OK. Layla *and* friends?" Jon tried again, but saw from her face it was another 'no'. He shrugged. "How hard can it be to come up with a name?"

No one answered, and then above them something special happened. The afternoon had been cloudy, but suddenly a gap appeared in the greyness, allowing a beam of sunlight to break through, illuminating a shaft of air in a deep white-gold shaft of light. It was both such an everyday sight that none of them mentioned it, yet such a beautiful spectacle that it left them all absorbed for a few moments. Gale felt his eyes drawn towards it, and noticed how his parents breathed a little deeper as they took in the sight. And then he glanced at Layla too, to see if she had seen it, and noticed instead how the colour of the sunlight exactly matched the glow that was still radiating from somewhere deep within Layla's presence. For a moment the coincidence of it surprised him. And then he knew. He tipped his head onto one side, wondering how to say it. Then he turned to his mother.

"All of the children the charity is going to help, they're going to come after Layla, aren't they? I mean they're going to die after she did?" He sensed more than saw the unease on his mother's face, and went on quickly.

"What I mean is, Layla will always be the first of them. Kind of showing the way."

Rachel kept frowning, but she was listening carefully. She wrapped her hands around the hot chocolate mug.

"I suppose so. Do you have an idea?"

Gale drew in a deep breath. He looked at his sister, it was funny, she didn't seem to know what he going to say, yet she was still glowing, so it was obvious.

"Well maybe." He drew in a deep breath. "How about we call it... *Layla's Light?*"

Rachel was still for a long time, but then she sat back in her chair, eventually she nodded. "Layla's Light." She glanced at Jon, a thoughtful look on her face.

Gale turned to his sister, who nodded excitedly, the same yellow light was pouring out of her now.

SEVENTY-THREE

The next day was Sunday, so Gale was allowed to stay up late, but when nine o'clock came around he didn't mind going upstairs, and he knew his parents would let him leave the light on for a little while. He cleaned his teeth and put his pyjamas on. Then he lay on the floor, on his new rug, and absently fiddled with his Lego.

"Do you mind?" Gale asked after a while.

"Mind what?" Layla was floating horizontally, facing him across the room.

"That I've got your room now?"

She looked puzzled. "No. Why would I?"

"Because it's your room. And now you can't have it." He thought for a moment. "And you can't even have my room. Because Mum's going to be in there."

She shook her head. "No. I don't need a room."

"Because you're a ghost." Gale gave a knowing look. "And ghosts don't need rooms. They can be anywhere." But his expression changed when she went on.

"No. Not because I'm a ghost. Because..."

He sensed something in her voice. "Because what?"

Layla looked away. "Because I don't think I have long now."

"What do you mean? Not long?" Gale looked up and glanced at her, his heat was racing suddenly. "I don't know what you mean." But he did know.

"Yes, you do. You know what has to happen now."

He stared at her. "No I don't. I don't know what you're talking about."

"I want you to help Mum with my charity. I think it's going to be good for her. But it'll be hard too, and you need to remind her that it's worth it."

Gale was silent.

"Will you do that? Will you promise me? For when I'm..."

"For when you're what?"

Layla shook her head. "Please, Gale. Just promise me? Promise me you'll help her."

"I don't—"

"Just promise me."

"OK. I promise."

Layla smiled. "Thank you."

"Is that it?" Gale looked anxious, and Layla gave a light laugh.

"You know it isn't it, Gale. We both know." She stopped, and watched him, a resigned look on her face. Then she went on. "You know, having *him* out there, when he wasn't caught..." They both knew who she meant. "It was hard. It was like a bath with the plug in, when the water needed to drain away. It stopped me from going where... wherever it is I need to go."

Gale was angry now. Tears running down his cheeks. "But he's been caught now. The police have got him, and you haven't gone anywhere. Doesn't that mean you can stay? After all?"

Layla didn't reply.

"Or maybe... maybe it means that you might have to go there, but you can come back. To see me. Like, not every day, but just sometimes. Just so that I don't have to be alone?" Gale was shaking his head now, pleading with her.

"You're not alone, Gale. You've got Mum and Dad, your friends at school. People like Joe. And all the other people you're going to meet still. There's loads of people that will help you. Lots of people who are good and kind."

"No... but I won't have *you*. I don't understand why I can't have you."

"It's because I died, Gale. I *died*. You know that."

"Yeah but..." Gale was shaking his head, tears flowing freely down his cheeks, too upset to even wipe them away. "I just don't understand."

"I don't either. Not really, but it's like the bath. All the water doesn't go at once, but you still know it's going. These last weeks have been like that. The water's been going. Since they caught him. The water's been draining out, and we both knew it. And it's nearly gone now. Gale, it's nearly gone.

Gale turned away, but Layla kept talking.

"Do you remember how we used to have baths together? You and me? You would take up all the space, and Mum would shout at us because of all the water on the floor?"

Gale turned back to look at her, face screwed up with grief. "Can't you put the plug back in?"

"*We* took it out together, Gale. We took it out when we caught that man."

Gale suddenly noticed the Nintendo on the floor, and he reached out to pick it up. For a moment he toyed with the buttons, turning it on, and off again, as if they might start playing once more. But then he dropped it back on the bed. Now he did wipe his eyes, using one hand for each of them, and not stopping until he'd cleared his vision. Finally, he nodded.

"Does it hurt now? Being here? Is that why you want to go?"

Layla gave a strange smile in response. "It always hurt. But it's less now. Because I know that you're safe. Maybe that's the

real reason I couldn't leave before? Because you weren't safe."
She reached out to touch him, but of course she couldn't.

"But now I know you're going to be alright. So maybe that's
why I'm free to go now."

Gale rubbed the tears from his eyes again. He wouldn't look
at her.

"There's something else I need to tell you, Gale. Something
important. I don't know if I can say it in a way that really makes
sense, but I'll try."

Gale nodded. He turned back to face her, waiting.

"Where I'm going – where we all go – I've seen it. I've *been*
there. Early on, when I first died, I sort of saw it then, but I
didn't get to go there. But then later on, when we were together
in that horrible place, and he was choking you, I went there
again then. And I didn't want to say anything, because it's kind
of scary. But it's also the most amazing place. It's filled with
energy, and light, and love. And there's so much peace and
compassion, and... I don't know, I can't describe it. But it's
perfect, and it's beautiful. There's no need to be afraid for me,
Gale. And there's no need for you to be afraid, when it's your
turn. I promise you that. I swear, on Mum's life, and Dad's life.
And mine. The place you go to when you die. It's a good place.
And I'll see you again there. We'll be together again."

As she spoke Gale was running his hands through his hair,
and continuing to wipe his eyes, but he was doing his best to
listen. Trying to understand.

"Hey!" he said suddenly, looking at her in alarm. "Hey,
you're changing."

And she was.

Layla looked down at her own hands, and must have seen
how they were more translucent than before, and how the very
tips of her fingers had almost disappeared. The two of them
watched, and as the seconds passed they shrank back, as if the
very air were dissolving them. She bit her lip.

"Oh Gale, we have to be quick. The water's going. It's almost gone now."

For Gale the tears came flowing right back, blurring his vision, stealing his last glimpses of his sister.

"No. Not yet. *Please not yet.*" Furiously he wiped, as his eyes let him down once more.

"It's OK, Gale. It really is. I'm going now. But you'll be OK. And I'll see you again. *I can't wait to see you again.*"

"No... you *can't* go. I don't *want* you to go."

It wasn't just Layla's hands that were strange now, the entire apparition of her was coming in and out of focus, and flickering. For whole seconds she was almost not there at all, and each time she reappeared, she was weaker, her voice further away.

"What are you up to tomorrow? Have you got any plans?"

"What? Why does that matter?"

"I want to know, Gale. Please tell me. Please tell me what you're doing?"

"I don't know!" Gale had to search his mind for the answer. "Dad said he wanted to take me swimming. And then Becky and Auntie Erica are coming over for lunch. And we're going to play a board game."

Layla smiled.

"What board game?"

"What? I don't care. That doesn't matter..."

"I like Catan. Can you play that?" Layla held up her hand in front of her face. But there was no hand there, just the sleeve of her top.

"I have to go now Gale. I love you, and I always will."

"No—"

"They're calling me, Gale. It's my time. *It's* calling me. *I love you, little brother.* Make me proud, won't you? And Mum and Dad too. Tell them I love them, and tell them I'll see you all again."

Gale shook his head. He stared at the space his sister occupied. Had occupied, on and off, in the two years since her death. He wiped a final tear from his eye. Then he nodded. And then his face collapsed into grief one more time.

And then the room changed.

The air shifted.

And Layla was gone.

A LETTER FROM THE AUTHOR

Dear reader,

Thank you so much for reading *Little Ghosts*. I hope you were hooked on Gale's journey. If you'd like to join other readers in keeping in touch, here are two options. Stay in the loop with my new releases with the link below. You'll be the first to know about all future books I write. Or sign up to my personal email newsletter on the link at the bottom of this note.

You'll get bonus content, a free novella, and get occasional updates and insights from my writing life. I'd be delighted if you choose to sign up to either – or both!

www.stormpublishing.co/gregg-dunnett

Join other readers in hearing about my writing (and life) experiences, get a free novella, and other bonus content. Simply head over to my website:

www.greggdunnett.com

Gregg

ACKNOWLEDGMENTS

This is my first proper published book – after ten or eleven (I've lost count) self-published efforts – so I'd like to thank everyone at Storm Publishing for taking a chance on me. But especially Kathryn Taussig for the belief she's shown, and for her insightful and brilliant editing, in particular for not just pointing out the problems, but suggesting solutions too. With her help I'm also sure this is my best book to date.

I dedicated this book to my children, Alba and Rafa. I didn't really have a choice, since they, and the relationship they have with each other, breathed life into the initial idea, and then gave it the vital energy it needed to become an actual book. Thanks kids. Now go and tidy your rooms.

I'd also like to thank all of my readers who have supported me so far in my efforts to become a 'proper' writer. I don't know what I've done to deserve it, but I have a loyal base of fans who have followed me over the years, helping me to choose covers, working unpaid as 'beta readers' and laughing at the terrible jokes in my email newsletters. It feels a bit like having a supportive family all around the globe, and that's helped make the world feel a much friendlier place. I'm sure it's helped me pluck up the courage to take on our big adventure of moving the family out to the north coast of Spain. I'm eternally grateful.

And finally to Maria, my partner and my best friend, and now my Spanish translator too. I promise the next one will be shorter.